MW01234612

J.S. Ryan

Tolkien's View:
Windows into his World

2009

Cormarë Series No. 19

Series Editors: Peter Buchs • Thomas Honegger • Andrew Moglestue • Johanna Schön

Editor responsible for this volume: Peter Buchs

Library of Congress Cataloging-in-Publication Data

Ryan, J.S.
Tolkien's View: Windows into his World
ISBN 978-3-905703-13-9

Subject headings:
Tolkien, J. R. R. (John Ronald Reuel), 1892-1973 – Biography and interpretation
Tolkien, J. R. R. (John Ronald Reuel), 1892-1973 – Language and style
Mythopoeic fiction, English – neo-mediaeval legend and story
Middle-earth (cosmology of last things)
Recension of European history and culture

© Walking Tree Publishers, Zurich and Jena, 2009

All rights reserved. No portion of this book may be reproduced, by any process or technique, without the express written consent of the publisher.

Cover illustration: picture of Merton Meadows, facing south from Prof. Tolkien's former study, taken by John Gibbons 2008

Illustrations by Anke Eissmann

Set in Adobe Garamond and Shannon by Walking Tree Publishers
Printed by Lightning Source in the United Kingdom and United States

In Memory of

Graham G. Hough

Contents

Part B
The Young Professor and his Early Publishing

Appendix
Othin in England

The present volume of essays by Professor J.S. Ryan of the University of New England, Australia, has quite a long publication history behind it – something which appeals to me, as editor and historian, and which I want to comment on in the preface for this collection.

In early May 2006, Thomas Honegger, medievalist at the English seminar of the Friedrich-Schiller-University at Jena and mainly responsible for the academic aspects of our publication programme, was doing some research on Professor J.R.R. Tolkien's academic papers and curriculum at both Leeds and Oxford universities and came across two essays J.S. Ryan had written about this subject matter, one of which is the ninth in the present selection. When contact was made, John was very happy to provide these essays and other similar materials. Soon after he suggested that a number of like essays of his might well merit reprinting with us, since they were in quite scattered locations and had appeared over many years. When we had a look at the two essays and the Modern Language Association publication list of his work on Tolkien, we were soon convinced that a volume of these essays would be a worthy addition to our publishing list.

This was so for three reasons: First his special interests are closely connected with Professor Tolkien's own subject matter, philology, a field towards which not too much Tolkien scholarship is directed these days. The second reason is that he is one of the few students of the Professor now left who can tell us something not only about the author, but also his regular professional work, while the third is that his own studies in Oxford and Cambridge gave him a detailed and profound insight into Tolkien's academic environment, both regarding the atmosphere in which he worked and prospered as well as the teachers and students surrounding him. Thus our author is uniquely well positioned to give us insight into a world that, today, is long gone and that is not so easy to recreate in our own twenty-first-century minds.

When we started on this compilation of essays, we faced some quite unusual conditions. For once the material was already there and waiting, but, on the other hand, it had been produced in an age before the advent of computers, and was largely available in the form of printouts or off-prints. This meant that it took an unusual amount of time to collect the potential 'ingredients' for the book from all over the world, have them typed in, add consistent publishing conventions and obtain the necessary copyright permissions. But "all's well as ends Better," as they say.

The hunt for the source material was also, however, a fascinating one as it brought back to mind the tortuous history of (earlier) Tolkien studies. Having been a student in the Oxford English Course One from 1954 to 1957, under Professor Tolkien and those who taught the syllabus Tolkien had designed, J.S. Ryan handed in a pioneering doctoral thesis on the Inklings in 1967 and had been publishing on Tolkien and Tolkien-related matters over the period, in all from 1963 to 2002. There is a small selection of these items, as well as one entirely new piece, Essay Four, in this current collection. While a certain proportion of his Tolkien- and Inklings-set essays are to be found in such academic journals as *Folklore, Orana, Quadrant* and *Seven*, many others appeared in publications that were aimed at a more general readership.

Until fairly recently, Tolkien, the author, was not quite an approved subject-matter in academia and so Tolkien-scholarship reached a larger readership mostly by means of the 'academic' journals of the Tolkien Society (*Mallorn*), the Mythopoeic Society (*Mythlore*) and the Inklings Gesellschaft für Literatur und Ästhetik e.V. (*Inklings-Jahrbuch*), but also in other publications – these perhaps best regarded as society bulletins – such as *Amon Hen* (also from the Tolkien Society), *Angerthas* (from Arthedain, the Tolkien Society of Norway), *Anor* (Cambridge Tolkien Society), *The Book of Mazarbul* (Dwarf Postal Smial), *Minas Tirith Evening-Star* (American Tolkien Society) and *Quettar* (Linguistic Fellowship of the Tolkien Society, in England). In them scholarly material was often published alongside fan-art, fan-poetry and fan-fiction.

The third last item in this list also brought back a smile to me personally as *The Book of Mazarbul* was where my humble self published a couple of items, one of them, 'The Dwarves' Wifes', appearing alongside a J.S. Ryan piece on

the remarkable excavation c. 1930 in Lydney Park, Gloucestershire. It was the
heady days of the mid-1980s international Tolkien fandom that brought into
life the Swiss Tolkien Society. This last group, little more than ten years later,
in 1997, would give birth to an independent academically-orientated publishing
house, the Walking Tree Publishers, which today in its own turn, is publishing
a volume of essays by Professor J.S. Ryan. A full circle round.

After these musings – perhaps more reminiscent of a hobbit historian than a
follower of the Frankfurt School, I must admit – I would like to make the reader
aware of three specifics of this publication. First of all, that it does not contain
everything that Professor Ryan and the Walking Tree Publishers deemed worthy
of issuing now. Such a book would have become too unwieldy, and so it was
decided to split it into two volumes, the second to be published next year. The
second point concerns the present editing of Professor Ryan's essays. As these
were published over a long period of time, and in different journals – all having their own specific editorial conventions – it was decided to harmonize the
references, etc. in accordance with today's standards, and to add a consolidated
bibliography. Further J.S. Ryan also took the opportunity of updating various
essays or parts of them as he saw fit – although the vast bulk of the text has been
left in its original state, as testimony to the progressive historical development
of Tolkien studies – and added a new, as yet unpublished item.

This present volume would not have been possible without the fine technical, clerical and editorial advice and support received from my fellow senior
editors Thomas Honegger, Andrew Moglestue and Johanna Schön, as well as
Doreen Triebel, Stephanie Luther and Ulrike Ellguth from Friedrich-Schiller-
Universität Jena, Pat Reynolds, the Tolkien Society archivist and Peter Gilliver
and Jeremy Marshall from the *OED*. Further, we would like to thank equally
the kind editors of *Angerthas, Folklore, Inklings-Jahrbuch, Mallorn, Minas Tirith
Evening-Star*, and *Seven* as well as the University Press of Kentucky and the
University of New England who granted us permission to reprint essays that
have already been published with them as part of the present volume. Ample
thanks are also due to John Gibbons who provided us with his picture of Merton
Meadows taken from Prof. J.R.R. Tolkien's study, the Warden and Fellows of
Merton College with whose permission the picture was taken, as well as Anke
Eissmann who drew the 'Norse-Germanic' illustrations you'll find throughout

the book. Finally, I would like to thank Dr. Robert Haworth, a colleague of
J.S. Ryan's at the University of New England in Armidale, New South Wales,
Australia, who has given John and us enormous support over the last couple
of months in dealing with numerous small and large questions and without
whom it would not have been possible to finish this book.

On this note, we would like to send our readers on their way through this book,
wishing them much enjoyment, and in the hope that they can learn many new
things about J.R.R. Tolkien, his background and influences and so savour his
creations the more.

Peter Buchs
Zollikofen, June 2009

This volume may best be read as a clustered collection of essays, these all arising from an ongoing and reasonably informed Oxford experience of the cultural and academic mindset behind, and in the variety of scholarly writings of, John Ronald Reuel Tolkien (1892-1973). That long time Oxford professor of 'English' and most eminent Indo-European languages scholar has now become perhaps the world's most popularly regarded author. And yet I had met him and studied under him and his colleagues and pupils before the explosion of the 'cult' which, from its American campus beginnings, would make him a bestseller of ever increasing renown. However, the scholarly context of Tolkien's mind that informed his creative narratives was not always perceived clearly by his new audience. Thus, my early researches, and so ultimate thesis about what I had read, became a scholarly concern for me, still somewhat removed from all of this, as I was then lecturing in northern New South Wales.

The present text, one containing a score of reflective and topic-focused papers, has been largely selected and ordered by a most sympathetic team of current European scholarly publisher-editors. For they have selected and arranged these groupings from many earlier 'Tolkien' writings of mine, as variously issued, over more than thirty years, and in several countries – notably the United Kingdom, the United States of America, Germany and Norway. They have deemed them to be now more usefully issued together, and so a degree of refinement of particular details has been variously attempted, the better to achieve this aim of illumination of various personal or traditional aspects of the Tolkienian 'view' of our sublunary world.

Accordingly, in many cases the select papers as now re-issued have been slightly amplified or clarified, to be better understood by those who may well now be coming to Tolkien's world of 'Middle-earth' via their post-millenium contact with perhaps only his two best known creations, *The Hobbit* and *The Lord of the Rings*.

However, the biographical and critical knowledge base would not have been possible without my ongoing membership of Oxford's Merton College (for many years the preferred Oxford College for New Zealanders). My close study contact with its distinguished fellowship had begun even before my departure from New Zealand, as I had been lectured there by Merton's Emeritus Professor David Nichol Smith, in whose attic at 20 Merton Street, Oxford, I would live in my last year at Merton. Thus it was that my own 'colonial' nurture and a strictly classical education there had been followed – somewhat similarly to Tolkien's own – by a discipline move back to the west of Europe, to the older Germanic languages, and Old English and Old Norse in particular, and, similarly, to the actual physical landscape of 'England'.

For this academic course I had gone to Merton College, also the institution where Tolkien's second professorship was officially located. Further, and most fortunately and significantly, I 'lived in' – first in St Alban's Quad, and, later, close by for more than two years. In addition to official scheduled classes in term time in the nearby Examination Schools and elsewhere, this easy propinquity facilitated many unplanned and more social meetings with Professor Tolkien, many walks and pacings together with him around the College Garden, discussions about possible areas for my researches later, and then his acting as a referee for me for two academic postings. My last Oxford year was spent, as indicated above, in 20 Merton Street, the home of Professor David Nichol Smith, in a sparrow-visited attic looking out over the Botanic Gardens towards Magdalen College – and so onto some of Tolkien's favourite trees. Overall at that time, and in subsequent academic work, I had made many fruitful associations with Mertonians – such as Sir Basil Blackwell – both in Oxford and worldwide who had been trained in Merton in the academic areas of the Classics and of 'English language and literature' and of England's shaping culture, both of the earlier and, indeed, from all the major study periods.

After some serious thoughts about close analysis of the Old English treatment of the Dark Ages theme 'the birds and beasts of battle' as a thesis research project (and the piece that Tolkien inspired by insightful remarks on this matter in his lectures is now included as an appendix), I later elected to return to England from Australia to research into the Oxford-located group of 'Modern English Mythmakers' (i.e. Charles Williams, Owen Barfield, J.R.R. Tolkien and C.S.

Lewis). For some better perspective on the whole cultural milieu, I decided to do this research at and through Merton's brother college, Peterhouse, within the University of Cambridge.

This base was a particularly useful one, giving me easy access to many Mertonians living in Cambridge – notably Professor J.A.W. Bennett, R. Macgregor and Dr. Chester White –, as well as to many Fellows of the smaller college, Peterhouse, who had met with and entertained the visiting J.R.R. Tolkien in earlier years, notably Sir Herbert Butterfield, Dom David Knowles and the Danish scholar, Dr Elias Bredsdorf, and to several of the older members of Blackfriars, the Dominican community in Cambridge. Further, in the time between these Oxbridge forays, when at the University of Nottingham – and later – I had much contact with the so based headquarters of the landscape-scrutinizing English Place-Name Society, and thus with the infectiously generous Professor Hugh Smith of University College London, a fine Norse scholar who was the doyen of place name studies, and, earlier, had been a student of Tolkien at the University of Leeds in the 1920s and one of those participating in the somewhat roistering 1936 volume *Songs for the Philologists*.

The more applied, or slightly earlier, summer seminar entitled 'The Golden Age of Northumbria', one led by Dr Frederick T. Wainwright of St Andrews University, had also introduced me in situ to the culture of Old Northumbria (i.e. in the Old English period), to the Roman Wall, to its archaeology and, a matter proving to be crucial for Tolkien studies – to the Celtic scholar, Mrs Nora Chadwick. This gave me vital access to her knowledge of the challenge and significance of the archaeology of Lydney, in Gloucestershire, which had direct relevance for my researches and so to the importance of the 'Houses of Healing' motif in *The Lord of the Rings*. Furthermore, most of my mentors in Cambridge regarded Tolkien as far more immediately representative of English myth and story than the other three 'mythmakers' identified in my draft research plan.

Other greater awarenesses that came in these years were of various developments and researching in such areas as: Anglo-Saxon archaeology, and the currently active (field) workers and developments in English place-names study; the location and contents of the personal libraries of many of the 'Great Age' philologists, and particularly that of Sir Oliver Elton; and a fascination with the Kingsley-led Eversley school of eminent Oxonians, as gathered there in Berkshire, to the south of Oxford, in the mid-nineteenth century, and including Max Mueller.[1] Further, in the daily round, I had much tuition by a number of Tolkien's former students, many of them both University Lecturers and College Fellows and so teachers[2] to such small tutorial groups, perhaps the most notable of whom was E.O.G. Turville-Petre. Another, also a New Zealander, was the then Middle English research scholar, Robert W. Burchfield who was about to become the editor of the *Supplement to the Oxford English Dictionary*.

The most important aspect of all this was that my first time in England – and its research sequel – had again given me holistic studies comprising language, literature, archaeology, landscape and culture, and the 'folk memory'. These, together with their inter-relationships, provided me with a comprehensive foundation for my further academic career, much as Classical Studies and visiting British academics had done earlier for me at the University of Otago. This first time in the 'home country' was one of focused concentration on the Germanic 'Dark Ages', on the saga age in Iceland as presented so mesmericly by Professor E.O.G. Turville-Petre, and the earlier part of the Middle Ages as they impacted on the literature of Western Europe. And, fortuitously, a further period in Oxford, working for Sir Basil Blackwell – bookman, scholar and Fellow of Merton – had much developed my curiosity about and knowledge of all sorts of bibliographic aspects of Oxford humanism and culture from the High Victorian period on, as well as of the unchanging countryside around Oxford and much explored by Tolkien and his friends over many years.

Further, I was – and am still – much assisted by the generosity and very relevant researches and insightful writings of the following antiquarians and influential folklorists of both custom and lexis, much of whose work has been outside formal academe: Christina Hole (1896-1985); Katharine M. Briggs (1898-

---

1 This topic is to feature in the sequel volume of my papers as an instance of the mental climate of language research available in Oxford before World War I and experienced by Tolkien while studying with Professor Joseph Wright.
2 Since J.R.R. Tolkien had been a professor in the English Faculty since 1925, he had been involved closely with almost all the lecturers and other teachers of English language and earlier literature in the 1950s, something which is apparent in the fatherly remarks in his Farewell Lecture to the University, and also in the presentation volume accorded him for his seventieth birthday.

1980) (both then living in Oxford); the Cambridge academic, Hilda R. Ellis (Davidson) (1914-2006); the late Professor Stanley Wiersma (1930-1986), a distinguished and peripatetic American scholar of the semantics of the 'monster vocabulary' to be found in *Beowulf*; Dr Barbara Reynolds, the gracious founder and Cambridge-based editor of *Seven: An Anglo-American Literary Review*; and, later, (Emeritus) Professor John D.A. Widdowson, once a fellow-student in Oxford and later the founder and long the Director of the National Centre for the English Cultural Tradition, at the University of Sheffield.

Clearly I would have fared but ill without the continuing and generous support of the Folklore Society from the earliest stages of my ongoing work, and also from the staff of the Library of the Taylor Institution for Modern Languages at the University of Oxford, long the home of the teaching and resources in the older Scandinavian languages, and where Tolkien had insisted that I attend the lectures of the famed French scholar, Georges Dumézil, as had E.O.G. Turville-Petre for various visiting Scandinavian scholars.

The Mertonians who have contributed to my perception of so much of the Tolkien mental climate are too numerous to list, but to the late Professor G.V. Smithers, Douglas Gray (later the foundation Tolkien Professor), Dr Roger Highfield and G.M. Green, a son of the College, I owe a debt that can never be repaid.

The significance of the thought and writings of all these and so many other scholars and thinkers was in their sharing of various parts of the Tolkien mental climate essential to my own research. They illuminated the rich and powerful basis in older cultures for so many of the literary forms adapted and explored in the world of the earlier preserved scholarship and story, as well as in the vast world of creative writing which J.R.R. Tolkien has bequeathed to us.

*   *   *

A large number of my own Tolkien-focussed research papers were originally drafted to help me to clarify a particular issue or linguistic matter – and there are now included here none from the perhaps slighter journals in the field, *Amon Hen*, *The Book of Mazarbul*, *The Ring Bearer*, *Anor*, or *Ipotesi* (in Italy). However, the present selection and ordering will, I hope, shed some light on particular and intriguing corners of the Tolkienian world of word, thought and often elusive but so far spreading and yet subtly 'ramified' further story.

Clearly I have long been appreciative of the excellent support of – and publications from – the Tolkien Society (in England), the Cambridge Tolkien Society, the American Tolkien Society and the Mythopoeic Society, the Norwegian Tolkien Society, *The Cambridge Review* and the editors of *Seven: An Anglo-American Literary Review*, as well various major newspapers in Australian cities.

For the interpretations afforded and for any misperceptions of the nuances of sense or emphasis, or of the architectonic patterns present or implicit, I am, of course, solely responsible.

Finally, it is my very great pleasure to be able to thank the Board of Editors of the Walking Tree Publishers, in Germany and in Switzerland and particularly my patient and tireless series-editor, Peter Buchs, for his assistance with working from old typefaces. His is a generosity of time and effort which has been more meticulous and supportive than I have experienced before.

*   *   *

I would like to close this introduction with some words concerning the cover photograph, which is of enormous symbolism. In front, in the trees, to the south runs the Thames River, moving from the west down to the sea. On the near right lies Christ Church where Alice in Wonderland was penned by Lewis Caroll, and to the far right lies Lydney, the famed Romano-Celtic shrine on which Tolkien advised as to the inscriptions. To the far left, and so to the further south-east lies Rome, the Rome of ancient history as well as that of the Popes and of the Christian faith and the eternal symbol of Christian eschatology.

J.S. Ryan
University of New England
Armidale, New South Wales
Australia

BLT I	*The Book of Lost Tales*, Vol. 1
Beowulf	'Beowulf: the Monsters and the Critics'
EDD	*English Dialect Dictionary*
E.E.T.S	Early English Text Society
Essays and Studies	*Essays and Studies by Members of the English Association*
EW	'English and Welsh'
FotR	*The Fellowship of the Ring*
H.E.	Bede, *Historia Ecclesiastica Gentis Anglorum*
Hobbit	*The Hobbit*
Leaf	'Leaf by Niggle'
Letters	*The Letters of J.R.R. Tolkien*
MCE	*The Monsters and the Critics and Other Essays*
NED	*New English Dictionary*
OED	*Oxford English Dictionary*
OFS	'On Fairy Stories'
RotK	*The Return of the King*
SGGK	*Sir Gawain and the Green Knight*
SGGK, Pearl and Sir Orfeo	*Sir Gawain and the Green Knight, Pearl, and Sir Orfeo*
TL	*Tree and Leaf*
Bombadil	*The Adventures of Tom Bombadil and other verses from the Red Book*
TT	*The Two Towers*
UT	*Unfinished Tales*
Valedictory	'Valedictory Address'
YWES IV	*Year's Work in English Studies*, Vol IV
YWES V	*Year's Work in English Studies*, Vol. V
YWES VI	*Year's Work in English Studies*, Vol. VI

Part A

Early Biographic Pieces and Emerging Tastes

Those Birmingham Quietists: J.R.R. Tolkien and J.H. Shorthouse (1834-1903)

Since the 'official' publication, in 1977, of *J.R.R. Tolkien: A Biography* by Humphrey Carpenter, most of those interested in the life and thought of the Oxford professor and mythic writer have been very familiar with the sad story of the young boy's early life, after his birth in Bloemfontein, South Africa in 1892, return with his mother and brother to England at the age of three and then loss of his father a few weeks after his fourth birthday.[1] Their modest life in Birmingham is outlined with specific reference to their time in: the hamlet of Sarehole,[2] on the southern edge of the city; Hall Green village; St. Anne's Catholic Church in the slums near central Birmingham; the suburb of Moseley; or 26 Oliver Road, "a house that was only one degree better than a slum" (Carpenter 1977: 27); and their later removes after Mrs Tolkien's death in 1904.

Yet as the biographer hastens over this period of his subject's life, – and the writer himself was never particularly forthcoming about books read then, or the special tastes of those years, – scholars have had to resort to a certain amount of ingenious re-creation of their writer's mental climate of that period – as to what else filled the young boy's mind, apart from an interest in botany, legends, the language of the area (Carpenter 1977: 21), his classical studies and the like. An extended example of this type of speculation is to be found in *J.R.R. Tolkien: The Shores of Middle-earth* (1981: 21), by Robert Giddings and Elizabeth Holland, who quote with approval Carpenter's observation in his *The Inklings* (1978: 157-58) that:

This essay first appeared in *Minas Tirith Evening-Star* 17.3 (1988: 3-9) and is here reprinted with the kind permission of its editors.

1 A convenient chronology of these events is given by Carpenter (1977: 264).

2 The history of the mill there, one dating from 1542, is given in the pamphlet (no. 14) written by Stephen Price and issued in 1981 by the Department of Local History of the Birmingham Museum. The text corroborates that mill as the source of many details of the Mill in the Shire towards the end of *The Lord of the Rings*.

> Tolkien [...] could scarcely be called a modern writer. Certainly, some compara-
> tively recent authors made their mark on him: men such as William Morris,
> Andrew Lang, George MacDonald, Rider Haggard, Kenneth Grahame and
> John Buchan [...] He read very little modern fiction.

In their book, which does not make easy reading or afford many luminous insights, there are many references to: George MacDonald's *The Princess and Curdie*; Haggard's *Allan Quatermain*[3] and *King Solomon's Mines*; Kenneth Grahame's *The Wind in the Willows*;[4] and John Buchan's *Thirty-Nine Steps*. There are also some highly speculative links made, as between the Dead Marches and the approach to Mordor, to the Doone Valley and to the battle descriptions in R.D. Blackmore's *Lorna Doone* (1869).[5]

While such investigations have a certain interest, yet they do no more than identify obliquely story-motifs of the type classified, originally in Finland by Antii Aarne, and much revised and enlarged by Stith Thompson in his six-volume *Motif-Index of Folk-Literature* (1955), the subtitle of which was 'A Classification of Narrative Elements in Folktales, Ballads, Myths, Fables, Mediaeval Romances, Exempla, Fabilaus, Jest-Books and Local Legends'. And one must admit that the masterly collection of and analysis for less than a hundred items by (the late) Katharine M. Briggs,[6] and Ruth L. Tongue, *Folktales of England* (1965), affords us more assistance[7] in identifying Tolkienian patterns of plot and thought than the modern work under discussion.

*   *   *

With this background of few specific Tolkienian clues[8] and the desire of many persons of non-mediaeval cultural background to find influences familiar from their own readings, in more recent periods, any pointers provided by Tolkien

---

3 Wrongly cited by Giddings and Holland (1981: 45-46) as source for the barrow-wight episode. Much
   better antecedents are to be found in the *Saga of Grettis the Strong* and elsewhere in Old Icelandic
   literature.
4 It is generally agreed that MacDonald and Grahame afford much to *The Hobbit* (1937).
5 See chapters VII, 'Hard it is to Climb' and LXIV, 'Slaughter in the Marshes' concerning the bodies in
   the fen after the Battle of Sedgemoor and on their tragic slaughter as reflected on by John Ridd.
6 Later president of the Folklore Society (London). She was one of Tolkien's early research students in
   the 1920s. The book also had an American edition.
7 See for example, riddles asked by an ogre (47); wild riders (52-54); running water as protection against
   evil (53), etc.
8 Most, like the references to Christopher Dawson, historiographer and religious apologist, in *Tree and
   Leaf*, are usually either ignored, or not realized for what they are.

himself to familiarity with texts written since the seventeenth century are of considerable potential significance. One such hitherto neglected reference is the one, a few weeks before his own death, to J. Henry Shorthouse (1834-1903) and to his book, *John Inglesant* (1880).

The matter of this specific knowledge was first drawn to the attention of the reading public in 1975[9] by Canon Norman S. Power, M.A., in an article, 'Tolkien's Walk', which concludes:

> I feel sure that in the young Tolkien's daily walk past the house 'Inglesant', we have an unnoticed influence, but one of which the great man was himself aware. (Power 1975a: 22)

Canon Power, as vicar of St. John's, Ladywood, was recording the link of his church with Joseph Henry Shorthouse, a local resident, a People's Warden at his parish church and

> (with others) instrumental in founding the first school for Ladywood children, St. John's School, which is still flourishing, though in a new building. (*ibid.*)

He also referred to No. 6 Beaufort Road,[10] Edgbaston, (i.e., 'Inglesant'), where in the 1870s Joseph Henry Shorthouse was writing *John Inglesant* at the same time as running his vitriol[11] factory in Great Charles Street. The relative crowding of houses about 'Inglesant' is also recorded after Shorthouse's death, by his wife in a 'Memoir'[12] of her husband (1905a: 102).

The link with Tolkien (Power 1975a: 23) is expressed thus:

> As a child, Tolkien lived at 26 Oliver Road, Ladywood, with his widowed mother and brother. This was a few hundred yards from 'Inglesant', a house the boy passed often on his way to the famous and beautiful Oratory Church, for he was a devout Catholic. Incidentally, at the Oratory, Tolkien must have

---

9   It appeared in two places, (a) *The Library Review* 25.1 (Spring 1975: 22-23), and (b) in *Mallorn* 9 (1975: 16-17), in which it is subtitled 'An Unexpected Personal Link With Tolkien?' Quotations are taken from the first place.

10 At that time several Edgbaston Streets "were part of the poorer" Ladywood parish, according to Power.

11 I.e., sulphuric acid.

12 This text comprises vol. I, 'Life and Letters,' of the two volume set (1905), edited by his wife, and entitled *Life, Letters and Literary Remains of J.H. Shorthouse*. The first volume (1905a) is prefaced by an 'Introduction' by the Rev. J.H. Smith, while the second volume (1905b) is largely a collection of Shorthouse's essays.

seen the manuscript of Newman's *The Dream of Gerontius*, which is on permanent display there, including that superb hymn, 'Praise to the Holiest in
the Height'.

The stress on Newman's presence at and influence on the Oratory is particularly significant, for there Newman endeavored to give a "certain leaven of
Anglicanism and religiosity to the [...] distant Roman Catholicism of the new
mission field" (Ryan 1969: 11), and "one feels that Tolkien must have sensed
something of Newman's ideals and defeat there." (*ibid.*) Then, too, there was
the Papal Brief of 1847 which stated explicitly

> that the Oratory was to address itself mainly to the educated or upper classes.
> [...] they were allowed to make the Sermons at the Oratory more intellectual
> and controversial topics of the day could be discussed.[13]

However much of the Newman influence had survived in Tolkien's time there,
several of Newman's own disciples were still associated with the Oratory, one
of whom, Father Francis Xavier Morgan was to become the orphans' guardian
from 1904. And it was from Morgan that

> Tolkien learned of the dream behind the foundation of that Oratory School,
> and at some considerable sacrifice he was later to send his three sons to Oratory
> although he did not long attend it himself. (Ryan 1969: 11)

Indeed, before we leave this matter of the tone and style of the Oratory, Church
and School, we may recall R.W. Church's comment on Newman's greatest loves
and so bequeathed influences:

> his chief interests were for things English – English literature, English social
> life, English politics, English religion [...] (1897: 479-80)

*   *   *

As Canon Power had observed of the schoolboy's walk to church

> On the way to the Oratory, Tolkien would glance with interest at Shorthouse's
> church, St. John's Ladywood, a fine Victorian Gothic building [...]
> (Power 1975a: 23)

---

13 See Addington (1966: 14).

The Anglican Canon quoted from Tolkien's last letter to him,[14] with its reference to the two boys being "penniless and orphans" after the death of their mother, "from which plight we were rescued by Fr. Francis Morgan of the Oratory."[15] He continued

> Lodgings were found for the boys in various houses selected by Fr. Morgan of the Oratory, including one at 1 Duchess Road, nearby.

Tolkien's own letter of July 8, 1973 – penned some 56 days before his sudden death – also refers to it:

> One of these addresses is of supreme importance[16] in my personal history: 1 Duchess Road (I think: at any rate, the first house on the left across [sic] descended a slope into a rather gloomy road [...]). If you would be so kind as to tell me whether that house has been demolished (as I expect) or not, I should be greatly obliged.
>
> In the meantime [...] I send you a copy of [...] *Essays by Divers Hands*, no. XXIX issued by the Royal Society of Literature.[17] It is a spare copy and I would be pleased if you would accept it. It contains an interesting account of J.H. Shorthouse and *John Inglesant*, his book. JHS being a resident of 6 Beaufort Road and People's Warden of your Church.

*　　*　　*

Since it is the purpose of the present paper to focus on the association between the two writers, and indeed on the remarkable parallels between them, it will now serve best if we return to Shorthouse himself, with the encouragement of Power's assertion that the book, *John Inglesant*, may well be "an unknown early influence on Tolkien" (Power 1975a: 23) and that

> in the young Tolkien's daily walk past the house 'Inglesant' we have an unnoticed influence, but one of which the great man was himself aware. (*ibid.*)

In the introduction to Mrs Shorthouse's 'Memoir' of her husband, the Rev. J. Hunter Smith, as longtime friend, stresses: Shorthouse's deep and wide

---

14　Footnote 2 explains their actual relationship: "I used to send my scribblings to him: sparrow's eggs to an eagle, but the eagle was always most kind and gracious about them!" (Power 1975b: 19)

15　The full text of the letter is given in *Mallorn* 9 (Power 1975b: 19).

16　Since Tolkien continues directly on to the reference to Shorthouse, we may well assume, with Canon Power, that this relates to *John Inglesant*. It is, of course, true – see Carpenter (1977: 38) – that in 1908 the Tolkien boys had moved to 37 Duchess Road, where Ronald met Edith Bratt, his wife to be.

17　Edited by E.V. Rieu and issued in 1958. Morchard Bishop's piece, '*John Inglesant* and its Author', fills pp. 73-86.

culture;[18] his being encouraged by "the example and precept of his parents, themselves, cultured members of the [...] Society of Friends" (Shorthouse 1905a: x); his singular hospitality; that his life was

> as noble a protest as could be made against the banality and frivolity that are too apt to characterize the lives of the English Middle Classes (*ibid*. xi);

his reserve and modesty; the long time a-writing of his masterpiece, some ten years in all; his unfashionable 'Broad Church Sacramentalism' (*ibid*. xii); his sympathy for 'Friends of the Light' and his favourite word being 'mystic'; his being "in some quaint way an onlooker" (*ibid*. xiv) of English commercial life; his ability to satirize extremism in politics or religion; and his being, in Hunter Smith's opinion, "the chief lay and literary exponent in our days of cultured Anglicanism" (*ibid*. xv).

Smith concluded his overview by stressing certain perceptions that were central to Shorthouse's thought –

> 1) that the relation between the invisible spirit of man and the invisible God is immediate;
>
> 2) that Puritanism in its narrowness[19] failed to see God as not merely of right-eousness, but also as the God of joy and beauty and of intellectual delight;
>
> 3) that Quakerism, as in the thought of Charles Fox, was wrong to see the past as "a long and dismal night of apostasy and darkness"[20] (*ibid*. xvi);
>
> 4) that Inglesant was right to stress "the good blessings of God – the painter's and the player's art, action, apparel, agility,[21] music – without these life would be a desert" (*ibid*. xvii);
>
> 5) "the somewhat fantastic regard for the sacrament as a vehicle of grace" (*ibid*. viii); [and]
>
> 6) that in all the work of Shorthouse face to face with the Epicurean idea of beauty and pleasure is the counter-charm of purity, truth and duty.

---

18 This was the more remarkable in view of his lack of a university education or even a professional career.

19 The broad path, as in *John Inglesant*, is not necessarily damnable. See John's speeches, ch. 28.

20 Compare various remarks by Tolkien in his 'Beowulf: The Monsters and the Critics', first published in the *Proceedings of the British Academy* 22 (1936) and also available in *MCE* (5-48).

21 Compare Tolkien's stress on play in 'The Cottage of Lost Play', or on dance, particularly in relation to Lúthien, the complement of his own wife.

In his concluding remarks Smith endeavours to equate Shorthouse's stance with that manifested by Edmund Spenser[22] in his *Faerie Queene*:

> I venture to think that the *Faerie Queen*, and in a humble degree *John Inglesant*, show how 'to make the best of both worlds' in a nobler and more generous sense. Mr Shorthouse was neither a professed theologian nor a systematic philosopher. Yet, perhaps, no one in our time more forcibly than he brought home to men's minds the reality of the immanence of God in all the works of His creation, the sacramental spirituality of the ordinary facts of life. (*ibid.* xxi)

It should be obvious to readers that all of these qualities, as well as respect for inherited rank, are to be found in greater or lesser extent in the personality and writing of J.R.R. Tolkien.

*   *   *

It will be appropriate now to glance at various details given in Mrs S. Shorthouse's considerable 'Memoir', not least because of that text's including many letters to and from her husband. Like Tolkien, Shorthouse (b. 1834) was exposed in his early life (indeed, until 24) to the life of the unspoiled country and also there to his grandmother's "cheerful temperament, real love of good literature, active beneficence[23] and unfeigned piety" (*ibid.* 2). From his father he inherited: "tenacious memory" (*ibid.* 3), powerful intellect and "his recollections and anecdotes of the old English society and habits which are long passed away" (*ibid.*); a love of travel,[24] especially in Wales, a rejoicing in nature "and a humble dependence upon nature's God" (*ibid.* 6). His mother loved romance and had a remarkable gift of imagination which she bequeathed to her son. She was prominent among Quakers and bore her many years of blindness with remarkable Christian meekness –

> I have desired to have no will of my own in this matter [...] Shall I receive good at the hands of the Lord, and shall I not also receive evil? (*ibid.* 7)

---

22 This is, itself, of considerable interest since in the 1980s holistic interpretations of the creative writings of J.R.R. Tolkien are more and more likening his temper and significance to those of Edmund Spenser.

23 Compare the generosity of Frodo in the Shire and Tolkien's own legendary kindness to his students and to the old and the humble of Oxford.

24 Shorthouse, like Tolkien, did not travel in Europe but relied for such settings, notably those in Italy, upon his own reading and the tales of others.

Henry's wife-to-be met her younger husband when they were children, at which time his delicacy[25] and lifelong handicap of stammering were already manifest. Her many lucid memories of those years include his reading of Mrs Sherwood's *Infant's Progress* and his excited delight when at the age of four "his parents were reading Bunyan's *The Pilgrim's Progress* aloud" (Shorthouse 1905a: 11). She also recorded Joseph Henry's easy dialogue with God and communion with nature, notably at his father's Thimble Mill,[26] his schooling with the Society of Friends and his ability at the age of twelve to mix with refined and cultured adults (*ibid.* 13).

*   *   *

Joseph Henry Shorthouse's quiet writing career began when he was twenty with various essays[27] prepared for a Quaker Society, but *John Inglesant* took from 1866 to 1876 to complete, and it was then "allowed to lie in the drawer of a favorite cabinet for four years" (Shorthouse 1905a: 102). The next stage is well recounted by Canon Power (1975a: 22-23):

> In 1880 Shorthouse brought it out again: a hundred copies (now valuable) were published at the author's expense. The book was admired by a discerning few. So Shorthouse sent it to Messrs. Smith and Elder, who returned it. It was 'not the sort of book' they 'cared to publish'.

> However, a Birmingham schoolmaster admired the book enough to send a copy to a Mr Johnson at Oxford; he showed it to Mrs Humphrey Ward. She took it to Mr Alexander MacMillan. Dubiously, Messrs MacMillan agreed to publish the book [...] the demand was overwhelming [...]

> In its first year, nine thousand copies of *John Inglesant* were sold. In the nineteenth century, eighteen thousand copies were sold, and the book was reprinted every year until its MacMillan 'Caravan' edition in 1930.

The reception by literary figures, like Mrs Humphrey Ward, F.T. Palgrave, F. Pollock, Matthew Arnold, Lord Rosebery and Mrs Craik, or public figures such as the Archbishop of Dublin, Mr Gladstone, Lord Halifax and Dr Talbot, Warden of Keble College, Oxford – was both sensitive and enthusiastic. All

---

25 J.R.R. Tolkien's own early ill health is discussed by Carpenter (1977: 13ff).
26 Compare Sarehole Mill at the beginning of this article.
27 A number are in vol. II of the *Life, Letters and Literary Remains* (Shorthouse 1905b).

agreed that it was a remarkable portrait of the character of one who showed himself above all things to be a 'Christian *gentleman*'.

The love story between John Inglesant and Mary Collett[28] surprised late Victorian England by both its rare delicacy and its considerable poignancy. Equally pleasing was the evocation of the English countryside and the spiritual odyssey of John Inglesant, a veritable quest-progress of an Anglican in the troubled decades after 1537 when John first went to London at the age of 15, to serve as a page in the Royal Household of King Henry VIII.

In two letters of the summer of 1880, Shorthouse had explained to Mrs Margaret Evans of Llandudno some of his artistic intentions:

> 1) we are none of us, I hope, too old to take an interest in some of the subjects which are very inadequately touched upon. I have left the book to tell its own tale and read its own lesson to everyone according to their own liking, but I may tell *you* that my *own* reading of the book is that God prefers culture to fanaticism, and
>
> 2) I intend the last chapter[29] to represent John Inglesant as having attained to an atmosphere of complete mental rest and peace [...] One of the principal objects of the book is to show that to the children of God [...] there is no temptation without a way of escape. (Shorthouse 1905a: 121-23)

Yet other comments of the writer may await their place until a brief outline be given of the actual content of *John Inglesant*, an historical romance of the time of Charles I and the great civil war which is prefaced by a swift survey of the previous hundred years and beginning with the account of the actual closure of an inoffensive western monastery in 1537.

The book is also the spiritual biography of a very rare spirit, first the servant of Charles I, and then a go-between to the Anglican and Romanist ecclesiastical parties. Thus it also chronicles the uprising and suppression of the followers of Molinos in Rome, as well as telling of the hero Inglesant's being interwoven in the mesh of European politics. Historical events are subordinate, however, to the subjective narrative and the complex inner mental and spiritual life of the central figures. Thus Puritans, Quietists, the Nicholas Ferrar-led community at

---

28 Niece of Nicholas Ferrar of Little Gidding, and a member of his community there.
29 This one is discussing John's return to England after many years of residence in Italy, marriage and bereavement in that country, and the vilification of his friends there.

Little Gidding, as well as the Molinos type of mysticism all feature prominently. The protagonist is always depicted as immersed in and at times led astray by worldly affairs, but, guided by saintly counsellors and his own inner light, he devotes himself to a sacred mission, that of reconciling the Anglican and Roman communions, while, like his forefathers, holding firm to the church founded by Henry VIII.

While the seventeenth century plot was seen as very close to the problems of the Oxford and Tractarian movements of his own day – and these, doubtless, inspired the work – the historical distancing refreshes well the dilemmas of modern churchmanship and of retaining one's essential English inheritance in the face of selfishness,[30] secular pressures and the threats to the traditional English identity. As Canon Power (1975a: 23) so well put it:

> In *John Inglesant* [...] we have an imaginary world in which [...] the battle between good and evil has a terrible reality [...] and there are 'strange satyr faces that leer at us from the fringes of the wood' [...]

*   *   *

As in *John Inglesant*, so in his many essays and letters, J.H. Shorthouse ever focuses on "quietness, peace of mind, self-sacrifice, the illumination of a divine light, the idea of devotion,"[31] a personal sacramentalism experienced most perfectly in Holy Communion[32] and to the consequent "finding oneself the centre of life and love."[33]

His own general theories of myth are particularly interesting, since they are only touched on at the end of the 'Preface' to *John Inglesant*:

> Amid the tangled web of a life's story I have endeavored to trace some distinct threads – the conflict between Culture and Fanaticism – the analysis and character of Sin – the subjective influence of the Christian Mythos. [At the foot of the page he glosses Mythos as 'External Truth manifested in Phenomena'.]

---

30 At one level, *The Lord of the Rings* may be read as a fable of the renunciation of 'empire' by members of the Fellowship as opposed to the desire for ever more power by Sauron, Saruman, etc.
31 Phrases used by Shorthouse in a letter of November, 1880 – see 'Memoir' (1905a: 126).
32 See particularly a letter of his quoted (Shorthouse 1905a: 150).
33 Phrase in Shorthouse's essay, 'The Agnostic at Church', first included in the *Nineteenth Century* (the issue for April, 1882), and reprinted in the *Life* (Shorthouse 1905b: 151). A little further on, he observed "sunshine upon the grass [...] is a sacrament of remembrance and of love" (*ibid.* 152).

An expansion of this occurs in his letter, May 10, 1882 to Lady Welby, (author of *Links and Clues*, a Platonic religious text concerned with the ultimate reality), endorsing her views:

> That the *idea* is the reality, the fact nothing but its outward garb and voice [...] that the ideal and not the material is the province of faith; and that the source of faith so defined is free thought (and has ever been so, notably in the case of Christ himself), – is what has long seemed to me a certainty of supreme value [...] so far from a mythos being false, *it is impossible to start a false myth*. A man cannot sit down in a back parlour and make a myth. No mythos ever yet grew up except from the needs and aspirations of the people among whom it flourished, and to whom it brought spiritual nourishment and help. (Shorthouse 1905b: 157)

His conclusion, alluding to the notion of the 'Pilgrim in the Unseen World', stresses the importance with God of the self-sacrifice and devotion to which human nature constantly attains (*ibid*. 158-59).

*   *   *

Elsewhere in both letters and essays there are many remarks[34] about Molinos and Quietism. Thus, on December 23, 1883, he wrote to Dr Talbot, the Warden of Keble College. He refers to the fact that Quietism "produced the effect of a poem rather than of a theological treatise" and that "mysticism is the *poetry* of religion" (*ibid*. 214). That same year he had written the Preface[35] to a Molinos anthology, entitled *Golden Thoughts from the Spiritual Guide of Miguel Molinos, the Quietist*, in which he stressed that

> this message from a foreign country and a bygone age is not without a singular appropriateness at the present time, (*ibid*. 281),

and adding that

> the faith of which he speaks is faith in an eternal principle. (*ibid*. 282)

He stresses anew both 'the Sacramental principle' (*ibid*. 283), and the needs of "erring [...] wandering [and] perplexed Humanity" and concludes that, instead of individualism,

---

34 In some measure these are also very similar to his views on the poet George Herbert – also referred to in *John Inglesant* – as in the early poem, 'A Shadow of George Herbert' (Shorthouse 1905b: 407-8). He also contributed a Preface to Herbert's *Poems* (Shorthouse 1905a: 398).
35 Reprinted in Shorthouse (1905b: 281-84), from which the quotations are taken.

is presented the god-given Humanity as God Himself restored it, and offered it before the universe as a sacrifice again. (*ibid.* 284)

*   *   *

While it is hoped that this survey will lead to scholarly investigation of the various levels of meaning in *John Inglesant*, and the many echoes of Shorthouse's novel in the major works of Tolkien, it is important now to underscore anew the significant details in the article by Norman Power and in Tolkien's own (to be linked) letter of July, 1973.

It is intended, however, that the matters already discussed will direct readers of Tolkien's work to an associated spiritual autobiography of remarkable eloquence. Like all of Shorthouse's work, it leaves a sense of deep satisfaction at temptation overcome,[36] at the will to refine one's conduct, at the ennobling influence of a valorous past and at a considerable range of communings with nature and responses to music. Matters such as: Shorthouse's respect for Cardinal Newman;[37] his patriarchal manner; his distress at all forms of noise and vulgarity; his deep personal reticence and artistic pleasure in having a ceremonious and decorous life-style; his deep love for the spirit of England; and his own enormously sane and everyday mysticism; – all of these cannot but remind us of the real temper of Tolkien's life and writings. How likely, too, that the young and deeply religious schoolboy would have been fired by the knowledge that he was thereby at Shorthouse's death and that a similar literary taste had been bequeathed to him, using his own knowledge of earlier cultures for creating his own mythic world, one also a spiritual background.

We may, indeed, agree that Shorthouse's comment on George Herbert[38] and past culture is not merely true of that poet, but also of both Shorthouse and Tolkien.

> The note he struck has never ceased to vibrate, even in the darkest and foulest of times [...]; we may [...] well believe that this peculiar mission [...] is not without its supreme value, not without the special seal of approbation from

---

36 The Evil One actually appears in his *The Countess Eve*.
37 Referred to at many points by Shorthouse, and Mrs Shorthouse, and corroborated by Miss J.D. Montgomery in *Temple Bar* (and reprinted at the end of the 'Memoir', Shorthouse 1905a: 403).
38 Quoted by Miss Montgomery (Shorthouse 1905a: 407).

on high; for [...] in the long course of years that which is in accordance with the highest instincts of the finest natures will be taken as the type and flower of the whole.

The Oxford Undergraduate Studies in Early English and Related Languages of J.R.R. Tolkien (1913-1915)

The student of J.R.R. Tolkien's creative writings is well aware that his subject was the Oxford professor of Anglo-Saxon for an important period[1] but likely to be much less familiar with the nature of his own early courses of study as a student in the same university. These are of particular interest for the light which they can shed on the early moulding of mind for the writer-to-be.

As is explained by Humphrey Carpenter, the future professor and fantasy writer had encountered Sweet's *Anglo-Saxon Primer* while a young schoolboy (1977: 34, 46), had later (at seventeen) actually spoken at length to his class-mates in both Gothic and Anglo-Saxon (*ibid.* 48), and in 1913 had taken Comparative Philology[2] as an option in his First Public Examination, better known as Classics Moderations or 'Mods' (*ibid.* 63), and then worked on Old and Middle English with Kenneth Sisam and on Old Norse with W.A. Craigie for his finals in English.

His own final examinations

In the years 1913-1915, Tolkien had chosen on a composite syllabus consisting of various papers[3] from both the literary and linguistic sides. In the following paragraphs there is given some analysis of the papers set for the small wartime class[4] for the 1915 Second Public Examination, in Trinity Term, in *Literis Anglicis* (i.e., in English). His chosen papers were entitled as follows, and representative numbered questions are then cited from the largely rubric-free papers:

This essay first appeared in *Minas Tirith Evening Star* 20.1 (1991: 3-7) and I am grateful to the editors for permission to reprint.

1 J.R.R. Tolkien (1892-1973) held the Rawlinson and Bosworth Chair of Anglo-Saxon from 1925 to 1945.

2 See Appendix.

3 See University of Oxford, *Examination Statutes* for the year ending June 1915.

4 Consisting of seven men and seventeen women, as contrasted with the very large classics Mods groups of 1913, when some 148 students (including Tolkien) had obtained honours. (See the *1900-1920 Supplement to the University of Oxford [...] Historical Register.*)

Beowulf and Other Old English Texts (Paper 1)

1) Some seven short passages from *Beowulf* are given for translation, five of which also ask cultural or textual questions about the general and specific content, e.g.: What is the meaning of *Scefing*?; what is the link between Sigmund and Waels?; who were the *Eotena bearn*?; what is alluded to by *Metware* and *sunu Ecgþeowes*?

2) Translate four short passages, one prose (from the Orosius, 'Voyage of Wulfstan'); from a riddle (about a bookworm); from a poetic elegy; and from the poem, *The Dream of the Rood.*[5]

3) What members of the Danish royal family are mentioned in *Beowulf*? Do any of them occur in the Scandinavian records?

4) Where was the home of the various peoples who play a part in *Beowulf*?

5) Discuss the metre of the passages in 1 [...]

6) What is a kenning? Give instances.[6]

Middle English Authors (Paper 2)

(This paper was largely concerned with thirteenth and fourteenth century Middle English, containing as topics: many short pieces for translation [qq. 1-3]; rhyme endings, in *Pearl*; construction and syntactical problems; metre; orthography [in the *Ormulum*]; and dialect forms.)

Chaucer (Paper 3)

This paper had very open-ended questions, e.g.:

1) Cite as many as you can of passages in which Chaucer refers directly to himself or his writings.

2) Comment on the following [5] allusions to 'sources'.

3) Consider the view that the character of Criseyde is not drawn consistently.

4) Show how medieval literary tradition or convention is represented in the themes of the *Canterbury Tales*.

5) Trace the growth of realism in Chaucer's poetry.

---

5 In later lectures of his own he would call it 'The Vision of the Cross'. (See various lecture titles in the *University of Oxford Gazette* for terminal public lectures.)

6 There followed three grammar questions, one on preterite-present verbs.

6) Discuss Chaucer's interest in science.

7) Write on the art of Chaucer's landscapes.

8) 'Chaucer's mind is never satisfied with any one single aspect of any matter'. Discuss.

9) Point out some of the main differences between the language of Chaucer's poetry and the language of his prose.

10) Write (6) contextual notes on these (6) passages.

N.B.[7]

History of English Literature (Paper A.5)

This paper had twelve essay questions with topics from Old English to Wordsworth. While Tolkien did not take all of this A.5 option, the early questions were close to Professor Napier's lectures and would have been done by him, viz.:

1) "A gluttonous race of Jutes and Angles, capable of no grand combinations; lumbering about in potbellied equanimity; not dreaming of heroic toil, and silence, and endurance, such as lead to the high places of this universe, and the golden mountain tops where dwell the spirits of the dawn." (Carlyle) To what extent does Anglo-Saxon poetry refute this opinion?

2) Trace briefly the growth of the Arthurian legend in English literature.

3) Compare Langland's picture of contemporary English life with that given by Chaucer.

4) Estimate the importance of Caxton as a writer and translator.

Historical English Grammar (Paper A.6)

This paper does have a rubric, viz.: "Not more than TEN questions [i.e. of the seventeen] should be attempted." While many of the set questions are closely etymological, or phonological, or dialectal, or concerned with varied conjugations and declensions, several are remarkably 'cultural', viz.:

1) What is known concerning the continental home of the Germanic tribes who emigrated to England? Were Frisians amongst them?

---

7 He also had to take a paper on Shakespeare as No. 4. (It is not treated here). The syllabus was: *Love's Labour's Lost*; *Henry IV Part 1* and *Part 2*; *Hamlet*; *Anthony and Cleopatra*.

2) Was the influence of French on English after the Conquest exerted by the Norman dialect exclusively? Illustrate your answer by examples.

3) Pronunciation of various place-names derived from or having the second element of the O.E. *ceaster*.

6) The influence of O.E. inflexions on Southern English of the thirteenth century.

11) Compare and contrast Old Mercian[8] and Old Northumbrian.

Gothic (Paper A.7)

In view of his 'moderations' work on philology, he would have savoured the A.7 paper, 'Gothic and Germanic Philology' and he would have been excitedly aware of its deliberately comparative nature in many of the questions. Thus, after translation of some four passages from the six taken from the Gothic Bible, the candidate could attempt not more than NINE from the next thirteen. Very teasing and partially cultural queries were concerned with –

3) [...] the distinction between North and East Germanic.

5) the development of meaning, etc. shown by the O.E., Latin and Greek cognates of *kiusan*.

6) "Give a brief account of *Ablaut* and illustrate as fully as possible the various grades of [specified] Indogermanic bases [...]"

10) "In what respects is the vowel system of Gothic more primitive than that of West Germanic, and in which less so? Illustrate from OE and Old High German."

12) "Account for the occurrence of the diphthong *au* in Primitive Germanic, yet not in the other, non-Germanic Idg. languages or in Primitive Aryan."

14) "Mention some features of the Gothic vocabulary which differ completely from West Germanic, confining your examples to quite common words."

Clearly the paper would have expected – and elicited – many comparative comments on the migrations, legends, etc. of the early Germanic people, such as were preserved in passing classical reference, heroic lays, etc.

---

8 I.e. the antecedent dialect for West Midland of the Middle English period. Tolkien later made many pioneering studies of this language, and its texts from the eighth to the fourteenth century.

Old English and Middle English Set-Books (Paper A.8)

His paper A.8 'Old English[9] and Middle English Set-Books' had six questions, no instructions to the candidates, and an open style of question. No. 1, – the five short pieces (four in verse) inviting speculation as to the 'nature' of one poem; identification of a teasing passage – from *Waldere*; or, a Weland piece, from *Deor's Lament*, which asked:

> What is here alluded to? Are there any traces of the same saga in Old Scandinavian literature? etc.

There followed sight translation pieces from Old English and various fairly easy questions on Middle English, testing the candidate on grammar and dialectology.

The Middle English texts set for Tolkien were largely based on Morris and Skeat's *Specimens of Early English*. For paper 2, he had had to study from this work (1913-14 Regulations 1913: 135):

from Part I (second edition) –

> No. 5, viz.: – 'Jewish and Christian Offerings', from the *Ormulum*;
>
> No. 6, viz.: – 'Hengist and Horsa', from Layamon's *Brut*;
>
> No. 8, viz.: – *The Life of St. Juliana*;[10]
>
> No. 9, viz.: – 'The Seven Deadly Sins' and 'Directions how a Nun should live';
>
> No. 11, viz.: – 'A Good Orison of Our Lady', a short rhyming poem of 171 lines, called an 'English lay', but probably translated from a Latin poem;
>
> No. 13, viz.: – 'Sermo in die Epiphaniae' and 'Dominica Secunda post Octavam Epiphaniae', from the *Old Kentish Sermons*;[11]
>
> No. 15, viz.; – Passages from the *Life of Joseph*, from the English Version of *Genesis* and *Exodus*;[12]

---

9 These were – according to the *1913-14 Regulations* – *Deor's Lament, Wife's Complaint, Waldere, The Ruin*, the *First Riddle, Exodus, Elene, Gregory's Dialogues*, Bks. I and II (MSS. C and O), Sweet's *Anglo-Saxon Reader*, Nos. 30-34 [...] Candidates will also be required to translate passages from Old English authors not specifically offered. His first paper had had as set texts: *Beowulf, The Fight at Finnsburg*, and Sweet's *Anglo-Saxon Reader*, ed. 8, Nos. 1-29.

10 He would work on this text for much of his life, supervising a research thesis on it by S.T.R.O. d'Ardenne, and introduce her edition of it, when, later, it was published by the Oxford University Press.

11 These would be much referred to in his lectures later (1945-59) as Merton Professor of English Language and Literature.

12 He lectured regularly on the O.E. *Exodus* from 1925 on, and returned to it in the spring of 1957.

No. 17, viz.: – Two different southern dialect versions of 'A Moral Ode'; and

No. 19, viz.: – A pre-1300 text of *King Horn* (1568 lines).

The same paper required close work on the same anthology's Part II (fourth edition[13]) –

No. 1, viz.: – Sections on William the Conqueror and St. Dunstan from Robert of Gloucester;

No. 7, viz.: – The Visit of the Magi, and the Flight into Egypt, from *Cursor Mundi*;

No. 9, viz.: – Sermon on Matthew xxiv, 43 and the Paternoster, Ave Maria, and Credo, from the Middle Kentish of Dan Michel of Northgate;[14]

No. 10, viz.: – Extracts from *The Pricke of Conscience* by Richard Rolle of Hampole;

No. 15, viz.: – Excerpts (from the A-text) from *Piers the Plowman,* Prologue, and from Passus I, II, III and V; and

No. 16, viz.: – Extracts from Book VII of John Barbour's *The Bruce.*

The other texts set here were *Havelok* and *The Pearl*, while Paper 3 (Chaucer) set out to examine: *Troilus and Criseyde*, the Prologue to the *Canterbury Tales*, 'The Pardoner's Tale', 'The Franklin's Tale' and 'The Clerk's Tale'.

Students such as Tolkien "whose main study is in the English language" (p. 135) were to be examined also on the outlines of literary history, philology, etc. of the following Middle English works:

An Old English[15] Miscellany, ed. Morris (1872: 1-138);
The Owl and the Nightingale;[16] and *The Tale of Rauf Coilyear.*

Old English and Middle English Unseen Translations (Paper A.9)

Tolkien's ninth paper was a long one and required literary, metric and textual comments on the five Old and five Middle English texts, with a compulsory question on M.E. historical prose requiring that the candidate

---

13 1898, etc.
14 A portion of this linguistically important text would be included in K. Sisam's *Fourteenth Century Verse and Prose*, to which Tolkien would provide the 'Glossary' (separately issued in the first instance).
15 I.e. late texts. It was an E.E.T.S. volume, no. 49, (1872) and edited by R. Morris.
16 The editions then available included those of: Rev. J. Stevenson (1838); Thomas Wright, for the Percy Society (1843); and by Francis H. Stratmann, of Krefeld (1868).

compare the language of [the] extract with late O.E., and point out the chief differences due to the course of time in sounds, accidence, and sentence structure.

Tolkien also did as 'Special Subject'[17] – necessary for those aiming at a place in the First Class – Scandinavian Philology, with special reference to Icelandic, together with a special study of:

> *Snorra Edda, Gylfaginning* (chapters 20-54);
>
> *Vǫlsunga-Saga*[18] (chapters 13-31), *Hallfreðar saga, Thorfinns saga karsefnis, Hrafnkels saga.*

Its actual examination paper[19] consisted of twelve questions – all to be attempted, presumably, since there is no rubric – which will now be cited *seriatim*:

1) Four prose passages of 12-14 lines for translation;

2) Three short context pieces from the prose set, to be translated "with explanatory notes";

3) "Over what area were the Scandinavian tongues spoken about 500 AD and 1000 AD? Give some account of the principal changes which took place in them between those dates."

4) "What exactly is meant by Old Icelandic? How far can it be taken as typical of Old Scandinavian?"

5) A requirement to comment on "the differences between the Old Icel. and OE. forms which correspond to [the] Gothic [forms of eight common nouns, adjectives and verbs]."

6) "Give a general account of the Old Icel. vowel system as contrasted with that of OE."

7) To comment on the 'noteworthy' in the declension of eight Old Icel. nouns;

8) To discuss *u – umlaut* in various specified contexts and forms;

9) To explain six specified pronominal forms and the origin of the negatives *ekki* and *engi*;

10) To distinguish the types of Old Icel. verbs represented by five pairs of present tense forms;

11) To illustrate, from three short passages (scaldic[20] and heroic) some of the chief features of Old Icel. metre and poetic diction; and

---

17 No one chose the theoretical alternatives: Old Saxon Philology; or Old High German Philology, with a special study of Braune's *Althochdeutsches Lesebuch.*

18 Carpenter refers to Tolkien's early delight in this text (1977: 46).

19 Reference 4M8, Trinity Term 1915, 'Honour School of English Language and Literature'.

20 As Rawlinson and Bosworth Professor he would lecture regularly on *Carmina Scaldica* and/or *Prolegomena to Old Icelandic.*

12) "Contrast Icelandic saga-writing of the classical period with Middle English literature of the same date."

In view of the very small classes in English in 1913 to 1915,[21] and of the smaller numbers of language students, it is more than clear that Tolkien both studied hard and had generous and almost personal tuition in all his preparation for the 'Second Public Examination', held at the end of some seven terms of close work. While he had initially wondered if there was enough to do in the selected courses,

> I cannot see how it is going to provide me with honest labour for two years and a term, (Carpenter 1977: 63)

it was not "as easy as he had expected" (*ibid.* 64), and demanded much of his energies. Over that time of study, Tolkien had reflected with H. Carpenter (*ibid.* 63-65) on the idea that retrospectivity is a highly selective style of romanticism. It lacks the particularity of the historical records, while enhancing the general significance of past years and ages. This period was a time of consolidation of faith for the formation of taste, cultural preference, attitude of mind, and of embryonic imaginative visions of what the Germanic and Northern European peoples had once had in common, a distinctive cosmology, a world view, and a fresh sense of awe and mystery as they first contemplated the certitudes of the Christian religion.

*   *   *

While it is not the purpose of this pilot survey to do more than make available an account of the formal content of Tolkien's Oxford language studies in the realm of 'early English' and in related fields, it is clear that the texts then scrutinized closely had the most considerable potential to suggest:

> modes of historiography and conflicting real or fictional 'sources' for documents;
> complex manuscript traditions;
> the 'appeal of authority' to older accounts;

---

21 His army call-up was somewhat delayed so that he could speak for the Exeter College Junior Common Room in the six hundredth anniversary year, the College having been founded in 1314 by Walter de Stapeldon, Bishop of Exeter. [Common assertion to the present writer by friends of Tolkien – e.g. H.V.D. Dyson – in the 1950s.]

giving 'equal weight to language and literature';[22]

and the association of the Germanic world with those of Greece and Rome,[23] and of the poignant and glorious conversion of those same Northern peoples to their new religion, Christianity.

The first statute of Honour School of English Language and Literature enjoined on its students the study of "authors or portions of authors" belonging to the different periods of English literature, and the second statute that such texts be scrutinized "in their relation to the history and thought of the period to which they belong" (*1913-14 Regulations* 1913: 133), and "of the history, especially the social history, of England during the period of English literature" offered by the particular candidate.

It would seem that Tolkien made the fullest use of this exhortation and the further opportunity, in due course, would carry it into his creative writings which could, and did, distinctively change modern man's perception of his place in the cosmos, by the revitalized notion of the term, Middle-earth.[24]

Tolkien, from his own work on the *New English Dictionary*, would have been more than aware of the famous definition to be found therein:[25]

> *Middle earth.* 1. The earth, as placed between heaven and hell, or as supposed to occupy the centre of the universe. Now only *arch.*, sometimes applied to the real world in contradistinction to fairyland.

Yet it is only when his writings are set against the corpus of his training – and of his main career work in the period 1920-45 – that we are able to see how faithfully he re-created (or sub-created) from the precious documents of Germanic antiquity. Indeed, there is now available a helpful framework of his preferred texts which, used judiciously, will further enlighten those who study closely the major canon, the works published or largely complete during Tolkien's own lifetime.

---

22 See *1913-1914 Regulations* (1913: 134).
23 The better students were encouraged to: the comparative study of English and Greek tragedy; the epic, with a general knowledge of Homer and Virgil, and special knowledge of the *Faerie Queene* and *Paradise Lost*.
24 It was long used in Norse literature. Christopher Tolkien has used the title, *The History of Middle-earth*, for his twelve-volume edition of his father's materials.
25 See under letter M in the *OED*, vol. VI (1908: 421).

Appendix

This philological work is described in *The Examination Studies – together with the Regulations of the Boards of Faculties for [...]1911-1912* (1911: 42) in the following way:

Candidates must also offer one of the following subjects [...]

> 5) [...] the elements of Comparative Philology as applied to Greek and Latin, with a special knowledge of either Greek or Latin philology.

Tolkien's preference was for the Latin option, although he was particularly interested in Greek which he would take in his diploma in Comparative Philology work in 1919-20. He was also generally interested in the alternative option for paper (5), viz.: "the Historical and Analytical Syntax of the Greek and Latin languages" (*ibid.*), and would treat of this material in his Oxford philological lectures from 1925 to c. 1940.[26]

---

26 See my article on this in *Seven* 19 (2002: 45-62).

An Important Influence: His Professor's Wife, Mrs Elizabeth Mary (Lea) Wright

It is a commonplace of academe that prize students get to know their professors' wives due to the special teaching devoted to them,[1] a truism especially valid in Oxford with its small language classes and much teaching at the don's own home. The pupil in this case is Ronald Tolkien and the friend Mrs E.M. Wright.[2] Humphrey Carpenter refers both to Tolkien's 1912 studying at "Joe Wright's dining-room table" (1977: 56) and "the huge Yorkshire teas given by the Wrights on Sunday afternoons" (*ibid.*), and to Lizzie Wright as someone "expert in [her] husband's subjects, and [who] could assist in [his] work" (*ibid.* 154). In that same year 1912, when Tolkien was still working in the Classics field – his studying with Professor Wright was in Greek philology, not Germanic as yet – Mrs E.M. Wright was putting the finishing touches to her own book, the dialect-based *Rustic Speech and Folk-Lore*, issued the following year by the University Press.

It is the contention of this note that that un-indexed text, read first by the student in odd moments prior to his 1915 Oxford Public Examinations and then war service, was to have a specific influence on the mind of the creator of Middle-earth. For, even more than her husband's somewhat unwieldy six volume *English Dialect Dictionary* (1896-1905), it focused on the key collections of regional dialectical usages (1913: xvi) such as G.F. Northall's two publications namely,

> *A Warwickshire Word-book* (1896), comprising obsolescent and dialectical words, colloquialisms, etc., gathered from oral relation, and collated with accordant works; and his earlier
>
> *English Folk-Rhymes* (1892), subtitled: *A collection of traditional verses relating to places and persons, customs, superstitions, etc.*

This essay first appeared in a shorter form in *Minas Tirith Evening Star* 14.1 (1985: 6-10) and then in the *Shaping of Middle-earth's Maker* (1992) and is here reprinted with the kind permission of their editors.

1 Consider, for example, D.H. Lawrence's friendship with, and later marriage to Frieda Weekley, wife of Ernest Weekley, Professor of English, Nottingham University College.
2 Joseph Wright had held the Corpus Christi Professorship of Comparative Philology from 1901. His wife would later produce the two volumes of biography and illuminating tribute, *The Life of Joseph Wright* (1932).

While the latter may be shown to have influenced the style and mode of much hobbit versifying, the emphasis now is focussed more on the vocabulary specifically treated by Mrs Wright.

Of particular interest is her discussion of *brat*, an early Celtic word borrowed into Old English, which was the surname[3] of the young student's intended bride.

> *brat*[4] (occurring in Scotland, Ireland, Northumberland, Durham, Cumberland, Westmoreland, Yorkshire, Lancashire, Isle of Man, Cheshire, Staffordshire, Derbyshire, Nottinghamshire, Lincolnshire, Worcester, Shropshire, Pembrokeshire), a child's pinafore, a large coarse apron made with sleeves, worn by workers in factories, is found in the Northumbrian Gospels of the Tenth Century, *bratt* 'pallium', *Matthew* v. 40. (1913: 105)

Various Orc-type demon names are discussed in Chapter XII 'Supernatural Beings' (1913: 191-213), under ghosts, boggarts, mine-goblins (*ibid*. 199-200), fairies, pixies and witches, e.g.:

> the simple form *Bug*, a bogie is apparently obsolete, remaining only in the phrase *to take a bug* (Midl.), to take fright; [or]
>
> *bucca*,[5] *gathorn*, *nuggie*, *shagfoal*, and many others.

Then follows an intriguing Tolkien-like discussion of the 'Knockers' who "haunt the tin-mines of Cornwall" and are "mining on their own account, out of sight" (*ibid*. 199).

She continues in phrases that must remind us of those greedily ransacking Bag End as well as of the ancient dwarves of both the Kingdom-under-the-Mountain and those whose days had been spent in Moria –

> They are generally hard working deep underground, but at no great distance, for the rolling of barrows, the strokes of pickaxes, and the fall of earth and stones are distinctly heard, and sometimes voices seem to mingle with these sounds. Some say that these phantom toilers are the souls[6] of the Jews who formerly worked the Cornish tin-mines, and who, for their wicked practises as tinners, have never been allowed to rest. (*ibid*. 200)

---

3 Compare Tolkien's own bemused discussion of her Christian name, Edith, in *YWES V* (62-63) and, again in *YWES VI* (39), which I treat in Essay 6 of this volume, pp. 55-58.

4 This is a selective reference to the *EDD*, vol. I (1898: 381-82). The present writer heard the word in the late 1930s in southern (i.e. Scottish) New Zealand.

5 An Old Cornish word for hobgoblin (Wright 1913: 199). One is reminded, in sound at least, of the *-buck* suffix in many Shire names.

6 'Undead' Cornish miners, damned to eternal toil, are also found in Edgar Allan Poe's *The City in the Sea*.

There is a long section following this on the dialect terms for the *ignis fatuus*, or Will-o'-the-wisp, which reminds us of what Gollum calls in the Dead Marshes "The tricksy lights. Candles of corpses, yes yes" (*TT* 234). Wright herself calls them the "*corp-candle, corpse candle* (Scotland, Lancashire, Lincolnshire); *dead* [death]-*candle* (Scotland) – regarded as an omen of death" (1913: 200.). There follow a number of names for the 'false light' and the tempter to one's doom.

> This lantern-bearing sprite haunts bogs and swampy meadows where it gambols and dances by itself, [or]:
> Hovering and blazing with delusive light,
> Misleads th' amaz'd night-wanderer from his way
> To bogs and mires, and oft through pond or pool.
> There swallow'd up and lost, from succour far. (*ibid.* 199)

Hence we can now comprehend the reason – otherwise unexplained – for Gollum's caution, repeated by Sam, against Frodo's looking at the "misty flames" (*TT* 234-35).

Passing over the many other items specifically found in *The Lord of the Rings*, – such as the occult power of the ash (1913: 234); *Wang*,[7] a Yorkshire and Midland word for "a field, a meadow, low-lying land" (*ibid.* 76); or the magic potency of the number nine (*ibid.* 235-36), we may notice two typical items which occur at the end (*ibid.* 336) of her text, namely *way-bread* and *withy-wind*. 'Way-bread'[8] (found in Scotland, the northern countries and Worcestershire) is described thus as

> the greater plantain, *Plantago major*, O.E. *wege-breita*, the plantain.

Her husband's dictionary, vol. VI (1905: 407) had noted *way-bread* as a variant on "*way-berry*, plantain, *Plantago major*."[9]

Withy-wind (1913: 336) she gives as western and southwestern, continuing –

> the great bindweed, Convolvulus sepium, and also the field bindweed, *C. arvensis*, O.E. *wipewinde*, bindweed,

---

7 Found in the Old English poetic compound *neoxna wang*, a 'plain of paradise' or in the place-name, Wetwang, late in *The Fellowship of the Ring*. See Ryan (1983: 10-13).
8 One discerns an element of scholarly humor in Tolkien's following this folk-etymology when it is used as an equivalent of *lembas* (*FotR* 385).
9 So also the *EDD*, vol. VI, (1905: 526).

and illustrates this with the following couplet from Langland

> He bare a burdoun ybounde with a brode liste,
> In a witherwyndes wise younden aboute.
> (*Piers Plowman*, ll. 524-25)

While the place-name is probably derived from Old English *windol*, 'winding brook',[10] there is no doubt that Tolkien intended the pun, or, if you will the deliberate use of Old English homonyms, since the river could equally be a 'willow-banked winding rivulet' or a 'convulvulus-choked streamlet'.

*   *   *

It but remains to stress that Elizabeth Wright's book proved most helpful at earlier stages in the young scholar's work for both lexis and linguistic philosophy. Thus she had noted memorably among the archaic literary words in the dialects –

> *attercop* (Scotland, Ireland, Northumberland, Cumberland, Westmoreland, Yorkshire, Lancashire, Cheshire and Wiltshire), a spider. This was in Old English *attercoppe*, a spider, from *ator*, *attor*, poison, and *coppe*, which probably means head, the old idea being that spiders were poisonous insects. In the Middle English poem *The Owl and the Nightingale* (c. 1225), the owl taunts the nightingale with eating "nothing but attercops, and foul fliers, and worms." Wyclif (1381) has: "[...] the webbis of an attercop thei woven". (1913: 37)

It is, doubtless, the literal sense, 'poison-head' which is so offensive to the spiders in Bilbo's taunt-song intended "to make them curious, excited and angry all at once" (*Hobbit* 170).

Finally, it is to be noted that Mrs Wright was concerned to make a larger stylistic point, stressing that dialect speech is not necessarily 'archaic' or quaint, but rather 'delightful' for:

> Numbers of words used by Chaucer [...], by Shakespeare, and by the translators of the Bible, which are now treated as archaisms [...] still live and move and have their being among our rural population today. (1913: 36)

Later, in her praise of perhaps the most accomplished writer in the West-Midland dialect, the composer of *Sir Gawain and the Green Knight*, she offers

---

10 This is the interpretation given by Shippey (1982: 82).

something of the ideal to which Tolkien himself albeit unconsciously, was to aspire closely –

> [...] through his works, [...] he appears to have been a literary country gentle-man, born and bred in Lancashire, a man equally at home in his study, pen in hand, describing armed knights, and embattled castles, the tumultuous surg-ings of the Deluge [...], or in the saddle, [...] to the sound of horn and bugle [...] and the yelping cry of a pack of hounds.[11] He possessed, on the one hand, a real vein of poetic imagination, coupled with learning and knowledge, and on the other, all the instincts of a keen sportsman. He was a lover of nature and outdoor life, with extraordinary powers of accurate observation, and an artist's eye for picturesque detail. Thus his memory was stored with a rich and varied vocabulary [...] the skillful handling of which characterizes this unknown poet, sportsman and man of letters. (1913: 68-69)

Apart from the obvious parallel sympathies of Elizabeth Wright and Ronald Tolkien, it may be significant to quote from his words graciously echoic of hers, surely, at many points, when discussing[12] that same West Midland culture in the early thirteenth century and the manner of elegant prose expression of the unknown author of the *Ancrene Wisse* –

> It is not a language long relegated to the 'uplands' struggling once more for expression in apologetic emulation of its betters [...], but rather one that has never fallen back into 'lewdness,' and has continued, in troublous times, to maintain the air of a gentleman, if a country gentleman. (1929: 104)

*   *   *

Thus it is that Elizabeth Mary Wright's charming book may be seen to be a potent influence in Tolkien's evolving linguistic aesthetic, as well as the gateway to the vast field of English dialectology, as presented by Professor Joseph Wright which Tolkien was to work so persistently, like one of Elizabeth's unseen goblin miners over the next sixty years of his career as literary artist. Since Mrs Wright lived on, after the death of her much older husband in 1930, until after the publication of the three-volume epic, it would be gratifying to believe that she had seen some of its echoes of her work as well as the earlier use by Tolkien of *attercop* in *The Hobbit*.

---

11 In Oxford lectures in the mid-1950s, Tolkien expressed his zest for hunts conducted near his regiment in Yorkshire (c. 1916).

12 His article was entitled '*Ancrene Wisse* and *Hali Meithhad*' and was published in *Essays and Studies* XIV (1929: 104-26).

Epilogue

As is often pointed out, Elizabeth Wright was the spirit inspiring her husband's *English Dialect Dictionary*, doing most of the secretarial work for the dictionary, and, as helpmate, creating "the happiest couple in Oxford" (Kellett 2004: 466). She is also acknowledged for her work on West Yorkshire dialect in volume 1 of the *EDD* (1896, 1906: xiv).

Trolls and Other Themes – William Craigie's Significant Folkloric Influence on the Style of J.R.R. Tolkien's *The Hobbit*

> Three very large persons sitting round a very large fire of beech-logs. They were toasting mutton on long slits of wood […]. (*Hobbit* 44)

> […] through artful combination of [dragon] themes contributed […] by Andrew Lang and William Morris, Tolkien advances fantasy narratives. [Yet] […] there is something in Tolkien's use of traditional sources that transcends [the Victorian recensions]. (Evans 2000: 22)

This second quotation, a more recent and reflective critical reference to the fantasist's style and its possible antecedents, serves to remind us that the secondary creations from the famed twentieth century writer should be probed continually and very closely for the vast array of illuminating and fascinating possible sources and analogues for his massive body of new-fashioned 'legend for England'. Earlier literary research, notably that close work from the mediaeval studies' trained scholar, T. Shippey (1982), has, very properly focused on the significant Germanic and mediaeval texts well known to the fabulist from his professional teaching and supervisory duties[1] and related reading.

Many careful scholars of Tolkien's creations have profitably read around in Old English literature and in the more obvious Old Norse materials, such as Snorri's *Edda*, in search of analogues to and earlier forms of story motifs to be found in *The Lord of the Rings* and, earlier in the Tolkien writings, in *The Hobbit*. Yet there remain many haunting passages still not adequately or quite precisely 'sourced', the distinctive and ancient tones of which continue to tease both the intrigued source-hunter and the more general reader.

It was such a vague recollection – of remembered as once read and, seemingly, highly relevant, analogous materials – which led to this painstaking re-inves-

---

1 See Ryan (2002: 45-62).

tigation of the work of another Oxford mediaevalist-teacher of long ago and so to the more than likely source for numerous dramatic details of the world as depicted outside the Shire in the classic fantasy quest book of 1937, namely *The Hobbit: or, There and Back Again.*

One largely and critically neglected source-field from which so much may be shown to be derived is a lovingly and insightfully compiled folkloric text of some bulk, and, in fact, a specific book that was very close – and peculiarly accessible – to Tolkien from his first student days in Oxford, as will be shown below.

*   *   *

Thus, while the formal source of Tolkien's dragon lore and dragon behaviour as focussed on Smaug, is very correctly stated by Jonathan Evans[2] to be the Dragon in the Old English epic, *Beowulf,* – a text on which Tolkien had been lecturing so very regularly from 1925,[3] – no one has, to date, produced an obvious, let alone a closely detailed source for the fabulist's accounts of the great menacing trolls. These were, of course, startlingly encountered by Thorin's party in the early part of *The Hobbit,* and, much later, 'found' again in the early part of *The Fellowship of the Ring,* in the places where they had been caught off guard and so petrified by the onset of the daylight many years before.

Most interestingly, both the troll passages and innumerable fascinating details of dragons and their wiles may be found similarly treated in the long-neglected volume, *Scandinavian Folk-Lore: Illustrations of the Traditional Beliefs of the Northern Peoples* (1896: xx, 454).[4] This fascinating and illuminating work, a compilation correctly labelled as "Selected and Translated" by W.A. Craigie, was published by Alexander Gardner, Paisley, and at Paternoster Square, London. Library records of various sorts suggest that it was much read and savoured in Oxford in the next

---

2 The reference is given in the motto quotation at the head of this essay.

3 See the early such occasions in the J.S. Ryan article, as cited above, p. 49.

4 There is a mis-numbering in the end papers at the rear. Although trolls are mentioned in another recent Norse background text available to Tolkien as young student, namely E.E. Kellett's *The Religion of Our Northern Ancestors* (1914: 84), all the folklore is presented in a somewhat terse and unsympathetic style, as to be expected in a (Scottish) series of 'Manuals for Christian Thinkers'. Craigie's book was reviewed most sympathetically by F.Y.P. (i.e. Professor York Powell), in *Folklore* 10.4 (Dec. 1899: 459-61).

two decades or so, at least up to Craigie's departure for North America and his various, heroic and demanding lexical tasks there. (See below.)

It is however, important, in view of the current almost complete neglect of consideration of the content and engaging narrative style of the older man's writing on Scandinavian matters – let alone on his most stimulated Oxford pupil, Tolkien, – to explain first in some detail the highly influential Craigie-Tolkien association. For the link between the two men, master and pupil, seems to have been one long influencing both the latter's taste and literary style. Indeed, this personal association is perhaps as significant for Tolkien as those later with C.S. Lewis, Hugo Dyson and others regularly listed as fellow Inklings, with their considerable knowledge of classical, mediaeval and later literature, as well as of the manifestations of religious beliefs to be found in such story.

*   *   *

William Alexander Craigie,[5] a Lowland Scot, born in 1844 in Dundee as the son of a jobbing gardener, was generously and successfully educated at St Andrews and Oxford Universities. There he read for degrees in Classics and Philosophy, and would, from his student days in Scotland, spend much time in the independent study of German, French, and other languages. Danish and Icelandic would also be added to these after he had received a deeply significant mind- and imagination-priming gift from a friend, the present of a small book of Norwegian songs (Wyllie 1961: 273).

When up at Oxford – he was there from 1888 to 1893 –, despite his being a student in the realm of Literae Humaniores, first at Balliol College and then at Oriel, he had also purposefully continued his childhood-commenced Celtic studies, now under the tuition of Professor Rhys of Jesus College. Further, since there were no Icelandic lectures in Oxford at the time, – owing to the illness and death of that professor, Gudbrand Vigfusson, – Craigie had worked on the Scandinavian languages on his own, to remarkable effect (*ibid*. 274-75).

---

5 For convenience, many specific biographical details and interpretations will be referred to in their insightful treatment in the 'Memoir' (Obituary tribute) on Craigie by J.M. Wyllie in *Proceedings of the British Academy* 47 (1961: 273-91).

And so, when he already had excellent Moderations and Greats [Literae Humaniores] examination results behind him, Oriel College, much impressed by his scholarship, would offer him the financial means of pursuing his already strong Norse bent. This consequent academic year, 1892-1893, he would spend in Copenhagen studying ancient manuscripts and improving his Icelandic, reading ancient texts in both the Royal and University Libraries there, and copying texts that interested him, including *Skotlands Rímur*. Of this particular 'colonial' Scandinavian collection he would produce a fine scholarly and critical edition in 1908.

However, on his return to Scotland in 1893, the classics were still his official academic field, and so he was appointed as assistant to the Professor of Latin at St. Andrews University, remaining there for the next four years, collaborating with Andrew Lang (b. 1844), both a classicist and a folklorist, in an edition of Robert Burns. And soon after he would himself be supplying not inconsiderable (comparative) materials from Scandinavian sources for Lang's *Fairy Books*.[6] He would also produce at much the same time his own engaging *Scandinavian Folk-Lore* in 1896.

Then, in 1897, he was offered a post, back in Oxford, on the staff of the *New English Dictionary*, and so he would have for the rest of his life as his main task that of a lexicographer, working sequentially on the *New English Dictionary*, and then on the *Dictionary of American English on Historical Principles*, as well as collecting possibly suitable quotations for the *Scottish National Dictionary* to-be.

However, his passion for things Scandinavian bore immediate fruit. For, three years after his arrival in Oxford, he was also appointed to a lectureship there in Scandinavian languages at the Taylor Institution, and then, in 1916, he became the University's Rawlinson-Bosworth Professor of Anglo-Saxon, the first of these appointments making him Tolkien's official tutor in Old Norse[7] and related literatures.

---

6 See, for example, 'Hermod and Hadvor'– from the Icelandic – in *The Yellow Fairy Book* (Lang 1894: 301ff).

7 For a more detailed treatment of this, see Ryan, 'The Oxford Undergraduate Studies in Early English and Related Languages of J.R.R. Tolkien (1913-1915)' on pp. 17-26 of this present volume. Tolkien, by then an English student at Exeter College, was taking classes in Old Norse from the autumn of

It is this somewhat terse account of a wonderful linguistic aptitude and a teacher's infectious shared love for all things Scandinavian that explains the sort of contact that Tolkien would have with Craigie, both as student doing the Honours School of English, and then, in 1919-20, when back from the war, as apprentice colleague on the *New English Dictionary*. Appropriately, when Craigie was called to the University of Chicago to work on the *Dictionary of American English* (Wyllie 1961: 275), the young academic, in Leeds since 1921, would be found succeeding his teacher and strong supporter in Oxford's Chair of Anglo-Saxon in 1925.

And the much younger man would follow his mentor in the same Norse teaching,[8] since there was no one else to do this, and the two positions had been linked in actuality, even if not publicly bracketed together.

Indeed, we may even speculate quietly to ourselves that, at one level, aspects of Craigie's homely Scottish family background may well be hinted at in the character of another gardener, the humble Sam, or, perhaps also, the wisdom of his well-informed and much travelled professor[9] in the equally well-informed great wizard, Gandalf.

Back to Scandinavian Lore

However, we are on much more solid ground with the book of 1896 as a close source and influence for Tolkien, and, indeed, marvelous quarry of seminal folkloric materials for the future delineation of Middle-earth. For it was a text – if not read earlier – then first perused closely by Tolkien in 1913 and 1914. And he would continue to read and refer to its engagingly presented clusters of folkloric pieces for many years thereafter, not least since he would give all the

---

1913 until his finals in 1915 with Old Icelandic, then styled 'Scandinavian Philology, with Special Reference to Icelandic' as a chosen option (22). We must assume that he had read about the time of its publication Craigie's fine essay, 'The Oldest Icelandic Folk-Lore', in *Folklore* 2.2 (June 1893: 219-32), with its passages on dead warriors, ravens, sacred trees, trolls and burial mounds.

8 We may note in comparison Tolkien's somewhat later spirited defence of the teaching and study of Old Icelandic in his apologia essay, 'The Oxford English School' in *The Oxford Magazine*, May 29th 1930 (778-82).

9 As the 'Memoir' (1961: 284-85) tells us, far beyond his early Scandinavian travels and years in the U.S.A., Craigie had become an inveterate traveller, visiting Romania, India, China, and Japan, as well as Frisia, and many other fascinating linguistic and cultural corners of Europe.

Old Norse lectures himself for the next two decades from the time of Craigie's departure for Chicago in 1925.

For, as the new Rawlinson-Bosworth Professor, in addition to his duties in Old English, Ronald Tolkien was required to give all the university lectures in the Norse field[10] for those who sought tuition in this optional study area. Yet it was also one very much encouraged by him in the English School's Course I from c. 1930 and for almost the next three decades, there regularly being talented students as takers for two such optional papers.

*   *   *

Craigie's *Scandinavian Folk-Lore*, a volume clearly identified as "selected and translated by William A. Craigie," and subtitled "Illustrations of the Traditional Beliefs of the Northern Peoples," is a substantial manual of more than 470 pages, in 10 major sections, with the various items carefully focused, labelled and ordered, and with a reflective 'Preface', parts of which must remind the thoughtful reader of various turns of phrase in Tolkien's deservedly famous British Academy Lecture, *The Monsters and the Critics*, of 1936. For Craigie was much concerned in his informative and, indeed, engaging compilation to stress – as did his pupil so regularly – : the richness of Scandinavian "tradition and folklore;" the long memories of the people, and how saga-writing piquantly contained "an element of the supernatural," this making "the legend more impressive, more picturesque, and less easily forgotten" (1896: v), and so retaining "its inmost [pagan] nature," despite "the rise of a new faith."[11]

*   *   *

This first published Norse book from Craigie – for there were several later ones – is a young man's enthusiastic and even cunningly assembled compilation and an ingenious ordering of folkloric scraps,[12] all now carefully clustered

---

10 As the 'Memoir' (1961: 275) tells us, Craigie had had "the duties of the chair officially extended to enable him to continue teaching on Old Icelandic." This situation regarding the additional duties in the Norse field would continue for most of Tolkien's time in the Old English chair, until he was progressively relieved of this by E.O.G. Turville-Petre, to whom would long be accorded the courtesy title of Professor.
11 These phrases come from the 'Preface' (1896: v-x).
12 In the 'Memoir', Wyllie commented on Craigie's remarkable powers of memory (1961: 288), and referred to his subject's ability to make 'a convincing pattern' (*ibid*. 290), from hitherto disconnected scraps.

and linked, and quite distinct from his better-known and powerful study of the major Icelandic prose, *The Icelandic Sagas*. For this last small manual, issued in a comparative series, was compiled in 1912, – in effect, throughout the period of his pupil's comparative philology studies with him – and then published in 1913.

In his 'Preface' to the earlier book, Craigie – in a fashion that serves to remind us of his close friendship with Andrew Lang, and even echoes the 'Preface' to the latter's *The Yellow Fairy Book* – stresses the significance of the rise of folklore studies in Great Britain (1913: v), and then explains how he is himself trying to flesh out the design of Benjamin Thorpe in 1851, in the other's second volume of *Northern Mythology*. For both men were concerned with supplying specific instances of each separate conception or belief. Both, too, were concerned with grouping themes, yet ever stressing the great importance of each and every perhaps conflicting variant of essentially similar manifestations of belief and magic.

As Craigie put it so memorably of his own work,

> Wherever possible, the belief has been brought out by a narrative embodying it, not by a mere statement of its existence. [For] the story is the soul of folk-lore, by which the general concept is made living and interesting [...].

> How the story in many cases preserved the belief we may see in our oldest sources, the sagas [...]. These tales served for both instruction and amusement [...] where the interest they excited, and the imagination they called forth, were a salutary relief from the pressure of real life. (1913: vii)

Craigie's Structure, Classification and Analysis

In this personally compiled manual, one clearly derived from the great libraries of Copenhagen, William Craigie chose to both assemble and re-assemble his numerous sources, these scraps and tantalizing fragments coming from Iceland, the Faroes, Norway, Sweden and Denmark, and, more generally, from the Icelandic sagas, the peasants' folk-tales and from the several Viking areas' folk poetry (Wyllie 1961: 274). Yet the compiler and arranger was always concerned to tease out and stress "the conceptions retained in the memories of the people"

(1896: 419). Thus his more than 400 pages of grouped tales, legends, lays and beliefs, he had elected to cluster thus:

The Old Gods (pp. 9-39);
Trolls and Giants (pp. 40-92);
Berg-Folk[13] and Dwarves (pp. 93-141);
Elves or Huldu-Folk (pp. 142-88);
Nisses or Brownies (pp. 189-219);
Water-beings (pp. 220-48);
Monsters (pp. 249-75) [these last tales feature powerfully the motifs of caves, dragons, and gold];
Ghosts and Wraiths (pp. 276-334);
Wizards and Witches (pp. 335-89);
Churches, Treasures, Plagues (pp. 390-416).

Craigie-influenced Narrative and Imagery in Tolkien's Story Telling

While it will be very obvious that this approach to the people's lore and the adopted grouping suggests many parallels to the better known materials of the Tolkienian corpus, or Legendarium, it is perhaps enough for the moment to emphasize that the classifying and subtly guiding Craigie 'Index' picks up many strangely familiar examples of such important and recurrent narrative themes as :

silver cups;
crows, the speech of;
dragons;
elves, their (various) ages;
wizards;
mounds opening;
restless spirits;
dragon's treasure;
trolls; and stone-throwing (p. 133);
were-wolves; [compare Tolkien's wargs];
the wood-man, etc.

---

13 These feature fallen angels, fairies, brownies and nisser (1913: 93).

In short, many of the motifs that give the ancient and powerful heroic tone to the initial explorations immediately beyond the Shire – in both *The Hobbit* (1937) and the earlier parts of *The Fellowship of the Ring* (1954) – may be found already clustered here in most helpful (folkloric handbook) fashion.

For the moment, it is enough to focus on the many troll sections, particularly those telling of how these nasty creatures might be turned to stone by the light of the new day, should they then be caught in the open. Thus he tells us,

> [as] it is sudden death to night-trolls if day breaks upon them, the dawning was their destruction, so that each of them became a pillar of rock, and are now those which stand there (1913: 62).

Even more pleasing to Tolkien researchers is the series of footnotes, pp. 422-24, in which other troll transformations are linked with landscapes across the whole Scandinavian region. Indeed, it is arguable that several of these passages contribute small details to, or are echoed in, the second chapter of *The Hobbit*, or in the details noted by the company traversing the same region early on in *The Fellowship of the Ring*.

*   *   *

Like other malign creatures of the wastes, Tolkien's creations are always much more ominous and violently elemental – demi-urges, even, – rather than of the gentler treatment accorded them in another similar and popular Victorian period manual, the handbook *Norse Mythology: Or The Religion of Our Forefathers [...] Systematized and Interpreted* by R.B. Anderson, 2nd edition, Chicago, 1891. This somewhat bland contemporary work to Craigie's makes them "extremely rich" (1891: 202), "but they are not generally regarded as malignant" and so must seem more like somewhat secretive dwarves.

And Craigie – for he allows various intrusions from more significant folk details to be found in the *Kings' Sagas* – also tells us of how King Olaf went to Halogaland "which was so over-run by trolls that he could stand it no longer" (1913: 44), of their "sitting round a fire in a cave mouth," or of how a female troll was turned to stone "as the day broke in the east" (*ibid.* 49). For

> [s]he turned into a stone on the top of the ridge, which has since been called Skessu-stein ('The Giantess's Stone'). (*ibid.* 50)

In all, there are in his manual some six memorable passages on countryside trolls who are always nasty, as with the accounts of :

> "an ugly troll from Dragehoi" roasting toads on the fire and then eating them "one after the other" (*ibid.* 65);

> their cowardice at encountering the unexpected (*ibid.* 69);

> their confusion when stones are thrown towards them (*ibid.* 133); or

> their being turned to stone, variously, as in this passage on Drang-ey:

> As it is sudden death to night-trolls if day breaks upon them, the dawning was their destruction, so that each of them became a pillar of rock and are now those which stand there. (*ibid.* 62)

Further Influences from Craigie's Handbook of Germanic and Norse Folklore

A general point made by Craigie – and one, surely, extremely apposite to the shaping of Tolkien's best-known prose style – is that

> [when] saga-writing began in Iceland[14] [...] it rested upon a mass of traditional lore, which comprised not merely genealogy and history, but also an element of the supernatural [...] [which] made the legend more impressive, more picturesque, and less easily forgotten. (1913: v)

Craigie's further contention then was that the basic concept and later (individual story) variants bore witness to the transmission from early times of core folk beliefs, notions illustrated – and attested – by the presence of both early and much later varying versions. For, indeed, as he would say of the corpus:

> The work is a constant alternation of the new and old, but the two are seldom at variance, and both together bear witness to a unity of faith that underlies them [...] . The story is the soul of folk-lore, by general concept [for it] is made living and interesting [...] [and we can note] [...] how the story in many cases preserved the belief we may see in our oldest sources [...]. (*ibid.* vii)

In the several hundred (folk) tales summarized in his lucid yet richly textured, and even densely, presented book, or referred to by Craigie, there are so many

---

14 It has not been possible to discuss here the finer and fascinating details of Craigie's long and happy exposure to Iceland and its people, as this is recorded by Wyllie (1961: 277, 278, 282-84, etc.). See, however, the essay discussed in fn 7, above.

like situations, incidents and motifs very familiar to those reading *The Hobbit*, or the earlier sections of *The Lord of the Rings*:

trolls sitting around a fire and talking ponderously;

the reasons why mortal men can never see elves, unless the latter wish it;

the elf-king carrying music wherever he goes;

the berserkr who puts his treasure in a mound and guards it still;

a treasure cave where dragons may be found; or

a precious goblet stolen from a mound; etc., etc.

Craigie on 'Dragons in Norway'

By now it will be abundantly clear that Craigie's book constitutes an ordered and layered compilation, one concerned to classify the available folk tales and enforce the re-telling by inserting relevant scraps of ancient legend, as with the following piece which had, fascinatingly, survived to the seventeenth century:

'Dragons in Norway'

Stories of dragons which fly through the air by night, and vomit fire, are fairly common, and in various places all over the country there are still shown holes in the earth and in the hills, out of which they are seen to come like blazing fire, when wars or other troubles are to be expected.

When they return to their dwellings where they brood over immense treasures which as some say, they have gathered by night [...], there can be heard the clang of the great iron doors that close behind them. As they are fierce and vomit terrible fire, it is dangerous to meddle with them [...]. [...] a priest of the name of Anders Madsen (supposed to have lived about 1631), shot a dragon which lay upon silver [...]. (*ibid.* 255)

[This last piece is, surely, a close analogue to, if not the actual passage utilized by Tolkien in so much of his memorable account of Smaug – and of his nemesis, Bard – in *The Hobbit*.]

*   *   *

This last apocryphal, critical and also folkloric story, even if scholarly and antiquarian in its presentation, was, doubtless, one of serious interest for both Tolkien and for his Old Norse tutor. For it contains – amongst numerous parallel details of motifs – some remarkable analogues between the tales from both men of the lore of trolls and dragons.

A Fresh Field for the Source-hunter

The present exposition began with a reference to the Clark and Timmons edited collection of essays entitled *J. R. R. Tolkien and His Literary Resonances*. Further, it cited the recent and eminently valid critical intuition that Tolkien's seemingly 'new' heroic and monster-centred texts went back beyond the various popular, non-threatening and 'literary' recensions of earlier tales as frequently rehearsed in the Victorian period.

However, the general narrative point now to be made is that serious study of Tolkien's creative writings should look beyond the literary narratives and popularisers in the decades of his nurture and so focus much more sharply on the great Victorian close scholars of the texts of the Germanic North, like R. Cleasby or William Craigie. It is to their scholarly work that we should be turning for the folkloric story elements and motifs that constitute the everlasting appeal to all recensionists and students of the heroic tales and settings of the North.

For these, alike, it may be argued, gave the challenges and character-building experiences for those who leave the Shire to go on the great quest to destroy the One Ring. The same effect operates for all those readers who are fired by both Craigie's and Tolkien's tales of the Fellowship members' quiet heroism. Indeed, one might well reflect on Wyllie's encomium on Craigie, that "he taught us by the sheer force of his example,"[15] a sentiment which we might re-phrase as "the power of his stories was able to fire the imagination." For the Scotsman had also distilled so much of the spirit of the old tales in his book, one so influential for nurturing his pupil's creative genius.

For so very much of the texture of Tolkien's prose has closely phrased and structured analogues from the suggested, if vestigial, race memories, in fact, from the otherwise nearly lost corpus of ancient 'legends', – as his lengthy

---

15 This quality is called by Wyllie (1961: 291) "the very staple of genius."

1951 epistle to Milton Waldman would say.[16] All of this mass of story, it is argued, underlies the younger folklorist-fabulist's myriad tales, even as it fires the imaginations of his readers. For Tolkien did create his body of available narrative, which, as he said, "[he] could dedicate simply to: to England; to [his] country" (*Letters* 144) – as he had purposed, – so much of that great corpus had an inspiration and perdurable appeal that may so often be shown to lie in the old tales of much earlier, the people's stories from the North which he had heard, read and loved.

And so one of the scholar fabulists so central to Tolkien's training, William Alexander Craigie, should never be forgotten, or his engaging book, of *Scandinavian Folk-Lore*, one compiled before his own thirtieth year. For it constituted a richly veined source that would be so frequently mined for so many of the motifs for the great stories at the core of Middle-earth's perdurable appeal.

Indeed, we must rejoice that Tolkien had his lectures and almost individual tuition from one of the finest Victorian classicists-become-mediaevalists, a simple and humble man, a genuine folklorist, one steeped in traditional story, and someone, like himself, become converted to a great love of the unmodified corpus of Scandinavian legend. And, very satisfyingly, it was so often preserved in all its power in the anecdotal versions that the peasants told for relief in dark times, and in their own powerful and inimitable folkloric style.

And now, some Words of Folkloric Appeal from Professor Tolkien in his Prime

In the early summer of 1930, Tolkien had contributed to *The Oxford Magazine* a revelatory musing,[17] one entitled 'The Oxford English School', in which he made a strong plea for the place of the early Germanic language and literature studies – 'Dark Age Studies' and 'First English' were the designations he used. Further, he deemed that they presented "a curriculum with a rational and exciting discipline."[18] However, in his subsequent – and so derived fictions – he had

---

16 See *Letters*, letter no. 131, especially pp. 144-45.
17 It appeared on 29th May, 1930, and ran from p. 778 to 782.
18 This appears in the essay on p. 782.

sought a far greater audience than the select few studying the earliest language and literature in the University's English School. From the folk materials, both surviving and surmised in fact, he would now make a vast integrated construct, nothing other than a highly accessible mythology for the English people.

*   *   *

But to return to our opening, – we agree most emphatically that Victorian scholarship of folk tales and story-telling were important for the nurture of Tolkien's mind. However, it is to William Craigie's compilation of the many fragments of lore that we should turn for enlightenment about the sources for and analogues of his talented pupil. Tolkien's powerful retellings of the beguiling tales of trolls and other 'monsters' were drawn, through Craigie, from the cherished possessions of the north's plainest folk.

*   *   *

As he would write in 1951 of his passionate urge to write stories:

> I was an undergraduate […] I sought and found […] legends of other lands. […] But once upon a time […] I had a mind to make a body of more or less connected legend […] which I could dedicate simply to: to England. (*Letters* 144)

It is the contention of this present essay that a valiant mentor for the folkloric writer to be was his tutor in all matters Scandinavian, William Alexander Craigie, a simple man who inspired so many facets of the style and tastes of his worthy successor as both scholar and folklorist.

Homo Ludens – Amusement, Play and Seeking in Tolkien's earliest Romantic Thought

In March, 1965, the Oxford doyen of Booksellers, Sir Basil Blackwell, pointed out to me the existence of the very early Tolkien poem, 'Goblin Feet', published by B.H. Blackwell in *Oxford Poetry* for 1915 (64-65). There it appeared, soon after a Lay, 'Orford and Iseult' (50-58) by Dorothy Sayers of Somerville College, as being by J. R. R. Tolkien (then still a student) of Exeter College, Oxford. Despite its importance as an early piece,[1] Tolkien's dislike of it (*BLT I* 32) caused his biographer to quote only part of it (Carpenter 1977: 74f).

But its significance is now much more enhanced by the publication in 1983 of other early Tolkien works, namely, *The Book of Lost Tales, Part I* (*BLT I*) and the lecture, 'A Secret Vice' (*MCE* 198-223). The first lost tales volume contains much material concerned with the writer's earliest thought, while the lecture on private languages does much to substantiate Tolkien's own often repeated claim that the basis of all his creative writing was linguistic. Some of the points made in that paper to an unspecified linguistic group merit teasing out. These are: His belief "in an 'artificial' language [...] as the one thing antecedently necessary for uniting Europe" (*MCE* 198); and the idea that inventing languages is "a New Art, or a New Game," concerned with "the splendour of words" (*MCE* 198-99). Unlike cants or argots which "serve the needs of a secret and persecuted society," "the linguistic faculty, strong in children" is "purely for amusement, and pleasure" (*MCE* 201) and, when more highly developed, may lead to poet's craft and it is "an art for which life is not long enough" (*MCE* 202).

Invention in language "is probably always going on – to the distraction of 'etymology'" (*MCE* 204). In such new words there is a true making, not a creation,[2]

This essay first appeared in a shorter form in *Inklings-Jahrbuch* 6 (1988: 113-21), to whose editors I am grateful for the permission to reprint it.

1 The third in sequence in the list of the published writings, as given by Carpenter (1977: 268).

2 One assumes the Aristotle-inspired concept of the poet as 'maker' as opposed to the notions of God as Creator, and man in making up fairy stories as sub-creator. [Tolkien's terminology in his 'On Fairy Stories' (1947, *MCE* 109-61)]. *MCE* is a collection, edited by Christopher Tolkien, of his father's papers.

since such a word "is a group of sounds temporarily more or less fixed + an associated notion more or less defined and fixed in itself" (*MCE* 204). Once one has determined on a set of sounds, "the idea proposed for association with them gave *pleasure*" (*MCE* 205). "This idea of using the linguistic faculty for amusement is [...] deeply interesting to me" since "it is the *contemplation* of the relation between sound and notion which is a main source of pleasure" (*MCE* 206). In considering "what *pleasure* or *instruction* or both the individual maker of a play-language" derives from his hobby, he concludes that "for perfect construction of an art-language it is found necessary to construct at least in outline a mythology concomitant [...] because the making of language and mythology are related functions" (*MCE* 210); and in discussing some of his own considered linguistic efforts, he described them as being "in the one language which has been expressly designed to give play to my own most normal phonetic taste" (*MCE* 212), concluding of this process of expression and fixing of taste: "Just as the construction of a mythology expresses at first one's taste, and later conditions one's imagination, and becomes inescapable, so with this language" (*MCE* 212-13).

His concluding section (*MCE* 217-19) is concerned with the endeavour to reestablish in new languages some of the possibilities available for the most ancient of poets, before the fixing of associations,[3] when they, like language inventors, "blended the more elusive delight of establishing novel relations between symbol and significance, and in contemplating them" (*MCE* 218). Modern poetry, or the ear of the poet, he felt, "runs on heard but seldom coming to awareness," lacking the "merry freedom" of word coinings, as in the *Kalevala* or in your own invented language (*ibid.*). There you are able to experience many of "the less subtle but most moving and permanently important of the strokes of poetry [...] and set the imagination leaping" (*MCE* 219).

The poem 'Goblin Feet' possesses an undeniable sureness of rhythm, Georgian vocabulary, and a notion that the road that passes one's door embodies temptation and allure, particularly on summer nights. In lines that are an anticipation of 'The Road Goes Ever on' (1967), he exclaims of the fairy lanterns

---

3 This notion glances at the concept of 'nonsense' verse, beloved of the later Victorians and the Edwardians.

> I must follow in their train
> Down the crooked fairy lane
> Where the coney-rabbits[4] long ago have gone,
> And where silverly they sing
> In a moving moonlit ring
> All a-twinkle with the jewels they have on
> They are fading round the turn
> Where the glow-worms palely burn. (ll. 17-24)

His cry of yearning, "Let me go! O let me start!" (l. 27), is followed by the anguish of the exile excluded from their experiences, in the refrain

> O! the warmth! O! the hum! O! the colours in the dark!
> O! the gauzy wings, of golden honey-flies!
> O! the music of their feet – of their dancing goblin feet!
> O! the magic! O! the sorrow when it dies. (ll. 29-32)

While this poem, of itself, might not be identified clearly with the memory of heaven possessed by the very young and innocent, – as is to be found in the poetry of Thomas Traherne, or in William Wordsworth's 'Intimations of Immortality' – this association is made much clearer and more certain by 'The Cottage of Lost Play' (*BLT I* 13-44). This place possesses various synonyms in the collection, of which the index (*BLT I* 278) gathers up: Cottage of the Children; Cottage of the Children of Earth; Cottage of the Play of Sleep; The House of Lost Play; and The House of Memory.

The editor, Christopher Tolkien, has presented together and most judiciously, the various prose and poetry variations of this vision which "underwent a continual slow shifting, shedding and enlarging" (*BLT I* 7) from its original composition in "the winter of 1916-17" (*BLT I* 13). In essence, the central figure is an early man, one not unlike either the narrator of 'Goblin Feet', the Frodo-to-be, or even Tolkien himself – or, should not one argue, the Christian exile from Heaven. For, as the editor notes of the third section of the collection, there is present "a rare and very suggestive glimpse of the mythic conception in its earliest phase; for here ideas that are drawn from Christian theology are explicitly present" (*BLT*

---

4 A possible anticipation of his own etymology for *hobbit* see as published in the *Supplement to the Oxford English Dictionary*, Vol. II. (Burchfield 1976: 111, column b). The editor, R.W. Burchfield, had obtained it from Tolkien years before, c. 1957, and kept it ready for this volume.

50

I 92). Indeed, he goes on to point out that the later fragment, 'The Coming of the Valar' is a "reflection of Purgatory, Hell and Heaven" (*BLT I* 92).

In his annotation of 'The Cottage of Lost Play', Christopher Tolkien is less concerned to add either theological or biographical details. We find, however, that 'Goblin Feet' and 'You and Me' were both written on 27-28 April, 1915 (*BLT I* 27, 32, 136) when Tolkien was 23. The poem on the second subject, 'You and Me and the Cottage of Lost Play' (*BLT I* 28-30) is a moving piece of seeming autobiographical speculation,[5] which opens thus:

> You and me – we know that land
>   And often have been there
> In the long old days, old nursery days,
>   A dark child and a fair.
> Was it down the paths of firelight dreams
> [...]
> That You and I got lost in Sleep
>   And met each other there –
> Your dark hair on your white nightgown
>   And mine was tangled fair? (ll. 1-12)

As a footnote suggests, there is a likely echo of the lines of Francis Thompson's poem 'Daisy'

> Two children did we stray and talk
>   Wise, idle, childish things. (ll. 11-12)

The 65 lines of this early revision are, however, notable for a recurring pattern of images – a lost land, voyaging in sleep, wandering on the shores of an inland sea, following "a warm and winding lane" (l. 22), the cottage by the sea, dwellings in the trees[6] (l. 48), children clambering and dancing, and the loss of both cottage and 'the magic track' (l. 61). These are repeated in the final version of the poem, and in its companion 'Kortirion among the Trees', versions of which survive from November, 1915 to 1962.

---

5 This is, of course, mere speculative empathy since Ronald and Edith only met when sixteen and nineteen respectively. See Carpenter (1977: 41).
6 An anticipation of the *flets* of Lothlórien (in *The Fellowship of the Ring*).

Despite the longer lines of this last poem, there are present many of the themes of both 'Goblin Feet' and of 'The Cottage', as when the Elves pass away, as in these lines (100-6) of the 1973 version:

> O holy Elves and fair immortal Folk,
> You sing then ancient songs that once awoke
>   Under primeval stars before the Dawn;
> You whirl then dancing with the eddying wind,
>   As once you danced upon the shimmering lawn
> In Elvenhome, before we were, before
> You crossed wide seas unto this mortal shore. (*BLT I* 38)

And the Deeper Meaning of these Passages?

Although my treatment of this diffuse and not inconsiderable material is selective and impressionistic, it should be apparent that there is already present a pattern of images, more close to Christian concepts of the Fall, the innocence of children, and of the After-life, than is explicit in the more familiar texts concerned with Middle-earth. The William Morris device of a sea-voyager, Eriol, who arrives at an unknown land where he is to hear many tales, may not be continued in precisely that form, but the profound spiritual concepts continue.

As the text of the winter 1916-17 puts it: "a traveller from far countries [...] was by desire of strange lands" brought to the 'Lonely Island',[7] 'the Land of Release' (*BLT I* 13). He was Eriol – 'One who dreams alone' – who saw at the foot of a little hill "a tiny dwelling"[8] from which "a most warm and delicious light, as of hearts content within, looked forth. Then his heart yearned for kind company, and the desire for wayfaring died in him." He is told that the place is 'The Cottage of Lost Play' and that "all who enter must be very small indeed, or of their own good wish become as very little folk" (*BLT I* 14). He then finds the chamber wherein tales are told to be 'The Hall of Play Regained', and that those who listen are children and a sprinkling of "folk of all manners and ages," with one common quality: "a look of great happiness lit with a merry expectation

---

7 Seemingly Britain before the coming of the Angles and Saxons. At another level, the Cottage is a place of the innocence otherwise lost at the Fall.
8 As Christopher Tolkien explains (*BLT I* 24-25), the place was Warwick, or its imagined ancient nucleus.

of further mirth and joy" (*BLT I* 15). The whole island looks to this place, for "wisdom and leadership", "song and lore", much of which is now embodied in narrated tales. The children rejoice as new comrades come down 'the Path of Dreams', a lane which also runs to the homes of Men, and is marked by deep banks, tall trees and the presence of glow worms (details very close to the images in the poem 'Goblin Feet').

Play for Tolkien

Clearly the core concept of these very early Tolkien stories and poems is 'play', which may be defined as a joyous innocence, the enjoyment of story, the sense of wonder, or happiness of children, and the "desire to understand [all the natural things about one]" (*BLT I* 140). As the later segment, 'The Tale of the Sun and Moon' makes clear, there must be told in the House of Lost Play "the travail of the Noldoli and the coming of Mankind" (*BLT I* 189), the pattern of which events may well imply Babel, the shortening of human life and the Christian story.

Yet it may be appropriate to close this note on the early thought of Tolkien with a stress on the similarity of the common concepts to those of Huizinga who also saw many of the most important human activities as forms of play (1970). In these early poems and prose tales of Eriol's visit to the Cottage there are also elements of the most serious parts of human life – law, poetry, war, philosophy and religion. Play is seen further as an irreducible quality of human existence, of myth-making, of poetry, of philosophy, and of art. Indeed, it may be relevant to quote some of Huizinga's conclusions in his last chapter:

> Real civilization cannot exist in the absence of a certain play-element, for civilization presupposes limitation and mastery of the self, the ability [...] to understand that it is enclosed within certain bounds freely accepted. Civilization will, in a sense, always be played according to certain rules, and civilization will always demand fair play (which is) nothing less than good faith expressed in play terms [...] (which) must be pure [...] must not consist in the darkening or debasing of standards [...] must not be a false seeming, a masking of political purposes [...]. True play knows no propaganda; its aim is in itself and its familiar spirit is happy inspiration. (1970: 238)

As with Huizinga, so in the earliest writings of the young Tolkien, the focus is on play as necessary human activity, where our moral awareness of conscience defines that which is a serious duty. And, as Huizinga (*ibid.* 240) also saw, "[o]ne drop of pity is enough to lift our doing beyond intellectual distinctions." Thus it is that Tolkien's early poems and stories reinforce the Christian morality of *The Lord of the Rings*, even as they show that the human mind can only disentangle itself from the magic circle of play by turning towards the ultimate. Ordinary life is to be lived *sub specie ludi*.

As George Steiner observes in his 'Introduction' to the 1970 edition of *Homo Ludens* (*ibid.* 11): "The Indo-European philologist will out. The inception and much of the evidence in Huizinga's thesis is linguistic." This links with the philologist, Tolkien's stress on the inter-relationship between creativity, language and mythology, and the fact that all three are subsumed in the concept of play, that primal activity of tremendous fun and enjoyment. As Tolkien shows us in these fables of the wanderer, of the innocence of children and of the memory of pre-existence, (sacred) play cannot be denied, for it contains in its harmony deep satisfaction and the abstractions of justice, beauty, truth, goodness, mind and God.

Appropriately, for Tolkien was still, at that stage, very much under the influence of his classics training, he is closely echoing Plato's *Laws* VII: "What is then, the right way of living? Life must be lived as play, playing certain games, making sacrifices, singing and dancing and then a man will be able to propitiate the gods, and defend himself against his enemies, and win in the contest" (Bury 1984: vol. 11, 26). Tolkien is also providing in advance – as did Plato, too – the justification for the eminently sane behavior of those totally integrated yet most childlike of his orders of being, the hobbits. They, like the children at the cottage, are most truly on the threshold of religion, having play consecrated to the Deity as the highest goal of man's endeavour. Like them we in no way abandon the holy mystery, while seeing play as a highly serious and earnest recognition of immanence. Rather is play of a higher order than mere seriousness, since it is the enactment of mortal respect for the ultimate "fair house and magic gardens," "a wondrous town" and a "music full of all beauty and longing" (*BLT I* 20).

Thus it is that these early poems and prose texts subsume the moral system of the hobbits and of all childlike believers in the One.[9] The daily manifestation of this wholesomeness of spirit is play, an intense activity which, like the contemplation of children, assures for all men refreshment of spirit, delight in everyday things and solace and comfort for those who weep. Wonder, the rehearsal of legends, the emotion of joy – all are to be savoured best by traversing 'the Path of Sleep or of Dreams' – for that will return us to freedom of spirit, to the lost beauty of the Eldar, and, ultimately, to our true destination, 'the Great Lands', where, as in the fifth book of Boethius' *De Consolatione Philosophiae*, we may find God, outside time, yet seeing everything simultaneously in the eternal present.

Play, as an absorbing activity, will restore a dimension of wonder for modern man, will defy the stand of both protestantism and atheism against the intrinsic intelligibility of the world as a way to God. For Tolkien was concerned to argue that man's capacity for knowledge lies in his cognitive powers, his acceptance of order, sacrifice, his expression of wonder, and his delight in play. That activity and the zest with which it is practised is the great support of the hobbits – and of Modern Everyman – in all troubled times.

---

9 This term, within *The Lord of the Rings* only found in the Appendices, is to be identified as the Christian Deity. See Ryan (1969: 186ff).

Edith, St. Edith of Wilton and the other English Western Saints

While all readers of Humphrey Carpenter's *J.R.R. Tolkien: A Biography* (1977) will be aware of the future writer's early affection for Edith Bratt and his subsequent marriage to her,[1] they are, in all probability not familiar with Tolkien's early fascination with her Christian name and with his explicit reference to it in print in the 1920s.

Thus, in 1924, he had written for *The Year Book in English Studies*[2] a chapter entitled 'Philology: General Works', which contained a discussion of a then recently issued edition of the 'Life of St. Editha' and related references to the Wiltshire dialect of the Old English period (*YWES V* 62-63). In the yearbook's sequential volume, VI, prepared for 1925 but not issued until 1927, he had discussed (39), 'new' fashion (or very old), baptismal names for the native English, such as *Edmund*, *Edgar* and *Edith*. He was then, and later,[3] prone to discuss excitedly the etymology of the name which had extensive revival and popularity in the (later) nineteenth century[4] after its eclipse since Norman times. In the *Doomsday Book*, undertaken in 1086, the (for Normans) hard-sounding *Eadgyth* had been softened to *Eaditha* or *Edeva* (from which comes the modern pet form, *Edie*[5]).

The (disputed but) possible etymologies for the name (or for several names lumped together by the Normans) were:

1) Old English *Eadgyth*, 'prosperous war';
2) Old English *Eadgifu*, 'rich gift';
3) Old English *Eadgifa*, 'giver of bliss'; and even

This essay first appeared in shorter form as 'Edith, and St. Edith of Wilton' in *Minas Tirith Evening Star* 18.2 (1989: 4-5) and I am grateful to the editors for the permission to reprint.

1 See that work, pp. 3, 38-39, 43-45, 153-57 and *passim*.
2 This volume, no. V, was not issued until 1926.
3 Personal knowledge.
4 Cp. Edith Cavell, (Dame) Edith Sitwell and (Dame) Edith Evans.
5 See Sleigh and Johnson (1966: 83; repr. from 1962).

4) Old English *Aelfgifu*, 'elf-gift'.[6]

Now while Tolkien was fascinated by the fact that all senses could have been, albeit subconsciously, in the minds of Edith's parents, as moderns, the scholar was well aware that Edith was an important and socially significant name in the tenth century. For this was the name of a very special person of that period, the king's daughter.[7]

St. Edith of Wilton

The virgin known to history as (Saint) Edith of Wilton (near Salisbury) was born in 961 at Kemsing (Kent) as the daughter of King Edgar and an irregular union with Wulfryth (also called Wulfrida), a concubine. Herself a novice of Wilton, Edith was brought up there, to which place her mother returned soon after her birth. Two chaplains of this royal convent undertook her education,[8] consisting of letters, script, illumination, sewing and embroidery. She knew many famed churchmen from her early youth and, as the king's daughter, could have attained an important position in society on three occasions,[9] but each time refused this, preferring the obscurity of the cloister.

When – in all probability due to her friendship with Archbishop Dunstan – she was nominated abbess of Winchester, Barking and Amesbury, she appointed superiors to each and remained with her mother, now the abbess of Wilton. When in 978, her half-brother, Edward the Martyr (962-78), was murdered, she was proposed as queen, but refused. Instead, she built an oratory in honour of St. Denys, having part of the building decorated with murals of the Passion of Christ. She was conspicuous for her personal service of the poor and her familiarity with animals. She died at the age of only twenty-three, and miracles at her tomb soon attested her holiness and helped to spread her cult. She was described as one "knowing not the world rather than forsaking it" and as be-

---

6 Partridge (1968: 34), and earlier issued, in shortened form (1959).
7 Her father, Edgar, had become King in 959 but had only been crowned in a richly liturgical ceremony in 973. Compare the crowning of Aragorn in *The Return of the King*.
8 See Farmer (1978: 120).
9 See Horstmann (1883).

ing one who preferred "to serve her sisters in the most humble capacities, like Martha herself."[10]

*   *   *

Clearly there are many aspects to the saint that would have appealed to Tolkien: humility; familial rejection (Edith Bratt was a homeless orphan); deep religious sensibility; the renunciation of great power (compare Galadriel's refusing the One Ring); love of animals and their feeling for her, etc. In addition to the 1924 reference to the saint's life,[11] Tolkien had also worked on related materials a little earlier. For in 1921 there had been published by Kenneth Sisam an edition of Middle English short texts and extracts entitled *Fourteenth Century Verse and Prose*, to which enterprise Tolkien had contributed "the preparation of the Glossary, the most exacting part of the apparatus" (1921: xiii).

The first text in the volume so assembled is an extract from Robert Mannyng of Brunne's[12] *Handling Synne*, a moral text combining good teaching with entertaining stories. The improving tale included is that of 'The Dancers of Colbek', whose shameless (and perhaps occult) doings in the churchyard cause God's wrath and various stern punishments including perpetual dancing. Toward the end we hear how only St. Edith could help them:

> Here cloþes ne roted, ne nayles grewe,
> Ne here ne wax, ne solowed hewe,
> Ne neuer hadde þey amendement,
> Þat we herde, at any corseynt,
> But at þe vyrgyne Seynt Edyght, (ll. 236-40)[13]

One of the sinners (later 'St. Theodric') got his cure on Our Lady's Day when he slept by St. Edith's tomb (*ibid.* ll. 241-44).

---

10 Skeat (1885: I, 2, 468), Wilmart (1938: 5-101, 265-307).
11 See also Godfrey (1962: 478).
12 The modern Bourn, in Lincolnshire.
13 Translated into modern English:

> Their clothes did not rot, nor nails grow,
> Nor hair lengthen, nor complexions sallow,
> Nor was there change from this,
> As we have heard of any saint's shrine
> But that of the Virgin, Saint Edith,

The textbook itself was set on courses at Leeds and Oxford for the remaining thirty-eight years of Tolkien's formal teaching career, and there is no doubt that he reflected many times on Robert Mannyng's mix of German story, French manuals on sin, and local legend and English hagiography. Indeed, it is even possible that he read the Middle English text with Sisam[14] who was later his tutor (1913-15) and so had some influence on that extract being included in the reader which the two would assemble some years later.

The Female Saints for and from West Mercia

Hopefully enough has been said to indicate how Tolkien seized on this personal name as he did on others[15] that aroused his interest, passion and imagination. Women no less than men had the obligation to follow the lifestyle and spiritual example of those whose name they were privileged to bear. And so this western saint, like Chad, Katherine, Margaret and others, was especially dear to Tolkien as husband, Catholic, storyteller and scholar.

For Tolkien had early on in his occupation of the Anglo-Saxon chair turned his attention to numerous Western texts, notably to the Corpus Christi MS. of the *Ancrene Wisse* and MS Bodley 34, and its

> versions [...] of the legends of *Juliene, Katerine, Margarete* and of the homilies *Sawles Warde* and *Hali Meiðhad*.[16]

In this area he focussed both syllabus work for students in courses I and II, lectured for more than thirty years, and pressed for the scholarly recognition of their quality, consistency of expression and dignity and spirituality, they all being written in

> a language [...] that has never fallen back into 'lewdness' [...] it has traditions and some acquaintance with books and the pen, but it is also in close touch with a good living speech – a soil somewhere in England. (1929: 106)

---

14 See Carpenter (1977: 63ff).
15 E.g. Earendel (Carpenter 1977: 64).
16 See p. 106 of his essay '*Ancrene Wisse* and *Hali Meithad*' in *Essays and Studies* 14(1929: 104-26).

Part B

The Young Professor and his Early Publishing

Tolkien and George Gordon:
or, A Close Colleague and His notion of 'Myth-maker' and of Historiographic *Jeux d'Esprit*

Biography and Background

In an essay[1] drafted a little earlier (1922) and published in the year 1924, when J.R.R. Tolkien's readership at the University of Leeds had just been converted into a professorship, his former head of department there (1921-22),[2] George Stuart Gordon (b. 1881), wrote in a way which, arguably, provides fascinating insights into the early dialogue between these two friends, as well as assisting us with many of the earliest concepts known to have been discussed with Tolkien as to the various historical, cultural and as yet unfulfilled spiritual needs for Englishmen in the centuries after the Renaissance. Significantly, it also tells us something of the mental climate of the eminent language and early English – and Old Norse – language-sympathetic and already fine scholars of Tolkien's period in Leeds. For then he was also closely associated there with George Gordon, as well as teaching A.H. (Hugh) Smith. [The latter was later to appear as participant in the joyous and mildly roistering *Songs for the Philologists*, as well as becoming England's greatest place-names scholar, and the Professor of English Language at University College, London.]

George Stuart Gordon (1881-1942) a Scot from Falkirk, and who, after some time at Glasgow University, again studied the Classics, this time at Oxford (1902-06), winning there a double first in the process. However, he had already won the Stanhope Prize for history in 1905, was elected to a Prize Fellowship

---

This essay first appeared in slightly shorter form in the journal, *Minas Tirith Evening-Star* 16.1 (Winter 1987: 3-7). The opportunity has now been taken to expand that paper somewhat, as well as to refer to and include certain details from the life of George Stuart Gordon by R.H. Darwall-Smith which appeared in the *Oxford Dictionary of National Biography*, vol. 13 (2004: 909-10).

1 Originally presented spoken, in Glasgow in 1910 and subsequently re-handled in a lecture to the English Association in London on November 17, 1922, fn. p. 9, to the revised text of 'The Trojans in Britain' in *Essays and Studies* IX (1924: 9-30).
2 See Carpenter (1978: 27).

in English at Magdalen College in 1907, and was lecturing there and in the University to many including Tolkien in English, in the period from 1907 to 1913,[3] while he was still a Fellow of Magdalen College. Then he was elected to be Professor of English Language and Literature at Leeds from 1913 to 1922, as well as also serving in the trenches as a second lieutenant in the Sixth Battalion, W. Yorks., another northern regiment very like Tolkien's own. It was, of course, George Gordon who had, later, as the Professor-in-charge, welcomed the younger man to Leeds, and, as Tolkien recalled and told Carpenter (1977: 103), "displayed great kindness to his new assistant, making space for him in his own office [...] More important, he handed over to Tolkien virtual responsibility for all the linguistic teaching in the department."

It is of his time in Leeds that Tolkien was referring when he called Gordon "the very master of men" (*Letters* 56). Interestingly, if we may anticipate, it was also the same Professor Gordon who had read *The Hobbit* in 1937, before publication, and said that he would recommend it to the Book Society (*Letters* 20).

Gordon's cultural interests – which were in many ways remarkably similar to Tolkien's – are very well represented by his 1912 editing of *English Literature and the Classics*, as well by as his Andrew Lang lecture of 1928,[4] and his *Virgil*, published in the same year. He would also publish his 'The Trojans in Britain' in 1924, after his work on Shelley in 1923, and on Charles Lamb. He also served as Oxford's Gresham professor of rhetoric from 1930 to 1933, then as professor of poetry from 1933 to 1938, his related collection, *Poetry and the Moderns*, appearing in 1938.

By now Gordon had left Leeds to become Merton Professor of English Literature (1922-28), and so, on Tolkien's return to Oxford in late 1925, Gordon would very naturally join the Tolkien-led saga reading-circle there, those called the *Kolbítar*.[5] Similar to his colleague, he had a strong interest in the field campaigns of war and of battles, as is witnessed by his *Mons and the Retreat* (1918),

---

3 See *The University of Oxford First Supplement to the Historical Register of 1900* (1921: 81). Other details of Gordon's life may be verified from the *Merton College Register 1900-1964* (1964: 149).
4 In this he preceded Tolkien by some ten years. His discourse was entitled 'Andrew Lang'.
5 See Carpenter (1978: 27). Tolkien's specific recollections of Gordon in Leeds are to be found in *Letters* (56-58).

and his simultaneous service on the staff of the Official Military History from 1919-22. But to return to the re-vamped essay of 1924, with the certain knowledge that it was very familiar to Tolkien as it was re-drafted and then issued in final form.

Gordon's 'Trojan' Essay

The revised version of this now almost forgotten but provocative paper opens with a challenge about the lack of a native literary tradition for the island of Britain from the time before the Roman arrival, similar to the lack of a genuine Anglo-Saxon pre-conquest tradition, one which was so poignantly felt by Tolkien, as against the much greater length of accepted continental traditions:

> [...] was Britain to be counted voiceless all this while? no message? no traditions? (1924: 9)

He then quickly proceeded to point out that "this dumbness, this British silence, is recent" (*ibid.*) and that "Archaeology now rules in the place of Brutus and his Trojans, to the notorious advancement, as I gratefully admit, of historical truth, but, as it has been managed, to the perpetual and inexcusable disadvantage of all boys, all lovers of old stories, and all readers of English literature" (*ibid.* 10), and with their nice affiliation with the beginning of Virgil's *Aeneid* and its notions of destiny being the force that would found the future city and glorious Rome, 'ut conderet urbem'. The idea of linking up Britain's (largely pre-historic) past with the events that were formative for Western civilisation – the flight of Trojan noblemen from the sack of Troy and the ensuing founding of Rome and other European cities – bears some resemblance to Tolkien's own attempt to link implicitly his vast corpus of tales or 'legendarium' by means of various transmission-figures to the pre- and proto-historic eras of England. For the idea of the 'translatio imperii' (transference of power) as well as the 'translatio studii' (of zealous application to letters) – the ancient world's notion of 'transmission' of a particular culture and so of a linear continuity in both culture and history – seems to have played an important role also in Tolkien's 'legendarium' – not just in the case of Númenor, but in the manifold rises and eclipses of peoples and their civilizations.

After reference to Nennius's stress on the coming of the Britons "to this island in the Third Age[6] of the World" (*ibid.* 11), – a similar movement of fate to shape the rise of a new nation, as he carefully pointed out, George Gordon had then launched into a spirited defence of Geoffrey of Monmouth's much expanded treatment of Nennius in his own Latin prose *Historia Regum Britanniae*, or *History of the Kings of Britain*.[7] He also referred to the writer's pretence of translating from an Armoric source (*ibid.* 13-14), a technique imitated by Tolkien by means of his elaborate fictional framework of the 'Red Book of Westmarch'-tradition. However, Geoffrey, like Tolkien, would seem to have been drawing largely on a fertile imagination for his materials which would become, directly or indirectly, the chief source for the later accounts of Arthur. And Gordon then added a definition of this fictive material, and its eloquence, its play of imagination and elaboration of detail as being "the borderland where fable and history dance together" (*ibid.* 14).

Never Forgetting the Power of the Classics

In 1912, Gordon had contributed to the inspirational collection, *English Literature and the Classics*, the chapter entitled 'Theophrastus and His Imitators' – an essay earlier given (iii) as a lecture in the English School in "the winter of 1911-12" – in which he discussed the life and work of that Athenian professor, observing of him the great irony of so many great writers that he would

> be remembered by the slightest of his performances. (49)

He then continued with a comment, one as true of him, as, in due course of Tolkien,

> that professors are admired in their own day for their learning, but, at the last for their jeux d'esprit; (*ibid.* 50)

and that

> from the writings of Geoffrey we see that: the man himself seems to have been of a generous and vivacious nature, passing into urbanity with age. (*ibid.* 51)

---

6 Compare this with Tolkien's remarkably similar 'Third Age' of Middle-earth, e.g. in *Letters* (230).
7 Verbal echoes would suggest Tolkien's familiarity with the antiquarian-style translations of Geoffrey's work by both Giles (1848) and Evans (1903).

While it is not the place here to tease out all its nuances, this paper is a most helpful introduction to classical (and Tolkienian) notions of character, of type, and of their (rhetorical) description – such Greek figures as the Unpleasant Man; the Garrulous Man; the Fussy Well-meaning Man – and on through to their appearance in "the mediaeval curriculum" (*ibid*. 65), and in "the style of the Character in England" (*ibid*. 72), an engaging phrase much in vogue in both Edwardian and Georgian Oxford – to say nothing of the much later work, *The Character of England* (1947), edited by Sir Ernest Barker.

Gordon's conclusions are, like those of Theophrastus, equally and joyously heroic – that "the whole notion of balance or the Mean is in fact a bourgeois notion" (Gordon 1912: 86), one unable to comprehend "the heroisms and excesses[8] for which it can make no provision" (*ibid*.). Clearly Gordon was not merely a friend and mentor, an older man whose temperament was both formative for Tolkien's own, and illuminating for the fascinating insights which it can afford into the years of young manhood of a pupil – in 1911-12 – but a close colleague well before the commencement of the major writings. As Letter 46, one drafted in 1941 for R.W. Chapman, makes clear, Gordon was both light-hearted and determined to foster the mediaeval and linguistic aspect of 'English', to make it into a dynamic School. Further Gordon is one who can lead us to various Georgian period thoughts amongst classicists teaching English – namely about the case for glorious lying, uninhibited but appropriate creativity, myth-making and for (neo-Greek) outlandish and exaggerated characters.

A Digression to the Scholarly Mindset of the Time

In all of this reflection and reasoning on the transmission of (mythic) stories and their creative extension, Gordon is remarkably close to the text that was a veritable bible and distinguished and highly influential handbook for the before-listed group in Leeds and also for the language scholars of Oxford for at least the next two generations. This was, of course, *A Manual of the Writings in Middle English, 1050-1400* by John Edwin Wells, a joint publication in 1916

---

8 One is reminded here of the inability of Frodo to understand the powerful and contrary passions working in Boromir, as he is described in the last chapter of *The Fellowship of the Ring*, when he would take the One Ring from Frodo.

by Yale University Press and the Oxford University Press. For this considerable
tome would categorise and cluster in luminous fashion the surviving Western
Europe-sourced romances of that whole period, 1050-1400, according to location and content, namely, as its initial framework set out such categories as:

1) English and Germanic Legends;
2) Arthurian Legends;
3) Charlemagne Legends;
4) Legends of Alexander the Great;
5) Legends of Troy;
6) Legends of Thebes; and
7) The Breton Lais.

In all of these literary kinds, – themselves very largely with putative origins
next to historical strands – the various subject fields were known as 'Matters'
or large blocks of interlinked variant stories of the evolution of the (inherited)
culture in a new setting, where whole tales, or single incidents or episodes
were thereby made available to the emerging Western vernaculars by means of
bardic or minstrel-based oral traditions, or by longer written Latin versions.
In all these cultural fields, these considerable fields of story – or narrative
'matters' – had each a style, one which influenced not only plot, but lexis,
form and attitude, and which had links back to earlier periods of European
history and even proto-history.

And to Return Now to Gordon

In his reflections on Geoffrey of Monmouth and his redaction of Nennius,
Geoffrey himself is categorized by Wells as

> the first and by far the most successful of our historical novelists; [and]
> a liar of temperament. (*ibid.*)

Gordon approved strongly of his treatment of Merlin, while two other choice
observations that he made are that Geoffrey's prime ingredients were his
impassioned patriotism –

> the legends of his country, and sympathetic invention – "reimagining your
> sources", (1912: 14)

and – a very Tolkien-like characteristic – his awareness of

> the potency of the onomastic or place and heroic names element, [for] [...] in his stylistic, Geoffrey had realized that names are the music of history. (*ibid.* 17)

A Comparison with John Milton, Especially in his Prose Legendary

Gordon also found, in due turn, that John Milton's methodology in the re-treatment of traditional and legendary Biblical material was sound philosophically, as in his literary approval of

> causes – attested by ancient Writers from Books more ancient – the due and proper subject of Story. (Birch 1738: ii, 2-3)

His own endorsement of the earlier poet's accepting such materials is followed by a plea for respect for the numerous apparently slighter stories within the corpus:

> I should like to see the Fables of the Britons restored to their place in the first chapter of our histories [...] Let the chapter be labelled – 'Legends', 'Fictions', Britonum nugae, [i.e. trifling matters/(fanciful) stories of the Britons] any [such] defamation [...] We do this for the Grecian and the Roman fables [...] why not for our own? They are as interesting as Livy's primordia; they were as devoutly believed; they were made from the same methods; and they produced a body of literature. (1912: 25-26)

Gordon on 'Myth'

A writer who would use such methods as Geoffrey and Milton Gordon labels a 'myth-maker' (*ibid.* 26), adding that such early fictional pieces comprise "the fables of a race" and that such material has necessarily to be taken seriously now "because it was officially believed" once. This use of the term 'myth-maker' is a particularly interesting one, not merely because of its early challenge to Tolkien's already active creative imagination, but because of its relatively rare use[9] in English letters.

---

9 Apart from Tylor's use in his *Primitive Culture* (1871), already cited in the first edition *OED*, vol. VI (1908: 818), the present-day *OED Online* has only five other citations. Perhaps of interest here is the

His final stress is both Tolkienian and ent-like, as well as folkloric:

> It is about the young that I am most concerned, for the historians can look after themselves, (*ibid.* 29)

approvingly stressing that once Englishmen "knew all the old stories" and "could tell them" and then appealing for

> not quite so much erudition and a better sense of the stories of the world. (*ibid.* 30)

Gordon and the History, Style and Evolution of the English Language

Any close reading of Gordon's many wide-ranging essays, his editions of some nine of Shakespeare's plays, or his influential essays contributed to the *Times Literary Supplement* will have noticed the numerous references to lexis, early writers and various philosophers who held pertinent views on language, its evolution and (later) English stylists and writers. Thus his classic volume, *Shakespearean Comedy and Other Essays* (1924; reprinted 1945) was long a recommended text for all students of English Literature in the famed Final Honours Schools 'A 4' paper on the language of Chaucer, and of renaissance and later texts. Significantly the book referred to John de Trevisa, the *Ormulum*, Holinshed, Thomas Rhymer, Pattenham and Coleridge, and G.W.F. (b. 1893) Hegel,[10] as well as concluding with the penetrating and enduring chapter, XII, entitled 'Shakespeare's English' which became a classic resource of students of the English School for decades.

It but remains to refer again to the great – and related – service that Gordon would bestow upon England's scholarship and recovery of (national-seeming) story, in that he had so much assisted the creation of the separate Faculty Board for English, this in 1926. Along with the Tolkien reforms of the syllabus a couple of years later, Gordon's initiatives were able to marry the language side

---

fact that the present writer entitled his 1960s doctoral thesis for the University of Cambridge *Modern English Mythmakers* – it referring to Charles Williams, Owen Barfield and C.S.Lewis – his Inklings friends – as well as to Tolkien as storyteller.

10 Hegel was very much to the fore in the thought of G.R.G. Mure (b. 1893), the later Warden of Merton, and the author of the not so dissimilar *Josephine* fantasies, at about the time of Tolkien's producing *The Hobbit*, the thought of Hegel being discussed by both men in the 1930s and later.

of the national and, indeed, European, heritage with the literary in a fashion hitherto unimaginable. Tolkien referred to this very pointedly in his 'Valedictory Address' to the University of Oxford in 1959 (*MCE* 224-40). In this paper, Tolkien applauds the later 1920s union of language and literature. Indeed, the creation of the Faculty Board for English would, during Gordon's professorship, cause the number of English honours finalists to rise by half again. In similar vein he would support two like-minded Fellows of Magdalen College, one C.S. Lewis, and the other that fine student of Shakespeare's lexis and compounding, C.T. Onions, the fourth editor of the *Oxford English Dictionary*.

Thus it is that T.A Shippey was able to write of Tolkien's career from c. 1930, both as Oxford scholar and as fantasy writer:

> With hindsight, one can see that a continuing theme in Tolkien's academic work was the conviction that language and literature are not divisible [...] the two aspects of language and literature of 'English' necessitated a consideration of both. (2004: 903-4)

In all of this, of course, 'language' meant the earlier pre-Shakespearean aspects of 'English', and also the mediaeval materials which had for long been outside the realm of English and largely taught in the Taylor Institution for 'Modern [i.e. Germanic and other Western European] Languages' in the periods before the renaissance.

It was indeed largely due to the joint efforts of two trained classicists, Tolkien and Gordon, close friends as well as particularly stylish writers, that both the Faculty of English in the University of Oxford – and, indeed, the field of English letters generally – came to embrace linguistic and some philological study. And so Oxford graduates in English, now in ever increasing numbers, learned to their surprise that the history of language and the corpus of the oldest stories was a vital part of literature and that the appreciation of 'English' in the widest sense necessitated a careful consideration of both. For the language defined the story, even as it enshrined its style and its meaning.

Another Significant Contribution from Gordon

Much more could be said about the two men: their meetings at Magdalen (where George was President of that College – also C.S. Lewis's College and home for many years – from 1928 to 1942); their similar views as to the significance of the Roman epic, *The Aeneid*, and on the story-telling and fairy-tales collecting by Andrew Lang; the influence of the older man's training and aesthetic theories on the slightly younger's methods of creating a 'legend for England', or the close friendship[11] from 1921 until Gordon's death, as Vice Chancellor of the University of Oxford, in 1942. However, George Gordon's real importance to Tolkien studies is for

> his love of the *Aeneid*, its epic structure, and its function as a foundation myth for so much of Western Europe;
>
> his concern for the classics and their influence on English letters;[12] [and]
>
> for his introducing to his younger colleague both the writing of Geoffrey of Monmouth and to the peculiarly loyal love that it enshrined for the land and indeed the 'soil of England'.[13]

---

11 See the photograph of him sitting beside Tolkien in the Carpenter biography (1977: 114).
12 Often stressed in his lectures as Professor of Poetry, 1935-38.
13 Tolkien's phrase, in his cultural essay on the 12th century homilies from the West Midlands in *Essays and Studies* XIV (1929: 106). Cp. "I love England" (*Letters* 65).

J.R.R. Tolkien: Lexicography and other Early Linguistic Preferences

In this essay I am concerned to treat of J.R.R. Tolkien's early lexical work, particularly in relation to the emerging patterns of his formal academic scholarship and, perhaps, as that work may well indicate, to its significance as the seedbed for so much of his later linguistic, aesthetic and major imaginative work.

The brief piece by Steve Wood is correct in its reference to J.R.R. Tolkien's stint on the *Oxford English Dictionary* under Henry Bradley,[1] in a team which worked on *S-T,* 1914-19, and on *W-WE,* from 1920-23. This is discussed on pages xix and xxiv of the 'Historical Introduction' to Volume I of the *OED* as issued in the revised version of 1933. There is no reference to Tolkien in two other places where he might have rated a reference, namely in the 'Preface' to the 1933 *Supplement* (vol. 13: v-vi), and in the 'Preface' of *The Shorter Oxford English Dictionary* (v-vi), also issued in 1933 in the first place, in the 'Historical Introduction'. Tolkien is, however, listed as one of the six assistants in the third group, the least important class, that grouping "indicative of the relative length of time during which they were engaged on the work" (1933: xxiv).

Yet that he knew Bradley and appreciated the value of his work very clearly is indicated by the fact that he was asked to write an 'Obituary' for him by the

---

This exploratory article first appeared in *Mallorn* 16 (May 1981: 9-12, 14-15, 19-22, and 22-26) and is here reprinted with the kind permission of its editors. It was prompted then by the recent appearance of a short note by Steve Wood entitled 'Tolkien and the *O.E.D.*' in *Amon Hen* 28 (1977: 10). My text has been slightly modified to take into account some later research. It was, of course, written long before the release in 2006 by Peter Gilliver, Jeremy Marshall and Edmund Weiner, *The Ring of Words: Tolkien and the Oxford English Dictionary* (Oxford University Press), a volume that explores individual words which Tolkien used in terms of their origins, development and so semantic and associative significance in his fictional world.

1   Wood had followed Kocher (1973: 181), in noting the verbatim 'blunderbuss' quotation from the *Dictionary,* vol. 1 (1947, column 3), in the much later tale, *Farmer Giles of Ham* (1949: 15), the words being said to be from "the Four Wise Clerks of Oxenford" [i.e. the four editors of the *OED,* and suggests that this may very well have been phrased thus by Henry Bradley (see 'Historical Introduction', p. xvii). In his 'Valedictory Address' to the University of Oxford in 1959, Tolkien referred to his enjoying his observation first hand of "the privilege of knowing even the sunset of the days of Henry Bradley" (*MCE* 238).

Modern Humanities Research Association, and this duly appeared under the heading, 'Henry Bradley, 3 December 1845 – 23 May 1923' in its *Bulletin* No. 20 in October 1923.

The best known of the other five Bradleian helpers listed with him is Kenneth Sisam, 1887-1971, a New Zealand-born Rhodes Scholar of Warwickshire stock, who had been Assistant to A.S. Napier, Professor of English Language from 1912 to 1915. In this position, he was involved in Tolkien's tuition on various of the set texts in the Honours School of English, as we are told in a letter to Edith Bratt (*Letters* 7). Interestingly, Sisam had also been employed on the *Dictionary* at various times from November 1915, when he joined Bradley's staff and worked particularly on *STER*-words and *STEWARD*. As H. Carpenter correctly tells us in the biography, Tolkien had Sisam as a tutor from 1913 to 1915 (1977: 63) and the biographer adds that the student, only four years younger than his tutor, "was particularly interested in extending his knowledge of the West Midland dialect in Middle English because of its associations with his childhood and ancestry" (*ibid.* 64). From Hilary Term 1912, Sisam gave university lectures or classes five or six times a week, and in the obituary for Sisam,[2] Neil Ker, the scholar palaeographer, adds:

> Professor Tolkien has told me how fortunate he considers he was to have been able to go to Sisam's lectures. (1974: 414)

The other tutor of the student's language studies (i.e. for the cluster including Old Norse, continental story, etc.), was William Craigie, who had joined the *Dictionary* in 1897 as an assistant, and had been doing separate editing for the *Dictionary* from 1901, in which activities he continued until 1925. [Craigie is referred to elsewhere in this present collection.]

---

2 Ker wrote a fine obituary for Sisam in the *Proceedings of the British Academy* for 1972 (see below). The somewhat later (i.e. post-war) duel between Tolkien and Sisam in 1925 for the chair of Anglo-Saxon in the University of Oxford is discussed by N. Ker (*ibid.*), and by Humphrey Carpenter (1977: 108). Tolkien had also by then created the fine glossary for Kenneth Sisam's *Fourteenth Century Verse and Prose* (Oxford University Press, 1921), a scholarly small dictionary variously issued by the Oxford University Press as *A Middle English Vocabulary designed for use with Sisam's Fourteenth Century Verse and Prose*, as well as in a form of appendix to the numerous reprints of the Middle English reader.

The Place of Kenneth Sisam in the Training of J.R.R.Tolkien

In his obituary tribute to Sisam, Ker stresses how the publication of *L-R* and half of the *S* fascicules of the *Dictionary* issued in the years 1901-1910, had roused the youthful Sisam, still in New Zealand, to a sudden and profound linguistic awareness, and how, in mid-1915, the recent Rhodes Scholar and now young Oxford don had produced in three weeks for the Clarendon Press a revision of Skeat's edition of the East Midland Middle English poem, *Havelok* (*ibid.*, 410-11). Although he was destined to become a permanent official of the Press from 1922, Sisam never forgot his lexical apprenticeship, and he remained a friend to the 1933 *Supplement to the OED*, where he is listed as one of those "who have made noteworthy contributions or have maintained a continuous interest in the collection of evidence" (vi).

Tolkien's academic friendship with Sisam continued after his own return to Oxford in 1919, and they collaborated on the production of a reader issued by the Clarendon Press in 1921 under the title *Fourteenth Century Verse and Prose*, a volume with a very healthy emphasis on texts with their provenance in the West Country and the West Midlands. For this work Tolkien contributed a glossary, at first (1922) printed separately and at various later times to 1946, but then usually issued with the main text. Of the reader, alone, or, as in the majority of cases, combined with the glossary, more than 60,000 copies had been printed in the first 50 years, and it has remained the most stimulating and widely used of all the Middle English readers ever produced. In the best sense, it is an example of the qualities of scholarly 'haute popularisation' which both men encouraged in others, whether fellow-scholars or antiquarians.

In his preparation for the separate work, *A Middle English Vocabulary*, Tolkien was concerned to be thorough and, as Carpenter observes, "this meant in effect compiling a small Middle English dictionary, a task that he undertook with infinite precision and much imagination" (1977: 104-5). The prefatory 'Note' by Tolkien indicates alike the effect of his own training on the *Dictionary* and his creative writer's feeling for language. The first paragraph may be quoted in full, not least for its obvious concern to enfranchise the (student) reader :

> This glossary does not aim at completeness, and it is not primarily a glossary of rare or 'hard' words. A good working knowledge of Middle English depends

less on the possession of an abstruse vocabulary than on familiarity with the ordinary machinery of expression – with the precise forms and meanings that common words may assume; with the uses of such innocent-looking little words as the prepositions *of* and *for*; with idiomatic phrases, some fresh-minted and some worn thin, but all likely to recur again and again in an age whose authors took no pains to avoid usual or hackneyed turns of expression. These are the features of the older language which an English reader is predisposed to pass over, satisfied with a half-recognition: and space seldom permits of their adequate treatment in a compendious general dictionary or the word-list to a single text. So in making a glossary for use with a book itself designed to be a preparation for the reading of complete texts, I have given exceptionally full treatment to what may rightly be called the backbone of the language. (1921: iii)

Apart from the cross references to the *OED* itself, some thirty languages or dialects are utilized in its pages to indicate relevant etymology or cognate forms. They range over the Germanic, Celtic, and Latin and Romance groups. But the most interesting aspect of the *Vocabulary* is the sensitivity of the nuances given to the glosses on specific lines.[3] The work also remains today as the only completed Middle English Dictionary whose entries have any degree of subtlety.

Other work published by him in those years is best represented by his unhasty 'Some Contributions to Middle-English Lexicography', published in 1925 in the *Review of English Studies*.

As to Tolkien's personal work for the *OED*, we need not doubt a contribution to the various words given by Carpenter (*ibid.* 101) – *warm, wasp, wick* and *winter*, even if the last two do not equate exactly with the sections reserved for Bradley's team. They were words in the C.T. Onions' section, *WH-WO*, completed in the period 1922 to 1927; but it is made clear by Carpenter that there was a close relationship with Onions, one which did indeed continue until the latter's death in Oxford in 1957 (1977: 101, 120).

---

3 This desire for precision and subtle glossing Tolkien always held to be as much a product of his many years' use of Lewis & Short's *Latin Dictionary* (1879) or of the Cleasby & Vigfusson *Icelandic-English Dictionary* (1874), as of his use of English dictionaries or of the slips of Joseph Wright's *English Dialect Dictionary* (1909 and with reprints in 1961 and later, as in 1981). Indeed, in his O'Donnell lecture, 'English and Welsh' (given earlier, in the 1950s, but published in 1963), he recalled his momentous change of studies: "Under severe pressure to enlarge my apprentice knowledge of Latin and Greek, I studied the old Germanic languages; when generously allowed to use for this barbaric purpose emoluments intended for the classics [...]" (*MCE* 192).

That Tolkien was personally interested in all the Dictionary's scholarly and etymological work and, indeed, onomastic investigation in the last part of the alphabet is made very clear if we read his chapters, each entitled 'Philology: General Works', in the English Association annual, *The Year Book in English Studies* (vol. IV, 1923 [which appeared in 1924]; vol. V, 1924 [issued in 1926]; and vol. VI, 1925 [issued in 1927]). His opening section (for 1923) may be quoted at some length:

> Of the directions in which English Philology has principally progressed lexicography is the chief; the study of place names, which is in many respects closely akin, has also in recent years been gathering force and acquiring precision […] though […] it has not yet acquired the same precision here as that study has in Scandinavia […] In lexicography, and in English philology generally, the appearance of new sections of the *Oxford English Dictionary* remains the chief annual event, though the Dictionary is too universally familiar to call for detailed review here.

> This year there is, however, a special reason for mention of the new sections: *Wash-Wavy* forms the last completed and official contribution of Dr Bradley to the Dictionary and to English studies, and is, fittingly, full of lexicographical problems. The suggestion of wetness made by the title-words of this section is not deceptive; thirty of its sixty-four pages are occupied by *Water* and its compounds; much of the remainder is given up to *Wash* and *Wave*. The number of primary words is comparatively small, but nearly all of them are of native origin. It will no doubt be a blow to some to find *Wassail*, that typical Saxon pastime in the legendary land of our heptarchic 'Saxon forefathers', among the six exceptions. The origin of this word is one of the chief points on which new light is here thrown.

> The very difficult words, both in etymology and in sense-development, of the *Wave*-group here find a new and careful investigation; if neither their etymologies nor the history of their senses are now made completely clear – they are not – this is because of the tangle that the language has itself devised. In this section occur one or two exceptions to the general rule of the exclusion of proper names. (*YWES IV* 20-21)

In this last section he has a flair for seizing on the puzzles that long teased the students of English onomastics, with a mind peculiarly sensitive to the possible nuances preserved in the earlier folklore of his country. He continues on with reflections on some of the puzzles:

> The most interesting of these is *Watling Street*. Beyond the OE. *Wæclinga stræt* (the c not the t forms are here held the correct ones, at least in the name of the Roman road) it does not seem possible to go, nor does it appear doubtful that the interesting sense 'Milky Way' that appears in ME. is an application of

the same name; but it seems to the present writer that the usual assumption, apparently also made in the *Dictionary*, that it is a secondary application, is not so certain, in spite of its later record and of apparent parallels as the widespread European name of the galaxy, the Way of St. James (the pilgrims' road to Compostella). *Ermine Street*, another Roman road name, is not recorded at all until ME., but it is at least noteworthy that it corresponds to the German *Irminstrasse* = Milky Way.

This, coupled with the fact that *Vatland Streit*, if we are to credit the author of the *Complaynt of Scotland* and Gavin Douglas, was a name given to the Milky Way by Scottish sailors, unlikely to draw their descriptions from the land-traffic of the North-West route away south in England, suggests that we have here an old mythological term that was first applied to the *eald enta geweorc*[4] after the English invasion. Its original sense is probably lost forever.

The section *WH-WHISKING* is perhaps even more severe in its demands on both lexicographical skill and patience: it is infested by the difficult but important 'interrogative' words; these (which include such problems as *What* and *When*) taken together with *While*, occupy three-quarters of this section. Most of the words are native, few of them have wide exterior connexions or even well-established etymologies; some are long-standing etymological puzzles. Of these *Whig* and *Wheedle* remain unsolved.[5] (*ibid.* 21-22)

The second such review, Chapter II of *The Year's Work in English Studies*, vol. V (1924), contains some interesting lexical remarks. There is an appeal for more study of Modern Colloquial English (45), and satisfied approval of European recognition of the "completion of Bosworth-Toller" (i. e. their *An Anglo-Saxon Dictionary*) by the issue of a *Supplement* in 1921, as well as the statement of a need – still to be filled – of "the 'real Old English dictionary'" with full etymologies and in one alphabet.

Again he is concerned to discuss the newest section of the *Oxford English Dictionary* (*Whisking-Wilfulness*: some 64 pages), drawing attention to: interrogative words; *whole, white, wild, wold, whisper, whist, whistle, whitler, whizz, whoo, whoop, whoosh, widdendream, whitlow, wich* (saltworks), *width, wick*, and *wile* (*ibid.*, 47-49). The first edition of *The Pocket Oxford Dictionary of Current English*, compiled by F.G. and H.W. Fowler, is also noted as an

---

4 For a gloss on his likely further understanding and use of this phrase, "the ancient creations of the giants," in his own creative writing, see Ryan, 'Germanic Mythology Applied – The Literary Extension of the Folk Memory' on pp. 199-213 of this volume.
5 *Wash-Wavy*: pp. 129-62 of vol. X of *NED* (i.e. *OED*), by H. Bradley. O.U.P. *Wh-Whisking*: pp. ii and 64, by C.T. Onions.

admirable little dictionary [...] including neologisms and everyday colloquialisms and reasonable slang [...] We are inclined [...] to think that the rudimentary or vestigiary etymologies [...] were better away [...] It is arguable that there is not much use in etymologies unless they are fairly full and can have space to hesitate. (*ibid.* 49)

There follows a two page discussion of E. Weekley's *A Concise Etymological Dictionary of Modern English* (published that year by Murray). This is filled with intriguing linguistic remarks on such words as *sufi*, *grig* (with reference to *Punch*), *irk*, *brimstone*, *minnow* and *blimp*. His comments on the last item, where Weekley had followed an air-officer's etymology from 'bloody' + 'limp', are of particular interest. The 1933 *Supplement* gave the word the meaning of "a small non-rigid dirigible airship invented early in the war of 1914-18" (87, col. 3), supported by quotations from 1916 (Rosher), 1918 (*Illustrated London News*), and 1928 (Gamble's *North Sea Air Station*). The second of these gave the origin as "an onomatopoeic name invented by that genius for apposite nomenclature, the late Horace Shortt." While not rejecting this outright, the editor R.W. Burchfield (himself a pupil of Tolkien's) in vol. I of the new *Supplement* (1972: 289), interpolates between the second and third illustrative quotations these words:

> 1926 J.R.R. Tolkien in *Year's Work in English Studies* [1924: 52]: It is perhaps more in accordance with their looks, history, and the way in which words are built out of the suggestions of others in the mind, if we guess that *blimp* was the progeny of *blister* + *lump*, and that the vowel i not u was chosen because of its diminutive significance – typical of war-humour.

Tolkien's third chapter, delayed and so published in 1927, opens with a passage which is remarkable for a philologist and anticipatory of *The Lord of the Rings*, but peculiarly satisfying to the reader who knows 'Leaf by Niggle', that fable of an artist first published in *The Dublin Review* (432ff) in 1945:

> It is merry in summer 'when shaws be sheen and shrads full fair and leaves both large and long'. Walking in that wood is full of solace. Its leaves require no reading. There is another and a denser wood where some are obliged to walk instead, where saws are wise and screeds are thick and the leaves too large and long. These leaves we must read (more or less), hapless, vicarious readers, and not all we read is solace. The tree whereon these leaves grow thickest is the *Festschrift*, a kind of growth that has the property of bearing leaves of many diverse kinds. To add to the labour of inspecting them the task of sorting them

under the departments of philology to which they belong would take too long.
With a few exceptions we must take each tree as it comes.[6] (*IWES VI* 32)

After listing several such congratulatory volumes presented to illustrious scholars
in token of their achievements and noting the peculiar facilities which they
offer for highly idiosyncratic research, he observes, ent-like, of these volumes
of piety:

> Chiefly they are due to affection and honour for great names and figures, and
> are a melancholy reminder of the age of the older generation of giants who
> have laboured in the service of Philologica and have deserved so well of her.
> (*ibid.* 33)

There follow several musings on the Dutch language and on Celtic and Germanic
roots, notably in the scholarship of M. Förster, W. Keller, E. Sievers and J.
Hoops, and including with approval a quotation which saw the late nineteenth
and early twentieth centuries as a time when the making of German-English
dictionaries became impossible, due to the

> general haste and fever of modern life, grasping at sensation, tearing ideas to
> pieces, turning ethical values upside down, and introducing finer nuances into
> the language of poetry, art, and science. (*ibid.* 35)

He goes on to observe that the volume *Germanica*, a tribute to E. Sievers at
the age of 75, "is a tree of altogether larger girth and bigger branches – a not
unworthy reminder of the honour and affection, the great tale of years, and the
great work achieved by Sievers" (*ibid.* 36). After many self-indulgent excursuses
on 'interesting side-issues', he continues,

> Of specially English lexicography the year under review is barren. But more of
> *W* is doubtless under active preparation at the Old Ashmolean for the delight
> and troubling of next year. None the less, this seems the place to record a new
> edition of Roget's *Thesaurus*. It is hardly lexicography, of course. Rather the
> pre-eminent example of the spirit of philately in words – with a side-glance at
> the assistance of authors in search of the mot juste or recherché. (*ibid.* 57-58)

---

6 Apart from the obvious link with Sir James Frazer's *The Golden Bough*, one feels that the lines of *Sir
Gawain and the Green Knight*, which Tolkien was co-editing with E.V. Gordon in 1923-24, are in his
mind:

> After þe sesoun of somer wyth þe soft wyndez
> Quen Zeferus syflez hymself on sedez and erbez,
> Wela wynne is þe wort þat waxes þeroute,
> When þe donkande dewe dropez of þe leuez,
> To bide a blysful blusch of þe bryȝt sunne. (*SGGK* ll. 516-20)

The Intrusion of 'Philately'

This 'philatelic attitude' to their language Tolkien also finds in L. Pearsall Smith's *Words and Idioms: Studies in the English Language*, and he deplores this style of language scholarship, one which denies the existence of semantics and seems to see philology as concerned "only with a limited phonology" (*ibid*. 58). He then makes the very revealing assertion:

> It is difficult to discern wherein lexicographer and word-historian is ultimately to be distinguished from the student of literary ideas. The boundary line between linguistic and literary history is as imaginary as the equator. (*ibid*. 58-59)

*   *   *

These three essays, covering as they do some 94 pages (19, 40 and 35 respectively) of culturally rich material, cogently and dynamically presented, as in the breathy style of his own rapid fire lectures to the University, contain a wealth of insights, aphorisms, and sudden glimpses of Tolkien's aesthetic philosophy of creativity. While lexis, semantics, loan words and a grand conception of philology are the dominant tones, there are many illuminations of the young professor's mind. Some of these – subjects of an editorial nature, and which are indicative of his thought and emerging sensitivity – may be listed here:

> Volume IV: Names invented by Dickens (23); the Christian name *Edith* (23) [and see Essay 6, pp. 55-58 in this volume]; Middle Kentish vocabulary (23); Essex speech (25); words in Roxburghshire (26); the importation of the American *spondulicks* (26); slang in Thackeray (28); *bumf* (28); *Billingsgate* (29); *tiffin* and other Anglo-Indian words (30); shadowy persons behind Anglian settlement place-names (30-32); approval of the series of 'Wright' grammars (33); the revival of Gaelic (34); René Huchon's ideas on the character of English prose (36); and the importance of the great philological epoch in England from 1850-1900. (37)

> Volume V: The mountain walls now confronting eager philologists (26); the shocks applied to Indo-European philology by Tokharish and Hittite (27); the fact that

>> [...] the pre-history of Europe and nearer Asia looms dark in the background, an intricate web, whose tangle we may now guess at, but hardly hope to unravel. All this we ought to take account of, however distant and cursorily. If our present linguistic conceptions are true, there is an endless chain of development between that far-off shadowy 'Indo-European' – that phantom which becomes more and more elusive, and more alluring, with the passage of years – and the language that

we speak today.[7] Germanic and Indo-European philology are part of the history of the English. (27-28)

And the torrent of observations and aperçus continues:

> Jespersen's ability to analyse the exact meaning of various English expressions (28); -th suffixes, such as Ruskin's unsuccessful *illth* and F. Thompson's *spilth* (30); Tolkien's observing of Jespersen's work, it being 'devoured on the top of a tram to the oblivion of fare-stages' (31); 'the need for the study of language as it is instead of bullying it for not obeying rules drawn up without its consent' (32); irregular preterites to (West) Germanic verbs of motion (35); dialect conflict in Low German (36); the difficulties of Lappish (37); Baltic place names (38); etc.

He waxes lyrical at the astonishing digging up of Hittite after an oblivion of over 3,000 years (38-39); the curious position of the prehistory of the Indo-European languages stretching in a line NW-SE on both sides of the Armenian highlands, where their weakest point lies (39); references to "the dark mystery of ancient Western Europe" (39); *cow*, having come "some 5,000 years ago from Sumerian" (40); or *star*, some 4,000 years ago from Accadian istar, 'Venus' (40); Sievers' theories of the 'motor' aspect of voice (41-42); a scholarly aside on academic gossip, with the engaging comment that "rumour is mythopoeic" (43); some general remarks, and a statement of *Silmarillion* significance:

> Here a point of interest is the evergreen problem of the relations of the 'Germans' (speakers of Germanic languages) to the rest of the 'Indo-Europeans' (speakers of Indo-European languages), and especially to the Slavs on the one hand and the Celts on the other [...] and [the question of] bringing home to the reader how complex are the linguistic and cultural events of Europe before the dawn of history (44);

the problems of the origin of the 'Standard English language' (45); the interesting question of Old English influence upon Old Norse (46); mining terms being influenced by possible (reciprocal) miner and dialect migration between

---

7 Whether or no we choose to extrapolate some of his notions of the ancient European fears of the east from his fictions, or remember the eastern nuances to the death brought by possession of material things, which he discerned in 'The Pardoner's Tale' by Geoffrey Chaucer, it is certain that Tolkien had thought long about the survival of roots, senses, and superstitions from the Indian subcontinent that might have come to the west in the course of trade or war.
Apart from odd references in his paper, 'Beowulf: the Monsters and the Critics' (1936), his most extended critical study is to be found in 'English and Welsh' (1963), where he explores the English and Welsh languages, particularly in relation to "the difficult and absorbing problems that are presented by the linguistic and archaeological evidence concerning the immigrations from the European mainland [...]" (*MCE* 173).

Derbyshire and North Wales (46-47); the Anglo-Manx vocabulary of c. 2,400 main words (47); *An Elementary New English Grammar* by Professor and Mrs Wright and its helpful inclusion of some 4,000 different words (52); the phonetics of Siamese (53), etc.;

British river-names are noted to be of Welsh, Goidelic origin and yet of Greek, Latin and Cornish form (53-55). He notes the foundation of the English Place-Name Society and of the issue of its first volume, *Introduction to the Survey of English Place-names*, ed. by A. Mawer and F.M. Stenton (55-60); his general comment is the hugely perceptive one that

> [t]his study requires specialists in Scandinavian, Old and Middle English, Celtic, Mediaeval History, and Archaeology, not forgetting the local enthusiasts who know and love their ground, and the willing drudgery of many searchers (56);

a discussion of the element *helm* – 'protective covering, especially overhead' follows (compare *Helm's Deep* in *The Two Towers*) (57); and a note on "the difficulties and toils of historico-philology,"[8] with his own revelatory comment that

> [p]robably the imagination of most people reacts quickest to the glimpses that are gained of England before the English-speakers and to the dark years of the new settlement. (58)

Yet other apercus in the cascade of insights, all delivered in the style of his own lecturing, especially on Old English topics, include those on: Germanic gods (58); village colonisation (58); the coming of the English to Britain (59); early Germanic personal name elements, e.g. *Hob* (59); Anglo-Scandinavian and Anglo-Norman names (59-60); 'mixed' dialect areas and the shifting of considerable groups of people, caused by natural barriers, important centres, political divisions (61); the mingled conservatism and innovation of Middle English spellings (62); the 'Life of St. Editha' and the Wilts. dialect (62-63); some charming remarks on 'Place-names and Archaeology' (64-65), including specific reference to the expression on *fāgne flōr* ['onto the brightly marked paved surface'], as found in *Beowulf* l. 725, plus comments on enclosure words, the

---

8 This is an admirable description of his O'Donnell lecture, 'English and Welsh' of *Angles and Britons* (*MCE* 162-97).

significance of mounds and ruins. He quotes with approval Professor O.G.S. Crawford's stated aim and intention in his archaeological work:

> We are gradually collecting facts in order to construct a series of maps of England, or parts of England, as it appeared in past ages. (65)

Tolkien's own apologia-conclusion to this vastly illuminating essay with its combination of the etymologist's search for the language and its root elements, and of the archaeologist's pursuit to recover the patterns of earlier man upon the surface of the earth is as follows:

> In other words this study is fired by two emotions, love of the land of England, and the allurement of the riddle of the past, that never cease to carry men through amazing, and most uneconomic, labours to the recapturing of fitful and tantalizing glimpses in the dark – 'Floreant Philologia et Archaeologia'. (65)

From the third essay it is again possible to offer a form of summary of the breathless and excited catalogue of the items presented:

> Celtic forms in English (33-34); the verbal noun and its uses in Celtic and English (34); the gentle self-revelation in the phrase, 'knowing how these little lexicographical chases open vista after vista, and one complication after another' (35); the cluster of names for the pole-cat in Germanic and Romance languages of Northwest Europe (38); *hawk* words in Old Norse; a new etymology of the name *Beowulf* as 'windwolf' (39); new baptismal names for the native English, such as *Edmund, Edgar, Edith* (again!), etc. (39); the critical issue of the treatment of O. E. verbs in *-ian* in Middle English (40); and the treatment of phonology in Middle English. (40-43)

He then comes out with a comment on difficult if useful theories, one that bespeaks the walker over dale and moor, that:

> The *Anfänger* need not rejoice. It will not make the bog less treacherous for tender feet to walk on; it will only learnedly expound to one up to his neck in it how the bog came there and what it is made of! In fact it seems that it may even tell him 'the bog is not bog, because of the dry land'! [...]. (43)

Scandinavian influence on the inflexions of English in occupied areas of Britain catch his attention (45); as do the Old English charm against elfshot (46); the scholarship as to the history and enigmatic character of Richard Coeur-de-Lion (47); the basic etymology behind O. E. *wīcing* (48); the first county-volume of place-names, that on Buckinghamshire (48-50), including, surely, some indication of a personal obsession with mounds, heathen Saxon settlement, Celtic survivals and continental Germanic settlers; place-names in the *Anglo-Saxon Chronicle* (50); English place-names "in a French garb" (51); the rise of initial *Sh-* in place-names, etc. (52); a questioning of the work of de Saussure and other new French language scholars, which contains

> an inexplicable weakness [...] the compensation, perhaps, for their wide range, penetrating thought, and imaginative vision [...] the book [having] an indefinable sense of hastiness [since] [...] the pace must be a gallop, the country is so wide (53);

the syntax of the Indo-European simple sentence (55); Holthausen's Old Frisian dictionary (57); the structure of English (59); the origin of the gerund (62); compounds of the Blue-beard or Greenmantle sort (62-63).

And the Philosophy Behind the Linguist

Two more general views of Tolkien the man may be given more space. The first is his obvious disquiet at the possibility (already prefigured by L.P. Smith 1919: 59) of English as the coming world-language, and his feeling that he must make a cultural stand against this tendency –

> Wherever it occurs we think it is time somebody said that as prophecy it is as valuable and certain as a weather-forecast, and as an ambition the most idiotic and suicidal that a language could entertain. Literature shrivels in a universal language, and an uprooted language rots before it dies.

> And it should be possible to lift the eyes above the cant of the 'language of Shakespeare', or to tear them from visions of the Parliament of Man, sufficiently to realize the magnitude of the loss to humanity that the world-dominance of any one language now spoken would entail: no language has ever possessed but a small fraction of [...] human speech, and each language presents a different vision of life. (*YWES VI* 59-60)

The Importance of the Words and Thoughts of Every People

> In the past the dominance of a language has been due to the often sheerly accidental, and even undeserved, material success of its speakers, rather than to its own merits as a medium. This was certainly the case with Latin, and expansion was bad for it. Few prefer the Koine to Attic. However imminent such a calamity to English may be imagined, it should be alluded to, not with self-complaisance, but in alarm and as a summons to resistance. The curse of

Babel is no less fundamental than that of Eden. Man's brow must sweat over
the everlasting spade, and over the everlasting grammar too. Without their
pain there shall be neither food nor poetry. (*ibid.* 60)

The above stern declamation ended with a further sentence: "If we say nothing
about American English here, it is only reserved for the end." He observes quite
mildly that: "It is impossible to teach [British students] American (though it
might be good for them) as a preliminary to Old and Middle English" (*ibid.*
62).[9]

The last three pages of the third essay are concerned with G.P. Krapp's *The
English Language in America*, treated there in "a place of honour" (*ibid.* 64-
66). While he is not uncritical of this significant historical work of more than
700 large pages, he is sympathetic to these parts of its generous treatment of
the rich mix:

the varied information and curious detail; [the treatment of] literary dialects
(e. g. rustic, Negro, Indian), American place-names, and American dictionaries; the remarkable interest of the seventeenth and eighteenth-century town
records;and of the supreme philological event of which we have certain knowledge, the transportation of the language of a small country and its spread and
ramification over enormous regions to find not one but a thousand new soils,
atmospheres, and homes. (*ibid.* 64)

Indeed, in this passage he is making some of the earliest and significant comments on the great linguistic diaspora which would result in the rise of 'World
English'.

But Language Conquest by the Strong is a Tragedy for the Spirit of Man

His concluding reflections are more personal and concerned to rally the English
nation. After finding that Krapp seems disappointing "on the subject, not unimportant, of the relations of the American and 'British' varieties of English in

---

9 Despite one offer of a lecture tour, Tolkien never visited the United States of America, although many
American Rhodes scholars did some language work with him in the English Language and Literature
School, Course III. There were always a cluster of American Rhodes Scholars in Merton, one of the
last he met being Brock Brower, later columist and man of letters. Similarly, Auden made many return
visits from New York to see him. Of course, his own earlier mentor, William Craigie, was already at
work in Chicago on the *Dictionary of American English*.

the most recent period," probably due to "the very judicial and non-committal spirit of his utterances" and to an apparently intentional minimizing of the real differences, Tolkien then launches into a deliberate peroration:

> If in careful and studied writing, of which this book is an excellent example, the differences are not very obvious, it is still possible to see in its very cold-ness and formality the dangers of an artificial uniformity veiling fundamental divergence.
>
> To some it seems obvious that petrification and death ultimately await it, if the attempt is made too long to maintain a language as a literary or cultural medium over areas too wide and of too divergent a history to preserve any permanent community. Whether we endeavour to maintain the different va-rieties of English in vigorous life now, or in the future seek to restore life after 'English' has become a universalized but dead book-Latin, divergence into distinct idioms is ultimately the only thing that will achieve the object.
>
> To the American author, of course, it does not appear so clear as it does to us that the problem is no longer that of the freedom of America and her 'illustrious vernacular', but of the freedom of England. Sir Walter Alexander Raleigh in a speech on 'Some Gains of the War' made in February 1918 did not escape the notice of Dr Spies when he said: "the clearest gain of all is that after the War the English language will have such a position as never before. The greatest gain of all, the entry into the War of America, assures the triumph of our common language and our common ideals."
>
> We have indicated above what we feel about linguistic triumph. Some even now are found to criticize the expression 'common language'; more might question 'common ideals' (and without necessarily implying any judgement concerning relative values); but to all it should be apparent that this triumph, if it takes place, is only likely to be 'common' if it is predominantly or wholly American. Whatever the special destiny and peculiar future splendour of the language of the United States, it is still possible to hope that our fate may be kept distinct. And it is possible in *The English Language in America* to find reasons for making that hope more earnest. (*ibid.* 65-66)

These sentiments reflect not so much his active dislike of American speech as distaste at the actual eclipse of a living language of long pedigree and his horror at the (linguistic) oppression which caused – and still works – to produce social uniformity. He was to say the same thing some thirty years later, when, after lamenting the Tudor oppression of Welsh, under such 'far-seeing civil servants' as Thomas Cromwell, he then went on:

> Governments – or far-seeing civil servants [...] understand the matter of lan-guage well enough, for their purposes. Uniformity is naturally neater: it is also very much more manageable. A hundred-per-cent Englishman is easier for an

English government to handle. It does not matter what he *was*, or what his fathers were. Such an 'Englishman' is any man who speaks English natively, and has lost any effective tradition of a different and more independent past. For though cultural and other traditions may accompany a difference of language, they are chiefly maintained and preserved by language. Language is the prime differentiator of peoples – not of 'races', whatever that much-misused word may mean in the long-blended history of western Europe. (*MCE* 166)

And our Response to these Breathless Reports?

The overall impression of this early and co-linguistic scholarship shows Tolkien, the young professor, to be a passionate student of words, and of their changing meanings even before the establishment of their likely or actual etymology; of place-names and personal names, both historical and literary; of the scholarship of ideas and of the heroic men who 'shepherded' these concepts into print and into literature; of [Western?] man in relation to his physical landscape as well as to his (actual/potential) mental climate.

For it may be fitting to close this brief survey of this surviving 'diary of concepts and fascinations' from the first decade of his academic work and writing with a glance at his great love for the Western Marches which manifested itself alike in his Mercian studies from the Old English period to that of the *Ancrene Riwle* in the period 1180-1220. Indeed, it was of the great cluster of West Midland (homiletic) texts written over that period, that albeit unconsciously he gave a self-characterization which is also prophetic of his later literary position and of a/his preferred regional style – both in language and in content:

> There is an English older than Dan Michel's [c. 1340] and richer [...]; one that has preserved something of its former cultivation. It is not a language long relegated to the 'uplands' struggling once more for expression in apologetic emulation of its betters or out of lack of compassion for the lewd, but rather one that has never fallen back into 'lewdness', and had contrived in troublous times to maintain the air of a gentleman, if a country gentleman. It has traditions and some acquaintance with books and the pen, but it is also in close touch with a good living speech – a soil somewhere in England [...]

> [The] language is self-consistent and unadulterated. It is a unity. It is either a faithful transcript of some actual dialect of nearly unmixed descent, or a 'standard' language based on one. ('*Ancrene Wisse* and *Hali Meithhad*', in *Essays and Studies* XIV, 1929: 106.)

The (Arranged) Marriage of Language and Literature

This was also to be the decade of his successful modification of the university's undergraduate English syllabus. For, as many of these quotations from his scholarly work make clear, he was a most unorthodox teacher of language, but now he was also declaring publicly the perspectives and philosophies on which his creative work would be so firmly based.

It is very much of this decade that, as his 'Obituary' in *The Times* has it,

> [...] he was, more than any other single man, responsible for closing the old rift between 'literature' and 'philology' in English studies at Oxford and thus giving the existing school its characteristic temper. His unique insight at once into the language of poetry and into the poetry of language qualified him for this task.
>
> Thus, the private language and its offshoot, the private mythology, were directly connected with some of the highly practical results he achieved, while they continued in private to burgeon into tales and poems.
> (*The Times*, September 3, 1973: 15)

The Work and Preferences of the Professor of Old Norse at the University of Oxford from 1925 to 1945

> Old Icelandic presents at once the difficulty of an ancient and alien inflected language, the philological value of an intimate relationship with English which can be revealed by analysis, and literary and historical value of the highest rank [...]
>
> the English School in Oxford has proved the [...] sole refuge of Scandinavian studies [...];
>
> the statutes of the Anglo-Saxon chair specially recommend among the older Germanic languages, Old Icelandic as a field of labour, while the chair is assigned to the English faculty [...]
>
> J.R.R. Tolkien, 'The Oxford English School', *The Oxford Magazine*, vol. XLVIII, No. 21, 29 May 1930, pp. 778-82.

The title of this exploratory article and its appearance in the present Scandinavian publication draws attention to the fact that J.R.R. Tolkien was officially and heavily engaged in teaching and research in the field of Old Norse/Old Icelandic during most of the time during which he held the Rawlinson and Bosworth Professorship[1] of Anglo-Saxon, i.e. from 1925 to 1945, and – more significantly for his creative writing – during the period of the gestation of *The Hobbit* and of the run-up to the larger planning of *The Lord of the Rings*. The chair itself was pledged in his will in 1755, and it took effect in 1795, according to the wishes of its founder, Richard Rawlinson, D.C.L., of St. John's College, University of Oxford.

This essay first appeared in *Angerthas in English* 2 (1992: 51-58) and I am grateful to the editors for permission to reprint.

1 To Tolkien's satisfaction, it had northern and Danelaw antecedents, having originally been endowed "with some annual or fee-farm rents, payable out of certain lands in Lancashire." See *University of Oxford, First Supplement to the Historical Register of 1900-1920* (1921: 37).

By a Statute, sanctioned by Queen Victoria in Council in 1858, the range of the Rawlinson Professor's lectures was no longer to be confined to the language of the Anglo-Saxons, but was made to include also "the history of that people, the old Low-German dialects, and the antiquities of Northern Europe." Joseph Bosworth, D.D., who had held the chair from 1858 until his death in 1876, had bequeathed further funds (available from 1910) to augment the chair's stipend. Meanwhile, from 1903-15, The Rawlinson Professorship was joined with the Merton Professorship of English Language and Literature, both being held concurrently by Arthur Sampson Napier,[2] M.A., D.Litt. In order to give effect to the Rawlinson bequest, the union of the two chairs was dissolved in 1915, and the Rawlinson Professorship was restored as a separate entity under the title of the Rawlinson and Bosworth Professorship of Anglo-Saxon. William Alexander Craigie, M.A., Fellow of Oriel College, was elected to be Rawlinson and Bosworth Professor from 1916 until his proffered resignation in 1924. His last scheduled lectures were given in Trinity Term 1925, on: Anglo-Saxon Poetical Texts; Anglo-Saxon Literature (Poetry); Old Icelandic Poetry; and The Old Saxon *Genesis* and *Heliand*.[3] On 21 July 1925, John Ronald Reuel Tolkien, M.A. of Exeter College, was elected Rawlinson and Bosworth Professor of Anglo-Saxon, as from 1 October 1925.[4]

In that first term, Michaelmas (October-December) 1925, Tolkien lectured only on Old English texts, including *Beowulf.* But the following term he offered a third strand[5] of official lectures entitled 'Introduction to Germanic Philology' and all three courses continued into the third university term, i.e. the Spring/Summer Term of 1926. In the first term of the next academic year he would lecture on:

1) Gothic (a class);
2) Old English Philology;
3) The Verse of Sweet's *Anglo-Saxon Reader*;

---

2 This made him one of Tolkien's own main teachers, since the student's work in Early English took place in the years 1913-1915, prior to his final B.A. examinations in June 1915.

3 See p. 556 of *The Oxford University Gazette* for April 24, 1925.

4 *Gazette* for 29 July 1925, p. 848.

5 This information comes from relevant issues of *The Oxford University Gazettes*. Michaelmas Term: October to late November/early December is the autumn session (of 8 weeks); Hilary (January to March) the winter term; and Trinity the Spring/Early Summer Term (April to May for lectures, with the University written Examinations in June, and oral examinations in July).

4) *Exodus* (the Old English poem);

5) Old Icelandic Texts (a class); and

6) an Icelandic Discussion class ("For not more than 12 selected undergraduates, their names to be received through their tutors.").

From this beginning he would continue to lecture regularly on a number of Norse and Continental Germanic matters until he changed chairs in 1945.[6] Then, too, as the members of his Faculty increased, he would, progressively, leave many of the lecturing tasks once carried by him to others. And thus this short account will be largely concerned to highlight the pattern of texts and topics determined by him and treated formally in his official university-wide lectures.[7]

The representative Norse items of the following years are given below in a tabulated form:

Year	Term	Topic
1927	Hilary	*Vølsunga-Saga*
1927	Trinity	The Heroic Poems of the *Elder Edda*
1928	Michaelmas	The *Vølsunga-Saga* and related lays
1929	Hilary	The Older Runic Monuments
1929	Hilary	*Vølsunga-Saga*[8] and related lays
1929	Hilary	*Carmina Scaldica*
1929	Hilary	Legends of the Goths
1929	Trinity	*Carmina Scaldica*
1929	Michaelmas	*Baldrs Draumar, Guðrunarkviða en forna, Atlakviða*
1930	Hilary	*Baldrs Draumar, Atlakviða, Haensnaþoris Saga, Hávarðs saga Halta*
1930	Hilary	Old Norse Texts (class)
1931	Hilary	*Carmina Scaldica*: introduction to the reading of Scaldic poetry
1931	Hilary	The Germani
1931	Hilary	Introduction to the *Elder Edda*

---

6 From that year until 1959 he held the Merton Chair of English Language and Literature and so lectured largely on authors and topics from post 1350.

7 All details are taken from *The Oxford University Gazette*, a bulky compilation with 800-900 double columned pages per year.

8 Both poems refer to legends or a possible ancient heroic lay concerning Weland the Smith.

1931   Michaelmas   *Guðrunarkviða en Forna*

As will be clear from the above, there was a pattern to the teaching, whereby
the new students took seven terms for preparation for their Norse papers in
their final or Second Public Examinations.

Other significant patterns may be noted:

> *Hávarðar saga sífirðinga*; and *Høsnapóris Saga* being studied together from
> time to time;
>
> the *Vølundarkviða* often being set along-side the Old English *Deor's
> Lament*;[8]
>
> the *Vøluspá* being first set in Michaelmas Term, 1932;
>
> the appearance of an assistant, Mr E.O.G. Turville-Petre, B.A., who, in Hilary
> Term 1933, would take the text *Hrafnkels saga*;
>
> the first listing, for Trinity 1933[9] of 'Prolegomena to the Study of Old English
> and Old Norse Poetry';
>
> various clusters of lectures on 'The Germani';
>
> (from its first listing for Michaelmas 1933) a fairly regular cluster of background
> lectures entitled: 'The Historical and Legendary Tradition in *Beowulf* and other
> Old English poems'; and
>
> the *Atlakviða* then being set with the *Atlamól*, etc.

It may also be noted that Tolkien was assisting the early career of E.O.G.
Turville-Petre by helping his visits to Iceland, publication of early research,
etc. And on July 11 1934 the student's edition of the *Viga-Glúms Saga*[10] was
examined by J.R.R. Tolkien and E.V. Gordon[11] who recommended the award
of the research degree of Bachelor of Letters. Professor Tolkien continued his
regular Norse lectures, slight variations of title, etc. being:

> Introduction of the *Poetic Edda*;
>
> The Legend of Wayland Smith, followed by a study of the text of
>
> *Deor's Lament* and of the *Vølundarkviða*; and

---

9 In this term Mr Turville-Petre would take the Old Norse class "for the Rawlinson and Bosworth
   Professor." He would also take the *Hrafnkels saga* again in Michaelmas 1934, and when the professor
   was Leverhulme Research Fellow in 1936. Turville-Petre had matriculated in 1926, been taught by
   Tolkien, and he would prove to be the most brilliant Scandinavian scholar produced by the United
   Kingdom.
10 It was further described as being "from the manuscripts, with introduction and notes." Tolkien would
   facilitate the edition's publication later.
11 Gordon had edited *Introduction to Old Norse* (1927), a work which owed much to his close friend and
   former Leeds colleague, J.R.R. Tolkien. They also together edited *Sir Gawain and the Green Knight*.

his Hilary Term 1937 lecture on *Hamlet*, in a sequence of lectures including Messrs. Coghill, Dyson, C.S. Lewis, C.L. Wrenn[12] and others.

In 1941, the Vigfusson Readership would be established in 'Ancient Icelandic Literature and Antiquities' and be occupied by Mr Turville-Petre who would be taking the Old Norse Texts classes from Hilary Term 1942. Yet Tolkien would himself take these classes again, until the Reader's return from war-service in the Iceland zone. The young man's more formal classes (as of Trinity Term, 1946), began with a series entitled: 'Introduction to Icelandic Literature'.[13] The differing tastes of the Reader – from 'The Professor' – were even more clear from the Michaelmas 1946 offering of a course of lectures on Ari,[14] or the later offering of 'Origins of the Heroic Lay', or 'The Book of the Icelanders' (as in Hilary Term, 1960).

The Culture and Artistic Significance of Tolkien's Norse Courses

It is clear from the matters revealed or teased out in the above account that serious scholars of Tolkien's life and work can no longer accept the somewhat jolly and simplistic account of his Norse scholarship as given by Humphrey Carpenter

> The *Kolbítar* [...] is an informal reading club founded by Tolkien [...] they meet for an evening several times a term [...] Tolkien [...] is easily the best Norse scholar of anyone in the club. (Carpenter 1977: 119-20)

In the 1930 essay with which this paper began, there were various more helpful comments on the importance of Old Norse/Old Icelandic for Tolkien. Then he had argued that, among the cognate languages to English "Old Icelandic is naturally and deservedly most prominent" (*loc. cit.* 779); that it was important for "The study of the ancient Germanic monuments and of their literary, historical and philological background" (*ibid.* 780); that "Old Icelandic should in

---

12 Presumably Wrenn and Tolkien treated ancient/heroic and Icelandic materials. From Hilary 1938, Wrenn would also take various Introductory Old Norse language classes.
13 See the *Gazette* of 22 March 1946 (375).
14 In January 1953, Turville-Petre would complete his *Origins of Icelandic Literature* (published 1953), in which work the author both treats of Ari at length (chapter iv) and thanks Tolkien for his "many useful suggestions" (vi).

any case be prescribed for all [English students] and made more central" (*ibid.*); that "unseens in [...] Icelandic should be set; and he pressed for the degree to have *two* papers on Old Icelandic language and literature" (*ibid.*), a reform which he would get through very soon and which both he and Turville-Petre exploited for many years.

For, of course, Tolkien desired that his students should have a sound grounding in Norse grammar, philology, translation, etc. and then proceed to the study of representative texts. As early on as he could, Tolkien had turned his attention to the Faculty Library and in the Report on that Library for 1931-32 it would be reported that

> The chief event of the year was the complete re-organization of the philological section of the Library carried out by Professor Tolkien, Mr C.L. Wrenn and the Assistant Librarian Mr J.L.N. O'Loughlin[15] (Quoted in the *Gazette*, vol. LXII, 9 December 1932, p. 184).

Thus it was that the English Faculty Library had a considerable linguistic strength, relative to the size of its collection.

The particular emphases made in Tolkien's teaching and thought is brought out by several factors. As a student he had studied for the Special Subject,[16] Scandinavian philology, which involved:

translation into English from various set sagas;

writing contextual notes on the last named texts;

presenting short essays on such topics as early Scandinavian sound changes and regional differences;

comparison between Old Icelandic, Old English and Gothic;

discussion of seeming irregularities in Old Icelandic declension and conjugation;

explanation of heroic and scaldic verse styles; and

contrasting "Icelandic saga-writing of the classical period with Middle English literature of the same date."

---

15 Both men assisted Tolkien and in the early 1930s would take courses for him.
16 This was required if the candidate sought First Class Honours. See the examination papers for the Honour School of English Language and Literature, Trinity Term, 1915.

This syllabus had been modified by Craigie, so that a typical 'Norse' course of his[17] is: Old Icelandic, with special study of the following texts:

> *Snorra Edda, Gylfaginning* (chapters 20-54);
>
> *Vǫlsunga-Saga* (chapters 13-31);
>
> *Hallfreðar saga*;
>
> *Þorfinns saga karlsefnis, Hrafnkels saga*; and
>
> *either* Scandinavian Philology
>
> *or* Outlines of Old Norwegian and Icelandic Literature.

Until the publication of Gordon's reader in 1927, the study text – used by Tolkien as both student and teacher – was G. Vigfusson and F.Y. Powell, *An Icelandic Prose Reader* (O.U.P., 1879, etc.), with the supply of various poems from continental editions.[18] The two most commonly used critical texts were:

> W.A. Craigie, *The Icelandic Sagas* (Cambridge University Press, 1913, etc.); and
>
> Bertha S. Phillpotts, *The Elder Edda and Ancient Scandinavian Drama* (Cambridge University Press, 1920).

While the Norse teaching before Tolkien had been concerned largely with the minor Icelandic Sagas and the *Prose Edda*, Tolkien's own preferences, as illustrated by the cited lecture offerings, were for:

> mythical and heroic sagas;
>
> Continental Germanic materials, especially as they tended to illustrate common Germanic legends[19] of great antiquity;
>
> written or runic materials which would offer clues as to the movements of the 'nations' across the face of Europe after the Roman Empire began to fade; or
>
> the texts, such as the Vǫluspá, which would shed some light on the most primitive form of Germanic/Indo-European religion.

In the passage cited from Carpenter (1977: 120) there is a statement of significance for its emphasis that

---

17 Quoted from p. 137 of *The Examination Statutes ... for the Academic Year 1919-1920* (1919).
18 Information confirmed from the English Faculty and Taylorian (i.e. modern languages) Libraries in Oxford.
19 E.g. the Weland the Smith, Sigurd, Atli and other legends and heroic lays by means of which they were transmitted.

Tolkien started the club [i.e. the *Kolbítar*] to persuade his friends that Icelandic literature is worth reading in the original language; and he encourages their somewhat halting steps and applauds their efforts.

Of course, some of his conscripted friends who were also students of the sagas would become illustrious Germanic linguists – notably the Oxbridge professors Norman Davis, J.A.W. Bennett, E. Stanley, E. Dobson, etc. to all of whom he taught 'Old Norse' with considerable zeal and success. But it will be enough to quote from the 1940 tribute of E.O.G. Turville-Petre, in the 'Preface' to his edition of *Víga-Glúms Saga*:

> It would be difficult to overestimate all that I owe to Professor Tolkien; his sympathy and encouragement have been constant and, throughout the work, I have had the benefit of his wide scholarship (*op. cit.* iv).

While the influence of the Norse side of his academic work is, perhaps, less immediately obvious from the major fiction,[20] there is no question that the many later volumes of Tolkien's story drafts edited by his son Christopher, reveal the breadth and depth of his reading of the texts and knowledge of the remains and antiquities of the Norse world. Nor is this surprising since he was, for some twenty years, Oxford's Professor of Old Icelandic and more than happy to 'labour' in that field.

---

20 But consider Beorn's hall in *The Hobbit* (1937) as a form of Norse hall familiar from many heroic sagas.

The Poem 'Mythopoeia' as an Early Statement of Tolkien's Artistic and Religious Position

In the second (and later) editions,[1] of J.R.R. Tolkien's *Tree and Leaf*, there are certain additions to the first edition, printed in 1964. These are, in essence:

the introduction by Christopher Tolkien, styled 'Preface' (v-ix); and

the publication for the first time of the poem 'Mythopoeia' (the making of myths), in which the author Philomythus, 'Lover of Myth', confounds the opinion of Misomythus, 'Hater of Myth'. (v)

In the first, Christopher Tolkien refers to the fact that, due to the Autumn, 1931 (September – October) encounters between the two Christian friends J.R.R. Tolkien and H.V.D. Dyson and the non-believing C.S. Lewis of Magdalen College, Oxford, his father, the Professor of Anglo-Saxon in the University and a devout Catholic, had written the first version of a poem with the title, 'Mythopoeia'. It would ultimately have some seven versions (vii-viii), with, on the fifth, the dedication, "J.R.R.T. for C.S.L." (vii), and on the sixth version "Philomythus Misomytho," now translated as 'Philomythus to Misomythus' (85). While various notes by Christopher Tolkien give a summary of the relevant details of the unpublished versions, it is enough to note

the continual extension of the poem, the early versions lacking the last's stanzas VII - IX; and that

the last, twelfth stanza, separated off by a break mark, was added at a later stage.

There had been available for several years an elegant and sensitive account of the actual post dinner walk in the Magdalen grounds in September, 1931 in

---

This essay first appeared in *Minas Tirith Evening Star* 18.4 (1989: 4-6) and I am grateful to the editors for their permission to reprint.

1 The text had been reset from its 1964 form in the following editions. In the 2001-edition of the text which I am using in this essay, 'Mythopoeia' is printed in unlined couplets of rhyming iambic pentameter verses on pp. 85-90. These may be referred to thus, with the actual lines involved: I, 1-8; II, 9-28; III, 29-44; IV, 45-52; V, 53-70; VI, 71-80; VII, 81-86; VIII, 87-90; IX, 91-106; X, 107-18; XI, 119-30; and XII, 131-48.

Carpenter's retelling of the event (1978: 42-45), from which may be excerpted these key sentences:

> 1) [Lewis] still did not *believe* in the myths that delighted him (*ibid.* 43).

> 2) [From Tolkien] But the first men to talk of 'trees' and stars saw things very differently. To them, the world was alive with mythological beings. They saw the stars as living silver, bursting into flame in answer to the eternal music [...] [Man] may pervert his thoughts into lies, but he comes from God, and it is from God that he draws his ultimate ideals [...]. Therefore, [man's] *imaginative inventions* must originate with God, and must in consequence reflect something of eternal truth (*ibid.* 43).

> 3) Had he [i.e. Tolkien] not shown how pagan myths were, in fact, God expressing himself through the minds of poets, [...] using the images of their 'mythopoeia' to express fragments of eternal truth [...] For, Tolkien said, if God is mythopoeic, man must become *mythopathic* (*ibid.* 44-45).

The poem 'Mythopoeia' is not mentioned here, but it is referred to, with the stanza beginning "Man, Sub-creator, the refracted Light" being cited in the 1939 lecture (*TL 54*).

The poem, for the first time printed in 1988, will now be paraphrased and then treated more closely as a model for the essay, 'On Fairy Stories', written down first in the period 1936-38 and published later.

> 1) You are a nonbeliever who sees earth as a 'minor globe' of Space, in some "cold, Inane" universe.[2]

> 2) We bow to God's will, accepting all of His creation – rocks, trees, earth, stars, men, the movements of the planets, and death.

> 3) Nothing "is" until perceived and "spirit" must be divined. Elves there once were.

> 4) Stars were once as wondrous for all as flowers, however science might interpret them later.

> 5) Man still remembers the Divine Wisdom, and though fallen ("Disgraced," l. 57), he can still 'sub-create' and use his imagination.[3]

> 6) Dreams are "not idle" and only Evil is so.

> 7) Blessed are those who hope.

> 8) Blessed are those who believe.

> 9) Blessed are they who accept the legends, and who hope for ultimate spiritual victory.

---

2 It is possible that Lewis would recall his own, H.G. Wells-like, early beliefs in the character of the rational scientist, Weston, in his own space novels, beginning with *Out of the Silent Planet* (1938).
3 Most of this stanza is quoted in the 1947 essay, it is found on p. 23 of the 2001-edition.

10) I would be with all of them questing, loyal to the "distant King" and "lord unseen".[4]

11) I do not accept man's evolution from "progressive apes" (l. 119), or the path of "progress", or a world without the "little maker" (i.e. storyteller sub-creating to God's glory).

12) The free may attain "the Blessed Land" which "crooked eyes"/Evil will not see. There choice will ever come from God, and poets and the saved will ever choose faultlessly.

*   *   *

The text itself is distinctive for many reasons, several of which may be listed *seriatim* as they occur:

1) the hater of story wants for his world: labels (1), mathematical astronomy (4-6), decay of planets, dusty paths (125), and Iron Crowns (129);

2) the lover of story savours and respects: trees (16-19, 36), Time (11), the variety of the creation (20-28), light, wind, grass, birds;

3) man sub-created when he used the power of speech to see and name (29-32) by divine intuition, to exercise free choice despite [God's] foreknowledge, and to enjoy the light;

4) Germanic and not intellectual classical words are used to denote the simple things of story and of spiritual certitude: tree, star, will, time, earth, men, light, grass, cows, birds, etc.;

5) a series of capitalized abstracts defines a theological system that becomes (the model for) being Christian – Will (9), Time (11), Origo (18), God (19), Wise (54), Artefact (60), White (62), as opposed to another threatening system[5] – Fact (72), Evil (79-80), Shadow (86), Night (93), Circe-kiss (96), Death (101), Now (105), or Iron Crown (129);

6) a thread of terms and images exist for healthful (folk-type) story: the elves (42), living silver (46), elf-patterned (51), creative act (59), sub-creator (61), elves and goblins (66), dragons (68), wraith[6] (89), the legend-makers with their rhyme (91), the lyre (103), legendary fire (104), minstrels (107), the mariners of the deep (109), the fabled West (112), heraldic emblems of a lord unseen (118), etc.; and

7) the rhetorical devices of initial repetitions are used for emphasis in the litany of praise: Blessed are the timid hearts that hate evil; Blessed are the men of Noah's race [...] ; Blessed are the legend-makers [...]; or the fine Blakean "I will not walk" (119), or "I will not treat" (125); and "I bow not yet" (129).

---

4 The couplet, "or in fantastic banners weave the sheen / heraldic emblems of a lord unseen" (ll. 117-18) is the antecedent notion behind the necessary ride along the 'Paths of the Dead' for the perjured army in *The Two Towers*.

5 These echo both Old English poetry and the cosmology of John Milton's epics.

6 Used in a good sense, unlike the ring-wraiths of the epic.

All these strands are caught up in the epic resolution of the twelfth section,[7] with its now explicit references to: Paradise, everlasting Day, the Blessed Land,[8] yet completely free choices of perfect love in Paradise (143-48).

The style of the poem is akin to that of earlier religious epic and has echoes of the ancient Greek of Hesiod's *Theogony*; Virgil's Latin epic of a hero's (stoic) course of duty and of the achievement of his destiny; a wiser-than Milton's Adamaic protagonist's treatment of evil, dark, temptation and shadow; a Blakean defiance[9] of shabby rationalism and of a fixed scheme of things (e.g. 125-28); a statement that the writer is not yet, like Shakespeare's Prospero, bowing out (130). It has also various stylistic features that will become the hallmark of Tolkien's distinctively mannered prose:

> nouns weighted with poetic or Bible-like qualifiers – dark beginnings (12), green grass (24), free captives (38), secret looms[10] (44), ancient song (47), jewelled tent (50), beleaguered fools (113), everlasting Day (132), mirrored truth (134), or faultless fingers (147); or, compound adjectives and compound nouns of an Old English poetic style: myth-woven (51), elf-patterned (51), sub-creator[11] (61), misused (69), graceless (79), far-off (85), forswearing (96), day-illumined (133), etc.

Perhaps the most significant aspect of the whole is the coda, stanza XII, – with its vision of Paradise, where one may see the perfect God-made things, each no longer merely "the likeness of the Tune" (134); and now that Paradise is indeed 'the Blessed Land' of Celtic story; that one may – like Niggle to be – still 'garden' there; that all are free to make their (once often 'malicious' but now) wise choice; where poets like angels shall "have flames upon their head" (146), and joyously and freely choose in wisdom for the rest of their days. While there is more of music here than in the essay of *Tree and Leaf*, there are fine foreshadowings of the religious and artistic philosophers of both 'On Fairy Stories' and of the epic itself. Thus 'Mythopoeia' shows forth Tolkien's early thought as to

---

7 Compare Book XII of Virgil's *Aeneid* or Book XII of Milton's *Paradise Lost*.
8 One of the Celtic terms in the text – compare "living silver" (46), or "the harps" (147).
9 Compare William Blake's 'Jerusalem'.
10 An echo of Matthew Arnold, or of George MacDonald, this. Compare "a clumsy loom" (85). There are also gleams of the wearing of destiny as in the Greek of Hesiod or in the ancient Germanic three Fates or Norns.
11 This is of course, Tolkien's term in 'On Fairy Stories' (1947), for the creative artist, especially the story-teller who, when presenting myths of morality and power is, indeed, copying God's creative acts. He uses the synonym "little maker" (l. 128).

the meaning of 'sub-creation' and illustrates how, in his early rebuttal of the then Lewis position, he was able to bind together classical,[12] Germanic and Christian thought, much as he would do later in both style and larger detail of *The Lord of the Rings*.

---

12 By the time of the epic, or in its actual text as published, the classical elements are more muted and come through more in the general structure and in the antecedent religious notions of the adumbrated First Age and Second Age.

Tolkien's Concept of Philology as Mythology

While there have been various detailed critical studies[1] of J.R.R. Tolkien's 1938 lecture, 'On Fairy-Stories',[2] a prestigious one then delivered to St. Andrews University, most of this exposition concentrates on the literary and spiritual effects of certain kinds of fairy-stories, and on the special Tolkienian language of 'Escape', 'Consolation' and 'Eucatastrophe', rather than on another equally distinctive theme, particularly pronounced in the earlier parts of the lecture, namely in the significant references to philology.

His Farewell Apologia

This other neglected emphasis is one which was taken up again by Tolkien – albeit in muted tones – in his 'Valedictory Address to the University of Oxford'[3] in 1959. In this very late reflective piece, he makes a number of specific comments on the same concept, e.g.:

> Philology was part of my job, and I enjoyed it[4] (*MCE* 225); [and]
>
> I have, indeed, become more [...] convinced that Philology is never nasty: except to those deformed in youth [...] Philology is the foundation of humane letters. (*ibid.*)

He also then made several side glances at Latin and Greek, observing that the Oxford School of Classics included, as a branch of its content, "Comparative

---

This article first appeared in *Seven: An Anglo-American Literary Review* 7 (1986: 91-106) and is here reprinted with the kind permission of its editors.

1 E.g. R.J. Reilly, 'Tolkien and the Fairy-Story', most accessible in Issacs and Zimbardo (1968: 128-50) (it had earlier appeared in *Thought* XXXVIII (1963: 89-106)); or: Ryan, 'Folktale, Fairy-Tale, and the Creation of a Story' in Issacs and Zimbardo (1981: 20-39), reprinted in a new form as Essay 15 of this volume (153-77).

2 These essays and the present study work on the slightly expanded text in Tolkien's *Tree and Leaf* (1964).

3 Quotations are from the text in *MCE* (224-40).

4 The enjoyment is conveyed most genially in the little known 1936 collection, *Songs for the Philologists*, of which Tolkien was the major author. Its tone of fellowship is caught at the end of the Grace:

   And when we have dined, wish all mankind
   May dine as well as we. (st. 2)

Philology as illustrating the Greek and Latin Languages" (*ibid.* 232), and he also recalled his own "learning the elements of Greek philology" (*ibid.* 238) from Joseph Wright[5] in 1912, when he was preparing for the Honours Moderations papers in that School.

Later in that departing text he chooses, then for his last special audience of faculty and colleagues, to equate philology more narrowly with language (*ibid.* 233), and then for all of his readers, to call that 'technical philology' and, further, to widen his personally held definition of his theme:

> [...] it is not incompatible with a love of literature, nor is [its] acquisition [...] fatal to the sensibility either of critics or of authors [...] If [it] seems most exercised in the older periods, that is because any historical enquiry must begin with the earliest available evidence. (*ibid.* 234-35)

He was concerned to stress also that it had earlier been (technical) philology that

> rescued [...] [the purposes of literary criticism] from oblivion and ignorance, and presented to lovers of poetry and history fragments of a noble past that without it would have remained for ever dead and dark. (*ibid.* 235)

His challenge and assertion – one not repeated at the end of the address – was that its philology would, more than even "the history of art and thought and religion [...] bring [...] to life poetry, rhetoric, dramatic speech or even plain prose" (*ibid.*).

The Real Meaning of his Remarks

Now, while these remarks might appear merely a natural defence of the language side of 'English Studies', one then – as now – sadly under siege from literary teachers, it would seem that for Tolkien philology meant very much more than its conventional sense. The proof of this perception is to be found in his 1938 essay where philology is equated with mythology, with history, and even with religion; where he quotes from the myth scholars Andrew Lang (*TL* 36, 39, 40,

---

5 Corpus Christi Professor of Comparative Philology from 1901 (*Oxford Historical Register Supplement, 1901-1920*: 50). Tolkien refers to his mentor many times in the *Letters* (397), notably in the statement that "Joe [...] grounded me in G[reek] and L[atin] philology."

etc.) and Max Mueller[6] (*ibid.*, as specifically on pp. 22, 67); and in which he tells us that "a real taste for fairy-stories was wakened by philology" (*ibid.* 42).

Other related quotations from that text, taken *seriatim*, may be listed now:

> to ask what is the origin of stories is to ask what is the origin of language and of the mind (*ibid.* 17);

> the fascination [...] of the [...] history of [...] Tales [...] is closely connected with the philologists' study of the tangled skein of Language (*ibid.* 19);

> the history of fairy-stories is probably more complex than the physical history of the human race, and as complex as the history of language (*ibid.* 21);

> History often resembles 'Myth', because they are both ultimately of the same stuff (*ibid.* 30);

And, perhaps most significantly:

> It was in fairy-stories that I first divined the potency of words, and the wonder of things. (*ibid.* 60)

The Link with Friedrich Max Mueller

While all this might seem merely florid or some form of linguistic enthusiasm or excess, it must be seen against Victorian scholarship's conceptions of the history of the language, particularly as they are found in the seminal and appealing writings[7] of Professor (Friedrich) Max Mueller (1823-1900), a German who went to Oxford in 1848, began to lecture there on comparative philology at the Taylor Institution in 1850 as the Deputy Professor of Modern European Languages, was soon to become a member of Christ Church (in 1851) and so meet regularly with many of its literary men, became Professor of Foreign Languages in 1854, a Fellow of All Souls in 1858, and, later, have his professorship converted into one of Comparative Philology, which he would retain until his death. Initially the main focus of his teaching was on the development of the modern European languages, but after 1860, like his publications then, it was mainly in the fields of comparative philology and comparative mythology.

---

6 The spelling of his name in English scholarship was long Müller, but most twentieth-century scholars prefer Mueller.

7 Read for pleasure but also as textbooks by the young student, Tolkien, both in his first degree and his studies for Oxford's Diploma in Comparative Philology (1918-19).

For Mueller had long sought to popularise comparative studies of Indo-European language, as well as stimulating widespread interest in the study of linguistics, mythology and religion. This was done in Oxford, and, notably, through his membership of the circle of scholars and close friends which often gathered around Charles Kingsley in Eversley, Hants., a village not too far south of Oxford. And Mueller brought to a then ailing and not notably intellectual Oxford "that lofty conception of the scholar's life which is none too common in England."[8]

Mueller's early university studies[9] at Leipzig and Berlin had been remarkably successful. He had been working initially on Indian philosophy and later on Sanskrit, Persian, etc. under Bopp, Fleisher, Brockhaus and others. He first had moved to Paris, studying under Eugène Burhouf, and then to London, where he was commissioned by the directors of the East India Company to translate the *Rigveda*, the sacred Hymns of the Brahmans and the foundation of Sanskrit literature. The task took some twenty years and was interspersed with many other popularizing works.

His books, chapters, pamphlets and significant articles number perhaps 300,[10] apart from his many contributions to serious journalism and his much-attended public lectures, particularly at the Royal Institution. A selection of the most relevant titles includes:

> *Rigveda Samhita*, The Sacred Hymns of the Brahmans (translated and explained 1869). (All related work appeared 1849-73);
>
> *Essay on Comparative Mythology* (1856);
>
> *Sanskrit Grammar* (1866);
>
> *Stratification of Language* (1868);
>
> *Introduction to the Science of Religion* (1873);
>
> *Lectures on the Science of Language*, vol. I (1861, 14th edition 1886);
>
> *Lectures on the Science of Language*, vol. II (1864);
>
> *Hibbert Lectures* (1878);
>
> *Biographies of Words* (1888);

---

8 'Obituary', *The Times* (29th October 1900). A recent and judicious and informative tribute to him is the life by R.C.C. Fynes, in the 2004 edition of the *Oxford Dictionary of National Biography*, vol. 34 (706-10).

9 The most accessible survey is Chaudhuri (1914).

10 For a fairly complete list see the British Museum *General Catalogue of Printed Books* to 1955 (1967). Helpful selections from that vast bibliography are included at the end of Rau (1974: 169-71).

Science of Mythology, two volumes (1897).

The sketch of his life, one entitled *My Autobiography: A Fragment* appeared after his death, in 1901, while correspondence and family papers are held by the Taylor Institution in Oxford.

Perhaps the remarkable Mueller contribution to human thought may be best summed up, as it was by R.N. Dandekar[11] some years ago, by quoting the professor's own words to the University of Glasgow in 1891:

> If I were asked what I consider the most important discovery that has been made during the 19th century with respect to the ancient history of mankind, I should say that it was the simple etymological equation: Sanskrit *Dyas - Pitar* = Greek *Zeus Pater* = Latin *Jupiter* = Old Norse *Tyr*.

These precise words, from that lecture on 'Anthropological Religion', may be said to embody the thrust of the principal writings of that remarkable scholar – philological, comparative, religious and mythological, and concerned, as is the history of ancient religions, with the divine education of the human race and with man's long pilgrimage in search of the Infinite.

At another level, the quotation is also illustrative of Mueller's grand concept – that the comparative study of religions can hardly be divorced from the comparative study of language, that both are 'sciences' needing the greatest exactitude and imagination in their study. Both are to be associated with the concept of the Infinite, as man's senses make continual distinction of concepts into three classes of sense-objects, each of which leaves in us very different impressions of reality:

1) *tangible* objects, such as stones, shells and bones;

2) *semi-tangible* objects, such as trees,[12] mountains, rivers, the sea and the earth; and

3) *intangible* objects, such as the sky, the stars, the sun, the dawn, and the moon.

---

11 At the outset of his essay in Rau (1974: 21).
12 These ideas are closely echoed by Tolkien in *Tree and Leaf* (58), when discussing 'recovery', and by C.S. Lewis in his significantly entitled article 'The Gods Return to Earth', a review of *The Fellowship of the Ring*, first printed in *Time and Tide*, vol. XXXV (August 14, 1954: 1082-83).

If Mueller evolved his (cosmological) ideas largely from Sanskrit and the Veda, this was because he saw Indian culture of the ancient period as the earliest available views of the Indo-European peoples in their attempts "at naming the Infinite that hides itself behind the veil of the finite" (1861: 473). Elsewhere he spoke of three types of religion:

1) Physical Religion, seeking to discover the Infinite behind the phenomena of nature;[13]

2) Anthropological Religion, seeking an absolute behind the reality of man; and

3) Psychological Religion, concerned with what lies implicit within man.

In all this discussion, hardly any distinction is made between religion and mythology,[14] and most interpretation depends on the interrelationship of comparative mythology and comparative philology and etymology, since his method is to treat comparative philology as a means to a knowledge of thought[15] about God.

Now while this popularised form of speculation, with its fascination with solar myths, aroused much criticism then and since, clearly the quintessential aspect of this mode of spacious thought is its power: to liberate the mind; to present the discipline of comparative study; and to refuse to become bogged down by the burgeoning social sciences with their industrial-age emphasis on warfare, politics, materialism and necessary social reform.[16] Mueller's romantic 'escapism' was determined to see as paramount the events and achievements of the cultural life of a language and so of a people; and the origins and growth of philosophical thought.

While there is not space to discuss the flaws in his popularizations, it may help to summarize the achievements and Tolkien-like limitations of Mueller thus:

---

13 This is the basic concept behind Latin *numen* and Modern English *numinous*. Mueller's analysis of *light* as religious phenomenon would also have been familiar to Tolkien.
   Interestingly the present writer once heard Tolkien, while discussing 'The Pardoner's Tale' by Geoffrey Chaucer, digress into a speculation about money and it being the death of man as an ancient Indian motif that had come west along the trade routes, to be fashioned by Chaucer in his own moral tale. Then, realising that the issue was inappropriate for his audience, he put his motif tracing aside.

14 This was a common equation in nineteenth-century thought – see sense 3 of 'mythology', *OED*, [first edition], vol. VI (820), as the dictionary shows by quotations from Gibbon (1781), Coleridge (1830), and Phillips (1880).

15 See, for example Chapter I of *Lectures on the Science of Language*, vol. I.

16 Like Tolkien, Mueller found processes of decay operative in contemporary society, despite his (conflicting) theories of evolutionary and cyclic patterns in history.

he did more to advance comparative philology than any man who has ever lived;

he wrote essays which are still the most splendid statements of the doctrines of the linguistic school of mythology;[17]

he was not a 'good scholar' but he was one of real genius for the sheer brilliance of his tumbling ideas and the lucidity of their popular expression;[18] and

he was always the student and researcher in a world of teachers and examinations.

The parallels to Tolkien himself need no underscoring.

And the Place of Andrew Lang and More Recent Folklore

One of the best known critics[19] of Mueller was Andrew Lang (1844-1912), as in his uneven *Modern Mythology* (1897), a work which speaks out for anthropologists and folklorists and suggests both that archaeology of ancient civilizations is not everything (viii) and that later "mythology as a disease of [ancient] language" is a vast over-simplification, denying respect for semantic and social change. For, like Professor William James, Lang was distressed that psychology had been ignored, and that comparativism had been ludicrously overdone in the period 1860 to 1880, as had the mocking (albeit unintentional) of modern European folk studies.

Yet, as Lang graciously wrote[20] later to Mueller's widow:

To the unlearned world at large he was the personification of philological scholarship [...] which he knew how to render accessible to his public in inimitably simple and charming style [...] his greatest service was to have made knowledge agreeable – nay, even fashionable.

Lang's own method – one derived from E.B. Tylor's *Primitive Culture* – was to compare popular tales and explore their diffusion, to analyse ghost-stories and

---

17 Tolkien's pupil, the late E.O.G. Turville-Petre (1908-78) (the Vigfússon Professor of Old Icelandic at Oxford from 1953-75) was another disciple, as was Georges Dumézil (1898-1986), the scholar of Indo-European civilization, friend of both post-war professors and frequent lecturer in Oxford in the 1950s. See Udo Strutynski's introduction to Dumézil's *Gods of the Ancient Northmen* (1973: xix-xliv).
18 Ronald Tolkien's own credo of his concept of himself as a populariser appears many times in the *Letters*, perhaps never more significantly than in the 1925 application for the Chair of Anglo-Saxon: "I should [...] continue [...] the encouragement of philological enthusiasm among the young" (13).
19 He is discussed here – somewhat out of chronological order – for convenience and brevity.
20 His letter of March 26, 1902, is quoted in *The Life and Letters* (Müller 1902, vol. II: 429).

study folk-tales closely.[21] It is highly significant that Tolkien would be one of the supervisors of a seminal Oxford thesis on Lang by Roger Lancelyn Green, published in 1946 as *Andrew Lang: A Critical Biography*. The book version of the thesis refers to "the demolition of Max Mueller" (71) and, simplistically, to Lang's "greatest feat [...] the overthrow of the philological interpretation of myths" (73). Not surprisingly, all these complex and controversial matters are to be found referred to in the definitive version of 'On Fairy-Stories'. There Mueller is twice referred to explicitly – first for his "prim way" (67) which managed to miss the point of the story of the princess marrying the frog (*ibid.*); and, secondly, in his approval of a storyteller-artist's borrowing widely (*inventio*), impelled by his own genius.

This last passage merits quotation in some detail for its unconscious respect[22] for Mueller, despite the earlier scholar's obsession with ancient form as opposed to later meaning:

> Philology has been dethroned from the high place it once had in this court of inquiry [about stories and their origins]. Max Mueller's view of mythology as a 'disease of language' can be abandoned without regret. Mythology is not a disease [...] It would be more near the truth to say that languages, especially modern European languages, are a disease of mythology. But language cannot, all the same, be dismissed. (*ibid.* 21-22)

Similarly the thought of Lang is included by Tolkien in his analysis of story and of its various potential qualities. Tolkien quotes, only to query, the words of the Scottish anthropologist:

> Andrew Lang said, and is by some still commended for saying that mythology and religion (in the strict sense of the word) are two distinct things that have become inextricably entangled, (*ibid.* 26)

continuing with the observation that they are linked, probably were once, and, if severed, will 're-fuse'. And he then re-phrases Mueller's notion of the three types of religion by allowing them to co-exist in fairy-story:

---

21 See his 'Mythology and Fairy-Tales' in *The Fortnightly Review* (May 1873), *Custom and Myth* (1884); *Myth, Ritual and Religion* (1887); or his introduction to Kirk's *Secret Commonwealth of Elves, Fauns and Fairies* (1893).

22 T.A. Shippey gives some indication of both his own and Tolkien's admiration for Mueller: "Müller's remarks [engendered] an awareness that some forms even of modern language took you back to the Stone Age" (1982: 11).

1) the Mystical, looking to the 'Supernatural';

2) the Magical looking towards Nature (both of which equate to Mueller's 'Physical' and 'Anthropological' (v. *supra*); and

3) the "Mirror of scorn and pity towards Man" for Mueller's 'psychological religion'.

Further, his 1938 lecture makes certain other points which relate to the great Victorian controversy:

1) Andrew Lang's twelve collections of folk-tales have always been told to children because they represent "the young age of man" still with "a fresh appetite for marvels"; (*ibid.* 36)

and Tolkien himself realizes like Mueller that

2) [it]is in fairy-stories that one derives "the potency of the words, and the wonder of the things, such as stone, and wood, and iron; tree and grass; house and fire". (*ibid.* 60)

Indeed one is driven to the feeling that Tolkien preferred 'fairy-story' to 'myth' as a critical term because of his desire, like Lang, to speak out to moderns, and because of his Christian reluctance to claim too much spirituality for any ancient pagan religion. His penultimate remarks here on 'recovery' and 'escape' (*ibid.* 57ff.) may be seen as a more formally Christian version of Mueller's notion of an exciting spiritual liberation (v. *supra*).

The Place of Archibald Henry Sayce (1845-1933)

The earlier Lang reference to 'archaeology' is a convenient link with the other name in this quartet of scholarly speculators about language, myth and story, namely Archibald Henry Sayce[23] (1845-1933), the orientalist and comparative philologist who had been introduced to both fields as a schoolboy of thirteen. By the age of sixteen he already knew Hebrew, and was working on Assyrian, Persian, Arabic and Sanskrit. Going up to Oxford in 1865 he had entered Queen's College[24] and began a lifelong friendship with Max Mueller, with whom he read the Vedic hymns, and who, as he put it long afterwards, "introduced me to the

---

23 A convenient short account of his life is the survey by Gunn in the 1931-40 volume of *The Dictionary of National Biography* (1949: 786-88).
24 He was to hold a Fellowship there for 64 years, from 1869 until his death in 1933.

seductive fields of comparative mythology" (Sayce 1923: 36). After obtaining a first in *literae humaniores* in 1868, and ordination in 1870, he was appointed a regular correspondent on oriental matters for *The Times*, had begun his long course of lectures for the Society of Biblical Archaeology,[25] and became one of the Oxford representatives in the revision of the Old Testament.

As a result in part of his taking up Germanic philology and because of pressure of work on Mueller, in 1876 Sayce took some of the burden of the other's teaching, to become Deputy Professor of Comparative Philology (*ibid.* 132), a post which he held until 1890, then moving to an extraordinary Chair of Assyriology which he held from 1891 until his 'retirement' in 1919. From 1877 on, his life assumed *inter alia* a remarkable pattern of travel throughout Europe, Asia, North Africa and North America; a flood of published decipherments of Middle Eastern inscriptions; his own archaeological work and the organization of many seminal excavations[26] by others; and numerous studies of the mysterious and linguistically significant Hittites.

Attributes of Sayce's that are more relevant to the present study may be tabulated:

1) a highly original mind, and a very active imagination;[27]

2) his insistence in 1874 on the principle of analogy,[28] from then on a cornerstone of linguistic science;

3) his forcing Old Testament scholarship to take careful notice of the evidence of all relevant oriental archaeological remains and discoveries;

4) his efforts, almost single-handed, to introduce successfully the forgotten empire of the Hittites and their language[29] to the modern world;

---

25 He was its president from 1898 until it ceased to be an independent body in 1919.

26 Thus, he helped Garstang with Meroe and was one of the very first to recognize the significance of Heinrich Schliemann's discoveries and wrote a splendid preface to the other's *Troja* (1884), the major account of the excavations there in 1882.
   He also furthered the careers – similarly based on Queen's College – of
   (a) Francis L. Griffith (1862-1934), reader in Egyptology at Oxford (1901-24) and Honorary Professor (1924-33); and
   (b) Thomas Eric Peet (1882-1934), Laycock Student in Egyptology (1923-32), and then reader (1933-34), alike a vital lecturer and an outstanding philologist.

27 This led him to various errors, as in his translation of Herodotus, *Books I-III* (1883), for which he was criticized excessively.

28 See Sayce (1892a: 99ff).

29 Problems with Hittite continued to fascinate those working in broader language areas. See, for example, the work on the language in the 1983 volume of the *Transactions of the Philological Society*,

5) his luminous public lectures, such as his Hibbert, Gifford and Rhind Series; and

6) his remarkable memory, and legendary courtesy, particularly to his students and ordinary workmen on the Middle Eastern sites.

In short, he was, perhaps, the best comparative linguist of all time in the joint area of classical and ancient Middle Eastern philology, as well as being the longest serving and most impressive scholar of the 'heroic age' of Assyriology.

In the field of general linguistics – in which most of his published work on the European languages may be found – his outstanding volumes were *The Principles of Comparative Philology* (1874-75) (a work which had four large editions), and his *Introduction to the Science of Language* (2 vols., 1880; 2nd ed. 1883; 3rd ed. 1890), both of which were used by Joseph Wright in his tutelage of the youthful Tolkien in comparative philology. While both texts are compendious works, they may now be quoted from selectively[30] to illustrate the Saycean cast of thought – one which may be said to both modify Mueller and embrace Lang, and to articulate luminously his burgeoning thoughts for a student who must have passed him in the street and Examination Schools many times in the second decade of the century.

The first work, in the 'Preface of the Second Edition', had allowed that "Language is the reflection of society, creating and created by it" (xxx), but – unlike the view of Mueller – not forcing a model on civilizations. His first chapter on the 'sphere' of Comparative Philology is full of splendid and spacious concepts:

the study appeals at once to our reason, our imagination and our curiosity (*ibid.* 2);

our concern is the development of the moral and intellectual life of mankind (*ibid.* 3);

now as much as ever Comparative Philology has need of [...] bold and wide-reaching conceptions (*ibid.* 6); or

---

by Gillian Hart (100-54). It will be recalled that Tolkien had referred to the linguistically significant place of the Hittites in one of the overview essays that he had contributed to the *Year's Work in English Studies* in the mid-1920s.

30 The quotations in the text are from the fourth edition of *Principles* (1892a: lii, 422). All editions are dedicated "To Professor Max Mueller, Whose Words First Kindled my Interest in the Study of Language and Who Has Since Been to me a Teacher, Guide and Friend" (v).

linguistic metaphysics [...] and phonology are [...] but the scaffolding of the higher and more comprehensive generalizations of the master-science itself (*ibid.* 9).

These perceptions are then followed by views and concepts more sympathetic to the modern derivative languages and dialects:

consider the excitement of realizing the complete force of a term which has come up from the patois where the life of language is still vigorous (*ibid.* 27);[31]

language itself is poetry, symbolizing the impalpable things of the spirit under the veil of metaphor (*ibid.* 34);

language, as we find it, is as much the creation[32] of man as painting or any other of the arts (*ibid.* 38);

words are of no value in themselves except [...] in so far as they reflect and embody thought; and the object of a true philological etymology is to illustrate or discover [...] the evolution of thought (*ibid.* 45);[33]

if we had a complete history [...] of society [...]; but [...] as we do not and cannot possess it we must endeavour to find out [...] by some other method (*ibid.* 49); and

in [...] Comparative Mythology, like [...] [in] Comparative Philology [...] we must collect our myths from every race (*ibid.* 312-13).

As he had proclaimed, at the end of his study of the meaning of "comparative philology" (*ibid.* 60), the search for ancient nuances would appeal of necessity to history, psychology and ethnology, with the grand vision that, by so doing, philologists

will be [able] to reconstruct the past history of man and to determine the character of those long-forgotten strata of society which our fossil-like records reveal to us [...]; to trace the gradual growth of the mind of man [...] and the embodiment of the relations between thought and the world of [...] the triumph of [...] the religious idea, – in other words [...] Comparative Mythology[34] and the Science of Religions. (*ibid.*)

---

31 Compare Tolkien's remarks about thirteenth-century West Midland culture in his paper, '*Ancrene Wisse* and *Hali Meithhad*', in *Essays and Studies* XIV (1929: 104-26).

32 Was this a subconscious stimulus to Tolkien's concept of 'sub-creation' in his 'On Fairy-Stories'?

33 Compare (a) Tolkien's remarks in quiet questioning of the first edition of *The Pocket Oxford Dictionary of Current English*, compiled by F.G. and H.W. Fowler in his *YWES V* (49):

We are inclined [...] to think that the rudimentary or vestigular etymologies [...] were best away. It is arguable that there is not much use in etymologies unless they are fairly full and can have space to hesitate.

and (b) The ents' dislike of hastiness (*TT* 67).

34 At various points in the book Sayce cautions against random comparisons of myths. He puts the point most cogently in his *Introduction to the Science of Language*, vol. II (1880: 260):

The Human Mind, and so the Move toward Semantic Change

While Sayce's ideas do not equate precisely to those of Mueller, already (in 1874) his stress was on archaeology, on respect for modern culture and on semantics (still called 'psychology of language'). Most of these ideas of *Principles* are stated to be the basis[35] of his later work, *Introduction to the Science of Language* (1880, 2 vols.), a compilation more than twice the length of its predecessor. While the focus is particularly on the Aryan languages (I: 88), the grand scheme is still focused on the history of the human mind and the riddle of mythology (I: 89).

Sayce's conclusion to the long chapter, 'Theories of Language', runs thus:

> Language is the reflexion of the thoughts and beliefs of communities from their earliest days; and by tracing its changes and fortunes, by discovering the origin and history of words and their meanings, we can read those thoughts and beliefs with greater certainty [...]. (*ibid.*)

Throughout the books there are modifications – albeit made respectfully – to Mueller's thoughts, as in the peculiarly Tolkien-like observation:[36]

> Mythology is not so much a disease of language as a misunderstanding of its metaphors and a misconception of the analogical reasoning of our early forefathers. (I: 183)

Sayce's interest[37] in the related clusters of language is central:

> An antiquarian study of philology will enable us to trace the history of words and forms, to group words into families. (I: 229)

His ideas touching the origins of myth (Book II, Chapter IX) are very much closer to Plato than were those of Mueller and there is infinite sadness in his notion that in Greece, after Aristotle, the old myths had lost their religious potency[38] (II: 233) and were "stripped of all that was marvellous in them"

> But care must be taken to compare together only those myths which belong to the languages shown by comparative philology to be children of a common mother.

35 See 'Preface', vol. I (Sayce 1892a: v).
36 See above, the discussion by Tolkien in *TL* (22) and by Shippey, footnote 22 (*supra*).
37 Again more cogently and sharply put than by Mueller.
38 He feels that something of the "beauty and attractiveness" of the Greek myths could be said to survive in the Norse legends (235). Compare Tolkien's sense of 'Northernness'.

(II: 235). He also bemoans the irreverence of Euhemerus, Lycian, Lord Bacon and Voltaire, and he then suggests that rationalists fail to understand that the origins of

> the myths with which early literature [...] is filled [...] must be combined with the inability of language to express the spiritual and the abstract without the help of sensuous imagery. (II: 248)

Such a time is indeed "a mythopoeic age"[39] (II: 249) when "curiosity to understand and interpret the outward world [...] takes the form of tales and legends, of hymns to the gods [...]" (*ibid.*).

Sayce also had much to say of both folklore and fairy-tales (II: 275-84), at many points quoting from Andrew Lang.[40] Some *obiter dicta* may be tabulated:

> folklore [...] embraces all those popular stories of which [...] fairy-tales are a good illustration (II: 275);

> it is only when the fable [...] has not been composed with the deliberate purpose of conveying a lesson that it ought strictly to be regarded as a part of folklore (II: 279-80);

> and the comparative philologist cannot escape from the study of those religions and religious systems which have their root in the mythopoeic age (II: 284).

All of this shows how, as in Christianity,[41] the old sense of a myth is restored by discovering the first meaning and import of its key words. In the appended 'List of Works' he had listed (chronologically) those of Mueller, A. de Gubernatis (*Zoological Mythology*, 1872) – an amazingly comprehensive folklore collection – J. Grimm, G.W. Dasent (for his *Popular Tales from the Norse*), R.H. Busk (*Folklore of Rome*,[42] 1874), as sources for mythology, and Max Mueller and E.B. Tylor (*Primitive Culture*, 1871) for the fruitful study of religion. The compendious index (365-421) contains many summaries of argument which

---

39 This word, resurrected by C.S. Lewis, is encountered widely in his criticism, e.g. "It was in this mythopoeic art that MacDonald excelled," in *George MacDonald, An Anthology*, introduced by C.S. Lewis (1946: 17). Sayce used the word frequently, one use of his being quoted in *The Oxford English Dictionary*, vol. VII (820):

> The mythopoeic age is the period of primitive unconscious childhood and barbarism. (*Comparative Philology*, 1874: 376)

40 E.g. his article on nursery tales, *Fortnightly Review*, May 1873.
41 He indicates here the illustration of this in Dr Newman's *Development of Christian Doctrine* (1845: 285).
42 This work can be shown to be a promising and influential source for various Shire customs.

will prove helpful to those seeking sources for or influences on the arguments of Tolkien's own 'On Fairy-Stories'.

Conclusion

It will be readily apparent that the Andrew Lang Lecture authorities at St. Andrews University – for such were the original commissioners and formal auspices of Tolkien's disquisition – received from the Oxford professor both a public statement of his own literary position and a most judicious assessment of the rights and wrongs of Lang's view of mythology. For Tolkien had agreed with Lang that Mueller could be foolish, as in his debunking of 'modern' legends and folk-tales in favour of grand 'solar' concepts from the dawn of ancient civilizations. But the contemporary interpreter of mythology had not really demolished Mueller, but rather taken up a position very close to that of the judicious and wise A.H. Sayce who has been shown to be very much one of Tolkien's most potent early and seminal influences.

And so it may be profitable to return again to the opening remarks drawn from the 1959 'Valedictory Address to the University of Oxford', for it is clear that those references to philology were really an artistic credo, one presented anew to those most hostile to his creative writings, as well as a restatement of the eternal need for us readers to see what the writer had meant[43] as well as what his stylistic had seemed to say. For his 1959 glosses on his own old-fashioned definition of philology were, it may be feared, not luminously clear to all of his relatively numerous auditors. Yet they had always been part of his own aesthetic, appearing in print in the most surprising places, as in his three review chapters on early language for the *Year's Work in English Studies*.[44]

Some of the thoughts which those essays of the 1920s reveal will prove startling to those not otherwise alerted to the Tolkien-Sayce meaning of philology; for example:

---

43 This element of quiet polemic is also to be found in his British Academy lecture of 1936, 'Beowulf: the Monsters and the Critics' (*MCE* 5-48).

44 *YWES IV* (20-37); *YWES V* (26-65); and *YWES VI* (32-66). The three papers and related matters are discussed in some detail by J.S. Ryan in his 'J. R. R. Tolkien: Lexicography and Other Early Linguistic Preferences' in the same volume (71-87).

1) reading earlier texts carefully is akin to "walking in a wood, with the responsibility of scrutinizing every leaf" (*YWES VI* 32) (much like the priest of the grove in James Frazer's *The Golden Bough*);[45]

> There is another and denser wood where some are obliged to walk instead, where saws are wise and screeds are thick [...] [and there is] the labour of sorting them under the departments of philology to which they belong [...] (*ibid.*);

2) the deaths of the earlier language professors are a melancholy reminder of the age of the older generation of giants[46] who have laboured in the service of Philologica and have deserved so well of her (*ibid.* 33);

3) there is very little distinction between the 'word-historian' and 'the student of literary ideas'; and the boundary line between linguistic and literary history is as imaginary as the equator (*ibid.* 58-59);

4) all philologists have as the ideal phantom [...] the pre-history of Europe and nearer Asia (*YWES V* 27] for Germanic and Indo-European philology are part of the history of the English (*ibid.* 28);

5) the conclusion to the second essay when he is apparently discussing the task and labours of the then newly-founded English Place Name Society – but really of his own field of study:

> In other words this study is fired by two emotions, love of the land[47] of England, and the allurement of the riddle of the past, that never cease to carry men through amazing, and most uneconomic, labours to the recapturing of fitful and tantalizing glimpses in the dark – "Floreant Philologica et Archaeologica" (*ibid.* 65).

Thus it may be seen that the public toasts to 'Philologica', made by Tolkien in 1925, 1936 and 1959 were also given a further and luminous glossing in his 1939 'On Fairy-Stories' and in many other places, but that their fullest meaning is only truly perceived in the light of the thought of those 'giants', the Oxford philologists, and so students of the stories of the past, Max Mueller and Henry Sayce, the Oxford teachers of "the great philological epoch in England." Like them, Ronald Tolkien held a passionate 'philological attitude' towards the vestigial records of the past of mankind, both in Europe and back to the dawn

---

45 This last is not stated but is strongly implied.
46 Since this follows the details of the older forests it may be inferred that the epic's senior ents and Fangorn were, at one level, professors of comparative philology, interpreting the leaves of the most ancient trees. Thus Sievers, later, is equated to one of the largest trees (*YWES VI* 36). Earlier Tolkien had talked of the "philological epoch as that of 1850-1900 in England" (*YWES IV* 37) and clearly these natural and folklore equations to human activities have more than quaint charm when they are found in later creative writings.
47 Compare his remarks about "the soil" and "the clime and soil [...] of Britain and the hither parts of Europe" in a 1951 letter to Milton Waldman (*Letters* 144).

of language, and so an awed realization of philology's "vast importance in the history of the human mind, and [...] of mythology" (Sayce 1880: 408).

And, finally, we may note that the *Oxford English Dictionary* had long ago given the necessary clues to the particular sense of 'philology' as mythology required for proper understanding of all the Tolkien opera, by two passages: first, the 1874 Sayce quotation on 'the mythopoeic age'; and secondly the first sense for 'philology' (vol. VII: 778) as

> love of learning and literature; the study of literature, in a wide sense, includ-
> ing grammar, literary criticism and written records to history etc.; literary or
> classical scholarship

noting that it is "now rare in this sense" and giving the following resoundingly illustrative usage:

> The fact is that philology is not a mere matter of grammar, but is in the
> largest sense a master science, whose duty is to present to us the whole of
> ancient life, and to give archaeology its just place by the side of literature.
> (Sayce 1892b: 816, col. 1)

While only Sayce as archaeologist giant as well as comparative philologist *par excellence* espoused the ideal twin tasks of the 'mythologist', he gave Tolkien the challenge to *haute popularisation* which was followed by the second genius both as lecturer and, with his "basic passion [...] *ab inito* [...] for myth" (*Letters* 144), in his own creative writings which he defined to M. Waldman ideal as

> my legends [...] [with their] illusion of [ancient] historicity [...] of which there
> is far too little in the world (accessible to me) for my appetite.

And so

> I had a mind to make a body of more or less connected legend, ranging from
> the large and cosmogonic, to the level of romantic fairy-story. (*ibid.* 143-44)

His final 1951 remarks that "the cycles should be linked to a majestic whole" (*ibid.* 145) are but the dream of all the heroic comparative philologists, of elves and of mortal men, and they remind us once again of God's "intricate webs, whose tangle we may now guess at but hardly hope to unravel [...] that phantom which becomes more and more elusive, and more alluring, with the passage of years" (*YWES V* 28).[48]

---

48 Of course, paradoxically, Tolkien was able to himself enter the field of archaeology in the help that he
   gave to Mortimer Wheeler in the interpretation of a key inscription in the late 1920s excavation at the
   late Roman site at Lydney in Gloucestershire.
   Similarly, Tolkien had had so many significant conversations with R.G. Collingwood, the historian
   of Roman Britain, in his own earlier years in Pembroke College, when he was the professor of Anglo-
   Saxon, with rooms close by in that same college.

By 'Significant' Compounding "We Pass Insensibly into the World of the Epic"

The quotation in the title of this essay contains in its second part an abridged stylistic reference from a highly significant essay, treating of J.R.R. Tolkien's *The Hobbit* (1937), from C.S. Lewis. The latter contributed a paper to a collection of pieces[1] issued as a memorial tribute to their deceased friend Charles Williams (ob. 1945) by a number of his Oxford and London colleagues and literary associates. The essay by Lewis was 'On Stories', and it was originally – perhaps as early as 1938 – "read to a Merton College undergraduate literary society[2] [...] in a slightly fuller form" (Lewis 1966: vii) with the title 'The Kappe Element in Fiction'. Towards the end of his speculative piece (which has many parallels to Tolkien's own 'On Fairy Stories', first written in 1938 for the University of St. Andrews), Lewis pulls his argument together with insightful reference to Tolkien's recently published story:

> *The Hobbit* escapes the danger of degenerating into mere plot and excitement by a very curious shift of tone. As the humour and homeliness of the early chapters, the sheer 'Hobbitry', dies away we pass insensibly into the world of the epic [...] we lose one theme but find another. We kill – but not the same fox. (*ibid.* 19)

Another unduly neglected text of that same period of formulative thought and writing is Tolkien's own essay entitled 'Prefatory Remarks on Prose Translation of *Beowulf*', which he wrote in 1939 for the (1940 issued) completely revised edition of John R. Clark Hall's *Beowulf and the Finnesburg Fragment, A Translation into Modern English Prose*.[3] These 'remarks' are described by the reviser, C.L. Wrenn (long his assistant, and in 1945, his successor to the Rawlinson and

---

This article first appeared in *Mythlore* 17.4 (1991: 45-49) and I am grateful to the editors for the permission to reprint.

1 The collection of essays was entitled *Essays Presented to Charles Williams* and published in 1947 by Faber and Faber. Lewis' essay was later re-edited and re-published under the editorship of Walter Hooper.
2 I.e. the Bodley Club.
3 The original appeared in 1911. The remarks were subsequently corrected by Tolkien in the 1950 reprint issued by Allan and Unwin and are given in this essay in the form given in 'On Translating *Beowulf*', forming part of Christopher Tolkien's edited collection of essays by J.R.R. Tolkien called *The Monster and the Critics and Other Essays* (1983: 49-71).

Bosworth Professorship of Anglo-Saxon at the University of Oxford), as both highly insightful and of abiding significance "for they must remain as the most permanently valuable part of the book" (1950: vi).

While Wrenn saw the quoted details, analysis and discussion of the verse style as the key to the modern's enjoyment of the translation and, ultimately, of the original text of *Beowulf*, we may be able to extract from the 'remarks' some other notions not without relevance to the style of Tolkien's own creative writing of those pre-war years. Our concern will be largely with the first part, 'On Translation and Words' (*MCE* 49-60), and more briefly with the second, 'On Metre' (*ibid*. 61-71).

The first section is concerned with the task of obtaining a "translation into plain prose of what is in fact a poem, a work of skilled and close-wrought metre" (*ibid*. 49), in order to give readers at the end "a drink dark and bitter: a solemn funeral-ale with the taste of death" (*ibid*.).[4] Tolkien, who was consulted by his Oxford teaching associate, Wrenn, over many details of the following modified 'competent translation', then refers to aspects of the original that must be retained in an appropriate prose rendering: "heroic names now nearly faded into oblivion" (*ibid*.); "recurring word[s]" which give important 'hints' (*ibid*. 50); the need for words "bearing echoes of ancient days beyond the shadowy borders of Northern history" (*ibid*.); some words at least normally to be deemed "already archaic and rare" (*ibid*. 51); the use of "descriptive compounds [...] generally foreign to our present literary and linguistic habits" (*ibid*.); and compounds whose "primary poetic object [...] was compression, the force of brevity, the packing of the pictorial and emotional colour" (*ibid*. 52).

Tolkien then went on to distinguish between the tones that might be required:

  1) the colloquial or 'snappy' (*ibid*. 54);[5]

  2) the literary and traditional, occasionally archaic but "elevated, recognized as old" (*ibid*.), a serious language "freed from trivial associations, and filled with the memory of good and evil" (*ibid*. 55); and

---

4 This is the tone of Chapter XVII, 'The Battle of Five Armies' (*Hobbit* 291-96). All references to *The Hobbit* in this essay are made to the 1951 second edition, the first version with the expanded text.
5 While not in the translation of *Beowulf*, this strand is to be found in *The Hobbit*, where it is to be seen as deliberate (*v. infra*).

3) an ethical tone suggestive of being "upon the threshold of Christian chivalry" (*ibid.* 57).

The remaining sections of the essay give much attention to the retention of compounds and kennings (particularly for nouns and adjectives), stressing how modern heroic prose should try by use of compounds and/or compressed phrases to 'retain the colour' and not 'weaken' the texture, since every such phrase "flashes a picture before us, often the more clear and bright for its brevity, instead of unrolling it in a simile" (*ibid.* 59). His conclusion on the Old English heroic style in implicitly Christian epic contains his tribute to the verses' 'unrecapturable magic', for "profound feeling, and poignant vision, filled with the beauty and mortality of the world, are aroused by brief phrases, light touches, short words resounding like harp-strings sharply plucked" (*ibid.* 60).

When we turn to *The Hobbit* itself, a text finally edited only two years before the writing of this essay, we find Tolkien's notions of a grand style appropriate to the epic or heroic occasion to be very close indeed to his own fictional and story-telling practice. Let us consider first the colloquial or snappy. This style in *The Hobbit* has several functions, in that it is the private manner of the hobbits, sometimes remarkably modern sounding and colloquial. Here we may list, *seriatim,* – *smoke-rings* (14, 23), *seed-cake* (18), *flummoxed* (21, 27), *confusticate*[6] (21, 104, 164), *clarinets* (23), *walking-sticks* (23), *the whistle of an engine coming out of a tunnel* (28), *the game of Golf* (28), a *pocket-handkerchief* (40, 225), *policemen* (43), *bashes* (50), a *pocket-knife* (53), *larder* (54), *picnics* (66), *football* (69, 168), the nearest *post-office* (72), meat *delivered by the butcher* (121), *matches* (121), *toast* (123), a *warm bath* (123), *jack-in-the-boxes* (133), *veranda* (140), *black as a top-hat* (153), *dart-throwing* (169), *slowcoach* (192), *toss-pot*[7] (193), *waistcoat* (240), *hide-and-seek* (246), *looking-glass* (251), *mantelpiece* (213, 281), and *tobacco-jar* (315). As this fairly exhaustive list indicates, the domestic tone or 'hobbitry' does indeed die away very quickly, once Bilbo and the dwarves are far from the Shire and the plot grows more heroic and the destiny of whole nations is at stake. As others have pointed out, the manner of a nursery tale

---

6 There and other are 'nonsense' or Lewis Carroll-type words, beloved of the later Victorians when jesting or when ostensibly writing for children.
7 The *New English Dictionary*, vol. XI (T, 174) gave the word as first occuring in 1568.

has fallen away. As usual, Lewis said it well, when, in his Kappa lecture he continued, after his phrase "we pass insensibly into [...] the epic,"

> It is as if the battle of Toad Hall had become a serious heimsókn and Badger had begun to talk like Njal.[8] Thus we lose one theme but find another. (1947: 104)

In Tolkien's text the mysterious ancient names and words, echoic of ancient threat and repression, are fewer than the 'snappy' elements, but there are enough for his purpose, as in this heroic list: *Mirkwood*[9] (30, 145, 147), *Necromancer* (36, 308), *Goblin wars* [...] *Orcrist* (63), *thunder-battle*[10] (67), *noble-hearted* (115), *battle-ground* (118), *forest-gate* (147), *Lob* (171), *Attercop* (175), *Lake-town*[11] (188), *mountain-shadowed* (204), *mountain-gates* (204), *battering-rams* (243), *stone-paved* [...] *pavement* (253), *mountain-spur* (255), *lake-town Esgaroth* (257), *sparks and gledes* (261), *spearmen* (265, 294), *Oakenshield* (281), *Arkenstone* (285, 287, etc.), *roundshield* (288), *Ravenhill* (294), *Elvenking* (295, 303), *Underhill* (311), or *Lake-people* (314). This list has overtones of an older Middle-earth or Europe, suggesting the ancient history of the Romans, the Celts, and of the Germanic peoples. The ancient religion of the Greeks is recalled from *thunder-battle*, or that of the Norse peoples in the ominous Othin-associated *Ravenhill*.

The elves' presence as an earlier race of talented but doomed people is found ubiquitously as in the following (ordered but not exhaustive) list of compounds: *elf-fires* (174, 176), *elf-friend(s)* (75, 304), *elf-host* (285), *elf-king* (179), *elf-maiden* (307), *elf-prince* (251), *elven-harps* (272), *Elvenking* (*passim*), *elvish* (272), *Woodelves* (180), *Woodelves' realm* (300), etc. The last compounds remind us of the various separate races, not distinguished especially for the moment, including *Deep-elves* (or *Gnomes*), *Sea-elves*, and *Light-elves* (178).

The potential and actual dangers of the world 'outside' the safety of Bag End gradually become more threatening and, finally, horribly real in the crescendo of: the wild *Were-worms*[12] (29), *greater workshops* (32), *troll-make* (63), *Goblin-*

---

8 The references are to the Icelandic Saga and heroic tragedy, *The Burning of Njal*.
9 The most venerable associations of the name, Mirkwood, suggest that it was thought to run from north of Constantinople all the way to the Baltic.
10 This is an exact translation of various terms in ancient Greek to denote the warring of the gods.
11 This term and the descriptions of the people's lifestyle suggest the ancient Villanovan or La Tène culture of ancient north Italy and Switzerland.
12 *Worm* is the old Germanic word for 'dragon', so called from p. 125.

wars (63), *stone-giants* (69), *explosions* (74), *the big ones, the orcs of the mountains* (99), *battle-ground* (118), *arrow-wound* (120), *skin-changer*[13] (126), *goblins, hobgoblins, and orcs of the worst description* (149-50), *spider-webs* (167), *mining-work*[14] (219), *half-burnt* (252), *watchmen* (26), *guardroom* (256), *grim-voiced* (256, etc.), *grim-faced* (260), *guard-chamber* (268), *banner-bearers* (276), *drums and guns* (300), or the home-again nonchalance of *nasty adventure* (310) or of *a bad end* (314).

As the text reveals, the second edition – the text published from 1951 on – shows the goblins (of George MacDonald flavour) slowly becoming orcs as in

   1) the reference to *Orcrist* (*Goblin-cleaver*; 63);

   2) the orc reference to the *mountain orcs* (99) and to

   3) *orcs of the worst description* (149-50).

Yet the goblins are malign enough, as this sequential catalogue reveals the *goblins* (36), *goblin-wars* (63), *goblin-drivers* (73), *goblin-cleaver* (75), *goblin-hall* (76), *goblin-chains* (77), *goblin feet* (78), *goblin-infested* (110), or the later phrasal units: *goblin-army, goblin blood, goblin swordsman* (all on p. 293), or: *goblins' mustering* (299). *Wargs* are not explained in this work, they first appear on p. 112 (twice), and then are associated with the *wolf-riders* (292).

The dragon Smaug is not quite the malign monster of *Beowulf,* yet the nature of these great *worms* is well suggested by the total impact of the items in this catalogue: *dragon-fire* (246, 263), *dragon-gold* (125), *dragon-guarded treasures* (225), *dragon-haunted* (253), *dragon-hoards* (226), *dragon-lore* (233), *dragon-mountain* (203), *dragon-noises* (249), *Dragon-shooter* (262), *dragon-sickness* (314), *dragon-slayer* (276), *dragon-slayings* (240), *dragon-spell* (235), *dragon-talk* (236), or *stone-dragon* (309). There is, likewise, the odd synonymous compound, as in *worm-stench* (246).

The dwarves, a passing race, are not accorded many descriptive compounds, apart from: *dwarf-kings* (204), *dwarf-ridden* (235), *dwarf-linked* (242), *dwarf-lad* (268), *dwarf-messengers* (290), or *dwarf-lord* (292). More interesting, not the

---

13 This word is descriptive of both Beorn and the *wargs* (cp. *wolf allies* and *warg-skin* on p. 143), although Tolkien never quite equates the latter with *werewolves.*

14 Echoic of the 'saps' under the enemy in the trench warfare of 1914-18.

least for the curiosity of older races about them, are the various phrasal units concerning hobbits, viz.: *burrahobbit* (46, 48), *hobbit-hole* (78, 166, 219, 220, 313), *hobbit-legs* (252), *hobbit-smell* (235), or a *hobbit's holiday* (314).

There is now appended a chronological list of some miscellaneous items from the text – a list which also indicated the increasing frequency of compounds or noun/adjective phrases: *mapmakers* (43), *manflesh* (45), *troll-make* (63), *moon-letters* (63, 64), *stone-giants* (69), *miserableness* (80), *riddle-competition* (105), *pine-roots* (109), *noble-hearted* (115), *meeting-place* (115), *eagle-lord* (120), *arrow-wound* (120), *easy-tempered* (126), *honey-smelling clover*[15] (128), *rush-bottoms* (137), *beeswax* (137), *smith-craft* (138), *beartracks* (141), *forest-path* (146), *autumn-like* (146), *water-skin* (150), *forest-floor* (151), *woodland king* (165), *forest-day* (166), *spider-webs*[16] (167), *torch-light* (180, 252), *low-spirited* (186), *river-door* (194), *cliff-like* (203), *river-tolls* (206), *raft-men* (208), *steep-walled* (218), *grassy-floored* (218), *rock-wall* (222), *dungeon-hall* (226), *red-golden* (226), *two-handled* (228), *mountain-palace* (228), *high-walled* (230), *snail-covered* (246), *pine-torch* (247), *silver-hafted* [axe] (251), *drinking-horns* (252), *timeless* (254), *south-pointing* (254), *arrow-storm* (259), *market-pool* (259), *town-baiting* (260), *swift-flying* (265), etc.

The Beowulfian proper names or synonym names, if they are not as grand as in the epic, show well the origins and thought[17] involved in their creation. Thus it is that *Were-worms* (29), *Mirkwood* (30, etc.), *Goblin-wars* (63), *Sea-elves* (189), *Front Gate* (252), *Dragon-shooter* (26), etc. reveal their bases for us. The last honorific reminds us of the class of like descriptive names and designations, sometimes boastfully self-bestowed, as in the catalogue *clue-finder*, *web-cutter*, *Ringwinner*, *Luckwearer* and *Barrelrider* (234).

---

15 This is another of the Greek type pastoral phrases, reminiscent of Hesiod, or of Theocritus. See also *bee-pastures* (*ibid.*)
16 This sections contains: *spider-colony* (169); *spider-rope* (171); *spider-string* (172); *spider-poison* (172); and *spider-threads* (175).
17 This is often obscured in the case of Old English for the modern reader, unfamiliar with the elements of compound names like: *Orcneas*; *Wederas*; or *Wedermearc*.

The total corpus of these compounds, hyphenated or phrasal, numbering between 700 and 1000, can be categorized in more subtle ways than those already used. Thus there are also subsets of the following kinds:

> Journeying Terms: *mapmakers* (43), *mountain-paths* (73), *meeting-place* (115), *forest-path* (146), *landing-place* (212), *river-tolls* (206), *hill path* (254), *narrow path*[18] (285), *dreadful pathways* (303);
>
> Tree Vocabulary: *pine roots* (109), *oak-trunk* (129), *pine-woods* (141), *forest-roof* (152), *tree-trunk* (173), *tree-top* (308);
>
> Bird Compounds: *thrush-language* (239), *bird-speech* (268), *carrion birds* (269), *bat-cloud* (292), etc;
>
> Seasonal Compoundings: *autumn-like* (146), *mid-winter* (304), *Yule-tide* (304), *May-time* (308); and
>
> Germanic Battle Descriptions: *battle-ground* (118), *arrow-wound* (120), *sword-blade* (166), *bow-string* (260), *spearmen* (*passim*), *iron-bound* (285), *vanguard* (292).

Clearly these categories could be multiplied considerably.

*   *   *

While concordances would be needed to quantify the relative contextual frequency of compounds in *The Hobbit* as against the more diffuse and long-sentence romance[19] prose style of *The Lord of the Rings*, there is no question that the earlier story achieves its surprisingly powerful effect from the compact and linguistically allusive phrases and units. Tolkien had spoken of the refreshing of language in his 1938 'On Fairy Stories', and in the 1939 written 'Prefatory Remarks' he had observed of the kenning that "the compound offers a partial and often imaginative or fanciful description of a thing" (*MCE* 59). He continued:

> I have called this the poetic class [...] But compounds of this kind are not confined to verse [...] We find 'kennings' in ordinary language, though they have then as a rule become trite in the process of becoming familiar. They may be no longer analysed, even when their form has not actually been obscured by wear. (*ibid.*)

He went on then to deplore the "emptying of significance" (*ibid.* 60) that time tended to effect, but then observed that the older (epic) verse contained kennings and "a host of similar devices" –

---

18 This is very reminiscent of the *ānpaδ* in *Beowulf.*
19 See the later part of Chapter XII of Ryan (1969).

If not fresh[20] in the sense of being struck out then and there where we first meet them, they are fresh and alive in preserving a significance and feeling as full, or nearly as full, as when they were first devised. (*ibid.*)

It is thoughts like these which explain the prose style of *The Hobbit*, a text completed when Tolkien had held the chair of Anglo-Saxon for some twelve years and had regularly been lecturing to large classes on the epic, as well as giving the Old Norse classes for the University of Oxford.[21]

This concern with Old Norse poetry, and scaldic verse in particular,[22] explains the largely Germanic compounding style of *The Hobbit* in many ways. In his lectures of the period 1955-57,[23] Tolkien referred to the Latin Christian mold of many (Cynewulfian) verse kennings, agreeing with the thesis[24] of James Walter Rankin to this effect.[25] The central images of Old English verse – those of God as King, of heaven as a city, the devil as a monstrous beast, or the cross as a sign of victory – were inappropriate in the folk style of the legendary tale, whose tone is secular and concerned with adventure and quest. Thus it is that so much of the poetry's moral and religious compounding was unsuitable for the fairy-story. The scaldic verse, so battle-focussed, or the early heroism of the *Kings' Sagas* in the *Heimskringla*, were much more appropriate places to search for compounds and to afford the thought associations suitable for the heroic nature of the latter parts of Bilbo's story.

In his 1939 essay, at several points, Tolkien is to be found lamenting the non-survival into *The Oxford English Dictionary* of meaningful old compounds like: *boat-guard*, *neck-ring* or *hoard(ed)-wealth* (*MCE* 59), observing sadly that: "Our language has not lost, though it has much limited, the compounding habit"

---

20 I.e. 'original' with the poet whose work we are reading.
21 Due to funding problems within the Faculties of English and of Modern Languages, Tolkien was the effective Professor of Old Norse for nearly 20 years. This work exposed him to even more texts filled with kennings.
22 Lectured regularly by Tolkien in the period 1926-40 (according to lecture lists in the *Oxford University Gazette*).
23 Attended by the present writer. Tolkien was particularly excited by ancient Germanic pagan battle overtones which he discerned behind the text of the Old English *Exodus*.
24 Stated in 'Conclusion' to his analysis, *The Journal of English and Germanic Philology*, vol. X (1910: 83-84).
25 This scholar's work, stressed by Napier in Tolkien's own student days, is published as 'A Study of the Kennings in Anglo-Saxon Poetry' in *The Journal of English and Germanic Philology*, vol. VIII (1909: 357-422) and vol. X (1910: 49-84).

(*ibid.*). Quite clearly he intended to retain – and extend – 'the compounding habit'. His own contributions to the *Dictionary* have been discussed in detail elsewhere,[26] but Tolkien's prose-style had yielded to *The Oxford English Dictionary* by 1976 in vols. I and II), from A-N: *barrow-wight*, *barrow-wightish*, *bee-hunter*, *beggar-bread*, *bone-white*, *dwarf-man*, the ordinary *elf*-compounds given above, *Elven-king*, *elven-tongue*, *elven-wise*, *half-line*, *hard-edged*, *herb-lore*, *herb-master*, *hill-brow*, *hobbit-lore*, *hobbitry-in-arms*, *hobbit-holes*, *house-dweller*, *in-falling*, *long-shanks*, *man-high*, *mill-yard*, *mithril-rings*, *mithril-mail*, *marrowless*, *night-noises*, and *north-away*. The first volume (1972) of *The Supplement to the Oxford English Dictionary* had recorded some 'new' *elf*-compounds from Tolkien, namely *elf-friend* from *The Hobbit* and *Elf-Kingdoms* and *Elf-Speech* from *The Lord of the Rings*; yet no Tolkien-inspired *dragon-* or *goblin*-compounds are listed in the volume covering A-G, in its additional twentieth-century usages and/or compoundings.

One assumes therefore, that the readers for the *Supplement* and the editor R.W. Burchfield, were not particularly concerned to record all Tolkien's compounds by any means. Indeed, the A-N volumes' list given above only gives *elf-friend*, *Elven King* and *hobbit* from *The Hobbit*, although it does contain, from before 1940 writings from Tolkien: *Blimp* (from *blister* + *lump*; 1927); *eyrie* (*Hobbit* 115); and *half,* or *half-line* (1939). Yet the full list given in *Ipotesi* (q.v.) shows a range of compounds that may be described as being concerned with folkloristic concepts – as in *barrow-wight*, *bee-hunter*, etc; the vocabulary of war – *knife-work*, *night-eye*; Romantic Georgian poetic style, as in the diction of de la Mare and Bridges – elf-compounds, *elven-*, *eyrie*, etc.; use of northern terms (many still in dialect in the late nineteenth-century), e.g. *hard-edge*, *hill-brow*, *longshanks*, *maybe*;[27] and coining new nonsense(-like) words, e.g. *halfling*, *hobbit*. Yet it is not just in *The Lord of the Rings* that Tolkien displays the habit of inveterate compounding. While most readers recall *herb-lore* or *mithril-mail*, they seem to have missed, as did *The Oxford English Dictionary* readers, the enormous range of compounds already to be found in *The Hobbit*.

---

26 See Ryan (1978).
27 This adverb, ubiquitous in Tolkien, has nothing to do with American usage, but comes from Northern England. (See Burchfield (1976: 866)).

There is no space here to list the subtle but differing characteristics of the prose of *The Lord of the Rings* – such as Biblical echoes, the (Spenserian) tendency to the ornate or the stately, or the numerous impersonal constructions, and a syntax based on an accumulation of main clauses. *The Hobbit*, by contrast, is more austere, with deliberate (Germanic sourced) archaisms, distinctive compound elements and epithets, and a vocabulary which is closest to Tolkien's contributions to *Songs for the Philologists* (1936). These last-mentioned poems include pieces on elves, trolls, the springing of flowers in a new year, the activity of the carrion crow and the elegy 'Ofer Widne Garsecg' ('Across the broad [and surrounding] Ocean').

Somewhere about the same time Tolkien had made his translation[28] of *Sir Gawain and the Green Knight*, noting approvingly that the author's "style, his vocabulary, were in many respects [...] off the main track of inevitable development, [...] dialectical, [...] includ[ing] in its tradition a number of special [...] words, never used in ordinary talk or prose [...] courtly, wise, and well bred" (*SGGK, Pearl and Sir Orfeo* 2). In 1929, he had referred,[29] with much approval, to a medieval prose style used in the West Midlands as having

> traditions and some acquaintance with books and the pen [...] [a] language at once self-consistent and markedly individual [...] a form of English whose development from an antecedent Old English type was relatively undisturbed. (*Essays and Studies*, XIV: 106-107)

As will be abundantly clear, *The Hobbit* was a product of Tolkien's more antiquarian period,[30] having a physical setting with the emptiness of the Dark Ages, related in a manner close to oral literature, with a remarkable feel for continental Germanic landscape markers, such as hills, fords, hedges and passes. As well it has the topographic almost map-making mode to be found in such Icelandic texts of harsh terrain traversal as *Hrafnkels saga*.

While the stock epithet is to be found too often in the hobbits' poetry – due perhaps to hobbit innocence and simplicity – and *The Lord of the Rings* as open to charges of escapism, privatism and self-indulgence, Tolkien was always most

---

28 However, only published, posthumously, in 1975.
29 In *Essays and Studies*, vol. XIV (1929: 106).
30 From 1945 he was Merton Professor of English Language and commented in his teaching and research on the (romance) texts of the fourteenth-century Middle English.

successful with his evocation of barbaric times, gaunt landscapes and combats such as the Battle of the Five Armies. When he was re-creating and enfleshing Dark Age tales,[31] rounding out gaps in its (surviving) folklore, he was the most confident, consistent and heroic in both tone and style. As Shippey (1982: 54) would observe more recently, Tolkien was responding to the "charm of the archaic world of the North," and so he "wanted to tell a story about it simply, one feels, because there were hardly any complete ones left." Such was his aim, and inventive compounding of the Germanic sort was the manner best calculated to achieve this objective. Further, an analysis of the type attempted in this article makes it very clear that Tolkien's story came from pivotal words, enigmatic names, descriptions and an urge to fill complex omissions in the inherited texts. Quite simply, words were the inspiration, words were the vehicle, and words, compounded for preference, gave the qualities which C.S. Lewis was so quick to identify in the later parts of a seeming tale for children. The editors of *The Oxford English Dictionary* (K, p. 673) under 'kenning' 5 and 6, had given two particular senses of the word:

> 5b. A recognizable portion; just enough to be perceived. [Scandinavian and northern dialect.]
>
> 6. One of the periphrastic expressions used instead of the simple name of the thing, characteristic of Old Teutonic, and especially Old Norse, poetry.

They then gave an English definition from 1889: "A characteristic ornament of Old English, as well as early Teutonic poetry, are the kennings." We might add that they are also the key stylistic device of Tolkien's most heroic prose.

Afterword

While there is not the space now to elaborate on this, *The Hobbit* is a prime example of Tolkien's subtlety in creating in his readers a notion of the (valorous) compounding that was part of the English inheritance. Like the use of asyndetic parataxis in heroic verse, his regular use of compound nouns and adjectives takes the reader back to more spacious and heroic times, to champions and foes, and to magnificient bravery and adventure.

---

31 As he was with the early penned accounts of raids and battles in *The Silmarillion*.

As this essay has made clear, the text of *The Hobbit* is more than heroic and its style replicates not only the courage of late Victorian adventure stories but the courage of Old English heroic verse. It is so much more heroic than the diffuse syntax to be found in the romantic style of *The Lord of the Rings*.

Barrow-wights, Hog-boys and the evocation of *The Battle of the Goths and Huns* and of St. Guthlac

> The Waking of Angantyr [...] expresses with extraordinary force the fear and mystery of the grim dead lying lifeless but sometimes wakeful in their burial-mounds [...] 'set between worlds' in the words [...] with which [...] the poem ends. (Christopher Tolkien (1960: xi-xii) in the introduction to his *The Saga of King Heiðrek the Wise*).

The verse in question, no. 43, spoken by Hervör, follows on the reference by Angantyr to the doom-bringing sword in the barrow, and it is translated thus by Christopher Tolkien:

May you all lie unharmed
in the howe resting –
to hasten hence
my heart urges;
I seemed to myself
to be set between worlds,
when all about me
burnt the cairn-fires.[1]

It is the contention of this present note that the eighth chapter, 'Fog on the Barrow-Downs', in the first volume of J.R.R. Tolkien's land-traversing epic about Middle-earth, draws its associations and narrative power from several areas of the (Germanic) folk-memory, viz.:

This essay first appeared in slightly shorter form in *Angerthas* 27 (May 1990: 23-27) and is here reprinted with the kind permission of its editors.

1 In his edition and translation of the Old Norse text, *The Saga of King Heiðrek the Wise* (1960). J.R.R. Tolkien's teaching of Old Norse verse and Christopher Tolkien's edition of this saga were, alike, much informed by *Anglo-Saxon and Norse Poems*, edited and translated by N. Kershaw (Cambridge 1922). *The Battle of the Goths and Huns* is Poem XIII (142ff). Compare, in *The Fellowship of the Ring* (1954: 154), Merry's recollection of his dream while in a bewitched sleep in the barrow, when "The Men of Carn Dûm came on us." Readers are also referred to the classic Victorian account of such haunted settings in *Ruins of the Saga Age* by Thorsteinn Erlingsson (1899), especially in its Research Question I, 'Mounds' (64-70), and, most notably to the reference to "the large stones that were on top of the body" (68).

1) the barrow-marked landscape of southern England, or Orkney;

2) the folklore associated with burial mounds throughout North Western Europe;

3) ancient Germanic concepts of the undead of (Bronze[2] Age) barrows (the lore of which is best preserved in the Norse concepts of the *draugr* and the *haugbúi*);

4) a very early Dark Age battle such as those of Gothic history, for example that on the Catalaunian Plains,[3] 451 A.D.; and

5) the cleansing from demons of his solitary hermitage by St. Guthlac, the eight century marshland solitary.

Since most readers might well be content with the first cluster of responses, it will be necessary to outline the clues given by J.R.R. Tolkien to the various layers of association familiar to him and, arguably, sufficiently suggested for the perceptive reader in the chapter in question.

1) In the actual context, Tolkien uses the place-name 'Barrow-downs' (*FotR* 147, 149), the term 'a great barrow' (*ibid.* 151), and the generic term 'Barrow-wight'[4] (*ibid.* 151, 152), while he has Tom Bombadil "standing large as life on the barrow-top[5] above them" (*ibid.* 154), able from there to release the victims from the spell holding them inside the 'chamber'. All these terms must remind us of the traditional (archaic) compounding of *barrow-* with *-hill*; *-mouth*; *-pence*, etc.,[6] even as they do also of the hundred or so earthen long barrows of Wiltshire,[7] (some of which have yielded rich burial goods of gold and bronze); the most remarkable Stone Age burial-place in Scotland – *Maeshowe*;[8] or the celebrated long barrow on the Berkshire Downs, one visited by Tolkien and his friends on weekend walking excursions out from Oxford, and for so long

---

2 The treasure items brought out by Bombadil from the ancient barrow (*FotR* 154) are said to include 'bronze' and 'beads'.
3 In it the Romans and the Visigoths defeated Attila and the Huns, with whom the Ostrogoths were allied. See further on in this present article.
4 As Elrond will observe later: "The Barrow-wights we know by many names"(*ibid.* 178).
5 In various Scandinavian sources, e.g. *The Saga of Harald Fine-hair*, ch. 8, a king actually sits on the top of a barrow making of it a temporary 'high seat'. Compare the ominous standing on top of his mound by the Green Knight in *Sir Gawain and the Green Knight*, l. 2217.
6 See Wright (1898: vol. I, 174).
7 See, especially, L.V. Grinsell, *The Ancient Burial-Mounds of England* (1936a), and his *The Archaeology of Wessex* (1958).Grinsell had also written an essay entitled 'Analysis and List of the Berkshire Barrows' in *The Berkshire Archaeological Journal* (1936b), an essay which used closely O.G.S. Crawford's *The Long Barrows of the Cotswolds* (1925) and *Archaeology of Berkshire* (1931) by H.J.E. Peake.
8 Excavated in 1861, and generally accepted as dating from the first half of the second millenium B.C.

known as *Wayland's Smithy*. It is probably valid to assume that we are dealing with such a 'long barrow' on the fictional Barrow Downs.

2) The complex folk-beliefs associated with barrows and other places of inhumation, both in England and Europe-wide, include, perforce, some degree of meshing with similarly sited:

legends of giants;

associations with fairy folk;

identification with: the Devil and/or Grim (i. e. Othin);

or with historical personages (e. g. ancient barrows linked with soldiers killed in 1643 in the Battle of Newbury, a site often visited by Oxford University members keen to explore this relatively adjacent and well-preserved site), or the Cavalier skirmishes on the north side of Otmoor, north-east of Oxford);

historical (i.e. Civil War) and mythical battles;

hidden treasure and its protection;[9]

the deemed sanctity of the site;

calendar customs;

ghosts and/or often related mysterious music;

movements of stones at night whether megaliths or ruins of barrows, these apparently endeavouring to fight, bathe or to drink;[10]

the curative properties of such places, etc.

Much of this fragmentary material is relatively 'late' and trivialized or distorted, whereas the Tolkien sequence is both grim and echoic of very terrible ancient battlers (*v. infra*).

3) The opening quotation related to an archaic portion of an Icelandic saga, of which the oldest manuscripts date from the fourteenth century. This fragmentary poem refers back to a possible memory of a time when the Germanic peoples were in south-east Europe, perhaps more than a millenium before.

---

9 Compare the two Old English kennings for dragon: *beorges hyrde* 'mound guardian', and *beorges weard* 'mound protector'.

10 These motifs have been reactivated effectively by such more contemporary writers as Mollie Hunter, Penelope Lively, and, specifically for Orkney, by George Mackay Brown. Lively's stories particularly relate to places in easy reach of Oxford, such as the Rollright Stones to its north.

Old Norse Details: Atmosphere and Scholarship Now Imposed on the 'English' Landscape

Since detailed barrow legends of the pre-Christian sort were not available in any form of English, Tolkien had turned to the cited reference works and various older Norse sagas, composed largely in the spirit of historical novels, where many texts include pre-Christian beliefs about the *draugr* or 'animated corpse of the dead man' (living on in the barrow in which he has been enclosed), or the *haugbúi* or 'barrow dweller' (Chadwick 1946a and 1946b).[11] As N. Chadwick made clear in a most helpful survey article (1946a: 50-51), the oldest (Norwegian) stories allowed relatively little movement away from their burial place, the *haugar* (sing. *haugr*), 'barrows' themselves, each of which contained "a stone-built burial chamber roofed over with wood and covered with a great mound of earth." The ghost, known as a *haugbúi* (pl. *búar*) or a *draugr* (pl. *draugar*) is, in fact, "the animated corpse of the dead man living on in the barrow in which he has been enclosed" (*ibid.* 51). Nora Chadwick (née Kershaw) in Cambridge, much like Craigie and Tolkien, later, in Oxford would turn for reference and verification to the great teaching work, Paul B. Du Chaillu's *The Viking Age: The Early History, Manners, and Customs of the Ancestors of the English-Speaking Nations in 2 volumes*, published in 1889. In the first of these volumes, an obvious focus would have been Chapter XVIII, 'Various Forms of Graves', and Chapter XIX, 'Burials'.

While no reason is given in the Tolkien text for the barrow-wight's taking of the two hobbits, it may well have been Tolkien's intention to remind us of the need for the barrow-creature – or his victim – to have a companion or companions in the barrow, a motif that is stressed in many of the oldest stories.

The Patterns of Behaviour of the *draugr*

The emergence of the *draugr* from the barrow is not uncommon, despite its being feared by the living. Chadwick refers very helpfully to such an appearance:[12]

---

11 The survival of the word and conception into modern times in Orkney and Shetland is attested by quotation (*Scottish National Dictionary* 1960, vol. V, 172-73). *Hogboon* is a Scots alternative form.

12 Almost all of this pertains to the detail given or adumbrated in the Tolkien chapter.

> This occurs most frequently in the evening; but it sometimes happens that a mist or temporary darkness heralds their approach [...] They are sometimes seen by the living in what appears to be a kind of dream [...] (1946a: 54)

The attitude of the *draugr* to the (threatening) visitor varies – from making a gift[13] to the living in some form of placation, to being the death of many who have tried to come near his barrow. There is also a common motif whereby a living man enters the barrow and cuts off the draugr's head – but only the hand[14] is severed in *The Fellowship of the Ring* (153).

There were even cases, in ancient story, of the *draugr* emerging from his barrow and giving up his treasure to a member of his own family. In the modern text this does not happen, but Bombadil exorcises the "old Wight" (*ibid*. 155), has the present victims "crowned and betted with pale gold, and jingling with trinkets" [...] to then "cast off these cold rags" (*ibid*. 155). The benign nature-spirit brings out all the treasure and spreads it out in the sun (*ibid*. 154), leaving most to lie there

> 'free to all finders, birds, beasts, Elves or Men, and all kindly creatures';[15] for so the spell of the mound should be broken and scattered and no Wight ever come back to it. (*ibid*. 156)

For those who survived a night in the company of the howe dead, there usually followed some form of re-birth, with enhanced (even super-human) strength as a warrior and consequent success in wielding the ancient and magically empowered weapons taken from the barrow. Other interesting related motifs are the chanting of a poem (as in *Hálfs Saga* or in *Ragnars Saga Lothbrókar*) by a huge *tré-mathr* (lit. 'wooden man'), not necessarily associated with the barrow – "he is merely discovered in a wood" (Chadwick 1946a: 60) – and the obtaining of the gifts of poetry and second sight as a result of visiting a barrow.[16] Both these consequences, it may be held, are destined to befall Frodo

---

13 Compare the sword lain across the hobbits.
14 One wonders whether Tolkien had known of the episode of the finger from the skeleton taken from the Manton (Wilts.) round barrow – although this was not connected with a ghost (Grinsell 1976: 36).
15 This is similar to the habit of *mathom*-giving in the Shire. That use of the Old English word for 'treasure with a curse on it' for vaguely useful items of no great intrinsic worth is an example of semantic amelioration or, in this case, of the exorcism of the malign senses of the word. See also 'Germanic Mythology Applied – the Extension of the Literary Folk Memory' by the present author in this present volume (199-213).
16 This is also true of Tom Bombadil.

in the course of his further trials in his attempt to take the One Ring back to its source and so destroy it.

And the Lore Associated with Ancient Battles

A terrible and significant battle of long ago is not usually associated with a barrow in the Icelandic texts which are more concerned with the threat posed by the revenant. Yet the treasures or 'grave-goods' – by their very value and hence antiquity – were inherently likely to have associations from some far-distant past. In his introduction to the edition[17] of *Hervarar Saga ok Heiðreks*, Christopher Tolkien refers to the poems included in it, stressing in particular that one, *The Battle of the Goths and the Huns*, contains elements at least that come down from a very remote antiquity (xi), and assessing the likelihood of the references echoing some actual event:

> The likeliest view is that the oldest 'layer' of the material of the poem goes back to ancient wars of the Gothic kingdoms on the northern shores of the Black Sea in the late fourth and early fifth centuries. (xiii)

Now while the battle experienced by Merry (154) is entirely fictional, it does provide an available analogue to the types of battles still echoing faintly as in the ancient Old English catalogue poem, *Widsith*.[18]

In 1922 the young Nora Chadwick, under her maiden name of Kershaw, had edited and translated the ancient Norse poem,[19] stressing:

> "the national features of the invasion which it describes" (142);
>
> the traditional "catalogue of treasures and possessions" (143); and that
>
> the *Myrkviðr*[20] of the poem probably was on the Vistula (144).

Her scholarship, then, like that of Christopher Tolkien much later, stresses the barbaric ruthlessness of the victorious (the Huns?), and the cruelty and the poetry of warfare of some 1500 years earlier.

---

17 Published by the Viking Society for Northern Research in 1956.

18 Chr. Tolkien (1956: xiii) discusses ll. 116ff.

19 In a volume entitled *Anglo-Saxon and Norse Poems*. It would have been used from its publication by Tolkien, not least because of its inclusion of the Old English elegies.

20 'Mirkwoods' presumably existed in northern and south-eastern Europe – cp. Chadwick (1946b: 145): "the name [...] may well be a general term for any part of the forest region of central Europe or what we may perhaps call the traditional forest land of heroic poetry."

And So to Tolkien Again

While J.R.R. Tolkien will reserve his imaginative construct of ancient battles for other contexts, it is clear that he chose to relate an invasion slaughter to the memories of the men of the past, or to the lingering and malevolent aura and potency of the treasures within the barrow.

Although these further layers of meaning to the Barrow Downs episode may seem elusive and even sub-textual, there is no doubt at all that the strange *satura lanx* or mix of ancient materials was both well-known and closely studied in the Tolkien family.[21] In the introduction to his translation of *The Saga of King Heiðrek the Wise* (1960), Christopher Tolkien refers to

> the opening of Thrain's[22] burial mound (vii);
> the fear of the grim dead lying in their mounds;[23]
> the third century migration of the Goths back from the Baltic to the Black Sea (xxiv);

and, later, he translates (ch. 3, strophe 26) (Hervör's words) thus:

> it becomes not ghosts
> costly arms to bear. (15)

Then Angantýr replies (strophe 37):

> The blade from the barrow
> I will bring, rather;
> young maiden,
> I may not refuse you. (18)

A Further Layer of Dark Age Association in this Barrow-cleansing Episode

The benign action of Tom Bombadil in cleansing the barrow cannot but remind the reflective reader of an eloquent analogue from Old English poetry, the text known as *Guthlac A*, one taught for many years by Tolkien. This sensitive verse

---

21 See in particular Chr. Tolkien's survey article on the possible historical basis of the poem, *Saga-Book of the Viking Society* XIV (1955-6: 141ff).
22 Compare the behaviour of the dwarves in *The Hobbit*.
23 See the quotation at the head of this article.

piece is concerned with the life of St. Guthlac, who, when he has withdrawn from the world and established a hermitage in the wilds of the fen, experiences many assaults from a host of demons who had formerly haunted those lonely borderlands. Their tumult distresses him as does their threat of death by fire, but he defies them to do their worst against his body since his soul is immortal. However, St. Bartholomew rescues him, and bears him back unharmed to his hermitage where he is hailed by both birds and beasts. Further, we are told that he will win eternal life in heaven by his words and works on earth.[24]

A Last Speculation on Tolkien's Purposes Here

In his concluding remarks on the Tolkien presentation of the wight, T.A. Shippey in his *The Road to Middle-earth* (1982) has referred to the "white robes, wriggling hand, sword across neck" (84) as "glimpses of an alien world" offering "the special thrill of fantasy beyond study" (*ibid.*). While that context of barrow lore may be alien to many readers, it is, of course, firmly based in the surviving documents and folk memories of the Germanic Dark Ages. Indeed, it is not too much to state that, armed with relevant details from appropriate analogues, the text of almost every such 'alien' incident of *The Lord of the Rings* can and does re-animate ideas and legends long familiar but temporarily forgotten by modern man, sundered from the timeless landscape – and the earlier reflective and haunting literature – which enshrined them.

Indeed this passage on the barrow-downs and its standard analogous scholarship – that on the Old English poem, *Guthlac A* – act in unison to imply that, aided now by Bombadil, Frodo is and will be a potential Christ figure, not least for all the nuances of the beloved story of St. Guthlac, his renunciation of the world and his conquest of all the threats of violence from the demons lurking around him.

---

24 Although it is subsequent to *The Lord of the Rings*, it is appropriate to mention the highly sensitive scholarship of Laurence K. Shoole on its analogue to the barrow-cleansing 'The Burial Mound in *Guthlac A*' in *Modern Philology* 58 (1960: 1-10); and his supplementary note, 'The Prologue of the Old English *Guthlac A*' in *Mediaeval Studies* 23 (1961: 294-304).

Dynamic Metahistory and the Model of Christopher Dawson

While most readers and critics of the major creative work by J.R.R. Tolkien, *The Lord of the Rings* (1954-55), are familiar with its language, narrative quality as a 'fairy story'[1] and with its many analogues in Old English and Old Norse literature, few consider particularly its style as a philosophical history modelled on and interpretative of the passage of events in Western Europe over perhaps 2,000 years or more. Although it is not formally on this, one may quote the following passage from Tolkien:

> variations [of life] rouse in me visions of kinship and descent through great ages, and also thoughts of the mystery of pattern/design as a thing [...] recognizable. (*Letters* 402)

There are many other *obiter dicta* of his to be found, concerned with Divine Purpose and the movement of history.

In this endeavour to document Tolkien's notions of grand pattern, researchers have some explicit clues in the various references in 'On Fairy-Stories' to a famous work by Christopher Dawson (1889-1970), namely *Progress and Religion* (1929), the subtitle of which was 'An historical enquiry into the causes and development of the idea of progress and its relationship to religion'. The book owed its form to a number of controversial essays by Dawson, over the postwar years, such as his:

1) 'Cycles of Civilizations', *The Sociological Review* XIV (1922: 51-68);

2) 'Progress and Decay in Ancient and Modern Civilizations', *The Sociological Review* XVI (1924: 1-11);

3) 'Religion and the Life of Civilization', *The Quarterly Review* CCXLIV (1925: 98-115); or

---

This essay first appeared in slightly shorter form in *Minas Tirith Evening Star* 18.3 (1989: 10-14) and I am grateful to the editors for the kind permission to reprint.

1 Tolkien's own special critical term as in the address, 'On Fairy-Stories' originally given in 1938 and published in 1947 and somewhat revised for the publication *Tree and Leaf* (1964). The references in this essay are to the 2001 edition of *Tree and Leaf*.

4) 'Christianity and the Idea of Progress', *The Dublin Review* CLXXX
(1927: 19-39).

(Henry) Christopher Dawson (b. October 12, 1889), who went to Trinity
College, Oxford in 1908,[2] was the son of an old-fashioned High Anglican
family from the Yorkshire gentry, a lover of the Church of England's religion-
culture with its easy access to the spiritual and intellectual treasures of an earlier
past, and a devotee of Catholic saints and mystics as mediated through the
Anglo-Catholic tradition.[3] All these forces urged him ever more strongly to
the Catholic Church, into which he was received in Oxford in January, 1914.
Reflecting on this step some twelve years later, he wrote:

> It was by the study of St. Paul and St. John that I first came to understand
> the fundamental unity of Catholic theology and the Catholic life. I realized
> that the Incarnation, the sacraments, the external order of the Church and the
> internal work of sanctifying grace were all parts of one organic unity, a living
> tree[4] whose roots are in the Divine nature and whose fruit is the perfection of
> the saints [...]. (*The Catholic Times*, May 21, 1926)

Dawson was engaged in historical research in Oxford before the First World
War, this followed by research for various Whitehall Government Departments
from 1916, and later spent much of his life as a free-lance scholar, although
he was also Lecturer in the History of Culture at University College, Exeter
(1925-33), and Lecturer in the Philosophy of Religion at Liverpool University
in 1934. He became in the 1930s an influential member of the group of writers
who formed around the new Catholic publishing house of Sheed and Ward. For
them he edited and contributed to a series of books entitled *Essays in Order*.

He was also much admired by such clerics as Cardinal Arthur Hinsley and
Bishop G.K. Bell of Chichester, and so became a vice-president in the Sword
of the Spirit, a proto-ecumenical movement which was, however, too ecumeni-
cal for its time. He became also the editor of *The Dublin Review* (1940-44),
a fellow of the British Academy in 1943, Gifford Lecturer (Edinburgh) 1947

---

2 Thus 'going down', with only second-class honours in modern history the term before Tolkien's arrival in
   Michaelmas Term (1911). See *University of Oxford Historical Register [...] for the Years 1900-1920*
   (1921: 227).
3 See the account of his love for Little Gidding in Knowles (1973: 441).
4 Here, (as elsewhere in Dawson), on the notation of the sacraments and the tree, the mode of expression
   is very similar to Tolkien's discussing the 'tree of tales' and the role of the sacraments (i.e. *lembas*) in
   the writings about Middle-earth.

and 1948, and Professor of Roman Catholic Studies at Harvard University, 1958-62. After ill-health compelled his retirement, he returned to England to Budleigh Salterton in Devon,[5] where he died on May 25, 1970.

*   *   *

If we may anticipate and summarize Dawson's position, it is possible to see him as a peculiarly English – and Anglo-Catholic[6] – 'meta-historian' or philosopher of history, concerned, even more than Toynbee, with both metaphysics and theology. Thus the Christian philosophers, Dufourcq, Pourrat, Rousselot are some of the continental writers cited in his earliest books. His enormous output of books and essays[7] was always concerned with the nature and meaning of history, and with the cause and significance of historical change especially in relation to the religious life of the people. For he held that Christianity could and does change the world, "so long as it is a living mind, not enervated by custom or ossified by prejudice" (1931: 110).

He would stress[8] that all historiography is pervaded by metaphysical influences, a stance that may be held to dominate the outlook and accomplishment of the great historians of the eighteenth and nineteenth centuries from C. Montesquieu and Edward Gibbon,[9] to G.W.F. Hegel and Lord Acton.[10] Yet while some of the great historiographies tended towards philosophical explanations for change, Dawson was concerned with a middle ground, implicitly theological rather than formally so, in the manner of J. Bossuet.

---

5 Indifferent health had compelled him to live much of his life from 1918 in this benign climatic region.

6 His *The Spirit of the Oxford Movement* (1933) was concerned to stress the strong spirit of prophetic witness. The best biographic account of him is C. Scott, *A Historian and His World: a life of Christopher Dawson, 1889-1970* (1984). Dom David Knowles of Cambridge would produce a fine tribute to him in the *Proceedings of the British Academy* 57 (1973: 439-52).

7 From 1920 to 1967 – see Claude Locas' bibliography published soon after his death in the *Harvard Theological Review*.

8 In his 'The Problem of Metahistory' in Mulloy (1957a: 287-93).

9 This giant was the subject of his address in 1934 to the British Academy (issued both in the *Proceedings* for that year, and as a separate publication). It was later expanded as his 'Preface' to Gibbon's *Decline and Fall of the Roman Empire* in Everyman Series, variously issued.

10 Compare his often quoted comment, on "Acton's sublime vision of a universal history which is something different from the combined history of all countries and which enlightens the mind and illuminates the soul" (1957b: 394).

Dawson's final perception of explication of the pattern of Western European Christian culture[11] may be schematized thus:

1) Primitive Christianity[12] (the first to fourth centuries, with expansion of belief beneath the surface of existing Graeco-Roman civilizations);

2) Patristic Christianity (fourth to sixth centuries);

3) The formation of Western Christendom (the sixth to eleventh centuries, and including the conversion of Northern Europe);

4) Medieval Christendom (eleventh to fifteenth centuries and including the full flowering of Christian culture);

5) Divided Christendom (with civil wars and the expansion of Christian Europe beyond Europe to the New World); and

6) Secularized Christendom (from the eighteenth century to the present, a period during which the Christian framework of society was swept away by the various revolutionary movements).[13]

For, despite his knowledge of and sympathy for many world religions, the great thrust of all his writings was towards the place of Christianity in the world, and the relationship between Christianity and Europe, as a mode of explanation of the nature and destiny of man and so 'The Spritual Tragedy of Modern Man'.[14]

                                    *   *   *

To return to Tolkien and his published perceptions of Christopher Dawson. The first of these occurs in 'On Fairy-Stories' (*TL* 26) when *Progress and Religion: An Historical Enquiry* (1929) is cited for his, Tolkien's belief, following Andrew Lang,

that mythology and religion (in the strict sense of that word) are two distinct things that have become inextricably entangled,[15] though mythology is in itself almost devoid of religious significance.

These sentiments paraphrase the middle portion (1929: 86-87) of Dawson's Chapter IV, 'The Comparative Study of Religions and the Spiritual Element in Culture', a larger section concerned to stress that the "inner aspect of a

---

11 In this, for convenience, reference may be made to Hittinger (1984: 1-56).

12 See, for example his *Mediaeval Christianity* (1935b) and *The Crisis of Western Education* (1961).

13 See, particularly, his posthumously issued *The Gods of Revolution* (1972).

14 The title of his paper in *Blackfriars* XXV (1945: 361-65). It was a review of Arthur Koestler's *The Yogi and the Commissar*. It appears in adapted form in Oliver and Scott (1975: 293-300).

15 This is referred to more briefly by the present writer in Essay 15, 'Folktale, Fairy Tale, and the Creation of a Story' (pp. 153-77).

culture [...] constitutes its most distinctive features" (1929: 75); and "primitive man [...] sees the external as a living world of mysterious forces greater than his own" (1929: 79).

Tolkien then, however, goes on to concede Dawson's position –

> Yet these things have in fact become entangled – or maybe they were sundered long ago and have since groped back towards re-fusion. (*TL* 26)

He then refers to the 'mystical' face of the fairy-story – which is described as 'cosmological' by Dawson (1929: 86), and then as

> a mysterious and intangible something of which they are only the embodiment [...] (1929: 90)

These last views of Dawson are, in fact, echoed by Tolkien in his further observations:

> History often resembles 'Myth' because they are both ultimately of the same stuff; [...] mythical stories [...] open a door on Other Time [...] outside our own time, outside Time itself, maybe. (*TL* 32)

> [...] leaves [...] from the countless foliage of the Tree of Tales [...] This recovery fairy-stories help us to make [...] I do not say 'seeing things as they are' and involve myself with the philosophers,[16] though I might venture to say 'seeing things as we are (or were) meant to see them' – as things apart from ourselves. (*ibid.* 56-58)

Thus it is clear that Tolkien is in considerable sympathy with Dawson's stress here that "the inner aspect of a culture is most important and distinctive" (1929: 11); "every culture possesses a distinctive view of life – its soul and formative principle" (*ibid.*); "religion is [...] the womb of civilization" (*ibid.*) and "a crude speculation [...] often contaminates and weakens religion" (*ibid.*). For Tolkien, like Dawson, explained religion to be the soul of a culture and indicated the fact that the British between the wars were singularly unaware of their own convictions, of their deep attachment to progress and to a liberalism which had arisen from within a Christian culture and was unlikely to survive it.

*   *   *

---

16 This must remind us of Tolkien's own formal studies, 1911-13, of the works of various classical philosophers.

The second section of Tolkien's essay which is closely based on Dawson's seminal book is that in which the young Oxford professor discusses his progressive colleague (*TL* 62) who welcomed Morris Motors in Cowley ("the proximity of mass-production robot[17] factories") and the fact that Oxford was becoming a "desert of un-reason" (*ibid.*), or as the other might put it, more in contact with 'real life'. This brought forth his famous cry of exasperation:

> How real, how startlingly alive is a factory chimney[18] compared with an elm-tree; poor obsolete thing, insubstantial dream of an escapist! (*ibid.* 63)

From this self-flagellation for an inability to respond to 'serious' literature, he notes how 'progressive' factories have

> machine-guns and bombs [...] (as) their most natural and inevitable, dare we say 'inexorable' products. (*ibid.* 64)

This is followed by a direct quotation from the end of Dawson's chapter:

> The rawness and ugliness of modern European life [...] is the sign of biological inferiority, of an insufficient or false relation to environment. (*ibid.*)

Tolkien's footnote[19] to the last then quotes some eleven lines from Dawson as to "the full Victorian panoply of top hat and frock coat" being "a kind of grim Assyrian beauty, fit emblem of the ruthless and great age that created it" (*ibid.*)!

In his close following of Dawson's text, Tolkien was paying his own tribute to what was perhaps the older man's most brilliant work of synthesis in which he examined the relationship between religion and social progress in different religion-cultures. Already it contained – as did Tolkien's essay – a clear perception of the problems of totalitarianism both in politics and in culture, a particular theme for his work over the next few years.[20] Dean Inge praised *Progress and Religion* from the pulpit and in pamphlets; and T.S. Eliot was himself inspired

---

17 The robots are, of course, the state to which regional craftsmen were reduced by their duties on the machine – and assembly-lines.
18 Compare: "towards Bag End they saw a tall chimney of brick in the distance. It was pouring out black smoke into the evening air." (*RotK* 283)
19 Actually p. 68, not 58-59, as stated in *Tree and Leaf* (*TL* 64).
20 As in his 'Communism, Capitalism and the Catholic Tradition', *Ave Maria* XXXIX (1934: 695), or in 'Modern Dictatorship', *The Tablet* CLXV (1935a: 509). Tolkien's treatment was, of course, symbolic, and not sociological and explicitly Christian as Dawson's was.

by Dawson in writing his *The Idea of a Christian Society* and later, his *Notes Towards the Definition of Culture*. Yet, while Inge was profoundly pessimistic, neither Dawson nor Tolkien were so troubled, being both concerned to stress – one literally, the other in his fictive world – the real treasures of Christian culture and the way to recovery of its core, what Dawson would call in 1951, while Tolkien was yet a-finishing his epic:

> a universal metahistorical vision [...] partaking more of the nature of religious contemplation [...] which lies very close to the sources of [former] creative power. (1957: 293)

*   *   *

The last portion of this exploratory paper must give brief acknowledgment to the other aspects of Dawson's work which shed light on Tolkien's grand vision –

1) a belief, like European Thomists, in intuition as a source of religious knowledge;

2) similarity to Frederich von Hügel's view of the approach to God through intuition;

3) a society's survival depends on its possession or loss of religious conceptions of reality;

4) the older elements in a culture assist man to a deeper insight into his relations with spiritual reality;

5) the secularization which the ideologies have made of religious motives is eventually self-destructive,[21] as well as undermining all genuine creativity; and

6) the solution of social ills lies not with man and his programmes but with the Holy Spirit.

As Christopher Dawson would later say so well, in the Second Series of Gifford Lectures –

> An ideology [...] is the work of man [...] But faith looks beyond the world of man and his works; it introduces man to a higher and more universal range of reality than [...] the State and economic order [...] thereby it introduces into human life an element of spiritual freedom which may have a creative and transforming influence on [...] man's personal experience. (1950: 7)

---

21 This is the sad tale of Saruman, both at Orthanc and in the Shire. It was also true of Boromir and of his father, Denethor.

The Mental and Spiritual Links Between Tolkien and Dawson

Although this matter is to some extent inference, – despite the many echoes of the views of both in *Time and Tide* in the middle third of the twentieth century – it has come to a much greater critical attention in the twenty-first century, notably in the work of Bradley J. Birzer, as in his *J.R.R. Tolkien's Sanctifying Myth: Understanding Middle-earth* (2003), where he explains the surprisingly specific – and Dawson-like religious symbolism that permeates Tolkien's Middle-earth. Thus he places its creator within the Christian humanist tradition, stating this neatly in his 'Introduction' –

> Tolkien fits in with a group of twentieth century scholars and artists which we might label collectively as 'The Christian humanists' [whose ranks include] such poets as T.S. Eliot, C.S. Lewis, Christopher Dawson, Eric Voegelin, Russel Kirk [...]

and adding

> Tolkien should be counted as one of their foremost thinkers and spokesmen. (2003: xxv)

In the same place Birzer has carefully paralleled the two men's thinking about truth, reason, science, art and myth and their hope for a renewal of Christendom and an end to "the ideologically inspired terror of the twentieth century."

For, while not an Inkling himself, Christopher Dawson was both known to Ronald Tolkien – not least from Dawson's various periods living near Oxford, on Boar's Hill, and long association with the Oxford Catholic community – and had sought to say similar spiritual and moral things from the viewpoint of a historian of European and Catholic culture and from his espousal of the significance of "the Rise of the Mediaeval Unity of Christianity," a society of free peoples "under the presidence of the Roman Pope and Emperor." Thus he was long the interpreter to England and, from 1958, to America, of a Catholic historical philosophy as well as of a Catholic social and political theory. He was and is at his best when writing on the social teaching of the Christian Church, writing with both a prophetic and practical purpose, much as that which inspired the Sword of the Spirit[22] movement during the Second World War.

It is appropriate to quote what the present writer had to say of Dawson in 1969 of the historian's moral standards and principles:

> He discovers in the interaction of Christianity and Western civilization throughout the ages a definite cycle of historic action: and age of intense spiritual activity in response to a new spiritual situation, a period of achievement in which new forms of life, art and thought are created, and a time of retreat when the Church is attacked from within or without. (Ryan 1969: 54)

Yet it was also stressed there that:

> His style of writing is vital and tingling, and there is a fine and generous liberalism in all [his work] and a power to rouse his readers out of comfortable optimism and to send them into action with a note of unquenchable hope. (*ibid.*)

Tolkien as the Integrator of Culture, Religion and Literature in the Honours School of English – and so in like Oxford Research Work – as well as in his Literary Creations

It is, surely, this quest by Christopher Dawson for the rediscovery of religious Western man which is closest to the thought and actions[23] of J.R.R. Tolkien when in 1931, after two years of campaigning, he successfully reformed the Oxford English undergraduate courses, and so their perceptions of inherited culture.

It is also a model, of a different sort, which, eschewing documented and narrow 'national' history, sought to define man's search for the essence of his being, much akin to the Christ-like quest of Frodo and his remarkable and selfless substitution for all the sinners and sufferers in his world at the end of the Third Age. Dogmatic secularism and its opposition to a belief in the transcendent were

---

22 He was Vice-President of this English organization concerned – according to its manifesto – "to promote common action between Catholics and Christians of other allegiances in dealing with the spiritual issues of war time."

23 It is relevant to instance here his success with the support of C.S. Lewis, in reforming the Oxford Honours School of English to both put early (Christian) culture into every syllabus, as well as to establish the famed Course I which ran for more than a quarter of a century and which was entirely a Mediaeval Greats, embracing several languages and literatures and coming no later than Langland. See also Carpenter (1977: 145).

the ultimate enemies for both Dawson and Tolkien. Each presented a view of history moving on steadily to its God-appointed goal. The attitude and position of the faithful Christian has always been difficult, often precarious, as he commits himself with courage and trust to the sublimely inscrutable purpose of Providence,[24] the centre of all man's faith, hope and love.

While many of their Catholic contemporaries, both theologians and philosophers, were concerned with the relationship of the Christian to the world, these two thinkers and writers of metahistory were summoned to rediscover and scrutinize the inherited past, the immutable idea of the sacred, and the present apocalyptic epoch of man's separation from man and of man's separation from God. Their concerns were ever with the dynamic,[25] unifying aspects of life and the possibility for all modern men of return to the source of creation, the practice of love, from which they have become estranged. Each saw God as the chief exemplification of metaphysical principles and present misery to be the illustration of the awful fallacy of deeming Him to be irrelevant in history. Both had the vision to perceive and the task to present the spirit of sacrifice and the responsibility of every individual, allied with a fine Boethian philosophy of human freedom which does not exclude God.

> This image of *Homo Cum Deo* implies the highest conceivable freedom [...] to step into the very fabric of the universe, a new formula for man's collaboration with the creative process[26] and the only one which is able to protect man from the terror of existence.[27]

Thus it is that one may read far and wide in the corpus of Dawson's splendid prose and ever come upon parallels to and so insights into the fictive yet grand historical and cultural construct of J.R.R. Tolkien. Like T.S. Eliot, Tolkien found Dawson's work deeply inspirational and illuminative for his own purposes as philosopher of history. Yet, paradoxically, his acknowledged debt to his con-

---

24 Or Tolkien's 'the One'.
25 Dawson rebutted the central thesis of Spengler's *Decline of the West* (1927), and the various pessimisms of Herbert Spencer, J. Huxley, Bertrand Russel, J.B.S. Haldane and many others. Tolkien's rejection of despair is nowhere better displayed than in his characterization of Denethor.
26 Compare Tolkien's notion of the (Christian) artist as sub-creator, working with God.
27 These words not merely apply to both writers but were seen and approved by a group including Dawson, as well as W.H. Auden, Martin C. D'Arcy, Mircea Eliade, Jacques Maritain and Paul Tillich. They are taken from the 'Epilogue' to all the texts in the Religious Perspectives series, first issued in 1960 by the Editor of the texts. Thus they also occur in Christopher Dawson's *The Historic Reality of Christian Culture: A Way to the Renewal of Human Life* (1960, 1965, etc).

temporary – albeit made clear in 'On Fairy-Stories' – has remained neglected for almost 70 years. As philosophic, theological and cultural panorama so analogous to Tolkien's work in his vast *Legendarium* of narrative and story, it deserves a better fate at the hands of all anti-modernist thinkers and students of Middle-earth, for each has been courageous and, in the face of extreme secular and ideological opposition, wanted and so mightily striven

> to prevent the crumbling twentieth-century Western world from fully entering the Abyss. (Birzer, 2003: xvi)

For both Dawson and Tolkien were concerned with the interaction of Western civilization and Christianity throughout the centuries, this giving a definite cycle, and a time of retreat when the church is under attack. Both saw religion as the dynamic element in culture and sought to send their readers into action by giving them a sense of the unconquerable hope that religion can engender. Each deplored the substitution of the idea of secular progress for religion as the guiding principle of human society. Both writers were remarkable theorists as to the power of Christian cultures to rouse their realms to faith in the spirit and eschew all faith in material wealth and power.

Folktale, Fairy Tale, and the Creation of a Story

In a form more compact than that of Charles Williams expounding the theories of 'co-inherence' and 'substitution',[1] and with a simpler, more consistently presented literary philosophy than that of C.S. Lewis, Tolkien has explained very luminously and memorably for us his own views of the function of myth. At the same time he has also shown himself to be the best critic of his own mature work[2] from very early on in his writing and scholarly careers. This is a feat all the more illuminating of his consistency of thought, when we realize that his theories appear to have been fully evolved when he had only just begun his great epic; for the original versions of his critical piece, 'On Fairy-Stories' and his charming exemplum, 'Leaf by Niggle', were both, as he said himself,

> written in the same period (1938-39) when *The Lord of the Rings* was beginning to unroll itself and to offer prospects of labour in yet unknown country. (*TL* vi)

Although they are not as specific to our purposes as one might have liked, it is helpful to note first the various luminous comments Tolkien had made in 1936, on the core of surviving Dark Age and folkloric stories, when he was giving an invited lecture to the British Academy on the Old English epic poem,

---

A version of this essay first appeared as Chapter VI in J.S. Ryan, *Tolkien: Cult or Culture?* (Armidale, N.S.W., Australia: The University of New England, 1969: 111-22); then it was modified for Neil D. Isaacs and Rose A. Zimbardo (eds.), *Tolkien: New Critical Perspectives* (Lexington, KY, The University Press of Kentucky, 1981: 19-39); and again, more recently, in a somewhat shortened form in *Understanding The Lord of the Rings: The Best of Tolkien Criticism*, edited by Rose A. Zimbardo and Neil D. Isaacs, (Boston: Houghton Mifflin, 2004: 106-21). It is here reprinted in a new form with the kind permission of the previous editors.
The first publication of Tolkien's 'Tree' essay was in 1947, in *Essays Presented to Charles Williams*. The first publication of the *Beowulf* essay was in *Proceedings of the British Academy* 22 (1937: 245-95), but the references are to the single text, issued as a monograph in 1958.

1 These ideas were much discussed in the Oxford group of writers, and both presented to the group and illustrated in his novels and essays by the unorthodox English romantic critic and wartime Oxford resident, and so their familiar romantic theological thinker, Charles Williams (ob. 1945).
2 W.H. Auden, for example, as critic of Tolkien, usually chose, early on, to stress the core motifs of the Quest, the Heroic Journey, the Numinous Object, and the victory of Good over Evil, as in his 1955, 1956 reviews of the several volumes of *The Lord of the Rings*, but he later built his criticism much more on Tolkien's own essay in his *Secondary Worlds: T.S. Eliot Memorial Lectures* (London, 1968), particularly on pp. 49-53.

Beowulf, in a paper even then – and most certainly since – widely recognized as a turning-point in *Beowulf* criticism. He was, even that early, concerned to stress the tragedy of the human condition and to show how that theme is set forth by the *Beowulf*-poet in artistic terms as "a balance of ends and beginnings," and focusing on "the moving contrast of youth and age," with the monsters, embodying the forces of evil and chaos, appropriately placed in the centre of the poem. In his already deeply reflective remarks on the style of inherited tales, Tolkien indicates that he is in the keenest sympathy with the Old English poet for using afresh ancient and largely traditional material, this giving something nearer to mythical allegory than the folktale. And he warns us that any intellectual snobbishness should not blind us to this –

> I will not [...] attempt at length a defence of the mythical mode of imagination [...] Folk-tales [...] do often [...] contain much that is far more powerful, and that cannot be separated from myth [...] capable in poetic hands of [...] becoming largely significant – as a whole, accepted unanalyzed. The significance of a myth is not easily to be pinned on paper by analytical reasoning. It is at its best when it is presented by a poet who feels rather than makes explicit what his theme portends; who presents it incarnate in the world of history and geography [...] myth is alive at once and in all its parts, and dies before it can be dissected. It is possible, I think, to be moved by the power of myth and yet to misunderstand the sensation, [to] refuse to admit that there can be an interest for *us* [...] in ogres and dragons. (*MCE* 15-16)

He goes on to stress the impact of the sinful mood of *draconitas*, the lust for power over possessions and people, a large symbol of malice, greed, and destruction, walking here in mortal history and incarnate in time, and he underscores the inevitable overthrow of man himself in Time, for *lif is læne*, [i.e. 'life is transitory'], a theme which, in its deadly seriousness, begets the dignity of tone. He notices that the Old English poem is by a great Christian just over the threshold of religious change, who has the sustaining hope which was denied his heroic but still pagan ancestors.

Interestingly Tolkien regrets that "we do not know more about pre-Christian English mythology" (*MCE* 24), – a gap, which he would refer to in his O'Donnell Lecture of 1955, and which, it has often been felt, this scholar has been concerned to limn in – and even to fill – in his own creative writings. He is also determined in this lecture to stress the impact of his story from its cosmic dimension:

> It is just because the main foes in *Beowulf* are inhuman that the story is larger and more significant [...] It glimpses the cosmic and moves with the thought of all men concerning the fate of human life and efforts; it stands amid but above the petty wars of princes, and surpasses the dates and limits of historical periods [...] during its process [...] we look down as if from a visionary height upon the house of man in the valley of the world [...] (*ibid.* 33)

In his conclusion, Tolkien notes that the poet is concerned to use materials then still plentiful, but from a day already passing – and to record a time now for ever vanished; using them for a new purpose, with a wider sweep of the imagination, achieving thereby a peculiar solemnity, so that, for all those of northern races, "it must ever call with a profound appeal – until the dragon comes" (*ibid.* 34).

As his better-known minor writings have shown,[3] Tolkien's imagination was nourished on the materials of Old Norse, Old English and Middle English literature; therefore it comes as no surprise to find that the strands and themes that are woven into the fabric of his major works are rich in Germanic and mediaeval associations. Yet other early indications of certain other powerful concepts (e.g. that both in its nature and in its processes man's imagination is like a tree) seem to have been overlooked. Thus his 1924 essay in *The Year's Work in English Studies* had placed emphasis on certain fields of important scholarship [that of archeology and place name studies – 'Floreant Philologica et Archeologica'] – much depended on "the two emotions, love of the land of England and the allurement of the riddle of the past," these being strenuously pursued all the more eagerly in the hope of "recapturing fitful and tantalising glimpses in the dark" (*YWES V* 65). And in the similar essay for the following year, he had begun his survey with lines which are a startling anticipation of 'Leaf by Niggle', as well as of the reverential wonder of Aragorn and others in the woods of Lothlórien. Interestingly, they also echo the thought and expression of both Dante and of Frazer's classical myth-probing *The Golden Bough*, as in his :

---

3 While these matters occur ubiquitously in various scholarly and creative pieces, the most interesting probing occurs in his 'English and Welsh', being published first in *Angles and Britons* (1963: 1-41), a collection of O'Donnell Lectures by various hands. [It is possible that Tolkien's one was modified slightly from its delivery several years earlier. In this volume, the essay is cited from *MCE*.]

It is merry in summer when 'the shaws be sheen and shrads full fair and leaves both large and long.' Walking in that wood is full of solace. Its leaves require no reading. There is another and denser wood where some are obliged to walk instead, where saws are wise and screeds are thick, and the leaves too large and long. These leaves we must read (more or less), hapless vicarious readers, and not all we read is solace. (*YWES VI* 32)

Yet it was the need to clarify his own specific earlier comments on *Beowulf* about "the mythical mode of imagination" (*MCE* 15) which may well be assumed to have prompted much in the slightly later theoretical essay, 'On Fairy Stories'. This is one wherein he is concerned to describe the genre fairy tale in a way that does not relate to many examples of the form, but which does apply very closely to his own writing – and it was so accepted by his friend C.S. Lewis, who uses it, without acknowledgement, when defending his friend's three volumes.[4] While it is indeed also possible to trace the lines of Tolkien's thought back through Chesterton's 'The Ethics of Elf-land' (1908: 66-102) – and earlier to George MacDonald's 'Imagination, Its Functions and Its Culture',[5] and thence back to Coleridge, in the *Biographia Literaria*[6] – it will be enough here to analyse what is a substantially new piece of work which goes much further than its several predecessors or mentors and argues its case with greater cogency and fuller development than they.

In actuality, both Chesterton and Tolkien are pointedly unconcerned about the origins of the fairy tale, the latter had concentrated his attention on its form, meaning and deeper purpose. Chesterton had himself become disillusioned about 'practical politics', but was committed to 'vision', 'ordinary things', and 'the sense of the miracle of humanity'. And thus he would aver that

Ordinary things are more valuable than extraordinary things. [...] Man is something more awful than men [...] The mere man on two legs, as such, should be felt as more heart-breaking than any music. (1908: 67-68)

---

4 Lewis, 'The Gods Return to Earth', *Time and Tide*, 14 August 1954 (1082-83); and 'The Dethronement of Power', *Time and Tide*, 22 October, 1955 (1373-74) – both essays variously reprinted since, especially by N. Isaacs and R. Zimbardo in the works referred to in the headnote above.

5 In his *Orts* (1882: 1-45). ['Orts' is a Scottish dialect word for 'roots', in this case, in the sense of 'nutritious vegetables'.]

6 See the Everyman edition of the *Biographia Literaria, or, Biographical Sketches of My Literary Life and Opinions*. The revised and accessible edition introduced by George Watson, 1975ff., has a particularly helpful critical approach essay.

He then goes on to stress that "a legend ought to be treated more respectfully than a book of history;" that "tradition means giving votes to the most obscure of all classes, our ancestors;" "I would always trust old wives' tales against the old maids' facts;" that "Fairyland is nothing but the sunny country of common sense;" and "we all like astonishing tales because they touch the nerve of the ancient instinct of astonishment;" or notice his emphatic assertion that "wonder has a positive element of praise."

However, Tolkien, in his 'On Fairy-Stories' piece, finds that no definition of them can be arrived at on historical grounds, and it must, rather, come from 'Faërie', "the realm or state in which fairies have their being" (*TL* 9), the 'Perilous Realm' itself which holds

> the seas, the sun, the moon, the sky; and the earth, and all things that are in it: tree and bird, water and stone, wine and bread, and ourselves, mortal men, when we are enchanted. (*ibid.*)

Further, most good 'fairy-stories' are about the *aventures* of men in that realm. Perhaps the best translation of this 'Faërie' is magic "of a peculiar mood and power" (*ibid.*) which operates to give us "the enchantment of distance" and "the satisfaction of certain primordial human desires [...] to hold communion with other living things" (*ibid.* 13).

The later three-volume epic, in its story, is full of echoes of the dim past, and of the earlier ages and the ancient forces, while it makes considerable use of borrowing in time. As is stated early on, "we stand outside our own time, outside Time itself, maybe"(*ibid.* 32). As well as "open[ing] a door on Other Time" (*ibid.*), there the language of the trees is a function of the story, as are the alien tongues of birds and horses, while the reader, enfranchised through the hobbits' experiences, is able to communicate with many different rational species, from the orcs and trolls, and eagles and horses, to the Elves and the High Elves who do not normally commune in words.

All of these processes satisfy the primal desire of 'imaginary wonder' (*ibid.* 14), the which emotion we, as readers, experience vicariously as the hobbits behold with 'wonder' the variety of Middle-earth: Goldberry (*FotR* 134); the "silence of the heavens" (*FotR* 142); or Strider, as one of the noble line of the old kings (*FotR* 233). Throughout the epic we see people bigger than we existing in a world filled with marvels both horrifying and beautiful, so that, like the hobbits, we can only gaze with astonishment. The men of Gondor marvel at the races of hobbits and dwarves, while the Elves themselves have this reverential attitude towards Númenor and to the Far West.

In his monograph's theory section on the fairy story's origins, Tolkien acknowledges the validity of the investigation of story elements as an exercise for folklorists but stresses that

> it is precisely the colouring, the atmosphere, the unclassifiable individual details of a story, and above all the general purport that informs with life the undissected bones of the plot, that really count. (*TL* 19)

In words that both recall his comments on philology cited above and anticipate much later writing, he links in several of his own yearnings :

> Of course, I do not deny, for I feel strongly, the fascination of the desire to unravel the intricately knotted and ramified history of the [meanings and developments of the] branches of the Tree of Tales. It is closely connected with the philologists' study of the tangled skein of Language, of which I know some small pieces. (*ibid.*)

In a change of image, he argues that the reader should be content with the "soup" as presented, or with "the story as it is served up by its author or teller" (*ibid.* 20), and not with the bones that went into the mix.[7]

In the making of the true fairy story he stresses three important ingredients – *invention, inheritance* and *diffusion* (*ibid.* 20-21). By the first, he probably means collecting up in a mediaeval – and serendipitous – fashion a cluster of separate, and hitherto unlinked, creative items already known and available, while the second is 'borrowing in time', and the third 'borrowing in space', usually from another 'inventor'. At the centre is an inventive mind, the nature of which Tolkien (in a manner similar to that of Owen Barfield)[8] would explore. This leads to his analysis of the creative imagination, a theory which

---

7 The 'cook' as artist, or even as an image of God as Creator and as the offerer of Choice to mortals, is the point of his *Smith of Wootton Major*, even as in it young Smith becomes an assistant to the Cook, and so, perforce, a Christ figure.

8 Owen Barfield, another of the Oxford circle of friends, was an anthropologist who held that the solid objects of the material world were but the antecedent condition for perceiving the 'unrepresented' numinous, so that man, in failing to acknowledge this Reality, has forgotten that all his knowing is ultimately a participation in the creative Word of God.

utilizes and goes beyond Coleridge's use of Platonic concepts, to an implicitly Christian romanticism. Faërie is a product of the 'esemplastic imagination' of the Secondary World, and this 'Secondary Belief' is much more than the 'willing suspension of disbelief' (*ibid.* 37).

For folktales, he believes, like all cosmologies, were once myths, or allegories "of the greater elemental changes and processes of nature" (*ibid.* 23) and only gradually became localized and humanized. Tolkien in this matter disagreed with the view of his Oxford co-denominationist, the slightly older Christopher Dawson (1889-1970), that they were once separate.[9] He rejected the notion that the cosmologies, or the various national folk-tales, were once allegories of the greater processes of nature, arguing that they were always together "there in the Cauldron of Story, waiting for the great figures of Myth and History, and for the nameless He or She," – a form of creator-Cook – waiting for the moment when they are to be cast into "the simmering stew." After considering History and Myth, and the power of many stories which "open a door on Other Time," he draws attention to the taboos in stories and has this to say of tales that are good enough:

> What really happens is that the story-maker proves a successful 'sub-creator'. He makes a Secondary World which your mind can enter. Inside it, what he relates is 'true': it accords with the laws of that world. You therefore believe it, while you are, as it were, inside. The moment disbelief arises, the spell is broken; the magic, or rather, art, has failed. You are then out in the Primary World again, looking at the little abortive Secondary World from outside. (*ibid.* 37)

This is the distinction between the outer, objective or Primary World and the inner world of myth, the Secondary World produced by the 'sub-creator'. Tolkien, in writing the epic, has imagined an entire world and told the story of certain significant events which took place during its imagined history.

He is also concerned to underscore the presence in all such stories of the element of desire. From the tales he read as a child, he says, there came a "wholly unsatisfied desire to shoot well with a bow" (*ibid.* 41) and "glimpses of an archaic mode of life, and, above all, forests" (*ibid.*). His taste for these stories,

---

9 See Dawson (1929: 86ff) and the Essay 14 'Dynamic Metahistory and the Model of Christopher Dawson', in this volume (141-51).

he tells us, "was wakened by philology [...] and quickened to full life by war" (*ibid*. 42). Later, when commenting on the enormous difficulties of being a successful sub-creator, he notes the many obstacles to commanding Secondary Belief and then comments that few attempt such difficult tasks

> but when they are attempted and in any degree accomplished then we have a rare achievement of Art: indeed, narrative art, story-making in its primary and most potent mode. (*ibid*. 49)

It is just this craft and fusion, it may be contended, which produces the widespread fascination with and the peculiar power of *The Lord of the Rings*.

Coleridge's thought always appealed to Tolkien, and his *Biographia Literaria* was much discussed in various Oxford literary groups. Indeed, an early paper of Tolkien's on the close inter-relationship between language and literature in some subtle characterization in the *Canterbury Tales*,[10] and delivered to the Philological Society in London, would seem to have closely influenced a little later published, and similarly auspiced paper by L.W. Willoughby on Coleridge as a philologist manqué, which may be summarized thus:

> He [...] even thought, for a moment, of turning to philology as his profession [...] His linguistic inquiries took on a psychological bend [...] His approach was philosophical, aesthetic, religious, and only rarely philological in the stricter sense [...] His linguistic observations and suggestions bear witness to the sharpness of his intellect, and the penetration of his intuition. He showed particular insight into the cultural aspects of language and a keen sense of aesthetic values. But his chief strength was the way in which linguistic training was put to the service of literary criticism. (1935: 75)

The influence of Coleridge is very much to be found in Tolkien's discussion of the concept of the creative imagination. Finding a need for a term other than 'Fancy', one "which shall embrace both the Sub-creative Art in itself and a quality of strangeness and wonder in the Expression [...] a quality essential to fairy-story," he proposed "to use Fantasy for this purpose" (*TL* 47).

---

10 This paper, originally entitled 'Chaucer's Use of Dialects', was given to the Philological Society's meeting in Oxford on 16 May 1931. The essay, when finally published in 1934, was not much revised, but given "textual notes, as well as [...] various footnotes, appendices, and comments naturally omitted in reading." It subsequently appeared in the *Transactions of the Philological Society* (1934: [1]-70), and also as an offprint. See, for the publishing story and particular details, Hammond (1993: 292-93).

In this mode, the images are of things not of the Primary World, but possessed of 'arresting strangeness', quite unlike dreaming, in which, as Tolkien admits, "there is no Art" (*ibid.* 48), or like Drama which "is naturally hostile to Fantasy" (*ibid.* 50) and which "has, of its very nature, already attempted a kind of bogus, or shall I say at least substitute, magic" (*ibid.* 51). For this precise reason – that the characters, and even the scenes are not imagined but actually beheld – Drama is an "art entirely different from narrative art" (*ibid.*).

In invented story, as distinct from 'adult' naturalistic ones, there were four peculiarly distinctive invented ingredients, namely: Fantasy, Recovery, Escape, and Consolation (*ibid.* 56). Needing a new term to express both 'Sub-creative Art' and 'a quality of strangeness and wonder', he used 'fantasy' and produced a thesis reminiscent of Chesterton's earlier one on the non-natural, namely that:

> We all like astonishing tales because they touch the nerve of the ancient instinct of astonishment. (Chesterton 1908: 80)

For he would treat of both 'Sub-creative Art' and a quality of 'strangeness and wonder', which suggest a motive for this urge in men, which he likens to the imagining of gods themselves. Yet:

> Fantasy remains a human right: we make in our measure and in our derivative mode, because we are made: and not only made, but in the image and likeness of a Maker. (*ibid.* 56)

'Recovery' which for him includes return to and the renewal of health, is the "regaining of a clear view" (*ibid.* 57). It is a means of "seeing things as we are (or were) meant to see them" (*ibid.* 58). For although all things once attracted us, we "locked them in our hoard,[11] acquired them, and, acquiring ceased to look at them" (*ibid.* 58). Seeing them only in relation to ourselves, we lose sight of their true nature, but by Recovery we again attain a fresher and a brighter vision, one "dangerous and potent [...] free and wild" (*ibid.* 59).

As C.S. Lewis had observed in his early review of the epic, Tolkien's theory had been used in *The Lord of the Rings* to considerable effect:

---

11 Again note the 'dragon' imagery so pondered on in his *Beowulf* paper and prominent in *The Hobbit*.

> The value of the myth is that it takes all the things we know and restores to them the rich significance which has been hidden by 'the veil of familiarity' [...] If you are tired of a real landscape, look in a mirror. By putting bread, gold, horse and apple, or the very roads into a myth, we do not retreat from reality: we rediscover it. As long as the story lingers in the mind, the real things are more themselves. This book applies the treatment not only to bread or apple, but to good and evil, to our endless perils, our anguish and our joys. By dipping them in myth we see them more clearly.[12]

One might add that the method had been applied to hospitality and courtesy, friendship and heroism, to the atmosphere along unfamiliar roads to the operations of greed and the inevitability of time, from the passage of the seasons, marked by holiday and joyous communal dancing in the Party Field (*RotK* 390), to "mortal summers that flicker and pass upon this Middle-earth" (*RotK* 303).

Closely related to this notion of Recovery, the regaining of one's clearer and true perspective on the meaning of life, is Escape, the positive, even heroic process of getting away from ordinary and drab surroundings that society may well seek to inflict on one, which is, in effect, the escape of the prisoner (*TL* 61). As Tolkien says, "The world outside has not become less real because the prisoner cannot see it" (*ibid.* 60).[13] He then answers one of the common critical charges against fantasy when he asks why man should be scorned for thinking of topics other than prisons, that is if he should think of transcending his actual world because he will not accept it; for his defiant action, like that of any Chestertonian hero, is one of rebellion compounded of "Disgust, Anger, Condemnation and Revolt" (*ibid.* 61). It is a response to the distortion that leads him to cry sarcastically, "[h]ow real, how startlingly alive is a factory chimney compared with an elm-tree" (*ibid.* 63). The need for such rebellion to restore one's true own perspective is well illustrated in 'The Scouring of the Shire', where the returning hobbits find a wilderness of hideous buildings, including just such a chimney stack.

Having come 'back again'[14] from a world where they have gained greatly in moral fibre, they proceed to set the Shire to rights by first fighting and rout-

---

12 See the references in footnote 4, above, *loc. cit.*, (1955: 1374).
13 Tolkien's between-the-wars' experience of Western Europe and his knowledge of the rise of totalitarian forces then, particularly in Germany – as well as the influence of Kafka's *The Castle* – may well have been in his mind at this time.
14 The sub-title of *The Hobbit* is 'There and Back Again'. This term from Hegel recurs in Tokien's work and indicates that the final value of distant *aventures* is their bestowal of moral fibre and so the ability

ing their enemies and then rebuilding and replanting the devastated areas. The lesson in the value of Escape does not need underscoring; in the epic it is seen in action, in the revitalizing of Minas Tirith, the rousing of Théoden, and the scouring of Orthanc, and, above all, in the destruction of the Ring, the actuality of Evil.

The vital element in Escape, however, is that of Consolation, the consolation of the happy ending, the Eucatastrophe – surely a parallel to the Christian concept of redeeming Grace – which by its very fantastic quality, the fairy story offers as solace for the pressing evils of the world. The Eucatastrophe is the opposite of tragedy, and in its sudden joyous 'turn' gives

> a sudden and miraculous grace: never to be counted on to recur. It does not deny the existence of *dycatastrophe*, of sorrow and failure: the possibility of these is necessary to the joy of deliverance. (*ibid*. 69)

Sorrow and evil can be as easily felt as in any other literary form and yet, perhaps more because of the clear outline of the fairy story, "it denies [...] universal final defeat and in so far is *evangelium*, giving a fleeting glimpse of Joy, Joy beyond the walls of the world, poignant as grief" (*ibid.*). And so it is that the fairy story, by means of its core of eucatastrophe, gives the reader a lifting of the heart, "a piercing glimpse of joy [...] that [...] passes outside the frame, rends indeed the very web of the story" (*ibid.* 70).

The relevance of the fairy story to reality lies in the "sudden glimpse of the underlying reality or truth," an "*evangelium* in the real world." (*ibid.* 71) For this is what the fairy story offers to Tolkien and other Christians. The Christian view of the happy ending of the world is significantly reflected in the fairy story. For Tolkien (who specifically states his faith (*ibid.* 71-72)), Christianity is a matter of historical fact and a philosophical interpretation of the universe as well as a religion. It is also the archetypal myth of which all others are but confused images. "The Birth of Christ is the eucatastrophe of Man's history. The Resurrection is the eucatastrophe of the [glorious] story [made manifest for us in the received account] of the Incarnation" (*ibid.* 72).

---

to enter an heroic (and Blakean) fight to restore one's community and its pristine and spirit-sustaining environment.

The conclusion to be drawn by us from this set of reflections is that Tolkien has much advanced Coleridge's claim for the priceless worth of the imagination. For him the Secondary Imagination is to be seen as an 'echo' of the Primary Imagination, which Coleridge had regarded as

> the living power and prime Agent of all human perception and as a repetition in the finite mind of the eternal act of creation in the infinite I AM (1975: 167).

The fairy story, in its making of a Secondary World,[15] is thus deemed a construct of the Imagination for Tolkien, just as God as Creator brought the world itself into being as His creation. Thus all stories of Faërie – and the epic is a notable example – look "forward (or backward: the direction in this regard is unimportant) to the Great Eucatastrophe" (*ibid*. 73), and partake of its epic and symbolic character. Since, for Tolkien, the Gospel story is true, by a transference of the transcending validity of the happy issue to the individual's battle with the World of Evil, Tolkien is to be seen to be declaring to modern man (as he does so implicitly in *The Lord of the Rings*) that

> God is the Lord, of angels, and of men – and of elves. Legend and History have met and fused. (*ibid*. 73)

And Other Stories and Folk Tales?

The many legends referred to in the *Beowulf* lecture – the magic land of Breasail in the West; Layamon's story of King Lear in his *Brut*; the 'Thrymskvitha' in *The Elder Edda*; the legends of the Shield-Kings of Denmark; the tale of Ingeld and his love for Freawara; or that Sigurd of the Volsungs – all of these traditional tales are desperately serious for Tolkien, and so, he argues, should they be for us. For they are, in a very literal sense 'legends' and so tales requiring to be understood as the essence of messages handed down from an earlier time or civilization. Similarly, magic must be taken seriously when it occurs in

---

15 As W.H. Auden, Tolkien's deeply sympathetic disciple, would put it in *Secondary Worlds*:

> Present in every human being are two desires, a desire to know the truth about the primary world, the given world outside ourselves [...] and the desire to make new worlds of our own, or, if we cannot make them ourselves, to share in the secondary worlds of those who can. (1968: 49)

mediaeval story (e.g in *Sir Gawain and the Green Knight*), in the eastern tale (e.g. the Egyptian *Tale of the Two Brothers*), or in a modern fairy tale. And Tolkien chides Sir George Dasent for forbidding children to read two of his more 'adult' tales, and quotes with approval the anecdote of Chesterton's concerning children who were dissatisfied with Maeterlink's *Blue Bird* "because it did not end with a Day of Judgement" (*TL* 44).

These thoughts indicate to us the moral and theological concern which Tolkien posited for a fairy story, and they are underscored by his concern that Elf-land depends on keeping promises and, ideally, on the fulfilment of "the oldest and deepest desire […] the Escape from death" (*ibid.* 68). It is finally made clear that ideally "every writer making a secondary world […] every sub-creator, wishes in some measure to be a real maker" (*ibid.* 70-71), to touch on the "serious and dangerous matter […] the Christian story" (*ibid.* 71). For, as he avers quietly, it "has long been my feeling (a joyous feeling) that God redeemed the corrupt-making creatures [by] the Great Eucatastrophe [,] the Christian joy" (*ibid.* 71-72). The religious and literary conclusion is that story or Art, the "Primary Art, that is, of Creation," are all come together in "the eucatastrope of Man's history," the Birth of Christ (*ibid.* 72). Thus it is made clear that it was Tolkien's artistic purpose in his own sub-creating to provide an analysis – even an eschatological parable for his own lost generation, and for those to follow – of the point of fusion of all Creation[16] and of its implications for the duty and destiny of humanity.

Tolkien had so early in his writing insisted that, to be complete, the fairy story or myth must have the eucatastrophe, since in its highest form myth dealt with universal or cosmic reality, and that there must be a moral and historical progression, for myth is meant to tell the whole story of the world from the beginning to the end. With the Eucatastrophe comes Joy for mankind, and that is really the beginning, the purpose of it all. While the formal and earthly process was brought to an end in Lewis's fictional world of Narnia, and it was there that the reality of the afterlife was the true beginning, the end for Tolkien's Middle-earth is still remote in time and space. As Gandalf says, "There are

---

16 I have adopted a certain measure of capitalization in order to bring out the moral – and
   eschatological – significance of the wording of the text and of the thought behind it.

other men and other lives, and time still to be" (*RotK* 87). Yet we are given to understand that the end is planned for Middle-earth, and that Elves and Ring-Bearers must await it in the undying lands. Already the process of history has removed whole civilizations, and even now we realize that

> much that was fair and wonderful shall pass for ever out of Middle-earth. (*TT* 155)

C.S. Lewis it was, who, when writing on George MacDonald, neatly summed up the attitude of his friend:

> All romantics are vividly aware of mutability, but most of them are content to bewail it; for MacDonald [and, we might add, for Tolkien] this nostalgia was merely the starting-point – he goes on and discovers what it was made for. (1955: 19)

Individual Responsibility and Divine Determinism

Although he does not discuss it in the expository essay, Tolkien is well aware of the related conceptual problem of the apparent conflict between Destiny and Freewill, between Divine Foreknowledge and Personal Choice and responsibility for one's actions, if the fruition of God's purpose is the true goal of man. This issue, like the seemingly inevitable recurrence of evil (and the task of every generation to attempt to remove it to the realm of future possibility, rather than present actuality), is not one discussed in Tolkien's critical work, but is allowed to make its own impact in the writing itself.

Because of the refusal of critics to take *The Lord of the Rings* as myth and so to accept it on its own terms, there has been considerable confusion as to its genre, and this doubtless explains the 1964 re-issue of the fairy-story essay, as well as the Oxford discussion-type explicatory sermons referring to his writings, and which Tolkien gave at various times, particularly at the High Anglo-Catholic Pusey House,[17] in the decade following its publication. It may easily be shown

---

17 This information was given to me by Canon Edward Arthur Maycock, of St Mary The Less Church in Cambridge about 1966. His own brother, Canon Francis Hugh Maycock, the Oxford cleric, had invited Professor Tolkien to speak about his literary purposes there at the Pusey House Chapel in central Oxford, in the years immediately following the issue of the three-volume epic. Tolkien had also variously visited Peterhouse, the ancient Cambridge college alongside St Mary the Less, and was

that Tolkien's aim in his major completed work was not to produce a realistic novel so much as to restore the Hero to modern fiction, and, implicitly, to bring the beliefs of Christianity to a central position in men's thoughts. For there is contained in it all the necessary materials for religion. Conscience is presented in the form of natural law, as the sense of fitness in their behaviour which is instinctive in the hobbits, and this is in a form that is intuitive and emotional rather than rational.

Lewis it was, who, elaborating on his friend's theory and so teasing out the themes implicit in the epic for those who would heed, was right to stress that "our victory is impermanent" and that the moral is for

> a recall from facile optimism and wailing pessimism alike, to that hard, yet not quite desperate, insight into Man's unchanging predicament by which heroic ages have lived. (1955: 1374)

In his review of the first volume, Lewis has most neatly summarised up the moral – and heroic – position which Tolkien posited for modern man:

> There was sorrow then too, and gathering dark, but great valour, and great deeds that were not wholly vain. *Not wholly vain* – it is the cool middle position between illusion and disillusionment. (1954a: 1083)

And so to the Deeper Meaning of Trees and 'Leaf by Niggle'

In the year in which he revised the text of the Andrew Lang lecture as 'On Fairy Stories' (1947), Tolkien published a most beguiling story – and one of the most subtle of the minor writings; a moral fable which may be related to the essay on the genre as an allegorical exemplum for it, since both were written in the same period as the early stages of *The Lord of the Rings*. Although it may be understood as an illustration of the writer's "wholly unsatisfied desire [for] forests," (*TL* 41), it is also related to his account of the student of fairy stories and his thoughts on all men's activities on earth:

---

known to many of its Fellows, notably Dom David Knowles, the Dominican and historian of Western Europe in the Middle Ages.

collecting only a few leaves, many of them now torn or decayed, from the
countless foliage of the Tree of Tales, with which the Forest of Days is car-
peted. It seems vain to add to the litter. Who can design a new leaf? The
patterns from bud to unfolding, and the colours from spring to autumn were
all discovered by men long ago. But that is not true. The seed of the tree can
be replanted in almost any soil, even in one so smoke-ridden (as Lang said) as
that of England. (*ibid*. 56)

Similarly, this must remind us of his chapter for 1924 in *The Year's Work in
English Studies*, where he had referred to *Germanica* as a "tree of altogether
larger girth and bigger branches" (*YWES V* 36).

But it is to his essay on fairy stories that we need to refer for an illustration
of his most profound statements and presentation of his reverential attitude
towards standing trees. The awe and the respect he has for them is part of "the
wonder of things" – the phrase used of another outside formal Christianity, the
Roman poet Lucretius. It becomes progressively more clear, as we read Tolkien's
various writings sequentially, that the hierarchy of the imagination for him was
to be found in the growing world. While a leaf is a new story, an attempt to
catch Faërie in a net of words – (although this is never quite successful in this
world, for the sought-after is "indescribable, though not imperceptible" (*TL*
10)), a tree or rather *the* Tree – that one knows so well and is there for one's
quiet contemplation – is the mass of tales which the individual mind can take
in. However, the Forest – our particular observed forest – is the continuous
manifestation of Time itself as it is there for us to enjoy and savour.[18] As Tolkien
the theorist had observed:

> Each leaf, of oak and ash and thorn, is a unique embodiment of the pattern,
> and for some this very year may be *the* embodiment, the first ever seen and
> recognized, though oaks have put forth leaves for countless generations of
> men. (*ibid*. 57)

And yet these further dimensions of the little illustrative tale should be put
aside for the moment, as Tolkien lets it slowly unravel.

---

18 One could well reflect here on the most ancient Germanic notions of a temple as being a flat space
   open to the skies and flanked by two rows of trees. Similarly, this was the time when his friend, E.O.G.
   Turville-Petre, was writing his powerful essay on the Scandinavian – and possibly Danelaw – association
   of Thor with tree worship. Originally written in Iceland and published there, it would appear in *English
   and Mediaeval Studies Presented to J.R.R. Tolkien on the Occasion of his Seventieth Birthday*, ed. by
   Norman Davis and C.L. Wrenn (1962: 241-49), and again in *Nine Norse Studies* by E.O.G. Turville-
   Petre (1972: 20-29).

The moral fable with its touches of satire so manifest in the opening to 'Leaf by Niggle' and in certain of its details will, perhaps inevitably, suggest C.S. Lewis's *The Great Divorce* (1946), a kind of parable of the [necessary] Harrowing of the Hell which Man makes of his own world, and a text which many have seen as a rebuttal of George Santayana's conception of immediate joy and an assertion of our too easy sensuous pleasure in beautiful objects, whereby the mind is freed from 'supernatural interference'. Yet the concept of the [necessary] 'journey', now mentioned here in the very first sentence, is much less specific, and the notion of its being that of death itself is not made clear until the Tolkien tale's epilogue.

*   *   *

Niggle, as first presented to us, is a simple and very ordinary man of no social consequence, with an awkward journey ahead of him, privately a reflective if strictly amateur painter, whose preferred activity is continually interrupted by "things he thought were a nuisance; but he did them fairly well, when he could not get out of them, which (in his opinion) was far too often" (*TL* 93). In a fashion he was kind of heart, although he often ignored its conscience-like promptings, and would grumble and swear a little to himself. He had at various times somewhat reluctantly assisted his neighbour, Parish, a man with a lame leg, and even others further off, for

> [t]here were many things that he had not the face to say *no* to, whether he thought them duties or not; and there were some things he was compelled to do, whatever he thought. (*ibid.* 96)

In short, Niggle was a quiet little Everyman, insignificant, "a very ordinary and rather silly little man" (*ibid.* 96).

However, his painting is very important to him, – perhaps the attempt to paint this tree is symbolic of his reflective life upon earth, and he tries hard at it, although thoughts of – and even some worries and concerns about – the apparently necessary journey, these also slow down his work, as do the interruptions and obligations of having to perform various mundane tasks. He had started a number of paintings, and not got very far with them, since his skill was with rendering with sensitivity the fine veins of single leaves rather than trees, even though he did want very much to paint a whole tree. And then, finally, while he was working hard at "a leaf caught in the wind, [...] it became a tree" (*ibid*. 94).

The process of artistic creation is well – even miraculously – described in the way that the central trunk of his painted tree sends out more branches, fantastic roots, and then has birds on twigs, a more and more engrossing setting, until finally a whole country opens out, with glimpses of a forest marching away and even the distant tips of the mountains. Whatever else he has done is either discarded or incorporated into the new picture that soon takes up a whole shed, one that stands where once he had grown potatoes. Despite a certain lack of surrounding encouragement – for he lives alone, with no one to talk to – Niggle begins to feel that the picture, while "wholly unsatisfactory", is "very lovely" (*ibid*. 95), and that, if it can stop growing, it can and will be able to be finished. Yet the more he tries to concentrate, the more demanding interruptions there are.

At this point there comes the intrusion of the town which both wants him on a jury, and sends him sundry distant acquaintances, all of them very happy to take tea in his "pleasant little house, miles away from the town" (*ibid*. 96). Although he resents this outside contact in the summer and when he is joyously painting, he had been glad enough to go there for the shops and to visit his acquaintances in the winter. The town serves as the greater symbol of Mankind in society, and so of the duty one has to one's fellows, of whom one is always a part. Thus he may not cut himself off from them, even as he may not ignore the continual complaints about the weeds in his garden. The lesser society of which he is a part consists of his neighbour, Parish, and the latter's selfish wife, who is ill, at a time when the wind has blown many tiles off their roof, and her husband is unable to cycle to get to the builders.

Once he has set out on this quite unsought errand, Niggle is suddenly granted a vision of the way to paint the "peak of a snow-mountain" (*ibid*. 97), a challenge which had long been one so tantalizing to him – although he still doubts that he will have the opportunity, or perhaps the ability, to effect the insightful strokes. Now the ride in the rain had given him a fever, during which there were "marvellous patterns of leaves and involved branches forming in his head and on the ceiling" (*ibid*. 100), and so he buries himself in leaves. Then, after an apparent recovery of his health and confidence, he is summoned to give up his large canvas to repair the roof of Parish's house, and then sternly ordered to begin his obligatory journey immediately, although, as another voice observes: "it's a bad way to start on your journey, leaving all your jobs undone" (*ibid.* 102).

Still the best-known reflective critic of *Tree and Leaf*, the English intellectual Colin Wilson had pondered the original and exemplum in his essay, *Tree by Tolkien*, originally published in later 1973, at about the time Tolkien died.[19] Apart from his stressing the influence of Chesterton (12), Yeats (14), and de la Mare (16), he draws attention to its Kafka-like mode and details of 'Leaf':

> While [Niggle] is in bed, a strange Kafka-esque official calls on him and tells him that his neighbour's house is not satisfactory – the implication being that it is Niggle's duty to take care of his neighbour. Niggle's picture would be just the right size to mend a hole in Parish's roof. When Niggle protests: 'It's my picture,' the Inspector replies, 'I dare say it is. But houses come first. That is the law.' The bewildered artist is ordered to start on his journey, and he sets out quite unprepared. The journey is pure Kafka. (23)

Niggle is soon off and on his way, although he does manage to loose the few possessions he has with him, when he gets out of the train, and so, destitute, he has to be put in the Workhouse Infirmary. There he is made to work hard – "This turns out to be a kind of prison where he is made to do boring manual tasks (it sounds like a Soviet labour camp) and to spend hours locked in his room in the dark" (*ibid.* 23). While he endures these corrective disciplines, Niggle reflects that "he should have acted sooner for his neighbour, since then so many of the unfortunate consequences of his selfishness need not have followed" (*ibid.*). Significantly he is now employed at the very practical jobs he had not turned his hand to for his neighbour, but, after a period of more willing service, he learns how to become master of all his time, now without any sense in inner tension. His next bout of therapeutic treatment is the task of digging until he is on the point of collapse, after which, as he rests in the dark, he listens to a judgemental Court of Inquiry on himself.

The weakness of his position is put by the First Voice: his heart did not function properly; he hardly ever thought at all and did not get ready for the journey;

---

19 The actual limited English edition which came out in 1973 is not followed, but, rather, the more available American edition of 1974, as published by Capra in their Chapbook series.

although he is moderately well off, he arrived there almost destitute; he neglected the things ordered by the law;[20] he resented 'interruptions' and uttered complaints and silly imprecations. The Second Voice, defending, notes that his heart was in the right place; he was never meant to be anything very much, and he was never very strong; his painting, 'A Leaf by Niggle', had a certain charm, and "he took a great deal of pains with leaves, just for their own sake. But he never thought that that made him important. [...] he did answer a good many Calls, [...] [and] never expected any Return" (*TL* 106).

His last act, the ride for assistance in the wet, is held to weigh the scale, and make the case for a little gentle treatment, at which Niggle blushes: "that Voice made Gentle Treatment sound like a load of rich gifts, and a summons to a King's Feast" (*TL* 107). His basic decency is made clear by his first question, which is for Parish's welfare. Niggle awakens to radiant sunlight, fresh clothing, and a light repast, which is in the form of a communion, although nothing is so explicit. His new journey with a ticket takes him by train, bicycle, and path, over the turf to a tree:

> Before him stood the Tree, his Tree, finished. If you could say that of a Tree that was alive, its leaves opening, its branches growing and bending in the wind. (*ibid.* 109-10)

Here the sun is "very bright," colours brilliant, the wind invigorating, everything seems new and the smells are delicious. It is all familiar as from a dream, "that Niggle had so often felt or guessed, and had so often failed to catch" (*ibid.* 110).

It is perhaps this realization of his deepest aspirations which really suggests that Niggle is indeed dead, for now the Imagination, the comprehension of the deeper meaning of life – and of his own awed act of creativity – is truly realized:

> 'It's a gift!' he said. He was referring to his art, and also to the result; but he was using the word quite literally. He went on looking at the Tree. All the leaves he had ever laboured at were there, as he had imagined them rather than as he had made them; (*ibid.* 110)

---

20 Stern as it sounds, this probably refers to no more than the customary (Christian) courtesy to others which is innate in the hobbits and practiced almost instinctively.

What is most surprising is that some of the most beautiful, characteristic and perfect leaves are seen to have been produced in happy collaboration with Parish. Now, too, the further vistas are clearer – birds, the Forest, and the Mountains glimmering far away. Niggle – the hitherto fussy somewhat querulous man – has experienced a form of spiritual recovery and awed wonder, in that he is, for the first time, able to walk into the further distance without turning it into mere surroundings. His artist temperament immediately discerns that there are "a number of inconclusive regions" (*ibid*. 111), these still needing his work on them, while the Mountains are another picture, one still to be clearly perceived and perhaps by grace and favour captured.

On sitting down to ponder how to approach his tasks, all of which have a further quality which needs to be apprehended, "something different, a further stage" (*ibid*.), he now thinks charitably of Parish as flower lover and gardener, and the latter appears, whereupon they both set to work without any talk. Now their roles are reversed, each compensating for his previously limited perspective, so that Niggle is better at ordering his time, while Parish often wanders about, looking at trees. Then, as in Naming Day in Eden – a famed Renaissance trope of the identifying role of Adamic Man, that of formally – and first – naming and finding good the things created by God, Niggle, no longer a niggler, is now made to imagine into existence "wonderful new flowers and plants" (*ibid*. 113), while his forgiven and now close friend, Parish, always knows exactly how to set them in their beds.

And Parish now explains that he was able to come there because Niggle had wanted him with him. He has now lost his limp, which was perhaps a sign of a deeper spiritual malformation, and all tension between them ceases after they have drunk from the pristine Spring in the heart of the Forest. [This act will, surely, recall the similar refreshment of the two young hobbits after they have drunk from the Ent's great bowl.]

In the Spring of the year, with the Great Tree in full blossom, they walk to the margin of the country, to the Edge (a phrase also used in *The Hobbit*), where they are met by a guide. While Parish who is not yet ready to go on waits there for his wife, Niggle passes on – in a sort of Bunyan-like fashion – into Niggle's Country, a little bit of which is now the wondrous and heavenly Parish's Garden.

Thus it is that the unimaginative and prosaic man has now, aided by his friend's selflessness, been blessed with imagination and so become a sub-creator himself. As the guide explains, it was all thought of by Niggle, although Parish and his wife had hitherto dismissed it, seeing it only as Nonsense, or "That Daubing".

> 'But it did not look like this then, not *real*,' said Parish. 'No, it was only a glimpse then,' said the man; 'but you might have caught the glimpse, if you had ever thought it worth while to try.' (*ibid.* 89)

To this Niggle immediately replies that he had not given Parish much chance to work with him, or know him, mentally calling him 'Old earth-grubber':

> 'But what does it matter? We have lived and worked together now. Things might have been different, but they could not have been better.' (*ibid.* 115)

For the acts of shared creation have brought mutual understanding and a deep and satisfying harmony.

Niggle now turns to go further in, like the man who was saved in C.S. Lewis's *The Great Divorce*, or his other protagonists experiencing a like spiritual growth, the survivors of Old Narnia, who were able, after many acts of selflessness, or substitution, and heroic courage, at the end to reach the real country. In the process of the further growth of the little man, he is able to achieve his largely self-repressed potential, to learn of the animals, of higher lands where the spirit expands, of a wider sky, and to go nearer the yearned for Mountains, and like Bunyan's Pilgrim to proceed "always uphill".

*   *   *

There follows an epilogue which is the dread and uncaring earthly inquest on Niggle, – an appraisal typical in Tolkien's mind of the bureaucracies of mid-century England – at which the man of affairs states that he would have put him away, and thus have had him "start on the journey before his time" (*ibid.* 116). For he had chosen to indulge in private daydreams, and did not live in the town, which is to be equated at last with the practical or severely economic use of all things. While dismissed out of mind by most, Niggle is remembered by the schoolmaster who, finding the corner of the canvas with the one beautiful leaf, had preserved it in a Museum, where it was finally burned in a fire and then "the leaf, and Niggle, were entirely forgotten in his old country" (*ibid.* 91).

Yet the fact of Niggle's existence and his greatest creative achievement have real meaning, for, as the two Heavenly Voices explain, that painted scene, an area of the mind's sensitivity and intuition, has a full reality in what we may now see as a transformed Limbo, where:

> It is splendid for convalescence; and not only for that, for many it is the best introduction to the Mountains. It works wonders in some cases. (*ibid.* 118)

The place has now been named by the Porter,[21] as Niggle's Parish, a title which has caused both of them to laugh so that the mountains rang.

And so to the Deeper Meaning of *Tree and Leaf*

'Leaf by Niggle' is, more than anything else that Tolkien wrote, an allegory of his own and the creative artist's exercise and activities on earth, and of such sub-creation's function in helping him and others on the spiritual journey towards the higher state represented by the Mountains.[22] It is, surely, too, a pointer to its interpretation that it had been linked with 'On Fairy Stories' several years after the massive reader difficulty with the 'trilogy', and before the great cult of his writings had exploded, as a result of the mid-1960s copyright issues in the United States of America.

The earlier part of the story of Niggle – like the curious epilogue with its conversation between unimaginative, practical men on the subject of the 'worth' of Niggle's life – represents the conflict between those who are of the spirit, – this indicated on earth by their creative imagination, – and those who are not. For the man of awed marvelling and creative intellect is often bothered by what appear to be extraneous influences which retard his attempts to reach out as he endeavours to realize his vision.

---

21 This figure has something of the shrewdness and yet fatherly, and like, compassion of the typical Porter of the Oxford Colleges of Tolkien's day. It is also, surely St Peter, and a pun on the name of Merton's sister college is a plausible Tolkienian conceit.

22 The Mountains have a focus that is inspirational, and some have even deemed them to relate to the Himalayas as some sort of ancient focus of the Indo-European peoples and their languages. This may well have been reflected in Tolkien's lecture room comments on the Indian antecedents of some of the elements in the story about Death in Chaucer's 'Pardoner's Tale'.

In terms of the story, even as the (potential) artist, writer or other visionary, has responsibilities towards his fellows, so the practical man of affairs needs to have deep sympathy towards his imaginative brother, without whose help he will never leave the Workhouse of this grim world, let alone be enabled to see the Forest – and all the tales that go to make up the Forest, – or be introduced to the Mountains,[23] which, surely, constitute the world of the spirit, Faërie, and for Tolkien, an allegory of the Christians' Heaven. As Colin Wilson would put it:

> The final judgement [...] is unexpectedly complex. In the conflict between the artist and society, Tolkien comes down on the artist's side, as is to be expected – but he also blames the artist, implying that if he were less vague and incompetent, he could become something more like a leader of society – without, however, compromising his own basic vision. (1974: 25)

*   *   *

The story is also critically important – and so highly significant – in that it shows that Tolkien, at this time, was actively engaged in putting his ideas into an allegorical form and here – and this is very distinctive – in fact, to be seen as drawing on no associations of the Celtic or Germanic past. For, rather, does the tale have its affinities – if these can indeed be discerned – with the mediaeval drama, *Everyman*,[24] with Bunyan, or, more specifically, with the several allegorical journeys in the writings of C.S. Lewis. Accordingly, the critic is clearly the safer in assuming that he might have been doing the same in *The Lord of the Rings*. This is particularly the case in the challenges suddenly posed to the imagination and understanding of the plain and everyday highly satisfying, if workaday, existence of the hobbits as they become drawn into the War of the Ring. For the meaning of the little tale must be the stress on the fact that the business of the artist is to create a kind of tree as given, beautiful and as

> alive as possible. The tree will serve its purpose in [i.e. to combat] a world that becomes increasingly urbanized. (*ibid.* 39)

---

23 Presumably this quality of vision and of beckoniong higher things is similar to the function of the Sea and of the far West in *The Lord of the Rings*.
24 We may recall that Tolkien had, in the early 1920s, compiled the linguistic and contextual sense glossaries for such mediaeval drama materials as in Kenneth Sisam (ed.) *Fourteenth Century Verse and Prose* (1921).

The story, then, and much more so than the essay, is an exploration of the difference between the states of: life lived prosaically, life with imagination, and of the radiant life possible for the selfless after death, for, by an intensification of some unselfish aspects of the earthly life, the individual is translated to a different plane. While for 'Leaf' "one of its sources was a great poplar tree that [...] was suddenly lopped and mutilated by its owner" (*TL* VI), this has surely been transmuted into the notion of the great 'Tree of Tales' which every man of vision[25] can glimpse and so be inspired by.

For, even if it is not in his earthly power to give representational or true actuality to a subtle and wondrous single leaf, the quiet contemplation of it in any man is the sure testimony to the value of the miraculous seed of reflective thought and so of spiritual salvation. For it and its vision symbolize momentously the wonder that such a perception may be planted even in the most arid soil, the muddled and bemused soul of 'a very ordinary little man'.

---

25 As the corpus of Tolkien's drawings and tales was progressively published, it is more than clear that so much of the quest and achievements of the querulous but imaginative Niggle is some sort of fable of Tolkien himself as both artist and story-teller or 'sub-creator'.

The Wild Hunt, *Sir Orfeo* and J.R.R. Tolkien

Michael Burgess, the eminent scholar and writer of fantasy, in his then recent article, 'Oromë and the Wild Hunt: the development of a myth' – and so a somewhat mythic and comparative piece for the Tolkien Society – had been offering a reflective comment on that mighty prince of Arda, Oromë (his name literally meant one 'who blows mightily on a horn'), a hero who loved the lands of earth while they were still dark and travelled far into the forests of Middle-earth, and so first discovered the Eldar. In these, Tolkien's proto-legends, Oromë is titled Tauron, or 'Lord of the Forests' (the forests, that is, of Middle-earth).

The first related matter of some moment is Tolkien's work on *Sir Orfeo*, the short fourteenth-century poem in Middle English, the literary kind of which is the 'Breton lai'. Tolkien himself had been taught the genre of the poem by and studied it closely with Kenneth Sisam, and so it was a part of his own degree studies and final public examinations in the Summer of 1915.[1] When himself teaching at Leeds University, in very quick time, Tolkien provided the glossary to his former tutor's volume, *Fourteenth Century Verse and Prose* (1921), in which volume the whole poem of 604 lines is included as text II (see pp. 13-31 and for the notes, etc., pp. 207-12). Later Tolkien had supervised the Litt. B. thesis of Alan J. Bliss

---

This essay first appeared in a shorter form in *Mallorn* 24 (1987: 16-17) and is reprinted here in a new form with the kind permission of its editors. At the time it was written in direct response to an earlier published essay by Michael Burgess (*Mallorn* 22, 1985: 5-11). The piece by M. Burgess had not discussed either Tolkien's scholarship on the 'Wild Hunt' theme in the early Middle Ages, or his varied use of the same device in his creative writings. However, there were certain related points which I had deemed might well be made in response to this article, and that is what was attempted in that 1987 exegetic text of mine, one somewhat expanded now. I have also added a form of Appendix, this last focussing on a particular – and seemingly somewhat 'Wild Hunt' influenced fantasy work by the now widely popular Susan Cooper (b. 1935), earlier an undergraduate of Somerville College, Oxford. She had attended Tolkien's public lectures in the years 1953-56, and would herself become celebrated for her fantasies on both sides of the Atlantic, certain parts of it having a southern English ethos, with a lower Thames Valley-Chilterns landscape and setting, and so peculiarly appealing to students of the creative writings of J.R.R.Tolkien.

1 See *In Literis Anglicis* result for that year, p. 255 of the 'University Honours – for years 1900-1920' in the *First Supplement to the Historical Register of 1900* [of the University of Oxford] (1921).

who subsequently prepared an edition of the text for his own research degree and Tolkien, from 1940 to 1958, being the senior general editor of the *Oxford English Monographs* series, was instrumental in having that scholarly work published in that same series in 1954. In the 'Preface' (vi) to his edition, Bliss refers to certain related matters, the first among the 'debts-incurred', being to –

> Professor J.R.R. Tolkien, whose penetrating scholarship is an inspiration to all who have worked with him

and again to the several editors who "agreed to include this volume in the series."

In 1975 in his preface to J.R.R. Tolkien's only then published translations[2] of *Sir Gawain and the Green Knight, Pearl* and *Sir Orfeo*, Christopher Tolkien said that his father's "version of *Sir Orfeo* was [...] made many years ago, and had been [...] for long laid aside" (v), and also observing: "I was not able to discover any writing by my father on the subject of *Sir Orfeo*" (vi). Accordingly, he adds the brief note of introduction, stressing only the likelihood that the poem "was composed [...] in the south-east of England in the latter part of the thirteenth century, or early in the fourteenth" and "translated from a French original" (14).

Yet one may see much of Tolkien's speculative thought reflected in the commentary in and annotation to his own pupil's admirable edition.

The poem[3] itself, describes how Heurodis, the wife to the lord Sir Orfeo, had in sleep been summoned by the fairy king, who, refused by her, had then appeared to her in splendid person –

> then came their king himself with speed;
> a hundred knights with him and more,
> and damsels, too, were many a score,
> all riding there on snow-white steeds,
> and white as milk were all their weeds. (ll. 142-46)

---

2 The history of the actual prose translation is given – as far as it can be – in Hammond (1993: 323), who tells us, cautiously, that

> It may be assumed that Tolkien translated *Sir Orfeo* into Modern English [...] circa 1920-40 – or perhaps c. 1944.

3 The translations are from the Tolkien 1975 collection, as cited in the text above.

She is warned that, although with her husband for the present, she will be taken off by the fairy king, willy-nilly on the morrow, and so it occurs, despite Orfeo's preparing mightily to guard the queen and then defending her "and full ten hundred Knights with him" (l. 183) –

> And yet from midst of that array
> the queen was sudden snatched away;
> by magic was she from them caught,
> and none knew whither she was brought. (ll. 191-94)

After this Orfeo becomes a hermit in the forest and

> There often by him would he see,
> when noon was hot on leaf and tree,
> the king of Faërie with his rout
> came hunting in the woods about
> with blowing far and crying dim, (ll. 281-85)

These hosts are of the fairy sort[4] and cast in a courtly and gracious mould, as is the 'hunt' of elegant lady hunters from Faërie which he also sees:

> And one fair day he at his side
> saw sixty ladies on horses ride,
> each fair and free as bird on spray,
> and never a man with them that day. (ll. 303-06)

In this the two excerpts follow both the elegant Breton style of the poems of Marie de France and, presumably, of the lost Breton lai on the same theme (Bliss 1954: xxxiiff.) and the Celtic mode of describing the fairy army and the fairy hunt, much as in the *De Nugis Curialium* of Walter Map. As Bliss goes on to illustrate (1954: 1), the story of Sir Orfeo passed into popular tradition and reappeared in Unst, Shetland, as the ballad 'King Orfeo'.[5]

But to return to the poem which Tolkien knew so well. As a variant on the hunting theme, or because they are 'dead', the male huntsmen observed by Orfeo take no kill:[6]

---

4 Some of these lines provide analogies to Tolkien's reflective descriptions of both Galadriel and of Arwen in *The Lord of the Rings*. See also Carlson (1998: 62-75).

5 See Child (1882, vol. i: 217ff.).

6 Interestingly this same hunt without slaughter is also provided in the hunts of another Fairy King, as observed by Bilbo in *The Hobbit*. Indeed, so much of the trance-like account of the experiences of the hobbits in the wood would seem to be derived from *Sir Orfeo*.

> There often by him would he see, [...]
> [where] the king of Faërie with his rout
> came hunting in the woods about
> with blowing far and crying dim, [...]
> yet never a beast they took nor slew,
> and where they went he never knew. (ll. 281ff)

This absence of violence and, perhaps, so a test of Orfeo's humility and acceptance of some form of divinely-planned ordeal is also seen by some critics as a
an index of many surviving themes, notably those to be found in the Breton
lai.[7]

Quite other is the next sight, the stern fairy host of warriors[8] in military
order,

> At other times he would descry
> a mighty host, it seemed, go by,
> ten hundred knights all fair arrayed
> with many a banner proud displayed.
> Each face and mien was fierce and bold,
> each knight a drawn sword there did hold,
> and all were armed in harness fair
> and marching on he knew not where. (ll. 289-96)

This pageant is more traditional and much akin to the classic analysis of the
Wild Hunt variants in transmitted story by Stith Thompson in the *Motif-
Index of Folk-Literature.*[9] Yet that major work contains the following intriguing
examples of the motif-subdivisions of the hunt to be found in various (largely
European) folklores treated in that comparative compilation:

E 501: Witches in wild hunt;

E 501: Soldiers in wild hunt;

E 501: Wild huntsmen wandering because of sin;

E 501: 3.4. Wild huntsman wanders because of unshriven death;

E 501: 4.1.3. Dogs with fiery eyes in wild hunt;

---

7 A compact statement of this clashing of motif and purpose is well treated by Grimaldi (1981: 147-61).
8 Compare Walter Map on the silent armies of Brittany, and Tolkien's Dead men at Dunharrow
  (*RotK* 53), and Burgess' own text on this matter (1985: 9).
9 Vol. 2, D - E (1955).
  Motif E 500 (pp. 463ff.) is 'Phantom Hosts'; E 501 is 'The Wild Hunt'; and E 502, 'the Sleeping
  Army'.

E 501: 4.2. Wild horseman's ghostly horse;

E 501: 4.2.2. Black horse in wild hunt;

E 501: 4.2.4. Horse in wild hunt breathes fire;

E 501: 15.1. Wild huntsman blows horn;

E 501: 17.3. Wild hunt powerless at crossroads;

E 501: 17.4.2. Power of wild hunt evaded by silence;

E 501: 17.5.4. Wild hunt avoided by throwing self to earth;

E 501: 19.6. Effect of wild hunt remedied by prayer;

etc.

All of these sub-categories and many others listed under E, 'the dead', may seem to have echoes in Norse Folklore and sagas as well as in the more fragmentary literary remains of the Old English period. Thus the motif of the Wild Hunt Procession of the Dead (E 491), the Abode of the Dead (E 480), etc. would be very familiar to Tolkien from his life-long work in mediaeval languages.

In this connection, the sub-title of the Thompson compilations is peculiarly revealing:

> A Classification of Narrative Elements in Folktales, Ballads, Myths, Fables, Metrical Romances, Exampla, Fabliaux, Text-books, and Local Legends.

Some of the ambivalences of the Orfeo story, as given in the Middle English poem, have recently been teased out in Carlson (1998: 62-75).

*   *   *

While it would be too long to list the many echoes of the theme of the Wild Hunt, or of its more demonic form – the Undead Army – in the Tolkien corpus, it may be noted that something of the ominous movement of such fell armies, on horse or foot, is to be found in the Helm's Deep Sequence (*TT*) and when the hobbits, Frodo and Sam, are at the opening of the Black Gate, or when we are told – again through hobbit eyes – of the last ride from Rohan, or of the violent hastening of the Uruk-hai. The original Hunt notion of terror (in the skies) is largely reserved by Tolkien for accounts of the Black Riders, particularly when the Lord of the Nazgûl is later on the wing, as in the account of 'The Passage of the Marshes':

a small cloud flying [...] a black shadow [...], a vast shape winged and ominous. It scudded across the moon, and with a deadly cry went away westward, [...] the shadow of horror wheeled and returned, passing lower now, right above them, sweeping the fen-reek with its ghastly wings. (*TT* 237)

Appendices

Appendix A

Michael Burgess, in the earlier *For the Wind, for the Wild* (1975: 9) refers very relevantly to the motive of the 'furious host' crossing to America and to (wicked?) cowboys condemned to "spend eternity chasing a herd of unearthly cattle across the sky." This was, of course, the country and cowboy-style song, '(Ghost)Riders in the Sky', written in June 1948 by Stan Jones, sung by Gene Autry in his 1949 film, *Riders in the Sky*, and by many others subsequently. In Australia, too, towards the end of the 1964-66 drought in the eastern states, the American motif was extended in both art and music, particularly in the sudden and ubiquitous popularity of the mournful American ballad, one which was then so widely used to describe the terrible pastoral grazing conditions, especially in the east.

William Butler Yeats much earlier had evoked the Wild Hunt in 'The Hosting of the Sidhe', the opening poem in his fairy collection, *The Celtic Twilight* (1893), much as, later, would Alan Garner, Diana Wynne Jones and Raymond E. Feist, the latter as in his fantasy *Faerie Tale* (1988).

Thus the image from that not quite post-modern period in both story and music, as well as in paintings, is of gaunt and burned drovers in the sky, driving un-dead cattle – who are literally skin and bone – on and on in search of the non-existent flowing waterhole. Since they never find it, gaunt as their pathetic charges, they too are doomed to an eternity of urging on their faltering herds and emaciated mounts across dust-filled clouds strewn across the empyrean.

Appenix B

And a pupil, the writer Susan Cooper, who may well have been inspired by her teacher.

This opportunity has been taken to draw attention to the long time British use of the motif, one which had been found all over Northern, Western and Central Europe, and involving a phantasmal group of huntsmen with hounds and horns, engaged in a furious pursuit. And seeing it was thought to presage some disaster like war or the plague. In southern England it had been associated with St Guthlac (683-714), and with Hereward the Wake (ob. c. 1070), while the monastic *Peterborough Chronicle* attests its appearance at the time of the appointment of a disastrous abbot for his monastery around the year 1132, according to its scribe.[10]

If we ignore the Othinic Scandinavian associations of the Wild Hunt, there are also the other eastern and southern English ones linked with Herne the Hunter, and the Thames Valley in particular, the area of nurture of Susan Cooper, which she features so memorably in her *The Dark is Rising* (1973), a folklore-inspired text with a haunting sense of both vast spaces and of specific places.

In this tale the central figure, the boy, Will, experiences with the reader the half forgotten British racial memory of the Wild Hunt, so that it and the related numinous place, Herne the Hunter's Oak in Windsor Great Park, come together to provide a specific locale for the events of the ostensibly modern plot. Thus place, time and natural forces are all perceived the more acutely by both Will and the narrator, assisting the boy to come into his largely innate powers to control violence in nature – for he is the seventh son of a seventh son.

Something of the quality of race memory of the local British folklore and, alike, the teller-recensionist's power to evoke atmosphere may be gathered from the following sequential quotations:[11]

---

10 The passage in the annal for 1128 may be translated thus:

> The hunters were black and large and hideous, and their hounds all black and broad-eyed and hideous, and they rode on black horses this was seen in the park itself, and in all the woods there were probably about twenty or thirty horn-blowers.

11 They are taken from the 1999 edition, published by Simon & Schuster Children's Publishing, New York. The original had been published by Chatto and Windus in 1973.

1) He saw suddenly with a flash of terror a masked man with a human face, the head of a stag, the eyes of an owl, the ears of a wolf, and the body of a horse. The figure leapt, tugging at some lost memory deep within his mind. (45);

2) It was a giant carnival head, brilliant and grotesque […] it was not the head of a man […] The head from which the branching antlers sprang was shaped like the head of stag, but the ears beside the horns were those of a dog or a wolf. And the face beneath the horns was a human face – but with the round feather-edged eyes of a bird. (131);

3) We go to raise the Hunt […] It is time for the Hunter […] the white horse must come to the Hunter […] This is the ordering of things, you have forgotten […] It was impossible to tell where they were. A wind was rising. (202);

[and from the penultimate chapter, 'The Hunt Rides']:

4) If the Dark can take you now, they take all they need to […] rise to power […] The great black column pursued them, rushing on the wind, and in it and through it rode the Black Rider on his fire-jawed black horse, spurting after them, with the Lords of the dark riding at his shoulder like a spinning dark cloud themselves […] Merriman said, Of course. Tonight the Hunt rides […] For the first time in more than a thousand years the Hunt will have a quarry […] (219-21);

5) An Old Way rings the Great Park, the way through Hunter's Combe; […] the Hunter's face told of cruelty, and a pitiless impulse to revenge […] from every point in the Park […] came an endless pack of hounds, belling as hunting dogs do […] huge white animals their ears were red, their eyes were red. Will stood alone. (221);

6) And the towering black column rushed to engulf him with all the monstrous forces of the Dark arrayed in its writing most, and at its centre the great foam-mouthed black stallion reared up with the Black Rider, his eyes two brilliant points of blue fire […] (226); and

7) But now, riding down towards it, out of the west with the speed of dropping stones, came Herne and the Wild Hunt. (227)

*   *   *

Some background references for the reader's appraisal of Cooper's folkloric text:

Briggs, Katharine, 1967, *The Fairies in English Tradition and Literature*, Chicago: The University of Chicago Press.

Guerber, H.A., 1909, *Myths of the Norsemen: From the Eddas and Sagas*, London: George G. Harrap. (Interestingly, both Tolkien and Cooper are reported to have had a considerable affection for this book by the British historian. The book was re-published 1992 by Dover Publications.)

Hutton, Ronald, 1991, *The Pagan Religions of the Ancient British Isles: Their Nature and Legacy*, Oxford: Blackwell Publishing.

Kay, Guy Gavriel, *The Fionavar Tapestry*, consisting of:
The Summer Tree, 1984, New York: Arbour House.
The Wandering Fire, 1986, New York: Arbour House.
The Darkest Road, 1986, New York: Arbour House.

Shippey, T.A., 1988, 'Breton Lais and Modern Fantasies', pp. 60-91, in Derek Brewer (ed.), *Studies in Medieval English Romances: Some New Approaches*, Cambridge: D.S. Brewer.

Swinfen, Ann, 1984, *In Defence of Fantasy: A Study of the Genre in English and American Literatures since 1945*, London: Routledge & Kegan Paul.

Mid-Century Perceptions of the Ancient Celtic Peoples of 'England'

In late 1955, just one day after the October publication of vols. II and III of *The Lord of the Rings*, J.R.R. Tolkien finally gave to the University of Oxford his somewhat delayed O'Donnell lecture,[1] 'English and Welsh'. The text (heard given by this writer) is of particular interest for students of Tolkien's creative writings for two ideas that it contains. The first is a footnote at the end of the printed version, where he has referred to the Modern Welsh language thus:

> [...] it remains [...] closer [to the Celtic patterns of our origin] than any other living language. For many of us [...] it stirs deep harp-strings in our linguistic nature [...] It is the native language to which [...] we would still go home. (*MCE* 194)

His footnote on this whole passage, and the appeal of the 'Celtic patterns' of Arthurian romance, runs as follows:

> If I may [...] refer to my work, *The Lord of the Rings*, in evidence: the names of persons and places in this story were mainly composed on patterns deliberately modelled on those of Welsh (closely similar but not identical). This element in the tale has given perhaps more pleasure to more readers than anything else in it.[2]

The critic must assume that this is a form of clue as to the foundations of the fantasy epic.

The second notion appears at several points earlier in the lecture and it emerges directly from his expatiation on "what I personally have received from the study of things Celtic" (*ibid.* 162), and what he called "the attraction of the ancient history and pre-history of these islands" (*ibid.*). His next concern was to stress

---

This essay first appeared in *Seven* 9 (1988: 57-65) and I am grateful to the editors for permission to reprint.

1 Printed in due course in *Angles and Britons: O'Donnell Lectures* (1963: 1-41). It was also included in 1983 in the collection of pieces edited by Christopher Tolkien, namely J.R.R. Tolkien, *The Monsters and the Critics and Other Essays* (1983: 162-97) from which the quotations are taken.
2 See footnote 33 in *MCE* (197). The note may well have the hindsight of 1963, when the essay was first published in written form.

that the Welsh language of Wales preserved the identity of that people,[3] and that he had always been fascinated by the linguistic contacts between the two languages.

This ancient cultural interrelationship had been of some fascination to Tolkien from early in his academic life, as is made clear by his review articles, entitled 'Philology: General Works' of 1923, 1924, and 1925.[4] In the first he had referred to shadowy personages behind Anglian settlement in the south of England (*YWES IV* 30-32); in the second, to "the dark mystery of ancient Western Europe" (*YWES V* 39) and to the Welsh and Goidelic origin of various British river names (*ibid.* 53-54); and waxing enthusiastic as to the foundation of the English Place-Name Society[5] (*ibid.* 55-60), quoting with approval the then Director's stated aim:

> We are gradually collecting facts in order to construct a series of maps of England [...] as it appeared in past ages. (*ibid.* 55)

The conclusion to this illuminating and revelatory essay is:

> In other words this study is fired by two emotions, love of the land of England, and the allurement of the riddle of the past [and so labouring] to the recapturing of fitful and tantalizing glimpses in the dark [...] (*ibid.* 65)

The third essay continued the interest in things Celtic, as in its survey of Buckinghamshire (*YWES VI* 48-50),[6] and indicates very clearly Tolkien's fascination with the late Celtic linguistic survivals in that shire (*ibid.* 50). Indeed, it is tempting to speculate that the Bree-land place-name *Chetwood* (*FotR* 161, etc.) is drawn from the British (i.e. Celtic) place-name of Buckinghamshire, *Chetwode*, which contains the Celtic *Kēton*, 'wood' (Mawer and Stenton 1925: xii, xiii, 62, 251). But let us return to the O'Donnell lecture.

Reflecting on the situation of late survival of British names, Tolkien remarks:

---

3 By temperament he was not attracted to Ireland, and so writing in 1955 observed: "I [...] find both Gaelic and the air of Ireland wholly alien" (*Letters* 219).
4 Each published in *YWES IV* (20-38); *YWES V* (26-65) and *YWES VI* (32-66).
5 He stressed the need for specialists in Celtic for such research work (*YWES V* 56).
6 I.e., the first county volume of the English Place-Name Society, *The Place-Names of Buckinghamshire* (1925), by A. Mawer and F.M. Stenton.

> [...] the view of the process which established the English language in Britain as a simple case of 'Teutons' driving out and dispossessing 'Celts' is altogether too simple. There was fusion and confusion. (*MCE* 169)

Further, despite the massive impact of the Teutonic or Germanic peoples in the east and southeast of the island

> [...] these parts [...] must once have been the most Celtic, or British, or Belgic. (*ibid.* 170)

For both Germanic and Celtic groups were "invaders"[7] (*ibid.*) entering "by similar routes." Yet, overall, despite these mythical notions of clear division,

> [...] the inhabitants of Britain, during recorded history, must have been in large part neither Celtic nor Germanic. (*ibid.* 12)

He had reflected briefly on the possible survival of a pre-Celtic and non-Indo-European language in 'Pictland,'[8] and then gone on to stress "the antiquity in Britain of Celtic language" (*ibid.* 171), the Celtic occupation having "probably some thousand years behind it" (*ibid.* 174), before the 'English adventure', itself to be "interrupted and modified, after hardly more than 300 years" by the intrusion from Scandinavia. While these incursions occurred in "historically documented times" (*ibid.*) and are known of, the same is not true of the

> similar things, historically and linguistically undocumented, though conjectured by archaeology, [which] must have occurred [...] in the celticizing of Britain. (*ibid.*)

This civilization must have had the most complex aspects – cultural mixes occurring in dialects, legends, archaeology – and yet, he stressed, so little had survived or been made luminous.

Tolkien's emphasis on this 'Belgic invasion' is another matter of considerable importance, for here, as elsewhere, he is following the (later regarded as controversial) scholarship of his friend T.F. O'Rahilly,[9] whose research work dated

---

7 In more romantic contexts, Tolkien uses the term *adventure* for a successful raid that leads to colonization, e.g., 'the English adventure'.

8 He referred to the then-fresh survey essay, 'The Pictish Language', by K.H. Jackson in Wainwright (1955: 129-66).

9 He had lectured in Oxford at various times and was well known to Tolkien's friends, Idris L. Foster, Professor of Celtic, and E.O.G. Turville-Petre, Professor of Ancient Icelandic Literature and Antiquities.

from 1940 but for whom it will be enough to refer to his *Early Irish History and Mythology* (1946),[10] a book mainly concerned with the early history of Ireland but relevant also for the neighbouring island of Britain. With regard to the Celtic settlement of Ireland in particular, he had distinguished four successive immigrations:

> 1. The Cruthin (or Priteni) after whom the islands were known to the Greeks as 'the Pretanic Islands'; in historic times they preserved their identity best in the North of Britain, where they were known to Latin writers as *Picti*; arrival some time before 500 B.C.;
>
> 2. The Érainn (= Fir Bolg) and also known as Iverni; their name (**Bolgi*) identifies them with the Belgae[11] of the Continent and of Britain; according to Irish tradition they were of the same stock as the Britons, and their own invasion legend tells how their ancestor Lugaid came from Britain and conquered Ireland; these events, perhaps occurring in the fifth century B.C.;
>
> 3. The Laginian invaders, including the Lagin, the Domnainn and the Gáloin, in the third century; and
>
> 4. The Goidil, the latest of the Celtic invaders who, coming direct from Gaul, reached Ireland between 100 and 50 B.C.

Of this vast and complex period of linguistic and social turmoil, and "the difficult and absorbing problems [...] concerning the immigrations from the European mainland [...] to Britain" (*MCE* 173), Tolkien will say little, concentrating rather on "points which have specially attracted me" (*ibid.*) – 'P-Celts' and "the speech-ancestors of the Welsh" (*ibid.*). He is also fascinated, as was K. Jackson, by the celticizing of Britain, the resultant of which was

> that the whole of Britain south of the Forth-Clyde line by the first century A.D. shared a British or 'Brittonic' civilization, 'which so far as language goes[12] formed a single linguistic province from Dumbarton and Edinburgh to Cornwall and Kent'. (*ibid.* 174)

Despite the flow of time since 'the Celtic adventures', Tolkien avers that, as to him, so to all his hearers –

> their surviving linguistic traces should be to us [...] of deep interest, as long as antiquity continues to attract the minds of men. Through them we may catch

---

10 And reprinted in 1957. Both printings were referred to by Tolkien in lectures. The book followed the ideas first put forward in a lecture given by O'Rahilly in 1929 and published as 'The Goidels and their Predecessors' in 1935.

11 Caesar (*De Bello Gallico*, Book v, 12) distinguished between the later arrivals, the maritime Britains, and those who had been in the interior from time immemorial, having ousted the earlier Priteni.

12 A qualification needed in view of the many different social units of the Celtic tribes.

a glimpse or echo of the past which archaeology alone cannot supply, the past of the land which we call our home. (*ibid.* 174-75)

He then cited as illustration of the survival of 'Celtic' legend the record of the stones of the Stonehenge monument having been carried from Pembrokeshire in Wales. This was followed by an intellectual and philological declaration as well as by his most explicit artistic statement as to the inspiration and challenge of preliterate Celtic and Welsh culture in Britain –

> then we must also ponder what that must imply: in the absorption by Celtic-speakers[13] of the traditions of predecessors, and the echoes of ancient things that can still be heard in the seemingly wild and distorted tales that survive enshrined in Celtic tongues. (*ibid.* 175)

He is equally excited by the concept that the whole transformation of British (Celtic)

> from a language of very ancient mode, an elaborately inflected and recognizable dialect of western Indo-European [...] has gone on in this island. (*ibid.* 177)

Thus that ancient thought became

> acclimatized to and naturalized in Britain; so that it belonged to the land in a way with which English could not compete. (*ibid.*)

Further,

> Latin and British appear to have been similar to one another. (*ibid.* 179)

This last observation, although not expanded, allows for Tolkien as philologist and student of pre-Christian mythology and religion to explore proto-Latin and Italo-Celtic religious beliefs,[14] as they might have been evolved and refined in England (or western Middle-earth) itself.

Now it will be clear that these philological (and philosophical) speculations, uttered as they were but a few hours after the launching of *The Two Towers* and *The Return of the King,* are almost certainly one of the most important authorial

---

13 He allows himself the thought that the archaic state of Celtic language in Britain *may,* however imperfectly, afford perceptions of "the hypothetical common Indo-European" (*MCE* 175), it being "far more archaic than [...] the earliest Latin" (*ibid.* 177).

14 Of course, all this fictive religion approximates even more toward a teleology, or doctrine of final causes and the view that developments are due to the purpose or design that is served by them.

statements surviving as to the purpose of *The Lord of the Rings*. Other evidence
survives to support this view. For the second half of the British millenium was
the time of Roman Britain,[15] and its records, archaeological and epigraphic,
were very easily accessible to the young professor of philology. There is evidence
to suggest that he was a very close reader of the journal *Antiquity: A Quarterly
Review of Archaeology*,[16] founded in 1927 and much concerned (then) with the
current developments in the archaeology and scholarship of Roman Britain. It
was these interests that led to his being invited to comment on an inscription
at an ancient site in Gloucestershire[17] by its excavator, Mortimer Wheeler. The
full details of that contribution are entitled

> 'Appendix I: The Name 'Nodens'', printed in R.E.M. Wheeler and T.V. Wheeler,
> 1932, *Report of the Prehistoric, Roman, and Post-Roman Site in Lydney Park,
> Gloucestershire*, London: Printed at the University Press by John Johnson for
> The Society of Antiquaries, 132-37.

The actual work had been done in 1928 to 1929, and had followed on earlier
excavations in 1805 and 1879. The Romano-British precinct of the god Nodens,
on the site of a prehistoric 'promontory fort', a later Roman iron mine, and
many German broaches brought there by the Roman army, are all discussed,
but the prime research is that of Tolkien.[18]

For this, no better assessment can be given than that of Christopher Hawkes, in
a pride-of-place review of the whole report. The relevant remarks run thus:

> The first five centuries of the site's history are thus instructive indeed, but undra-
> matic. The change that befell it in the years 364-67 is positively theatrical.

> The god Nodens, with his temple and all its appendages, appears on the site
> unheralded and unexplained. His name (on which Professor J.R. Tolkien [sic!]
> writes with learning and skill) appears to be Goidelic, indicating the same
> divinity that became in Irish tradition Nuada of the Silver Hand; its root

---

15 To which there are also many references in the three philological survey essays mentioned above.
16 The very first issue, that for March 1927, contained articles on: 'Lyonesse', 'The Roman Frontier in
    Britain' by R.G. Collingwood, 'Some Prehistoric Ways'; the second: 'Place-Names and Archaeology'
    by A. Mawer, an account of the 'Ancient Writers on Britain', and of palaeolithic man in Scotland.
17 The existence and significance of this scholarship of Tolkien's were first drawn to my attention in
    Cambridge in 1965 by the late Mrs N.K. Chadwick, the Celtic scholar. Her own interest in this work
    of Tolkien's may be found in Dillon and Chadwick (1967: 140 and footnote 2).
18 There seems little doubt that Tolkien was brought into the 'dig' by Robin G. Collingwood (1889-
    1943), a Roman Britain archaeologist like his father, W.G. Collingwood, and Fellow of Pembroke
    College from 1912, and thus overlapping with Tolkien there from 1925. Collingwood also visited the
    site and discusses various inscriptions in the official *Report*.

should connote 'catching', but as well as being a hunter and a fisherman he was worshipped apparently as a sun-god and certainly as a god of healing – an intriguing example of the syncretism of fourth-century mysticism working on a primitive cult. (1932: 489)[19]

He continues, referring to the secure coin dating of the building of the temple to the years 364 to 367, and to the basilical plan[20] with its unique peripheral 'chapels', and stressing that

the religious implications of the whole are admirably set forth and illustrated. (*ibid.*)

Toward the end, he observes:

The whole study makes a refreshing start on what should be a most vital approach to the rediscovery of our Dark Ages. (*ibid.* 490)

When, in 1932, Collingwood expanded the text of his classic *Roman Britain*[21] by half as much again, he gave special place in the chapter on 'Religion' (125-42) to Lydney, calling it "the most interesting temple in Britain" (*ibid.* 137), and adding:

The sudden development of this remote hill-top, on a spur of the Forest of Dean that overlooks the Severn Valley,[22] into an important religious centre, suggests that Lydney must have been one of the places in which a primitive cult had long been carried on by an un-Romanized peasantry in such a manner as to leave no trace for the archaeologist to find [...] The whole settlement was clearly a place of pilgrimage, and gives a vivid picture of the last phase of pagan religion in Roman Britain. (*ibid.* 139)

O'Rahilly, too, would pay some attention to Tolkien's comments on the god Nuadu, teasing out the sense 'cloud-maker,' and noting Tolkien's boldness in postulating for Celtic a root which "so far as is known, is peculiar to the Germanic and Baltic languages" (1946: 495-96).

Now, the point of all this research, and of the related reviewing of Tolkien's etymological contribution is that, as the young Germanic scholar manifests

19 Reviewing the whole report in a signed article of *Antiquity*, Vol. VI, No. 24, December 1932 (488-90). C.F.C. Hawkes would become Professor of European Archaeology at Oxford in 1946.
20 A reference to the building "where suppliants for healing probably repaired" cannot but remind us of this aspect of Aragorn's activities of peace in *The Return of the King*.
21 Issued first in 1923.
22 The altar is at the western end of the temple.

early in his lecturing and over some thirty years – forty if we allow for the likely
revision of the text of 'English and Welsh' – he has an informed interest in the
original 'Celtic adventures' which occurred in Britain over a thousand years,
all of them prior to the coming of the Saxons.

The final publication of the second and the third volumes of *The Lord of the
Rings* triggered off in him a public declaration of his abiding interest in "the
echoes of ancient things [...] still [...] enshrined in Celtic tongues" (*MCE* 175).
In 1932 Christopher Hawkes had pondered on the Lydney and Tolkienian
'vital' contributions to "the rediscovery of our Dark Ages" (1932: 490). It is
the contention of this present article that Hawkes had, all unwittingly, put his
finger on the fictional exploration by Tolkien of a culture with then only alluring
traces so far discovered. For in his search for a 'legend for England' – a phrase
occurring in the *Letters* to describe his artistic purpose – Tolkien was concerned
to explore both the pre-Saxon periods of British history and legend and the
subsequent dialogue between the English and the *Welsh* (his learned term[23] for
all the Celtic inhabitants of the island), particularly at the level of "village-talk
[...] what was going on beneath the cultivated surface" (*MCE* 184).

Further, he held that all the northwest of Europe[24] was and still

> is [...] a single philological province [...] interconnected in race, culture, history,
> and linguistic fusions (*ibid.* 188)

while, if one was speaking of Oxford or southern England,

> Welsh is of this soil, this island, the senior language of the men of Britain.
> (*ibid.* 189)

Indeed, in all honesty,

> It is the native language to which in unexplored desire we would still go home.
> (*ibid.* 194)

Hence it is that his last aside, quoted above, is not a credo but a statement of
achievement –

---

23 See *MCE* 183, "*wealh* was [...] a common Germanic name for a man of what we should call Celtic
   speech."
24 A useful definition of the general region fictionally known as Middle-earth.

the names of persons and places [in *The Lord of the Rings*] were [...] modelled on those of Welsh. (*ibid.* 197, footnote 33)

Clearly there is knowledge of and competence in linguistic matters British in the Tolkien academic career, as well as an inexhaustible appetite for more of the same. There is, too, a related vast area for necessary research in the early (fictional?) Gondorian history, the elvish history, and the Numenorian chronicles, for analogues, etymologies, speculative history and proto-religion of a sort that *might well* have been experienced in Britain over the 1,000 years prior to the Germanic incursions. It is, surely, the paucity of such legends – like the cited one of the Stonehenge monoliths – that Tolkien was determined to fill by his creative story. The unavoidable corollary would seem to be that this 'Welsh'/ Celtic strand to his writing,[25] "vistas of yet more legend and history,"[26] must be given the serious attention hitherto accorded only to his Old English and Old Norse analogues and borrowings.

Appendix A

Tolkien's use of the word *Welsh* would seem to be that found in Old English texts, i.e., 'foreign or non Germanic,' with the particular implication that this relates to the Celts in Britain. Thus the North Welsh are the Welsh of later history, while the South Welsh are the Cornish. Thus we should expect to find many possible Cornish elements in the (place-)names of Middle-earth, e.g.:

Middle Cornish *bar*, 'black'	- cp. Barad-dûr
Middle Cornish *du*, 'black'	- cp. Barad-dûr
[cp. Middle Cornish *bar*, 'summit']	

Middle Cornish *carn*, 'rockpile'	- cp. Carn Dûm
(for Welsh *carn*)	

Middle Cornish *bal*, 'mine', 'area of tin-working', raises further speculation about the writer's etymological intentions in the name *Balrog*.

---

25 Here, as in so many other areas, Tolkien was ahead of his time. And so, as a life vice-president of the Philological Society he would have read with delight in its *Transactions* for 1969 H. Wagner's masterly paper, 'The Origin of the Celts in the Light of Linguistic Geography' (1969: 203-50).
26 Written in 1954 (*Letters* 185).

Welsh *hen*, 'old' is to be seen in the river name *Hen Nant*, and, perhaps, in the name *Amon Hen*. [cp. Hen Barc, a locality in Carnarvonshire.]

Appendix B

Curiosity about the pattern of Celtic history and culture in Britain before the Germanic settlement was not, of course, confined to Tolkien. Famed and influential books of the period 1918 to 1950 include:

Collingwood, R.G and J.N.L. Myres, 1936, *Roman Britain and the English Settlements (The Oxford History of England, Vol. I)*, Oxford: Clarendon Press.

Kendrick, T.D. and C.F.C. Hawkes, 1932, *Archaeology in England and Wales 1914-1931*, London: Methuen & Co., Ltd.

Reed, T.D., 1944, *The Battle for Britain in the Fifth Century, An Essay in Dark Age History*, London: Methuen & Co., Ltd.

Reed, T.D., 1947, *The Rise of Wessex: A Further Essay in Dark Age History*, London: Methuen & Co., Ltd.

Sheldon, G., 1932, *The Transition from Roman Britain to Christian England AD 368-664*, London: MacMillan.

Germanic Mythology Applied – the Extension of the Literary Folk Memory[1]

Throughout all his critical and creative writing[2] Professor Tolkien has shown considerable awareness of the residuum of association in words and names from the Germanic world. Although his purpose in creating the vast world of Middle-earth[3] is an intensely moral one, it has not prevented this professional philologist from making considerable use of linguistic aesthetic. The whole theme of *The Lord of the Rings* has been cast in the form of the Heroic Quest, and made remote in its fabric from our own time and space.

The society there created (one strangely appealing and popular with many differing audiences), is continually varied and on a scale to rival the spectacle of Spenser's *Faerie Queene*. The endless perspectives of this world are quite new, yet completely familiar, and variously true in their reflections upon human experience. The mood, that *líf is lǽne*, while elegiac and so familiar from the Old English *Beowulf*[4] and *The Wanderer*, is different from the heroic pessimism of the pagan epic and the softness of later romance, since it presents a restrained hope which may be seen as having affinity with the Christian faith.

What is enormously attractive to a modern student of word lore is to trace the evocations of some of the special words and names, since these are more

---

The essay first appeared in an earlier form in *Folklore* 77.1 (Spring, 1966: 45-59) and is also found in its original form at http://www.jstor.org/stable/1258920. It is reprinted here with the kind permission of the editors of *Folklore*.

1 Both the late C.S. Lewis and his friend Professor J.R.R. Tolkien were concerned to present in the fictional form, through a mythological framework, points of view which were essentially spiritual, yet each most succeeded in their narration of adventure and quest when they enacted myths; the former used both the interplanetary sphere (for his 'science fiction' novels) and a Northern world which owed much to George MacDonald (in his children's stories about Narnia), while the latter gained success in his presentation of the world of hobbits by drawing on the peculiar richness of the traditions of Germanic mythology. While we will be concerned mainly with the latter's prose works, we cannot ignore the writings of his close friend and colleague in the faculty to whom much cross reference must be made.

2 E.g. in *Farmer Giles of Ham* (1949); *The Homecoming of Beorhtnoth, Beorhthelm's Son* (1953).

3 Handled briefly in the *The Hobbit* (1937), and more fully developed in his epic, *The Lord of the Rings*, published as: (i) *The Fellowship of the Ring* (1954); (ii) *The Two Towers* (1955); and (iii) *The Return of the King* (1955).

4 See J.R.R. Tolkien, 'Beowulf: The Monsters and the Critics' (*MCE* 19).

elusive than the scholarly apparatus, giving genealogies and tables of historical chronology, which appear at the end of the third volume. This ingredient of the whole, like the style of diction, is both heroic and evocative, and gives the dignity and remoteness needed to produce separation of the essential human soul and its general environment and condition.

Thus it is that Tolkien, being possessed of a mythopoetic imagination, has created or extended myth, both of the folklore type and that of literary associations. In the latter he may be likened to writers like Novalis, William Morris, George MacDonald, G.K. Chesterton and C.S. Lewis.[5] On the more traditional side, Tolkien, as a life-long student of Germanic stylistics, has adapted to his purpose all the formal eloquence of heroic romance: riddles, talismanic battle-cries, charms and incantations, efficacious names for weapons and horses, courtly address, parleys, defiances, curses, magical songs, exhortations to valour, the slimy speech of treachery. Growth and change[6] occur in the various languages from which the investigator pretends he draws his sources – Westron, the so-called Common Speech; Quenya, or High-Elven; Sindarin, or Grey-Elven – these last being magical tongues; the mutually incomprehensible dialects of Orkish; the slow and earthy communication of the Ents, the ancient tree-herds; and the magic lore, possessed by the various wizards.

Those who have been impressed by the epic's total impact need to have it pointed out to them that much of its nobility comes from the traditional associations, the familiar genre of heroic romance and a distinguished interpretation of the English inheritance of heroic poems and romances, in this creation of a work to deal with the various 'hideous strengths', that threaten and oppose humanity.

In his critical work, 'On Fairy Stories',[7] Professor Tolkien has shown the importance of Faërie:

---

5 Lewis may be said to overlap Tolkien at many points: talking animals, moving armies of trees (in his *Narnia* books); and in his notion of the colonization of Middle earth (sic!) by High Elves and men who escaped from Numinor (Atlantis?) in the Utter West, a mighty kingdom destroyed at that time. He specifically mentions 'Numinor and the True West' in the 'Preface' to *That Hideous Strength* (1945: viii), and states that he and Tolkien both write of the same world.

6 Although it is not possible to comment on linguistic process working in the names discussed below, the philologist will realize the relative age of many names by the absence of the Germanic sound changes of Grimm's Law, vowel fronting and the mutations.

7 A chapter in *Essays presented to Charles Williams*, (1947); also published in a slightly revised form in J.R.R. Tolkien, *Tree and Leaf* (1-81).

Fantasy, the making or glimpsing of Other-worlds, was the heart of the desire of Faerie. I desired dragons[8] with a profound desire. (*TL* 41)

This realization of the dragon symbol as a means of showing opposing evil in the world is to be found in his *Beowulf* paper (1936), *The Hobbit* (1937) and *Farmer Giles of Ham* (1949). The other monsters, wolves, trolls, goblins, dwarves, eagles are there because of a similar accretion of associations and because the author wants to say that the real life of men is of this mythical and heroic quality.

Also, the medieval world had an old-fashioned notion of characterization, here followed deliberately, although such is not fashionable with modern critics. Thus if the character is an elf or a dwarf the imagined being has his inside on the outside, his is a visible soul. This enables the qualities of men to be more to the fore, to be themselves. Because they have been dipped in myth we see them the more clearly for this essential masculinity.

While there are Celtic ingredients to this Germanic *satura lanx*, they are rather on the side and not in the foreground. The most obvious class to be so derived is that of the elves[9] possessed of a strange otherworldliness. Their immortality in the Western Land is very like the Gaelic *Tir nan Og*. Their interest in healing, the need for their ultimate passage across the sea to the West, and their language, even in its consonant clusters and syllabification, are all full of Celtic overtones. Frodo's mound and the way in which the Ring Bearers never grow older must suggest the Irish Bran.[10]

The 'Marriage of Aragorn and Arwen' is mainly Celtic in conception, particularly in its presentation of the fée losing her immortality by union with a mortal. It is like enough to the very confused situation of Pwyll, or Manawyddan, and Rhiannon in the *Mabinogion*. Especially Celtic is the pace and movement in the narrative, something very analogous to the later Arthurian romances in the *Mabinogion*. The writer's apparent editorial problems with the Red Book of Westmarch and the calendar difficulties of the Westlands, irresistibly suggest parallels with the Red Book of Hergest and the White Book of Rhydderch.

---

8 Representative studies of the dragon motif are: (1) Mackenzie (1936-37: 157-73); (2) Davidson (1950: 169-85). C.S. Lewis stresses the Dragon motif in *The Voyage of the Dawn Treader* (1952), chap. 6f.
9 Authority for various types of elves, such as the wood-elves of *The Hobbit*, is also to be found in the crusty Dark and Black Elves of the *Gylfaginning*.
10 See especially, *Bran the Blessed in Arthurian Romance*, by Helaine Newstead (1939).

Celtic names aside, the emotive associations engendered by mention of the ring
and the love of Faramir and Éowyn are those of thirteenth-century German
literature and an acquaintance with the world of the *Reginsmal*, *Fafnismal* and
the *Brünhildlied*. In passages like the mythic story of Isildur, Aragorn's ancestor,
swimming the Anduin, and losing in the river the ring of power, we have a situation reminiscent of the later poems of the *Poetic Edda* and the *Nibelungenlied*.
The sensation is one of dealing with materials drawn from archetypal versions
of the medieval treasure stories. The power of the treasure to kill is best seen
in Tolkien's work, *The Hobbit*, where lust for gold "upon which a dragon has
long brooded" (276), is the death of Thorin, the dwarf leader long exiled from
his kingdom under the Mountain.

The ethos of the Nibelungs comes across strongly in the 'Ring-world', with
the accumulated associations of Draupnir, Balder's ring, Sigurth's treasure, and
Siegfried's ring, the forests, the caverns and the dark mills of Saruman's Tower
and of the land of Mordor. It is impossible not to feel that the hobbits bring a
Parsifal innocence into this realm of shadows. Mirkwood is found on maps for
the epic, and is particularly well described in the journey of treasure-seekers in
The Hobbit. Mirkwood does not occur in the more northern writings of Snorri
Sturluson, naturally enough, since its associations are with Germanic peoples
still on the Continent and the *Nibelungenlied* in particular.[11]

From the Germanic world as revealed in the Icelandic Sagas, we have only those
features usually held to have been common Germanic: barrows and barrow
wights (malignant grave spirits which seem to prefigure the story of Glam in
Grettissaga); trolls of the mountains; the interest in horses, particularly among
the Rohirrim who dwell on a wide grassy plain: and the courage and chivalry
of this same race who will leave their homes to answer the summons of their
allies. They feel no fear since they do not dread defeat, providing that they
themselves die like heroes. Theirs is a more evolved chivalry than that of the
primitive Berserk, whose type is strongly evoked by the battle fury of Beorn,
half man half beast, in *The Hobbit*.

---

11 It may be noted that the most frightening aspect of Mirkwood is the eyes in the forest (*Hobbit* 152),
   and that this symbol is developed as the symbol of Sauron, the Dark Lord, in the epic.

The final battle sequences recall the Ragnarøk, where representatives of all races of men, the dead and even the wolves of the *Vøluspá* come against each other. A close reading of the *Gylfaginning* will suggest many parallels to *The Lord of the Rings*, as the movement of both is towards the Last Battle at the Coming of Darkness, even as the Misty Mountains remind us, in various ways, of Niflheim.

When Aragorn rides to the kingdom of the dead, we are inevitably reminded of Hermodr's ride to Hel after the slaying of Balder. Gimli's fall at the entrance recalls the "pit of Stumbling, Hel's threshold, by which one enters," (*Gylfaginning*, ch. XXXIV).

The sense of an earlier civilization passed into decay is pervasive. Valleys and plains are filled with the ruined cities of the former kingdoms. There lurk in the wasteland marshes the rotting yet half mummified bodies of warriors of old. The tombs of forgotten heroes dot the hill tops. Place-names[12] whose origin is obvious or explained recall battles of long ago. When the Fellowship leaves Lothlórien Frodo looks at Galadriel and she seems to him "a living vision of that which has already been left far behind [in Númenor] by the flowing stream of Time" (*FotR* 389). It is the presence of the past and constant reminder of the continuance of Middle-earth which gives such power to the mythic historical suggestions unobtrusively made throughout.

Yet the Tolkien world turns in the main to that of the Early English, perhaps before their departure from the Continent of Europe. Many names are formed from Old English roots which connect with this world simply by glossing their referends. Shelob ('she-spider') glosses the Old English *lobbe* and suggests to the linguist the associations with the psalms and the various pejorative contexts in which the word is used in Old English literature. (The popular horror at spiders is well used in *The Hobbit* (171), where Bilbo's insult word at the giant spiders in Mirkwood is 'attercop', from *atter-coppe*, poison head.) The primeval Balrog, one of Gandalf's foes, is indeed 'evil-exciter' (bealu, 'evil', and wregan, 'to arouse'), and the association is recalled of the Gnomic account of the storm:

---

12 The explanation of apparently prosaic place names as survivals of past glories is a feature even in the early *Farmer Giles of Ham*, e.g.; Farthingho (8), Worminghall (76-77), Oakley, etc.

hwīlum ic sceal ȳþa wrēgan
from time to time I (as storm) must needs excite the waves

A similar association is to be found in the name of the Goblin leader, Bolg (in *The Hobbit*). This anthroponym is derived from *belgan*, 'to cause oneself to swell with anger'.

Smaug, the great worm of *The Hobbit*, jealously guards the hoarded treasure he has seized from the dwarves of the Lonely Mountain, by means of fire and by such means (even as the *Beowulf* dragon) he would burn the city of the men of Esgaroth. The name is an old form based on the verb *smēocan*, 'to emit smoke'.[13]

The name *Arkenstone*, chief treasure in the Hoard beneath the Lonely Mountain, means 'peerless stone' and it is the one object for which the cold-hearted dwarf-leader Thorin is prepared to make any sacrifice. The supreme 'treasure' of the aristocratic and heroic world is a cold gem from the dragon's store. As the Prologue to *The Fellowship of the Ring* makes it clear, hobbits were devoted to *mathom* objects, defined thus:

> for anything that Hobbits had no immediate use for, but were unwilling to throw away, they called a mathom. Their dwellings were apt to become rather crowded with *mathoms*, and many of the presents that passed from hand to hand were of that sort. (15)

This use of the word is interesting since all the Old English references to the word suggest that it is a jewel, treasure, gold, or some sort of costly gift. Only in Icelandic do we find that the word may signify a more ordinary 'present' or 'gift'. Yet among the innocent hobbits the *mathom* is a set of spoons or an umbrella. This is a salutary corrective to the death-bringing presents and hoards, of the heroic and aristocratic world, as is the hobbit custom of giving simple and vaguely useful objects to all one's acquaintances as often as possible.

A second group of names adds a reality, if purely a scholarly one, by derivations: 'Middle-earth' recalls, deliberately, the Old English *middangeard* and the Old

---

13 Tolkien himself in a letter published in the *Observer* on February 20th 1938 and unknown to the author of this essay at the time of writing his article, provides an etymology to the name with the following words: "The dragon bears as name – a pseudonym – the past tense of the primitive Germanic verb *Smugan*, to squeeze through a hole: a low philological jest" (*Letters* 31).

Norse *miðgarð*; the name of Gandalf ('magic elf') is familiar from the *Vǫluspá* and *Gylfaginning* (ch. XIV), even though the word itself comes from a famed dwarf catalogue. Gandalf, inevitably, suggests the god Heimdallr, the White God, as warden, magician and rallier of the forces of good. The dwarf company of *The Hobbit* are nearly all found in the *Gylfaginning* catalogue – Kili, Fili, Dori, Nori, Ori, Oinn, Gloinn, Bifurr, Bafurr (for Bofur), Bomburr, and their leader Thorinn. Dvalin is given special significance by Tolkien, and this is appropriate in view of his fame in the Norse poetry and in Snorri's prose works.

It must, however, be stressed that for much of the detail in the depiction of the dwarves, the author has had to go far beyond the few extant references to that people. The *Vǫluspá* comment that "the dwarves are groaning before their stone doors" scarcely prepares us for the detailed world of the Kingdom under the Mountain, or the storied past associated with the Mines of Moria. The most prominent dwarf, Gimle (sic!), creates in his name a complex of associations.[14] Etymologically it must suggest 'gimlet', an appropriate notion of boring for a delver and rock cutter ("There are good bones in this country"). Yet Gimle is sad at heart, for his race is dying and finally he passes from the Western havens to the land of immortality across the sea. Although this otherworld is left suitably vague, it is to be associated in more than name with the pagan paradise:

> At the southern end of heaven is that hall which is fairest of all, and brighter than the sun; it is called Gimle. (*Gylfaginning*, ch. XVII)

An example of his whimsical use of great names is Garm, dog to Farmer Giles, and an endearing mixture of wisdom, cowardice, truculence and loyalty. This was also the name of the foremost of hounds, according to the Norse world (*Gylfaginning*, ch. XLI), an association which makes Garm's circumspect behaviour, whenever dragon Chrysophylax appears to be dangerous, the more ironical.

In other instances Professor Tolkien has taken a quite standard Old English word and elaborated it wondrously from a lexical point of departure, from which it was tempting to speculate. *Ent* is a perfectly good word for 'giant',

---

14 Here the activities, though not the temperament, of MacDonald's goblins are an influence. See *The Princess and the Goblin* (1872), passim.

and is so used in various glosses on the Latin. It is, however, very frequently used in the famed verse half-line, *enta geweorc*, 'the creation(s) of the giants', the Saxon comment on the massive stone ruins of Roman buildings. The word *ent* was also used, somewhat later by Ælfric in a comment on Goliath.[15] By rather a Druidic twist, ents are now giant tree-herds of great age, possessed of deep eyes, twiggy beards and rumbly voices. Although slow to act, they can be roused by the hewing of their wards and when the wizard Saruman begins the felling of the forests, they march to destroy his tower and fortifications and so produce a massive series of ruins, *enta geweorc*, par excellence. Something of the possible destructive forces of these ancient vegetation spirits is to be found not in the personality so much as in the title of Fangorn, whose name means literally 'harmful unhealthy clutch'. Because of their age and strength it is right to hold them in respect.

The home of black magic and destruction is Saruman's fortress of Orthanc. The slippery wizard's name is made up from a primitive spelling of *searu*, meaning 'device, design, contrivance, trick', and, in some contexts, 'treacherous art, wile, stratagem'. Appropriately his tower is Orthanc, 'inborn thought', a word which is used in Old English to gloss *ingenium* and *astutia*. Tolkien has made full use of this possible pejorative sense development.

Orc is an even more interesting term in this mythical stylistic. Although it does occur in the early work, *The Hobbit* (150), in the list of evil forces to the south of Mirkwood, "goblins, hobgoblins and orcs of the worst description," its main use then is in the name of the sword Orcrist ('goblin cleaver'). But the orcs in the epic are something much more sinister than the goblins. The Old English *orc*, a word taken early from the Latin *Orcus* (the god of the world of the infernal regions), and glossed as *hel-deofol*, seems to have had unnatural and ghastly associations. Its best known occurrence is in the famous (and disputed) Beowulfian *orc-nēas* (l. 112). The usual interpretation of this word is 'corpse from the underworld, phantom, spectre', and may also be associated with the

---

15 The influence of George MacDonald on Tolkien's tree men cannot be discounted. But the form of evil tree moving at dusk, in the former's Ash-tree (*Phantastes*, 1858), is rather to be found in the old grey willow-man (*FotR* 127-33 and *Bombadil* 12-13).

ghastly *ne-fugolas* (*Genesis*, l. 2158) 'carrion birds', of Old English pieces.[16] It seems to have originated from the practice of necromancy by which evil spirits were conjured by means of corpses back from the dead.

It is also possible that Tolkien's *orcs* owe something to Ariosto's *orco*, or to the character Orc, found in William Blake's prophetic works, where the evil character is needed in the transition between two ages.

The second syllable of the Beowulfian compound, *-nēas*, is usually held to be a cognate form of the (early) Gothic *naus*, 'corpse', and so the element **naz-* is not too far from this ghastly presence. Very appropriately, then, may we see the *nazgûl*, 'hovering birds of prey', as meaning etymologically 'corpse-ghouls', by a double suggestion of the horrific.[17]

Another involved but linguistically suggestive etymology is Gollum's original name, Smeagol and that of the brother he murdered (in Cain and Abel fashion), Deagol. The first name is to be associated with *smeagan*, 'to peer into, investigate'; the second with *deagol*, 'secret, hidden', and *dieglan* 'to hide'. This fits the early situation in that Smeagol was possessed of insatiable curiosity, while Deagol was secretive. *Smēa-wyrm*, 'a penetrating worm' (and an excellent description of Gollum), is a compound very familiar from the Old English *Leechdoms*.

Another interesting etymology is that for *warg*, a wolf-like creature, continually in league with goblins in *The Hobbit* (e.g. 112). Old English literature uses the word 'wearg' of human beings, as meaning 'villain, felon, criminal'; of other creatures, as meaning 'monster, malignant being, evil-spirit'. According to the *Blickling Homilies*, these creatures dwell under stones. By playing on both senses the reader is given the impression of shape-changers, outlaws, becoming bestial and so preying on humans and animals alike, yet able still to plot with evil-doers, and still going on two feet, like the goblins. This interpretation is strengthened by several passages where a distinction is made between 'wargs' and 'wild wolves'.

---

16 For a discussion of this aspect of the despoiling of the dead by carrion birds and beasts, see the Essay in the Appendix to the present volume, 'Othin in England – Evidence from the Poetry for a Cult of Woden in Anglo-Saxon England', on pp. 237-58.
17 Compare the grim battle atmosphere in *Exodus* (c. l. 160), where some form of spectre is implied.

A locus communis of Old English poetry, the 'birds and beasts of battle'[18] assembling as harbingers of the fray and 'greedy for carrion', is a feature of battles of the Heroic Age and as such is often used, particularly in the preliminaries for the Battle of the Five Armies (*Hobbit*); there wolves, ravens (268ff.) and eagles are to the fore. Perhaps because of their eminence in the bird kingdom Tolkien uses eagles as supreme forces of good which appear at decisive moments in both the great battle sequences.[19] As in Old Norse, where the ravens Huginn and Muninn were informants for Othin, so the raven (*Hobbit* 268), is made into a sage battle counsellor. In his dealings with raven and eagles, as well as in his often adopted disguise as an old man, Gandalf often suggests Othin, but it is only in wisdom and power that the war god influences the wizard's character.

The realm of evil towards which the quest takes the protagonist is Mordor, a noun which in Old English means 'mortal sin', 'great wickedness, torment, great misery', as well as the obvious 'murder'. It also has early glossary associations with 'perdition' and 'the devil'. It is difficult to avoid equating Mordor with the Scandinavian concept of Múspell: "That land is light and hot, burning and impassable, and in the south" (*Gylfaginning*, ch. IV); "The sons of Múspell shall go forth harrying" (*ibid.*, ch. XIII). And the final success of Frodo and Sam in destroying the ring (*RotK* 224) reminds us of the Norse verses:

> The rocks are falling,   and fiends are reeling,
> Heroes tread Hel-way,   heaven is cloven. (*Gylfaginning*, ch. LI)

The earlier panoramic view which Frodo obtains from a great peak south of the Falls of Rauros contains many vignettes that parallel the various tokens by which we are to know that the Ragnarøk is come:

> Horsemen were galloping on the grass of Rohan; wolves poured from Isengard. From the havens of Harad ships of war put out to sea and out of the East men were moving endlessly: swordsmen, spearmen, bowmen upon horses [...] (*FotR* 417)

---

18 See again the Essay in the Appendix of this volume. It is also suggested by C.S. Lewis, *The Horse and His Boy* (1954b: 164, 167).
19 The mountain eyrie to which Gandalf and the treasure seekers are carried in *The Hobbit* (120-23), is based on the Old Norse Hlidskjalf, 'cliff-shelf', which was one of Odin's abodes and a famed lookout. The phrase 'Great Shelf' (200) reinforces the identification. Similarly, Gandalf is carried away by the eagle, after the contest with the Balrog, to a mountain crest where he rests.

Much of the language has associations with the countryside and the every day life of ordinary folk. At the level of this more friendly and sociable existence the name 'hobbit' is interesting. It does perforce suggest the rustic *hob* (as in *hobgoblin*), and is familiar as a generic name for a clown or rustic. The custom of the race's dwelling in holes inevitably suggests that the second element may have something to do with 'rabbit'. The Great Eagle tells Bilbo that he need not squirm like a rabbit, even if he looks like one. (*Hobbit* 123), and Thorin, enraged, calls Bilbo "descendant of rats" (*ibid.* 286). The name is actually a vulgarism, *pace* Tolkien, from an original *holbytla*, which comes from *hol* 'hole, hollow, den', and *bytla* 'a hammerer, builder'.

Goldberry and Bombadil, being spirits of the countryside, do not have names with learned or heroic associations. The first is, perhaps, a reminder of Goldborough, the English heroine of that rather rollicking romance *Havelok* (see Skeat, 1889). Both characters and names suggest the mummers' play, the nature and spirit of which is repeated in the volume of poems, *The Adventures of Tom Bombadil*. He is a nature guardian and has existed from the beginning, "before the kings and the graves and the barrow-wights [...] when the elves passed" (*FotR* 142).

Sauron, the evil lord of Mordor, who is never seen, suggests by his name pain and suffering (O.E. *sar*), and some form of reptilian evil.

The name of the hero, Frodo, rather defies analysis and perhaps this is intended. By his action in carrying the Ring of Power back to its origins in the Mount of Doom (=Judgement?), he restores some sort of stability to the known world. In view of this, one is reminded of (King) Frodi the Peaceful of Denmark,[20] particularly famed for his contempt of death (Saxo Grammaticus, lib. xii). It is also the sort of name an old chronicler (like the putative compiler of the *Red Book*) would have delighted to give to his hero as an eponym, with the added advantage of Frodi of Denmark being a son of Fridleif, himself a son of Skjold, the son of Odin. Specific suggestions for the etymology in Old English would be the cognate *friðo*, 'peace', and the adjective, *frōd*, meaning 'wise' or 'advanced in years', both of which were eminently true of Frodo. Finally there

---

20 See Olrik (1919: 446ff) and the translation of Eirikr Magnusson and William Morris of *Grottasongr*, found in Morris (1915), esp. pp. 13-17.

is the vague but highly gratifying association with Frothi, the Dragon-Slayer (The Viking Saga of Frothi).

Themes made familiar to us from their recurrence in Dark Age literature are to be found continually in Tolkien's writing. In *The Hobbit* we find:

the *comitatus* loyalty in the dwarves of Thorin's band;

the splendidly heroic last stand in the face of the impossible odds (294ff.);

the bond between a warrior and his sister's son (for this reason Fili and Kili throw away their lives for their uncle, Thorin);

the heroic (and especially dwarvish) lust for treasure "the power that gold has, upon which a dragon has long brooded" (275).

The epic, being much more highly wrought, tends to avoid the simpler statements of the shorter works, yet almost all the practical and heroic sentiments (as listed, for example, in the *Hávamál*, or the *Gnomic Verses*) find memorable expression:

the unconsolable grief of a leader whose heir is (apparently) slain – Denethor over Faramir;

the need for the host to be hospitable to strangers (*passim*);

the false counsellor (Wormstongue) who casts doubt upon the valour of the visiting leader (Aragorn);

the courage and will of the hero must operate under the shadow of fate and he is doomed to final failure (not true for Frodo, but thought by Boromir to be the ethical system);

the need to respond when a call to duty is made – "when things are in danger someone has to give them up, lose them, so that others may keep them," (*RotK* 309);

the council of war where representatives of the several parties state their views (in the house of Elrond).

The feel for language goes far beyond the Germanic names and legends discussed. 'Right' names have been achieved for the many races of this landscape, and specimens of the distinctive speeches are given for every people, from the beauty of High Elvish, to the snarling gutteral cries of the monstrous orcs. The subtleties of language are seen to the best advantage in his nature descriptions. The allegation that Tolkien's prose style is a fabric drawn from William Morris and George Dasent indicates little imaginative response to the accounts of the streams and valleys of the paradisiacal land of Ithilien (e.g. the wood described in *TT* 258), and the wreckage of Saruman's fortress, or the harsh wasteland landscapes round Mordor:

> All dead, all rotten. Elves and men and orcs. The Dead Marshes. There was a great battle long ago, so they told him when Smeagol was young, when I was young before the Precious (the One Ring) came. It was a great battle. Tall men with long swords and terrible elves, and Orcses shrieking. They fought on the plain for days and months at the Black Gates. But the Marshes have grown since then, swallowing up the graves; always creeping, creeping. (*TT* 235)

All this complex creation, much of which is sheer invention, is myth, although it scarcely conforms to the broad definition of myth as being some sort of adumbration of what was once either fact, or felt to be fact, or even desired to be fact. We might add the further dimension of what, in antiquarian writing, was deliberately created to convey a sense of the past, as a Virgil or an Ovid, an Ariosto or a Spenser, or the *Beowulf* poet achieved – a mingling of past and present, to establish a sense of man's impermanence. The literary device of *contaminatio*, or the mingling of distinct sources, is all the more effective when applied to the legendary past and all the keener in its appeal, when the antiquarian realizes that a way of life and thought, which had much to commend it must needs be rescued from oblivion.

The fusion of elements from various sides, Celtic and the Arthurian preliminaries, Germanic primitive, Scandinavian and Middle High German, is necessary as a bridge between this literary world of Middle-earth and our world, the Age of Men, the Fourth Age. History, through the use of myth, is made to appear a cycle. The events of the epic close the Third Age and reach us particularly through the hobbits who can be seen as actual vehicles of the age change. Although this is only suggested in the vaguest fashion, we may like to think of the First Age as that of the Greeks, the Second as that of the Celts, largely departed, and the Third Age as a sort of Germanic Heroic period, viewed in an aristocratic Beowulfian twilight, before a Fourth Age, potentially Christian, where 'the One' really rules fate, and, as was the case with Bilbo, Frodo and the other hobbits, burdens of power and of choice, though not in the form of the 'Rings', will fall on ordinary people.

The real name, halfling, apart from suggesting persons half human size, indicates that they are half-fairy, half-man, yet neither. Possessed of almost ethereal qualities beside the dwarf sons of earth, they have in their simplicity and domesticity avoided the idealistic excesses of the Rohirrim and the Byzantine splendour and decadence of Gondor, in the last survivors of the old kingdom of Númenor, grouped about their capital, Minas Tirith. They will survive for the new age, while other races fall. And, as survivors, they have the responsibilities of the great dynasties they replace. As the appendices indicate, in several generations the descendant of a simple Sam or a Merry may have the authority of a noble born Faramir.

In a real sense we were prepared for the cyclic moment by the rise of Giles from relative obscurity to rank and responsibility, as the king and his knights ceased to fulfil their functions in that miniscule Middle-earth, Ham or Thame, in the early and simpler comic-heroic story, *Farmer Giles of Ham*.

Yet even the good must pass away. The immortal elves must go and cross the sea and Gandalf, the white wizard, will eventually leave Middle-earth for some land of immortality, as will the three Ring-bearers, Bilbo, Frodo and Sam, and the dwarf Gimli who seems to be allowed this in return for his dedication and slow purging away of the grosser dwarf fibre. But all the rest must die, with no hope of after-life, as must Arwen the elf-princess, who gave up her immortality to marry Aragorn, a king, but a mortal.

The total achievement of Professor Tolkien in his mythical works is to re-interpret the ethos of the Heroic Age, to stress for the English the cyclic nature of history by an imaginative construct of the world before our own, and by the careful linking of it with the Second and First Ages before, – and our Fourth Age, our age, the period of men immediately following. More specifically he has recreated a passing world, one well caught in the epic *Beowulf*, with its similar aura of the complex myth and history from all the Germanic past, and its awareness of Wyrd, or fate, which rules the universe.

By his skilled use of a linguistic esthetic he has made a number of highly ingenious and wholly plausible essays at materials, perhaps in the folk-memory, but never fully recorded. Unlike the far-traveller, the name-stringing poet of *Wīdsīth*, he has given us the close-knit fabric of a Germanic-type life, and in human fashion shown us what it means when peoples rise and fall. While much is hinted at which is not developed, enough is given to suggest a past rich as that depicted in the *Beowulf.* For both works, despite the vague suggestion of a Christian hereafter, are pagan and look at man's deeds and their inevitable destruction, at life and death, the presence of evil and doom, the necessary result of being human. The necessity for change and the inevitable return of destructive forces is well phrased at the conclusion of the earlier work

> 'Ere long now' Gandalf was saying, 'the Forest will grow somewhat more wholesome. The North is freed from that horror for many an age. Yet I wish he (the Necromancer) were banished from the world.' 'It would be well, indeed,' said Elrond, 'but I fear that will not come about in this age of the world, or for many after'. (*Hobbit* 308)

While the treatment is heroic and its formal affiliations romantic, the mood is elegiac, as in *The Wanderer,* and best summed up in the lines Tolkien[21] took from *Wīdsīth* to apply to *Beowulf*

> līf is læne: eal scæceð leoht and lif somod
> Life is fleeting: everything departs, light and life together

Professor Tolkien may be seen as the most complex of modern myth-makers. While the form of his writing is heroic-romance-elegy, the use of folk-epic and Northern mythological imagination produces a remarkable depth and so increases the force of his moral and theological scheme. Like all true myth the epic bears no specific message, despite its heavy overtones of moral significance. It has mythic scope and its quality of originality is all the more enhanced by being fused to materials which give it vast sweep and mythic timelessness.

---

21 See 'Beowulf: The Monster and the Critics' (*MCE* 19).

Perilous Roads to the East, from Weathertop and through the Borgo Pass

> 2 November, morning [...] There is a strange heaviness in the air - I say heaviness for want of a better word; I mean that it oppresses us both, it is very cold. [...] The country gets wilder as we go, and the great spurs of the Carpathians [...] now seem to gather round us and tower in front [...] By morning we shall reach the Borgo Pass.[1] (Stoker 1897: 313)

> [...] the Riders themselves do not see the world of light as we do [...] In the dark they perceive many signs and forms that are hidden from us. And at all times they smell the blood of living things, desiring it and hating it. (*FotR* 202)

These two quotations may serve very well to focus the reader of the early parts of Tolkien's great epic on the similar (textual) atmospherics of the world outside the Shire, as so soon experienced by Frodo and his party, in *The Lord of the Rings*, to that encountered by those who also venture from a safe land into a dangerous and threatening unknown, very much as occurs in Stoker's vampire novel, *Dracula* (1897). For the present, however, no more is suggested than the remarkable closeness of style and motif in various minatory parts of the last two chapters, 'A Knife in the Dark' and 'Flight to the Ford' in Book One of *The Fellowship of the Ring* to the last part (chapters XXVI and XXVII) of Stoker's *Dracula*. In both cases, the would-be removers of a demonic force experience a terrible shock when they leave their ordinary comfortable and civilized world far behind in their mission to the east to destroy a ghastly evil incarnate in their place and age.

This is a somewhat modified version of a paper, with the same name, which first appeared in *Minas Tirith Evening Star* 17.1 (1988: 10-12) and is here reprinted with the kind permission of its editors. Throughout this article all specific references are now made to the text of the Norton Critical Edition of Bram Stoker's *Dracula* (1997), as edited by Nina Auerbach and David J. Skal.

1 Compare: "The hills grew nearer [...] Often rising almost to a thousand feet and here and there falling [...] to passes leading to the eastern lands beyond." (*FotR* 197)

The justification for this proposed comparison and linked exercise in both possible source-hunting and similarly linked atmospherics must be, initially, to establish sequentially the closeness of Tolkien's text to the actual Stoker phrases or, more generally, to his plotted style. For the text, one earlier in date, is not apparently presented as one of cataclysmal threat to the home of those now venturing east to Rumania and beyond. These very plausible links are now given with some exactness of reference.

Similar details

From Stoker's climactic pursuit narrative in his novel's Chapter XXVI (that one being largely concerned with Dracula's attempt to escape from England to his native region), we may note :

> the departure for the East (from London) of the band of noble friends, on their mission to seek out Dracula's Castle east of the Slovaks and to destroy him there – a motif to be compared closely with the little band of hobbits leaving the Shire and Bree to return the One Ring to the source of its making in the dangerous and unknown East, and thereby destroy it;

> the taking back to its origins by both road and by water the most evil talisman, the undead Dracula himself in his coffin, the 'box' of Transylvanian earth, and so we may compare the like attempt at bearing back to its source for its destruction there (the terrible power vested in) the One Ring;

> Dracula's own frightening power at night to "summon fog and storm and snow and his wolves"[2] to threaten his foes – a like potency and power being possessed by both Sauron and the Witch-king of Angmar in *The Lord of the Rings*;

> the further transport east of the evil to its home region again, for "The Count in his box, then, was on a river [either the Pruth or the Sereth] running up round the Borgo Pass, in an open boat propelled probably by either oars or poles" (306) – a passage which may be compared closely with the later travel of Frodo and the Ring down the River Anduin in Tolkien's text;

> Dr Van Helsing's intention to take Madame Mina to the east (for her nature is now part evil due to vampire bite), for her cure, "right into the heart of the enemy's country;" an action which may well be compared to Strider's guiding the soon-to-be wounded Frodo east towards Rivendell, and then the wounded Frodo's own free decision to take the ring still further to Mount Doom;

and, similarly, many motifs of parallel structure between the tales, such as

---

2 This last is, perhaps, a more major motif in Tolkien's *The Hobbit* (1937), particularly in the various pursuits just before the climactic Battle of the Five Armies.

the guardianship of the vampire-hurt Mina by Dr van Helsing, a task which may be likened to the role of caring for Frodo that is assumed by both Gandalf and Strider.

Further, from the last chapter of *Dracula*, no. XXVII, we may note:

"the [vampire-given] scar on Mina's forehead," to be compared with the similar obscene contact wound on Frodo's left shoulder (*FotR* 208);

the need for furious speed in the pursuit/pursuers – "we are traveling fast [...] The Professor seems tireless; all day he would not take rest" (312), and then for the reader to compare this to Strider's urgings forward, and the later frantic ride to the Ford (*FotR* 195ff and 225); and then

"There is a strange heaviness in the air – I say heaviness for want of a better word; I mean that it oppresses us [...], it is very cold" in *Dracula* (313), to be put alongside "All seemed quiet and still, but Frodo felt a cold dread [...] he huddled closer to the fire" (*FotR* 207).

The closeness of these particular selected passages comes from the fact that both texts have those journeying far beyond their familiar safe world fearfully huddling close to a protective hilltop fire, as in *Dracula* – for "The morning is bitterly cold" (313) –, as they seek to undo demonic evil from the east (316). Yet these two hurt persons, both Mina and Frodo are now so peculiarly vulnerable to malign and occult influences, both, necessarily yielding to some form of 'hypnotic sleep' (as in *Dracula*, Ch. XXVII). The protector figure in each case nurtures a tiny fire, while the hurt figure can eat but little and is not entirely in the world of her/his faithful supporters.

Pursuit and Assault

The two most distinct situational and atmospheric parallels in both (eastern-set and so climactic) fantasies are those concerned with the movement of distant figures along the road from the west, and soon with ghastly undead assailants pressing toward the fragile circle of protection, although the pattern of events occurs in different order in the two texts.

I sprang up and stood beside him on the rock [...] From the height where we were it was possible to see a great distance [...] straight in front [...] came a group of mounted men hurrying along; in the midst of them there was a cart [...] two horsemen follow fast up from the south [and] on the north side two other men, riding at breakneck speed. (Stoker 1897: 322)

This account of Mina's view of the chase of the central group, of the move-ment 'home' of Dracula's box, and then the converging of the parties, is an uncanny anticipation of both Frodo's vantage sighting of "two black specks going westward, and three others creeping eastward to meet them" (*FotR* 200), and then the later furious pursuit of himself to the Ford by the ghastly Black Riders (*ibid.* 225-27).

Prior to the sighting of the terrible galloping riders, Mina is at grave risk, despite the presence of the wise Van Helsing, his use of the sacred wafer, broken fine (1897: 316), the marking of a protective 'Holy circle' on the ground, and the protective blazing fire, which needs replenishing, in "the cold hour, when nature is at its lowest" (*ibid.*). The terrible avenging vampire women with their trailing garments, as they are calling Mina, are described thus by Van Helsing:

> In the cold hour the fire began to die [...] now the snow came [...] and with it a chill mist; [...] it seemed as though the snow flurries and the wreaths of mist took shape as of women [...]. All was in dead, grim silence [...] their weird figures drew near and circled round [...] their laugh 'Come, sister. Come to us. Come! [...] through the silence of the night [...] At the first coming of the dawn the horrid figures melted in the swirling mist. (*ibid.* 316-18)

A like threat came to Frodo and his friends in a similar protective circle on Weathertop, where, backs to the central fire,

> each gazing into the shadows [...] they felt, rather than saw, a shadow rise [...] three or four tall black figures – the shapes slowly advanced (*FotR* 207)

In the Tolkienian passage, one person, Frodo, breaks out of the protective cir-cle, and so sustains the dire wound of the Morgul blade, a thrust which binds him even more to the wraiths who can now call to him so potently, "silently commanding him to wait" (*FotR* 225). And we may recall, to our profit and elucidation, the sober reflection to his readers of Van Helsing, on those who might essay to kill in such a place a ghoulish vampire,

> Ah, I doubt not that in old time, when such things were, many a man who set out to do such a task as mine, found at the last his heart fail him, and then his nerve. So he delay and delay, till the mere beauty of the wanton Undead have hypnotise him, and he remain on and on, until sunset come [...] and there remain one more victim to swell the grim and grisly ranks of the Undead! (Stoker 1897: 319)

It would seem clear that the recollection of the analogous passages in Stoker's *Dracula* much intensifies our concern for the possible fate of Tolkien's Frodo, when he is surrounded on Weathertop by a similarly undead circle of deadly foes.

Conclusion

It is not now claimed that the prime specific – or only – source for Tolkien's Black Riders is to be found amongst Stoker's circle of [women] vampires, still less that Sauron's minions and reign of terror may be equated with Count Dracula and his vampire followers and victims. However, there is no doubt that images very similar to those of the late Victorian psychological thriller are to be found throughout *The Fellowship of the Ring*, especially in his passages about the reluctant hero's journeyings to the east with the One Ring.

Further, the style of the vicious pursuit itself and a view down on the pursuers approaching fast may indeed also be loosely equated with certain Highlands sequences in John Buchan's 1915 thriller, *The Thirty-Nine Steps*, – much as has been done by Robert Giddings and Elizabeth Holland in their study of Tolkien's sources, *J. R. R. Tolkien: The Shores of Middle-earth* (1981: 37-39).[3] However, there is much less similarity between Buchan's and Tolkien's texts, than with Stoker's occult and demonic all-consuming furies, and their undead demonic urge for possession.

As was stressed at the outset, we may not assert with complete confidence that Bram Stoker's Gothic text did influence Tolkien, very possible though that is, but, rather, that both texts have a common pattern – as found in the late Victorian and Georgian mental climates – of near demonic motifs which seize the imagination in a horrible haunting fashion, namely,

> a deadly pursuit in a central European/Middle-earth unfamiliar setting of
> heroic and selfless visitors far from the safety of their home in the west;

---

3 These critics are astute in their discussion of Tolkien's debt of a possible (part-)motif to Buchan, but they certainly miss the much more demonic element in the Black Riders. We may not doubt, however, that both novels were read by the fantasist-to-be at a formative stage in his development, the vastly popular Buchan text being issued in his twenty-third year, and the Stoker one available to him when very much younger.

a lofty vantage point from which the pursued may see madly galloping pursuing horsemen far down below;

the (deliberate) journeying into the Enemy's territory to undo and destroy already unleashed and rampant evil;

the warm blood of the heroic venturers drawing upon them the pursuit of the ghoulish undead;

a deadly attempt at spiritual breaching of the (magic) circle and its protective fire; and

the (attempted) diabolic stabbing of the hated leader of the still living and now intended victim by the already undead.

This last motif, that of the 'Un-dead' (Stoker's term), points up the essential difference between the two, for whereas Frodo merely struck defensively at the Lord of the Nazgûl (*FotR* 210), in *Dracula* the stabbing knife would be used to put 'the King-Vampire' (320), the Count, to his final rest –

> But, on the instant, came the sweep and flash of Jonathan's great knife. I shrieked as I saw it shear through the throat; whilst at the same moment Mr Morris's bowie knife plunged into the heart. (*ibid*. 325)

Perhaps the spiritual significance of these late Victorian and Georgian comparisons is that, whereas Buchan's tale is one of high adventure and dangerous pursuit, both Stoker and Tolkien achieved their chilling effects by drawing on –

age-old (vampire) fears;[4]

the influence of occult powers[5] and the demonic hatreds of the undead for the living; and yet

the spiritual protection[6] available to the true believer.

Further, another layer of man's ancient fears of the enemy-invader is thus seen to be adumbrated in the treatment by Tolkien of the human damned, the erstwhile great lords of Middle-earth, all now bonded eternally to performing the Dark Lord's purpose as the ghoulish Black Riders. The great fear of the East and of its peoples in Middle-earth – and, for that matter, in all western

---

4 Stoker equates the vampires with the wolves, a notion similar to Tolkien's use of talking wolves, wargs, and the exile/outlaw/vampire.

5 It would seem that this may well be one of the occasions when Tolkien used some of the more demonic manifestations of evil much like those used in the spiritual shockers, the novels of his fellow Inkling, Charles Williams.

6 In *Dracula*, for Mina and Dr Helsing, the protections were garlic, the 'Holy Circle', and 'the Wafer'. For Frodo, in protection there were his friends, fire, the ancient powers of the hill circle, and "the name of Elbereth" (*FotR* 210).

mediaeval Europe – is not articulated here. However, it must suffice to stress again that there are story motifs of damnation aplenty in *The Lord of the Rings* that indicate terror at the possibility of assault by such undead forces. Not the least of these fearful dreads are the ghastly vampiric attacks and behaviour of the deathless, much as Jonathan Harker and his friends had experienced them in Bram Stoker's Gothic fantasy, *Dracula*.

Before Puck – the Púkel-men and the *puca*

In memory of Kathleen M. Briggs[1]

[...] languages (like other art-forms or styles) have a virtue of their own, independent of their immediate inheritors. (*MCE* 171)

[...] far off and now obscure as the Celtic adventures may seem, their surviving linguistic traces should be to us [...] of deep interest [...] Through them we may catch a glimpse or echo of the past which archaeology alone cannot supply, the past of the land which we call our home. (*MCE* 174-75)

The Púkel-men before Dunharrow

In the third chapter, 'The Muster of Rohan', in *The Return of the King*, the hobbit Merry comes, when squire to King Théoden, with his lord, to the ancient fortress or Hold of Dunharrow. As they climb the steep path from Harrowdale, the Riders of the Rohirrim pass at each turn of the road

> great standing stones that had been carved in the likeness of men, huge and clumsy-limbed, squatting cross-legged with their stumpy arms folded on fat bellies [...] The Riders hardly glanced at them. The Púkel-men they called them, and heeded them little: no power or terror was left in them; but Merry gazed at them with wonder and a feeling almost of pity,[2] as they loomed up mournfully in the dusk. (67)

Although these statues are not named again, they, or similar memorials, are presumably referred to[3] twice more, first on the following page as

---

This essay first appeared in *Mallorn* 20 (1983: 5-10) and I am grateful to the editors for permission to reprint.

1 The article is dedicated to the memory of the late Dr Kathleen Briggs, a fellow folklorist, not least because of her emphasis on the literary use of beliefs about fairy creatures in Part Three of her *The Fairies in Tradition and Literature* in which she refers to Tolkien's works as "the best of all the modern writings on fairy people" (1967: 209).

2 Cp. Ryan (1969: 186).

3 So Foster (1978: 321). Tyler (1976), is vague on the second passage but links the third (381) concerning the 'Wild Men'.

> a double line of unshaped standing stones that dwindled into the dusk [...]
> they were worn and black; some were leaning, some were fallen, some cracked
> or broken; they looked like rows of old and hungry teeth (*ibid.* 68)

and again by the Wild Man, when talking to Éomer, in his reference to the
earlier time when the 'Stone-house folk' "carved hills as hunters carved beast-
flesh" (*ibid.* 106).

As David Day comments in his *A Tolkien Bestiary* (1979: 206):

> The Púkel-men statues – have been compared to the Wild Men called the
> Woses of Druadan [sic]. Indeed it is likely that the Púkel-men were ancestors
> of the Woses [...]

The Silmarillion (1977) did not refer to these stone figures, or help in any way
with the problem posed by Tyler (1976: 381):

> What their relationship had been with the stonemasons of the White Mountains
> during the Accursed Years was never discovered.

The recent issue by Christopher Tolkien of his father's *Unfinished Tales*, however, assists us in various ways.[4] The editor tells us that the name Púkel-men
is "also used as a general equivalent to Drúedain" (*UT* 460) and that they,
presumably, held "the great promontory [...] that formed the north arm of the
Bay of Belfalas" (*UT* 263). As any inspection of Christopher Tolkien's map of
Middle-earth (such as that at the end of *UT* will make clear) the loose British
geographic equivalent of this area may be seen to be, either the area of Devon
and Cornwall, or the south and south-west of modern Wales.

Their Humanity

A further series of notes by both Tolkiens (*UT* 382-87) identify the race as
being

> tall, heavy, strong and often grim;
> sardonic, and ruthless;
> having, or being credited with "strange or magical powers" (382);

---

4 For example as in the confirming of the close association between the three passages linked by Foster
   (1978) from *RotK*.

as "eating sparingly [...] and drinking nothing but water" (*ibid.*);
as remaining in the White Mountains;
as paying no heed to the Dark One (i. e. Morgoth);
and as being driven from the White Mountains by "the tall Men" (383).

On this evidence, we must see these earlier people as being very much like

> 'P-Celts' and among those [who were] the speech-ancestors of the Welsh.
> (*MCE* 173)

The many notes of the Drúedain in *UT* link them with "the remote ancestors
of Ghân-buri-Ghân" (382) and describe them as

> at times merry and gay [...] but [with] a grimmer side to their nature and [they]
> could be sardonic and ruthless [...] with strange or magical powers [and like]
> the Dwarves [...] in build [... and] in their skill of carving stone. (*ibid.*)

and we are told:

> that the identity of the statues of Dunharrow with the remnants of the Drúath
> (perceived by Meriadoc Brandybuck when he first set eyes on Ghân-buri-Ghân)
> was originally recognised in Gondor [...] (*ibid.* 383)

As Ruth Noel (1980: 133) stresses, *drû* is the word for *wose*,[5] hence *Drúadan
Forest* is "where the Woses lived," and so we are not surprised to find Christopher
Tolkien's cluster of equivalents (*UT* 429) as including "*Drúwaith Iaur* 'The old
wilderness of the Drû-folk' in the mountainous promontory of Andrast", the
Old Púkel-wilderness and *Old Púkel-land*.

Anglo-Saxon Púcel

In his final annotation to these references in *UT*, Christopher Tolkien comments:

> It seems that the term 'Púkel-men' (again a translation: it represents Anglo-Saxon
> *púcel* 'goblin, demon', a relative of the word *púca* from which *Puck* is derived)
> was used only in Rohan of the images of Dunharrow. (387, endnote 14)

---

5 *Wose*, a word found in western Middle-English texts. Thus in *Sir Gawayn and the Green Knight*,
wodwos (l. 721), n. pl. 'satyrs, trolls of the forest', from Old English *wudu-wāsa*. Compare *wudewasan*
for *faunos*, Bosworth-Toller's *Anglo-Saxon Dictionary* (1898: 779).

This clue, which is more linguistically and culturally significant than the frequent easy scholarly identification of a word used by the Rohirrim with a form in Old English,[6] opens up a whole world of thought and exploration in linguistic aesthetics which is typical of so much of the sub-text of the so-called 'creative writing' of the late Professor Tolkien. It also fits well the unexpected reference to *The Lord of the Rings* in the opening paragraph of his Oxford oration, 'English and Welsh':

> [...] the years 1953 to 1955 have for me been filled with a great many tasks, [...] the long-delayed appearance of a large 'work', if it can be called that, which contains, in the way of presentation that I find the most natural, much of what I personally have received from the study of things Celtic. (*MCE* 162)

The 'way of presentation' in this context is not so much the mode of fantasy as his ever-present habit of etymological speculation and of searching for the cultural aesthetic behind surviving linguistic forms.

Puck's Antecedents

We are all familiar with Puck,[7] the sprite, otherwise called Robin Goodfellow, who first appears in Shakespeare in *A Midsummer Night's Dream* (Act II, scene 1, l. 40), and who categorises himself as a 'hobgoblin' in his speech to Titania's fairy, beginning

I am that merry wanderer of the night (1. 43)

This dramatic usage may be held to have given the sprite an individual character, so that it no longer seems natural to talk, as Robert Burton does in *The Anatomy of Melancholy* (1621), of *a puck* instead of 'Puck'. As is said of him,

> human follies are his perpetual entertainment, but like all hobgoblins, he has his softer moments, his indignation is always raised against scornful lovers [...]. Puck in Drayton's account of diminutive fairies in *Nimphidia* [l. 283] shows many of the same characteristics. For the rest, we shall find that Puck's traits correspond with those to be found in the Celtic parts of these islands, in the *pwca, phouka* and *pixies* (Briggs 1976: 337).[8]

---

6 See Tinkler (1969: 164-69).
7 "The earlier form was 'Pouke'; the Shakespearean text is the earliest evidence for the modern form" (Onions 1958: 171).
8 See also in this work pp. 33, 336 and 338. Dr Briggs had first gone to Oxford in 1920 and attended Tolkien's lectures over many years from 1925 onwards. Her general sympathy with his work can be

Dr Briggs also gives there many other details about these hobgoblins such as:

Pwca (*pooka*) being the Welsh version of English *puck* (1976: 337);

pwca as a *will o' the wisp* (*ibid*. 338); or

pouk-ledden,[9] as the Midland equivalent of *pixy-led* (*ibid*. 333).

She also quotes the mention of Robin Goodfellow, in seventeenth century literature, as in Rowland's *More Knaves Yet* (*ibid*. 342-43):

Amongst the rest, was a good fellow devill,
So called in kindness, cause he did no evill,
Knowne by the name of Robin (as we heare) [...]

Pouk – The Devil

This last quotation is of particular interest, since, as she stresses earlier (*ibid*. 333):

In medieval times 'Pouk' was a name for the Devil. Langland speaks of *Pouk's Pinfold*,[10] meaning Hell. By the 16th century, however, Pouk had become a harmless trickster, and only the Puritans bore him a grudge.

Yet Langland's vision, of Abraham showing this Lazar place controlled by the *pouke* to the Dreamer, has many later parallels, as with Golding's use of the word in an addition, which he makes in the ninth book of his translation of Ovid, to the account of the Chimaera:

The country where Chymaera, that same pooke,
Hath goatish body, lion's head and brist, and dragon'd tayle

---

found in many places in her publications in the field of British folklore. See in particular her *The Anatomy of Puck* (1959) or Briggs and Tongue (1965: 55-56).

Nancy Arrowsmith (1977) observes of hobgoblins in England: "They have become so rare that most people are only acquainted with them through stories and poems" (120); and "At one time they were known throughout England and into the Scottish lowlands" (122).

9   Compare the *pokey-hokey*, a frightening figure, mentioned by Mrs Elizabeth Wright (wife of Tolkien's teacher, Professor Joseph Wright) in her *Rustic Speech and Folk-lore* (1913). Tolkien was visiting the Wright's home regularly from from 1911 to 1915 to learn philology, and in the process he acquired from the editor of the *English Dialect Dictionary* his own love for these folk forms and meanings of the language.

10 This *Piers Plowman* association is discussed by Thomas Keightley (1880). In W.W. Skeat's edition (1886: 416) of *The Vision of William Concerning Piers the Plowman*, this is C-text, Passus XIX, l. 282, in the glossary to which Skeat observes of *pouke*: "A common word in Ireland, especially in the West, in such phrases as – 'What the *puck* are you doing?'"

Similarly Spenser had used the word in the prayer:

> Ne let the pouke nor other evil sprites, [...]
> Fray us with things that be not
> (*Epithalamion*, ll. 341-44);

while in Ben Jonson's play, *The Devil is an Ass*, the fiend of the title is called Pug.

Linguistic Cognates

In his most comprehensive manual Thomas Keightley (1880) gives many of the linguistic cognates to the *Pooke-Puck* root, viz.:

> Slavonic *Bôg*,[11] 'God' (315);
> Icelandic *Puki*, 'an evil spirit' (*ibid.*);
> Friesland *Puk* (233, 316);
> Irish *Pooka* (316);
> Welsh *Pwcca* (316);

and with the Northern German s-, the cluster

> Swedish *spöka, spöke* (a ghost);
> Danish *spöge, spögelse* (316);[12]
> Dutch *spook*; Low German *spoke* (ghost).

Keightley, following Sir Francis Palgrave, also indicates the links with

> Yorkshire *Boggart* (name and noun); the old English name *Puckle* (meaning 'mischievous' as in *Peregrine Pickle*, the Scotsman Smollett's name for one of his heroes);

and from *Bug, Bugbear, Bugleboo*, and *Bugaboo* (316).

In addition to these many derivatives found in mediaeval, Renaissance, and later dialectal usages in Western and Northern Germanic languages, there is

---

11 In his *A Concise Etymological Dictionary of the English Language*, W. W. Skeat (1882) gives as immediate cognates for *bug* (1) 'a spectre':
   Welsh *bwg*, 'hobgoblin', 'spectre'; cp. Scott *Bogle*;
   Gaelic, Irish *bocan*, 'a spectre'; cp. Lithuanian *bugti*, 'to terrify'.
12 Cp. Danish, *pokker*, 'devil, deuce', Norwegian *pauk*.

a most considerable use of the element *pūc-*, as in *pūca, pūcel*, 'goblin, demon' in Old English.[13] These words which do not appear in 'classical' Old English verse, and only occur in odd places in the prose, are quite a feature as an element in place names. In 1924, Allen Mawer (49) had noted in his survey of placename elements

> *pūca*, O.E., 'goblin', *puck*, dial. 'pook',

and gave as examples Poughill, Pophlet Park (Derbyshire) and Pownall (Cheshire). A similar note was provided in the revision of this work in 1956:

> *pūca*, O.E., 'a goblin', surviving as *puck, pook* as in Parkwalls (Cornwall); Pock Field (Cumberland); Poppets (Sussex); Puckeridge (Hertfordshire); Puckshot (Surrey); Purbrook (Hants.) [and] it is also found in M.E. minor names (Derbyshire, Essex, Sussex and Wiltshire).

> *pūcel*, O.E., 'a goblin'. (a) Popple Drove (Cumberland); Putshole (Devon); Puxton (Worcestershire). (Smith 1956: 74)

Indeed, many modern surveys of English place names include toponyms of this type. Thus the more popular book, *English Place-Names*, by H. G. Stokes, suggests that the early people pondered on

> Picklenash (The Fairies' Ash); Shuckburgh (The Goblins' Home), Puckeridge (The Goblins' Stream), Pokesdown (near Bournemouth) – and if we accept [it] that Pucklechurch was 'The Goblins' Church'. (1949: 53)

Kenneth Cameron in his *English Place Names* comments that the syllable, *puck, pook* (goblin) is especially common in the South of England, quoting Pockford (Surrey, 'ford'), Puckeridge (Herts., 'stream'), Pucknell (Wilts., 'spring') and Purbrook (Harts., 'brook').

Celtic Interface

This last reference to the southern regional frequency of the element is of particular interest, in view of the exhaustive survey of some 132 words or ele-

---

13 Old English *Pūca* is thought to be a nickname from *pūca*, 'goblin', and as such to be found in the Somerset place-name, Puckington. Similarly, the diminuitive, *Pūcela* is believed to occur in the ancient Gloucestershire name, Pucklechurch, found in the *Anglo-Saxon Chronicle* in 946. See Eckwall (1951: 357).

ments[14] identified for 'monster/demon' in English place names. R.A. Peters finds that 23 of the 132 Old English words so used occur in some 271 past and present English place names. The only words to occur in 10 or more instances are: *Grendel* (12); *scucca* ('demon/devil') (17); *þyrs* ('giant/demon') (23); and *pūca* ('spectre/evil spirit/demon') (103), with seven examples of *pucel*. A careful analysis of the names listed reveals that, of the 110 cases of *pūc-*, more than half occur in five counties, viz.: Cambridgeshire, 5; Essex, 14; Kent, 5; Surrey, 32; and Wiltshire, 17. Even more significantly, only one county not on this list (Derbyshire)[15] has a high number of monster words. While the common gloss of *pūca* is 'goblin' or 'demon', any analysis of the glosses from Latin where the word is listed, suggest a sense of 'evil spirit', with a Primitive Germanic anteced-ent form **pūkōn*. Whether the word was first in the Germanic languages and then borrowed into the Celtic, or whether it was in both clusterings from a very early date, it seems clear that its very frequent occurrence in southern areas of England is partly explained as Christianity's designation for non-Christian spirits, perhaps even surviving Celtic superstitions which would have been anathema to the missionary church. Then, too, the distribution of the element *pūc-* may or may not relate to Tolkien's point that the south and east (as landbridge) "must once, have been the most Celtic, or British, or Belgic" (*MCE* 170).

Etymology alone cannot explain the preference for the *pūc*-elememt or its peculiar distribution pattern which may well also indicate that it was used within the areas of the first converted Angles and Saxons in a dismissive way of a range of supernatural beings from Celtic folklore including goblins, banshees, ogres and others, as well as such supernatural powers as the Celtic *Deae Matres*. Certain it is that many varieties of local belief must have been lumped together under this head. In *The Return of the King*, the Rohirrim (i. e. early Angles and Saxons) are similarly dismissive – "The Riders hardly glanced at them [...] and heeded them little," whereas we are told that Merry "gazed at them with wonder and a feeling almost of pity" (67).

---

14 This data is largely derived by the present writer from the many localized examples listed in Peters (1961: 165-66; 203-4; 223-26; 234-35).
15 With *draca* 6; *scucca* 5; and *wyrm* 12, in a total of 37.

Lost Gods

Although the Púkel-men do not have a central place among the objects of veneration in Middle-earth, they once meant much more than they would seem to for Théoden's knights. Even before we learn from the *woses* of their earlier importance, Merry shows us that, for the sensitive viewer, and in their own place, they still possess an awesome and numinous power which may be intuited by one of a later and different race. Since they have faces, albeit battered, and a human shape, they were once intended to evoke human emotions of solemnity. Whether or no we accept the gloss on *priapos* of *pucelas* (Holder: 1878: 394),[16] a link with the better sense of Priapus as the 'god of gardens and vineyards', it is one of the associations known to Tolkien and it makes good sense in the context both of the ancient gardens[17] below Dunharrow and of the thoughts of the ancient men of the woods.

This 'Important Branch of Study'

While the above is no more than an essay in valid philological speculation, it may be held to fit Tolkien's definition of his text as that "important branch of study" with "no obvious practical use" (*FotR* 8). This ironic view of philology – or of the meaning behind the modern Puck – was not, of course, held seriously by Tolkien who would have agreed with his friend and fellow-Inkling, Owen Barfield that:

> The more common a word is and the simpler its meaning, the bolder very likely is the original thought which it contains [...]. (1956: 14)

Whether we are dealing with Proto-Celts, Druid-figures,[18] or some form of roadside fertility deities – or indeed a combination of all three – Tolkien's statues are not merely survivals from a distant past, but they suggest to us, as to the

---

16 See also Merit 1954.
17 The first description of the statues with their fat bellies is very much like those of fertility or vegetation deities or symbolic representations. See also the link with *faun* (above), and footnote 7.
18 The stones are much too human to be of the type in the circles of standing monoliths of the sort at Rollright or Avebury. Yet note of the following item from Kathleen Briggs (1967: 91) concerning the style of Midland fairies: "The last recorded Oxfordshire fairies are said to have been seen going down a hole under the King-stone at the Rollright Stones."

sensitive Meriadoc something of the intense and even poetic effort which went into their making as concepts and as statues. The *pūc-* word's Eastern European cognate forms from Slavonic and Lithuanian would imply that the root word may well have been Indo-European, with possible and plausible vegetation associations in both Italo-Celtic and Germanic, and as such it may well go back to the ancient notion of tree-gods which is held to be the possible etymology of the word Æsir.[19] It is also equally plausible that he is drawing attention to the tragic misunderstanding of Celtic religion[20] by the Angles and Saxons.

It is such etymological explorations as the above which are most in sympathy with Tolkien's continual assertion that the core of his work was language. For they are not only illuminating of his subtle use of aesthetic but are deeply luminous and satisfying in their own right. Again, as with such forms as *Middle-earth* and *mathom*, Tolkien has rescued otherwise lost words and significances and made them available for the modern reader's speculation and aesthetic satisfaction.

Conclusion

It should be understood from the body of the article, that Tolkien's use of 'the púkel-men' phrase (a) refers backwards from the Old English type society of Rohan; (b) relates imaginatively to the period of early contact with the Celts by the Angles and Saxons in the south and south-east of Britain; and (c) is largely independent of the considerable early modern (Celtic) speculation about the survival of *puc*-legends.

---

19 That is, Æsir from *ás* 'beam, standing post', i. e. the gods were once trees.
20 Cp. "in Celtic Ireland [pagan] dealings with the unseen were not regarded with such abhorrence, and indeed had the sanction of custom and antiquity" (Seymour 1972: 4) – in reference to the earliest periods of Christianity there.

Further Reading

Among the many works containing references to 'the Pooka' are:

McNally Jr., D.R., 1888, *Irish Wonders, the Ghosts, Giants, Pookas, Demons, Leprechawns, Banshees, Fairies, Witches, Widows, Old Maids, & Other Marvels of the Emerald Isle; Popular Tales as Told by the People*, Boston: Houghton Mifflin. Facsimile edition published 1977 by Weatheware Books, New York.

W.B. Yeats' two collections, *Fairy and Folk Tales of the Irish Peasantry*, 1888 and *Irish Fairy Tales*, 1892. (Given a modern format as *Fairy and Folk Tales of Ireland*, 1973, introduction by Kathleen Raine, Gerrards Cross, UK: Colin Smythe).

Haining, P., 1979, *The Leprechaun's Kingdom*, London: Souvenir Press.

Murray, M.A., 'The Puck Fair of Killorgen', In *Folklore* 64, June 1953 (351-54).

Appendix

Othin in England

Othin in England – Evidence from the Poetry for a Cult of Woden in Anglo-Saxon England

I t is a commonplace in the criticism of Old English literature to state that the whole poetic technique was a heritage from Germanic heathendom. It is, similarly, widely admitted, that the ideas, which were given heathen dress, meant a great deal – in some vague way – to the minds of the early English. It is not so generally agreed that a close analysis of this received material may still yield us some knowledge of the ways in which our ancestors regarded their deities. In the course of this paper I propose to confine my attention to the cult of the god Woden and to the various practices which were associated with his name.

From the many references to the god, both among Continental Germans and in Scandinavia, it is possible to pick out several aspects of his worship which recur and which we may take as giving us a general picture, with which to begin our analysis: he was a chief deity amongst the Germanic peoples; human sacrifices were made to him; he was a god of battles, victory being his greatest gift to men; those who died in war were his adopted children; he was the wisest of the gods, possessing supernatural knowledge which he had only gained at great personal sacrifice (being hanged on the gallows, and/or by pledging an eye); he was accompanied by two ravens and two wolves, who acted as bringers of intelligence, but who earlier seem to have been omen carriers, or even familiar spirits; he rode a grey horse, wore a long cloak and carried a spear; he was god of the storm and god of the wind. This catalogue of attributes is an inflated and rather artificial one, since the various aspects are not found in the Early German, the Norse, the Icelandic, or the Old English literatures in anything like uniform detail.

Scholars have long been reluctant to attempt any sort of synthesis of heathen practices in Early England, for the Cult of Woden or any other god. Indeed,

---

This essay first appeared in *Folklore* 74 (1963: 460-80) and I am grateful to the editors for permission to reprint. Most quotations in this essay have been translated.

both Professor Tolkien and Brian Branston (1957) have been dubbed frivolous for some of their more popular efforts in this direction. In a sense, this diffidence and scepticism is natural enough, for there is not a great wealth of written or other explicit material available, and we must glean from here and there to fill out the picture, but fill it out we can, as I hope to show.

It has long been recognized that this apparent paucity of evidence is due to several influences:

1) The passage across the North Sea may well have affected the quality of the faith, even before the coming of Christianity. This is a doubtful view, to say the least, since a longer passage at a later date had no such debilitating effect on the beliefs of the Norsemen who went to Iceland.

2) There was a lack of faith in England in the heathen period, because the transplanted Germanic peoples had no centralized places of worship, such as Leire in Denmark, or Uppsala in Sweden.

3) Writing only came with the Church, and the conversion of the Old English had taken place before they were able to put down their ancient beliefs and myths.

It is certainly true that writing, from the days of King Ethelbert down to the Norman Conquest, was a prerogative of the Christian clergy and that these did their best to suppress all native pagan lore. Thus, while we might have hoped to obtain a great deal of information from Bede, in fact, we find that this historian, being deeply Christian, and concerned with the strength of the heathen faith, as we shall see, cuts down very considerably on references to its practices.

From an earlier date we have a few references to the old gods by name, in the *Interpretatio Romana*, but there is little more. Other texts illustrate the tentative way in which the early missionaries sought to insinuate the new doctrines, and with what surprising results. Thus, for example, they tell us, as in the *Gnomic Verses*:

Woden created the false gods, but the all-ruler the gloriously wide heavens. (ll. 132-33)

4) It is often naively assumed because there are no references to heathen abominations in the *Anglo-Saxon Chronicle* – it speaks of the heathen, but does not dwell on their atrocities – that these could not have existed; and that the absence of serious strictures on the religious beliefs of the vikings in this same work, means that these later invaders were almost as orthodox in their religious beliefs as the English should have been, when the Danish raids began in the eighth century.

A much more plausible explanation of this state of affairs would seem to be that the Chronicle, like the more formal religious documents, was practising a policy of suppression, and that such pagan material was not suitable for a Church-inspired record.

*   *   *

There is plenty of evidence of various sorts to give proof, if it were needed, that the Germanic peoples in England were not ignorant of the gods of their heritage, or of Woden in particular.

The genealogies of the kings bear witness to the dignity of the god's name, and there were few which did not include it. He is given as an ancestor in the royal houses of Kent, Essex, Wessex, Deira, Bernicia, East Anglia, Mercia and Lindisfarne. This fact, which may be taken as a principal proof of the deeply rooted worship of the divinity, is of real value, for these records were made and continued in Christian times, in spite of what must have been certain clerical opposition to their inclusion.[1] It is of interest here that these lists, which do not stem from Woden, but start at a point about five generations earlier, all give the god a reign in the same relatively recent period, in the second half of the fourth century, or more exactly, in the decades between A.D. 370 and 390, that is to say not so very long before the invasion of England.[2]

More than one hundred years ago Grimm (1966: 157) stated of place names containing the name of a Germanic god as an element: "In what countries the worship of the god endured longest may be learned from the names of places which are compounded with his name, because the site was sacred to him." And as he points out of the Germanic Woden: "by their multitude and similarity, not to say, identity of structure lies the full proof of their significance." Whether the interest in lofty sites, hills and mountains, which these indicate, is indicative of the presence there of temples raised in honour of Woden, or not, it is to be related to the burial practises of Othinic worshippers, and the god as the leader of the dead, particularly those in the Wild Hunt discussed below.

---

1 I personally find it hard to accept the most sophisticated view that the descent from Woden was emphasized, since it had some propaganda value in conversation with, and conversion of, the Danes.
2 It may be noted here, in passing, that Thunor (the Norse Thor) does not appear in the royal genealogies, which is scarcely surprising, since he was the god of the farmer class.

While there are hardly any of these in Upper Germany, they are scattered fairly widely over the rest of the Germanic world:

> in Lower Germany and Hesse, (e.g. Wodenesweg, Wodenesberg near which Boniface ordered a holy oak to be destroyed);
>
> in the Netherlands, (e.g. Woensdrecht);
>
> in Schonen, (at Odensberg, where in a mound both Othin and Charlemagne live sequestered);
>
> in Scandinavia, particularly in the South, there are considerable numbers, as we would expect from an area where heathenism was longer preserved.

Many of these last have the element *ve*, (meaning 'a place of sacrifice'), and from what we know from the classical commentators and the *Fornaldarsaga*, we may be certain that human sacrifice would be practised at them.

In England there are to be found a number of place-names, in which the first element is the name of the god (these occur particularly in the southern counties, the East Midlands, and in the North-west, as far west as Derbyshire and Staffordshire):

> Roseberry Topping (West Riding of Yorkshire),[3] was in the earlier form, Othenesberg, 'Othin's hill';
>
> the tumulus now know as Adam's grave (Wiltshire) was called Wodnes beorg, in the ninth century;
>
> the great defensive work, Wansdyke (*wodnes dic*), running across Hantshire, Wiltshire and Somerset is known to have been constructed by the British in the fifth and sixth centuries;
>
> Wensley, a half hundred in Bedfordshire, was called Weneslai in the *Doomsday Book*, but Wodneslawe, in 1169;
>
> near Overton in Wiltshire, the *Cartularium saxonicum* has a spot, *on wodnes dene*;
>
> Woden was supposed to have a temple on the top of a conspicuous conical hill in Staffordshire, the name of which is now Wednesbury (while the tradition is probably true, there is no evidence for it, apart from the name);
>
> Wednesfeld (also in Staffs.) was the site of a great battle fought in 910 between the Saxons and the Danes, in which the Saxons were victorious;
>
> according to the main MSS of the *Anglo-Saxon Chronicle* there was a great slaughter in Britain in 592 at Woddesbeorge, but another MS records this event as happening at Wodnesbeorge.

---

3 In common with most philological and other historically-based research, I use here and elsewhere in this essay the county-boundaries before the local government reorganization of 1974.

Although this matter of various readings is a complicated one, it is, at least, of interest that battles are recorded as having taken place at sites whose names mean Woden's hill, in 592 when there was a great slaughter, in 715, and as late as 910, when the Saxons were victorious over the Danes.

Although the word, *Grim*, is not found as a by-name of Woden in England, we may accept it, on the analogy of the Old Norse Grimnir, as one of Othin's names.[4] While many personal names containing it are found in the Danelaw, such as Grimsby (Lincolnshire), Grimsthorpe (West Riding of Yorkshire), Grimston (Leicestershire), it may be taken as referring to the god in: *Grimsbury-burh* (Oxfordshire), a prehistoric earthwork, not now visible; Grim's Dike (West Riding of Yorkshire); Grim's Ditch (Wiltshire), where there is one in the north, and another in the south of the county; Grim's Dyke (Oxfordshire). As Stenton very reasonably observes, the attribution to Woden of these earth-works (for it is always the ramparts that are thought of), may have very well been made by a people not yet converted to Christianity (1990: 98-100).

As we have already seen (in the *Gnomic Verses*), the earlier proselytizing church had to make various compromises with the trappings of the older faith, and a mention, however derogatory, indicates a recognition. The genealogies, too, which commemorated Woden, were, doubtless, all written out by clerics, whatever misgivings these worthies may have had at such blendings.

Although there are no specific prose accounts of the worship of Woden, we need not be in much doubt about the fact of such worship of the main Germanic god in the face of the various documentary testimonies to such a survival:

1) Bede several times comments on apostasy among the people in times of plague and national disaster. Thus, for example, he describes the situation in Essex, when on the death of their father Saberht, his three sons profess heathenism and allow the people to worship idols (*H.E. ii* 5);

2) Redwald of East Anglia, while maintaining an altar for Mass, also had an *arula* for sacrifice to devils;

3) St Cuthbert had, in times of pestilence, to strengthen those who had recourse to the false remedies of idolatry. And there are other indications that

---

4 Its sense would be a masked person, one who conceals his identity; cp. ON, OE, *grima*, a mask, helmet, referring to the god's habit of appearing in disguise.

the populace of Northumbria were hostile to Christianity in the mid-seventh century (*H.E. iv* 27);

4) a belief in amulets is cited in the case of Imma (*H.E. iv* 22). These *literae solutoriae* may be compared with the *run-stafas* of *Beowulf,* ll. 1694ff and the sigrunar, or 'victory-runes', (mentioned in the Old Norse *Sigrdrifumal,* stanza 6); and

5) Bede's own letter to Archbishop Egbert in 734 makes one wonder if Christian teaching could have been so thorough in the remoter districts, as to eradicate all heathen practices.

Similar testimonies as to the tenacity with which the old gods possessed the mind of their adherents are likewise found throughout the Germanic world, as in the sermon of St Eligious in the middle of the seventh century, or in the attacks by Boniface in Germany on the unwisdom of allowing or condoning the use of Pagan charms by Christians.

Some of the later comments must be read with some caution. Thus the frequent denunciations of Germanic pagan practices by Wulfstan, who addressed himself vigorously to their suppression, may very well be levelled in great measure at the customs brought to England by the Scandinavian followers of King Eric. And neither he nor the gentler Ælfric have any first-hand knowledge of the details of these aberrations. And when we find Ethelwerd, the tenth-century chronicler and scion of the royal house of Wessex, reporting that "the pagans worshipped Woden as god, with sacrilegious honour, and offered him sacrifice for the acquisition of victory or valour" (Giles 1848: 4) we should realize that this may be the work of an antiquarian, who does not even confine himself to the customs of his own country.

Yet it would seem fair to interpret such comments as these as an indication of the way in which the church tightened its grasp on the minds of men, and had, as a result, to take more and more drastic steps to extrude heathenism from Christian worship – a tightening up which is reflected in the increasing harshness of the penalties listed in the legal codes for turning from the new ways.

The spells and other such lowly doggerel verse contain their share of pagan survivals. The *Gnomic* lines where we are informed that:

The Eucharist is for holy men, sins for the heathen;
Woden wrought idols (built shrines?), the Lord wrought heaven, (ll.132 ff)

may be compared with the *Leechdoms* where less obnoxious incantations were allowed to survive, the Æsir appearing alongside the elves, as in the charm for the stitch, with *færsticce*. In the *Charms* there are some half dozen appeals to Teutonic gods, one of which, to Woden, occurs in the metrical *Nine Herbs Charm*, itself redolent of Germanic lore:

> A snake came sneaking, it slew a man.
> Then Woden took nine glory-twigs (*wuldor tanas*)
> And struck the serpent so that in nine pieces it flew.

There is other non-literary evidence for the worship in England. We know from the *Ynglinga Saga* (Chapter 10) that Othin instituted the custom of cremation and ordained that all dead men should be burned on a pyre, and other Germanic comments make it clear that such a burning was a sacrifice to Othin. In harmony with this belief, we find in England that the location of the cremation sites in the heathen cemeteries, pre 600, are particularly on hills, whence the smoke and spirit might go to Woden. They are mainly – and appropriately – in the north of the country. Thunor was worshipped more in the south and it is in the Anglian area only that we find large scale cremation cemeteries.

In the arts there is no relief that has been positively identified as having a representation of Woden. But from the Sutton Hoo find, there is a purse clasp of East Anglian workmanship which may be dated before 650. Although it is held by some to be of Byzantine origin, and the British Museum Provisional Guide somewhat doubtfully feels the design to be 'Daniel in the lions' den', we may well wonder whether either of these views is the right one, for, on the basis of the similarity of design to a stamp for embossing bronze helmet plates from Torslunda in Sweden, it is just as likely (so stylized is the design) to be two wolves or ravens tearing at a fallen warrior.

*   *   *

From what we have seen so far, it is clear that there are certain traits of the deity, as listed earlier, that are not apparent from these references in England. Here Woden does have a variety of characteristics: but nowhere is he thought of as being the all-father; nowhere a one-eyed wanderer; he can in no sense be accounted as the heathen counterpart of the Christian deity, nor is he possessed of a well-appointed residence like the Scandinavian Valhall.

There are no specific statements that he is the god of war, could give victory, could be appealed to in battle, or appeased by a massacre.

He is, it might so far be argued, merely some one who can be employed in spells, who can be ornamental in the genealogies of royal families, who can make earthworks like the Wansdyke, or other *enta geweorc*.

As many critics point out, Woden has been quietened, diminished in stature, overcome as a person, by the successful white magic of the Church, by Augustine and Aidan, and that without much of a fight.

It is true that it is possible to argue this view, if we take the line that the fullest picture is the Old Norse one, and that what is in the Old English should only be subjected to close scrutiny if there is a wealth of evidence to support it in the later rationalized Icelandic accounts.

If we think this, we have been rather mesmerized by the most wonderful mythology, the work of a genius, Snorri Sturluson, and his school of litterateurs, working of course on old materials, who created a glittering Asgaard, in which Odin emerges as a god. But we have, as Chadwick (1899) showed, a large body of historic Scandinavian documents bearing on this cult and giving an altogether different picture. This is not to say that Snorri's version is false, but rather that this brilliant antiquarian utilized a vast amount of material, which heterogeneous mass he combined and standardized, and so he created something which had a currency in his own day and later periods, the glittering nature of which blinds us to the true form of the popular religion in the earlier times.

While various strands of this later, 'orthodox' cult may be discerned in the Old English literature, it is plain that another altogether more primitive Woden is to be found there – the god of wind and storm, the magician and necromancer, the abominations of whose worship are to be found in association with all the horrors of battle.

*   *   *

One aspect which is particularly to be associated with Woden is a theme which recurs in the literature, that of 'the Birds and Beasts of Battle'. It occurs so often that it is usually regarded as something inherited, traditional, a sort of literary pyrotechnic, which can be guaranteed to give some elan and spectacle to a set battle-piece. In order to bring out something of the atmosphere of these passages, I shall analyse several of the main ones.

The first occurs in the very early poem, *Exodus*, dated c. 700. The account is dramatically appropriate in that it heightens, by creating a mood or stock response, a feeling of terror at the Egyptians' menacing approach towards the retreating Israelites. The whole is an anticipation, since no battle has taken place, no one is killed, and it is not evening.

> The birds of prey, greedy for battle, dewy-feathered, the dark one who habitually picks over the slain, wheeled/screamed over the battle corpses. The wolves, in the hope of feasting, sang a terrible song in the evening, behind the track of the foemen, for the slaughter of the host. The guardians of the ways (i.e. wolves) cried out at midnight. The stranger, giving way to peril, turned to flee. (ll. 162-69)

The picture is a vivid one. It is in a most archaic portion of the poem as the vocabulary and the metre indicate. We might say of the style that it is new and unhackneyed, that the language has the freshness of a time when it was not a mere collection of traditional phrases and useful half-lines. The notion is of battle-birds wheeling, of the raven being regarded as a picker over of the slain (no golden haired goddess Valkyrie is choosing champions here). The wolves, devourers of all carrion, are circling around the action, and they grow bold in the evening.

Just a few lines before this passage, there was another, also in this older section, which is extremely relevant here. The narrator saw:

> Pharaoh's host come sweeping on, bearing a thicket (of spears)[5] overhead; war turned again and again. (ll. 155-58)

It has often been said that this last – "war turned again and again" – is not the sort of statement that is common in Old English verse, and this is true. The abstract is not used in this way. But in Old Norse, *guthr* was the name of a Valkyrie and it is possible that such a personified notion existed also in Old English, where it might have the sense of a bird-like shadow, a presence, which,

---

5 This phrase may well be significant for the dedication of a foe – see below.

like the raven, is wheeling overhead. We may recall another very early poem
The *Finnsburg Fragment*, where the raven was doing just this:

> *Hreafen wandrode*
> *sweart ond sealobrun.*
> (The raven dusky and dark brown wheeled.) (ll. 34-35)

The scene and the concept becomes more forceful if we consider that the two
nouns *guð and here fugolas* (i.e. ravens) are in apposition, and that the Raven is
Guth. Certainly the whole passage is one that is grimly vivid.[6]

While this sort of theme did become conventional in the later poems (for
example, see the *Battle of Brunanburh*), this was not the case for the older
poets. In a sense it may have been conventional before the Germans left the
Continent, but it had a reality for the people in pagan times. Here we may feel
that the detested cult of Woden and dark necromancy is not far away. And we
know, too, that the wolf, the raven, and the eagle were still seen – they were
all three numerous in 1066 – and that the association long survived. One of
its last examples is the *Twa Corbies* – anticipated in *Beowulf* where one raven
asks the other how he fared at the feast.

If these passages are examined in any detail, it will be seen that certain features
recur with an exactness that does not come merely from the naturalist, but from
the heightened observation of our ancestors who believed implicitly in the cult
of the god, and knew what to look for. Thus, though we as naturalists may
know that the eagle had his nest high on the cliffs, and would therefore be far
off when the battle started inland, the poetry always says that he is the last guest
at these grim banquets, and that the raven was always there before him.

In some of the other well-known passages on battle we may note variations on
the 'known formula'.

In *Beowulf*, ll. 3024ff, we have a picture of the desolation and miseries of war,
after the joys of this life:

---

6 This interpretation of guth would give added significance to such lines as this one from the *Fates of
Men* (l. 16):

> sumne sceal gar agetan,   sumne guð abreotan.

the sound of the harp shall not rouse the warriors, but the dark raven, ready above the fallen, shall speak many things, shall tell the eagle how he sped at the feasting, when, with the wolf, he spoiled the slain.

In *Genesis*, we have:

Then they came together, furious were the murderous hosts. The swart bird sang, dewy-feathered, beneath the skies, in expectation of the fallen [and then follows the description of the battle]. (ll. 1982-85)

In the Fragment of the *Fight of Finnsburg*, we have fighting at the opening of the poem:

But hither forth they fare, the birds of carrion are singing, the grey-coat howls, the war-wood clashes, shield answers to shaft. (ll. 5-7)

Other passages occur in *Elene*:

Spears shone [...] the host went forward. The wolf in the wood howled a song of battle; he did not conceal the spell for slaughter (*Wælrune*). The dewy-feathered eagle raised up its song in the track of the foemen. (ll. 27-30)

We are told of the noises of battle, and then the hosts come together:

The raven screamed aloft, black and greedy for corpses. (ll. 52-53)

There follows a third passage at the opening of the next day's hostility:

The trumpets rang loudly in front of the hosts. The raven rejoiced in the work; the dewy-feathered eagle beheld the going forth, the warring of fierce men; the wolf, the forest-dweller, lifted up its song. The terror of war was there. (ll. 109-13)

In *Judith*, when the Hebrews under her command meet the Assyrians of Holofernes,

[...] at the break of dawn battle-shields clattered, loudly did rattle. The lean wolf in the wood rejoiced at that, and the dark raven the bird ready for slaughter; both knew that the warriors purposed to provide them with a feast of fated men; and behind them flew the dewy-feathered eagle, hungry for food. The dark-coated one, horny beaked, sang a song of war. (ll. 204-12)

These constitute the best models, although they by no means exhaust the list. Of the *Battle of Brunanburh*, it has been justly said that it is something of an antiquarian effort, and has little force. After the battle there, when the victors went off,

> They left behind them the dark-coated swart raven, horny-beaked, to enjoy the carrion, and the grey-coated eagle, white-tailed, to have his will of the corpses, the greedy-war-hawk, and that grey beast, the wolf in the wood. Never yet before this was there greater slaughter [...] (ll. 60-66)

In the *Battle of Maldon*, there is a passage, short, but interesting, and realistic, in spite of there being no wolf:

> Then was the fight near, glory in battle; the time had come when doomed men must needs fall there. Then clamour arose, ravens wheeled, the eagle greedy for carrion; there was shouting on earth. (ll. 103-7)

There are some other pieces which do not occur in scenes of battle. In *The Wanderer*, we are given a list of the fates that befell the friends of the solitary survivor: "War destroyed some, bore them on far paths; one the bird bore away over the high sea; one the grey wolf gave over to death" (ll. 80-83). Another such list occurs in the *Fates of Men*: "To one unhappy man, it chances that his death shall come with sorrow in youth; the wolf shall eat him, the grey heath-stepper" (ll. 10-13); and then, lower in the same, of one who had been hanged: "There the raven pecks his eyes, the dark-coated one rends the corpse, nor can he keep the hateful flying foe from that malice with his hands" (ll. 36-39).

These and the many other references to the birds and the wolf may be classified in various ways. The passages from *Exodus, Genesis, Finnsburg, Judith* and *Maldon* are all concerned with the omens before a battle. The *Fates of Men*, the second *Judith* passage, and those from *Brunanburh* and *The Wanderer* describe the scene after the battle. Some are full set pieces in which all three creatures are referred to viz. *Beowulf, Elene, Judith*, and the *Brunanburh*. In the *Finnsburg* and the second *Judith* passage, there are probably all three present, although there may be one missing, as is the wolf in *Maldon* and *Genesis*, and in the opening piece from *Elene*, and in *The Wanderer*.

As we noted earlier, there is keen observation, of the wet wings of the eagle, to indicate that he has come from the eyrie on the cliffs; of the flash of white in his tail as he wheels (*Brunanburh*). The raven is usually dark, and often black. He arrives early, is ever ravenous, and ever in expectation of a banquet. Of him the word *ne-fugol* is probably used in *Genesis* 2158 – with the element *ne*; 'corpse' (compare *orcneas* in *Beowulf*). In this passage he is described as on the hills, stuffed with glutting himself from the armies. The wolf is ever there, following in the wake of the armies, now skirting on either side. In the *Elene* passage, he even raises a 'song', which doubtless refers to his call across the army to his mate on the other side.

*   *   *

And what conclusion are we to draw from all these references, where there is a distinct and recurring pattern? We know from the Norse authorities that Othin had two ravens, *Huginn* and *Muninn*, Thought and Remembrance, which he sent out over the world, to see all that happened, and bring the intelligence back to him. We know, too, that he had two wolves, *Geri* and *Freki*, names of both of which signify greedy or 'ravenous', and that the eagle was associated with him.

The inference to be drawn is that these relatively harmless references in the Eddic mythology are a much later version of an earlier and far more sinister aspect of the association of the birds and beasts of battle with the war god. In the *Exodus* passage first examined, we saw first that *guth* was abroad, wheeling in the sky, as an omen of battle, and then that the term *Waelceasega* was used of the raven, a few lines later. It is perfectly possible that both references are to the one presence, and that we can here see the terrible carrion birds of battle being slowly transformed into female followers and worshippers of Woden, whose rites were degraded and included practices savouring very much of necromancy. We shall see below some of the other beliefs about the Valkyries that were current in England.

*   *   *

Just as the theme of the birds and beasts of battle may be held to be associated with the worship of Woden as war-god, so may be the theme of the Wild Hunt with him as the God of Wind and Storm. The Wild Hunt is the name of a noise heard at night, as of a host of spirits rushing along, accompanied in later periods by shouting huntsmen and baying hounds. The Wild Huntsman himself is in cloak and great hat, Woden-like. Rhys, the comparatavist, had considered that many of the myths relating to Woden as the great Teutonic god could be traced to a Celtic origin, and compares the name Woden with the Celtic Gwydion. Whether this is true or not in the case of this belief, and it may be difficult to determine in some instances whether such a text as *Sir Orfeo* is more likely to have picked up the belief from Teutonic or Celtic sources, there can be little doubt that Woden was the immediate original of the various local heroes who led the hunt in Germanic lands, Dietrich von Bern, Berchtold, or King Valdemar.

In Old English literature, the 'Storm Riddle', in the *Exeter* Book, is distinctly reminiscent, both of the Valkyries, and of the Wild Hunt:

> It is the greatest of uproars, of noises over cities [...] dark creatures, hasten-ing over men, sweat fire, and crashes move, dark with mighty din, above the multitudes; they march in battle, they pour dark pattering wet from their bosom, moisture from their womb. The dread legion moves in battle; terror arises. (Gordon 1926: 322)

With this, let us compare the passage from the 'Charm for catching a swarm of bees': "Alight, victorious women, descend to earth; Never fly, wild, to the wood" (*ibid.* 97). Perhaps more promising is the following from the 'Charm against a Sudden Stitch in the Side': "Loud were they, lo, loud, when they rode over the Hill. Resolute were they when they rode over the lands" (*ibid.* 94). A version perhaps most close to what we imagine to be the nature of the Wild Hunt, as known in England – although we must allow for later influences – is to be found in the *Peterborough Chronicle*, for the year A.D. 1127:

> Let no one be surprised at what we are about to relate, for it was commonly told all about the country that after February 6th, many people both saw and heard a whole pack of huntsmen in full cry. They straddled black horses and black bucks, while their hounds were pitch black, with staring hideous eyes. This was seen in the very deerpark of Peterborough town, and in all the woods stretching from that same spot as far as Stamford. All through the night monks heard them sounding and winding their horns. Reliable witnesses who kept watch in the night, declared that there might even have been twenty or thirty of them in this wild group, as far as they could tell.

Unfortunately, the English references are not very specific, or so full as we could wish them. We may note here other Germanic details. Various stories refer to the two ravens which follow the Wild Hunt, and these may be associated with the two ravens of Woden, as may the night raven of Danish folklore which is said sometimes to precede the Wild Hunt, and personify the god himself. I shall not refer to the 'Fairy Hunt of Walter Map', discussed in Bliss's edition of *Sir*

Orfeo, but it would seem at least as likely, once the medieval elements are stripped away, that these stories could have a Germanic origin as a Celtic one.

The Glossaries are important for their interesting equivalents. Adam of Bremen stated in his *Gesta Hammaburgensis Ecclesiae Ponficum* that "wodan, id est furor", and this view is supported by the OE gloss of *wodendream as furor animi*, and the contemporary glosses of *wod* as 'rabidus vel insanus'. (We may also instance the glossing of the appellative *wotanas* as *Tyrannus*.) The language is too strong to refer to the frenzy of the *vates*. The valkyrie too is presented in much darker colours in the literature. We have seen from *Exodus* that the raven may be held to be a *waelcyrige*, and there is another similar reference (Caedmon, *Metr. Paraphrase of parts of Holy Script*). In the early glosses the word is equated with a Fury, a Gorgon, or the Goddess of War. Thus we find such equivalents as *Tisifone, Eurynis, Bellona, Allecto*. And one passage tells us that they are *Bestiae*, and have the eyes of Gorgons. Elsewhere the word has the notion of witch or sorceress, the pairing *Waelcyrigan* and *wiccan* being common (and is also found later in Middle English).

From the Old Norse sources, and as early as Tacitus, we are told that Woden was worshipped by sacrifices, often of the whole of the opposing army. There is some slight evidence that the first settlers in Britain practised the rite of total immolation of an enemy host. Certain entries in the *Anglo-Saxon Chronicle* in early years and for the late Danish invasions give this impression; for example the entry for 491:

> This year Ælla and Cissa laid siege to Pevensey and slaughtered everyone living there. Not one single Briton was allowed to remain alive.[7]

We have specific references in the Old Norse sources to the way of sacrificing an army, by dedicating them to Othin while a spear was cast over the opposing host. Although there are no detailed references to this in the Old English poetry, it is a fact that there is continual reference to the poising of spears, particularly by the army about to be victorious, following immediately on the descriptions of the birds and beasts of battle, and these occur before the hosts have engaged. Typical examples may be found in *Elene, Judith, Maldon* and in

---

7 Here in the translation of G.N. Garmonsway.

the 'Charm against the Stitch'. Confused, but still recognizable, is the reference
in the 'Storm Riddle':

> The fool fears not the spears of death; yet he dies if the true Lord speeds the
> [...] swift shaft [...] few escape whom the weapon of the swift visitant reaches.
> (Gordon 1926: 322)

It may be noted in this context that the reference to the spears is usually followed immediately by a reference to the standard or battle banner. Though
we are not told in the English sources of the details on it, we may recall the
banner of the vikings, with its raven, the wings of which spread, if victory was
in store, but dropped if it were not. (The Bayeux Tapestry shows William the
Conqueror under such a raven banner at Hastings.)

We know from the Old Norse accounts, and the long *Hávamál*, in particular,
that Othin hung on the gallows for nine nights and nine days, in order to in-
crease his *ásmegin* (or divine power), and obtain the runes. It is also clear from
the story of King Vikar in *Gautreks Saga* that hanging was a form of sacrifice
to Othin. (Compare the Shetland song, recorded by Karl Blind in the late
nineteenth century, and supposed by some to be an echo:

> Nine days he hang pa da rütless tree [...]
> A blüdy maet wis in his side [...]
> Nine lung nichts, i' da nippin' rime.[8] (Blind 1879: 1093))

In *Beowulf,* we have an interesting account of how Herebeald (son of Hrethel,
king of the Geats), was accidentally killed by his brother Haethcyn. Then
follows a passage on Hrethel's grief: "Thus it is grievous for an old man [...]
that his young son should ride the gallows. Then shall he utter a dirge when
his son hangs, a joy to the raven" (ll. 2444-48). Now, although we know from
the *Gnomic Poetry* that "the felon shall be hanged," the young man was not a
criminal or a prisoner of war, so it is difficult to see here how much we have
of a simile – or, perhaps – of a custom, such as that recorded by Procopius of
the Eruli.

---

8 Translated into modern English:
     Nine days he hanged on the rootless tree [...]
     A bloody wound was in his side [...]
     Nine long nights, in the nipping rime [i.e. freezing frost]

There are other references in Old English poetry to the hanging of a man, without the apparent explanation of his being a criminal.

1) Compare the passage quoted above, from the *Fates of Men*, where the corpse is torn by the raven;

2) In the same poem, there is another fate for man, which reads like a sacrifice, rather than a hanging for wrong-doing: "One in the forest shall fall, wingless, from a high tree; yet he does not fly, sport in the air, till the growth of the tree is no longer there. Then, reft of life, sad in mind, it sinks down to its roots, falls on the earth, its life has departed" (ll. 21-26);

3) Although the *Dream of the Rood* is Christian, there is a decidedly pagan background to the poem;

4) In *Beowulf*, the Swedish king, Ongentheow, after slaying Haethcyn, king of the Geats, while he is besieging the remnants, refers to enduring through the night, and then threatens to hang some of them in the morning on the gallows.

In several Old English passages, Woden is referred to as a magician. We have the passage, already quoted, in the *Nine Herbs Charm*, where he took the chips for divination, and struck the adder so that it flew into nine pieces. It is also possible that the Old English regarded him as the inventor of the (runic) alphabet, for this dialogue occurs in *Salomon and Saturn*: "Who first invented letters? Mercurius, the giant"[9] (the two gods were one and the same, according to the *Interpretatio Romana*). A similar passage to this last occurs in the Runic poem, where we are told that "Os is the beginning of every speech" (l. 10), etc., where 'os' could be the 'mouth', or, just as likely, the 'God', i.e. Woden. While it might be argued that the charms are late in their present form, and the references to the runes quite innocuous, it should not be forgotten that the language used in both is very archaic, *wuldortanas*, etc., and that these words and runes themselves were connected with magical habits both in England and among continental Germans. It is Othin's invention or possession of magic Runes which is emphasized in the Eddic poems.

One final indication of English identification with matters Othinic is that several of the heroes who are known from other sources to be dedicated to the god and under his special patronage, are found in the literature. In *Beowulf*,

---

9 See Kemble (1847: 192).

there are references to both Sigemund and Heremod, in conjunction with whom we may recall such a line in the *Hyndluljoth*:

> Othin gave Heremothr a helmet and a coat of mail, and Sigmundr a sword.
> (l. 2)

Finally, Starkathr, who was regarded by the Danes as the typical servant of Othin, cannot be dissociated from the account of the *eald aescwiga*, who goads Ingeld into revenge. On the whole, then, the acquaintance of the *Beowulf* poet with Othin heroes renders it more than possible that these men, known in Denmark in the first half of the sixth century, were known in England in the first half of the eighth, and associated with the war-god.

*   *   *

We can thus see that we have in the literature of the Old English period a considerable amount of material which is concerned with or reflects various aspects of the cult of Woden.

The references to the birds and beasts of battle are most important. They can scarcely be held to be the result of observation or ornithological lore. As time goes on, they become rather blurred, the most vivid accounts occurring earlier in the literary period. This is what we should expect to happen as the details of the cult fade, as they are handed down in the folk-memory. At the earliest period they are particularly vivid and horrific, for then the terrors of the heathen gods had still a strong hold of the popular imagination. If the references are to a literary convention, then we may marvel, for there is no convention in the poetic texts, which has such a long life, or is so pervasive.

The accounts of the Wild Hunt are not so clear, but what remains makes it obvious enough that this was associated with the wind god, the storm, and the carrying off of the slain. Just as in the 'Riddle for the Storm', we have the wild band of hags riding through the sky, thus linking the Valkyries and the Hunt, so, in the movements of the raven, and the wheeling of *guth* in the *Exodus* battle, there is the link with the Birds of Battle and the Valkyries, who may originally have been conceived of as ravens, like the *Wealceasiga*. And it would be a bold man indeed who denied the probability that the hounds accompanying the dark hunt, raven led, were a medievalization of the packs of howling wolves on the outskirts of earlier hosts.

The evidence of the early glosses makes it quite clear that the Valkyries were furies, debased and revolting. The equation with witch, a word of much greater potency in earlier periods, should make the association with necromancy and abominable practices with dead bodies, beliefs which we can consider to lie not too far behind the surviving texts.[10]

For other less pleasant and primitive rites of the cult, we have distinct evidence, even if it is not as positive as we could wish, in the references to the immolation of a foe, the poising of the spear before the armies engaged (this being a formal part of the rite of dedication), the hanging of warriors (for it is difficult to accept Professor Whitelock's reference (1952: 142f) to civil hangings as an adequate explanation of all passages), and finally the god being associated with the secret knowledge of the north, runes and spells, in passages where the language used is most archaic and most suggestive to the philologist.

This is not, of course, to assert that the Cult in outlying parts of England in, say, the seventh and eighth centuries, was flourishing in a form particularly dark and revolting, but rather that the earliest features of it, those mentioned by the various classical writers, may be seen to lie not too far behind the English literary texts. And that the cult must have long had a grip on the imaginations of the Angles and Saxons may be seen from the way in which the beliefs and customs associated with it continue through the centuries.

*   *   *

I have given some emphasis to the birds and beasts of battle, and, it might be felt, to the place occupied by the wolf and raven in relation to the Germanic god of battle. It is quite true that themes can become conventional, and persist right through the literature of a people. Of themselves there is nothing very significant for our purposes in the statement in the 'Creation riddle' as given by Aldhelm: "I can fly faster than could ever eagle or hawk;" or in the 'Riddle about

---

10 Here we may recall the picture of the *Edda*, where the witch rides upon the wolf, using eagles as reins. Even the glamorized Brynhild came from battle, riding upon an eagle.

the jay', when it claims, "Sometimes I scream like a hawk; sometimes I mimic the grey eagle, the laugh of the war-bird." We may not wonder particularly why the Soul in the *Address of the Soul to the Body* should say: "Thou art not more dear to me as a comrade, to any living man [...] than the dark raven." We may merely feel that the language is a little highly coloured when, later in the same poem, the body is told: "many earthworms shall gnaw thee, dark creatures, ravenous and greedy, grievously rend thee;" or when "Zealous worms strip the ribs; thirsty for blood they drink the corpses in swarms." We may not quite see the point of whole poems like the *Twa Corbies* and the *Three Ravens*, or why the Owl, in the thirteenth-century poem, *The Owl and the Nightingale*, by a transference of attributes defends its singing and its usefulness by the strange claim as of the battle-bird that:

> When bold men go to war and make their expeditions far and near, when they overrun many peoples, performing at night their good pleasure, then I follow in their train and fly by night in their company. (ll. 385-90)

All these and many other modes of expression are explained when we realize that we have to do with confused recollections of beliefs which were once for writers no mere conventions or animal lore, but very deep-rooted in their ancestors' emotions. We cannot deny the tenacity of these beliefs when we continue to find them, though in more attenuated form, in the works of Chaucer, Spenser, Sidney, Nashe, Greene, Shakespeare and many others.

If closer proof were needed of the strength and horrifying power these beliefs had over the imaginations of the Germanic peoples, we might note that similarly sinister overtones are associated with the wolf and the raven in the poems of the *Elder Edda*, and the later verses of the scalds. For example, in the early poem, the eighth century *Atlakviða*, alone, we have confused references to the wolf's way of being associated with anguish and death, with wolves devouring all the male members of a house, and strange women, referred to as 'corpse-norns' (stanza 17). These passages have just as much evocative power in spite of their formlessness, as those in the English literature.

The Anglo-Saxons had a love of the romantic, the mysterious, the vague, the half-expressed, and they did not readily cast aside all their heritage at the behest of the Church. We may accept the definition of their literature as being a fusion of pagan vocabulary and Christian ideas, but not that "the original meanings were so far forgotten [...] as to be more apparent to the modern Germanic philologist than to the Old English poet himself" (Tolkien in a lecture, c. 1956), for that same poet had a feeling for them, and a power to evoke half-sleeping memories.

If we do not make Snorri our guide through the heathen mythology of Old English, but make a sympathetic study of the old poetry for evidence of the cult of Woden, we can discover something very much older, from the folk-belief, something of the *myth* which *transcends* the poetry, of the world which was much closer with the coming of night, when

> shadowy shapes of darkness   came stalking,
> dusky beneath the clouds[11]

the which lines may not merely refer to Grendel and his race, but to the wolves, the Hunt, and to the Death which did not stalk in abstract form, but which manifested itself through the birds and beasts of battle.

If this paper has drawn attention to the possible recollection of the cult, that is perhaps all that is possible. For we cannot now know with certainty how much Woden was formally worshipped in England after the conversion of the seventh century.

But one hopes that, as for the original audience of *Beowulf*, the mention of the wolf, the eagle or raven, will rouse in readers some feeling for the past beliefs, some greater response to the poetry itself, and the primitive nature of the beliefs, in fact, more respect for the monsters, and less for the critics.

Postscript

No attempt has been made to completely re-cast this essay, by far the earliest written of those included in the present volume. Its general theme had been suggested by Professor Tolkien himself who was in no way responsible for its content. Later discussion has revealed that it had a certain appeal to Dr Hilda

---

11   *scaduhelma gesceapu   scriðan cwoman,*
        wan under wolcnum (Beowulf ll. 650-1)

R. Ellis Davidson of Cambridge, the British antiquarian and folklorist. Perhaps the scholarship of the early twenty-first century might well deem it an exercise in exploring cultural paganism,[12] or, more reservedly, an investigation of the range of possible uses and instances of the theme of 'the birds and beasts of battle'.

A few of the issues treated here are very helpfully touched on by the late Professor E.O.G. Turville-Petre, in Chapter II of his *Myth and Religion of the North*: The Religion of Ancient Scandinavia (1964), especially in the later sections, pp. 56-61, on 'Othin's Animals'.

---

12 This term is used variously in Cavill (2004), e.g. as by Judith Jesch, 'Scandinavians and 'Cultural Paganism' in Anglo-Saxon England' (55-68).

ADDINGTON, Raleigh, 1966, *The Idea of the Oratory*, London: Burns and Oates.

ANDERSON, R.B., 1891, *Norse Mythology: Or The Religion of Our Forefathers Containing All the Myths of the Eddas Systemized and Interpreted with an Introduction, Vocabulary and Index*, Chicago: S.C. Griggs & Co.

ARROWSMITH, Nancy, 1977, *A Field Guide to the Little People*, Gordonsville, Virginia: Farrar Straus and Giroux.

AUDEN, W.H., 1968, *Secondary Worlds: The T.S. Eliot Memorial Lectures*, London: Faber and Faber.

BARFIELD, Owen, 1956, *History in English Words*, Reprint, London: Faber and Faber.

BARKER, Ernest, 1947, *The Character of England*, Oxford: Clarendon Press.

BIRCH, Thomas (ed.), 1738, *A Complete Collection of Historical, Political, and Miscellaneous Works of John Milton*, vol. 1, London: A. Millar.

BIRZER, Bradley J., 2003, *J.R.R. Tolkien's Sanctifying Myth: Understanding Middle-earth*, Wilmington: Intercollegiate Studies Institute.

BISHOP, Morchard, 1958, 'John Inglesant and Its Author', In: E.V. Rieu (ed.), 1958, *Essays by Diverse Hands*, vol. 29, [Essay originally published 1934], London: The Royal Society of Literature, 73-87.

BLACKMORE, Richard D., 1869, *Lorna Doone: A Romance of Exmoor*, London, etc: Chambers.

BLIND, Karl, 1879, 'The Discovery of Odinic Songs in Shetland', In: *Nineteenth Century* 5.28 (June 1879), 1091-1113.

BLISS, Alan J. (ed.), 1954, *Sir Orfeo*, London: Oxford University Press.

BOSWORTH, Joseph and T. NORTHCOTE TOLLER, 1898, *An Anglo-Saxon Dictionary*, London: Oxford University Press.

BRANSTON, Brian, 1957, *The Lost Gods of England*, London: Thames and Hudson.

BRIGGS, Katharine, 1959, *The Anatomy of Puck*, London: Routledge & Kegan Paul.

1967, *The Fairies in Tradition and Literature*, London: Routledge & Kegan Paul.

1976, *A Dictionary of Fairies, Hobgoblins, Brownies, Bogies, and Other Supernatural Creatures*, London: Penguin Books.

BRIGGS, Katharine and R. L. TONGUE, 1965, *Folktales of England*, London: Routledge & Kegan Paul.

BRITISH MUSEUM, DEPARTMENT OF PRINTED BOOKS, 1967, *General Catalogue of Printed Books to 1955*, New York: Readex Microprint Corporation.

BUCHAN, John, 1915, *The Thirty-nine Steps*, Edinburgh and London: William Blackwood and Sons.

BURCHFIELD, R.W. (ed.), 1976, *A Supplement to the Oxford English Dictionary*, vol. II, H-N, Oxford: Clarendon Press.

BURGESS, Michael William, 1975, *For the Wind, for the wild, for all who love the earth*, private publication.

1985, 'Oromë and the Wild Hunt: The Development of a Myth', In: *Mallorn* 22 (1985), 5-11.

BURTON, Robert, 1621, *The Anatomy of Melancholy*, Amsterdam: Theatrum Orbis Terrarum.

BURY, R.G. (ed.), 1984, *Plato in Twelve Volumes*, vol. 11, books 7-12, reprint, Cambridge, Mass.: Harvard University Press.

CAMERON, Kenneth, 1961, *English Place Names*, London: B.T. Batsford.

CARLSON, C.M., 1998, ''The Minstrels Song of Silence': The Construction of Masculine Authority and the Feminised Other in the Romance *Sir Orfeo*', In: *Comitatus* 29 (1998), 62-75.

CARPENTER, Humphrey, 1977, *J.R.R. Tolkien: A Biography*, London: George Allen & Unwin.

1978, *The Inklings – C.S. Lewis, J.R.R. Tolkien, Charles Williams and Their Friends*, London: Allen & Unwin.

(ed. with the assistance of Christopher TOLKIEN), 1981, *The Letters of J.R.R. Tolkien*, Boston: Houghton Mifflin.

CAVILL, Paul (ed.), 2004, *The Christian Tradition in Anglo-Saxon England: Approaches to Current Scholarship and Teaching*, Cambridge: D. S. Brewer.

CHADWICK, H.M., 1899, *The Cult of Odin*, London: C.J. Clay and Sons.

CHADWICK, Nora, 1946a, 'Norse Ghosts (A Study in the Draugr and the Haugbui)', In: *Folklore* 57.2 (1946), 50-65.

1946b, 'Norse Ghosts II (continued)', In: *Folklore* 57.3 (1946), 106-27.

CHAUDHURI, Nirad C., 1914, *Scholar Extraordinary: The Life of Professor the Rt. Hon. Friedrich Max Mueller, P.C.*, London: Chatto and Windus.

CHESTERTON, G.K., 1908, *Orthodoxy*, London: The Bodley Head.

CHILD, F.J., 1882, *English and Scottish Popular Ballads*, vol. I, Boston: Houghton Mifflin.

CHURCH, Richard William, 1897, *Occasional Papers: Selected From The Guardian, The Times and The Saturday Review 1846-1890*, vol. II, London: Macmillan.

COLLINGWOOD, Robin George, 1932, *Roman Britain*, Oxford: Oxford University Press.

COLERIDGE, Samuel Taylor, 1975, *Biographia Literaria, Or, Biographical Sketches of My Literary Life and Opinions*, London: Dent.

COOPER, Susan, 1999, *The Dark Is Rising*, New York: Simon & Schuster Children's Publishing.

CRAIGIE, William Alexander (sel. and trans.), 1896, *Scandinavian Folk-Lore: Illustrations of the Traditional Beliefs of the Northern People*, Paisley: Alexander Gardner.

1913, *The Icelandic Sagas*, Cambridge: Cambridge University Press.

CRAWFORD, O.G.S., 1925, *The Long Barrows of the Cotsworlds: A Description of Long Barrows, Stone Circles and Other Megalithic Remains in the Area Covered by Sheet 8 of the Quarter-Inch Ordnance Survey Comprising the Cotsworlds and the Welsh Marches*, Gloucester: John Bellows.

DAVIDSON, Hilda R. Ellis, 1950, 'The Hill of the Dragon – Anglo Saxon Burial Mounds in Literature and Archaeology', In: *Folklore* 61.4 (1950), 169-85.

DAVIS, Norman and C.L. WRENN (eds.), 1962, *English and Medieval Studies Presented to J.R.R. Tolkien on the Occasion of His Seventieth Birthday*, London: George Allen & Unwin.

DAWSON, Christopher, 1922, 'Cycles of Civilizations', In: *The Sociological Review* 14 (1922), 51-68.

1924, 'Progress and Decay in Ancient and Modern Civilizations', In: *The Sociological Review* 16 (1924), 1-11.

1925, 'Religion and the Life of Civilization', In: *The Quarterly Review* 244 (1925), 98-115.

1926, 'Why I am a Catholic', In: *The Catholic Times*, (May 21, 1926), reprinted in *The Chestertonian Review*, 9 (May 1983), 110-13.

1927, 'Christianity and the Idea of Progress', In: *The Dublin Review* 180 (1927), 19-39.

1929, *Progress and Religion: An Historical Enquiry into the Causes and Development of the Idea of Progress and Its Relationship to Religion*, London: Sheed & Ward.

1931, *Christianity and the New Age*, London: Sheed & Ward.

1933, *The Spirit of the Oxford Movement*, London: Sheed & Ward.

1934, 'Communism, Capitalism and the Catholic Tradition', In: *Ave Maria* 39 (1934), 695.

1935a, 'Modern Dictatorship', In: *The Tablet* 165 (1935), 509.

1935b, *Mediaeval Christianity*, London: Catholic Truth Society.

1945, 'The Spiritual Tragedy of Modern Man', In: *Blackfriars* 15 (1945), 361-65.

1950, *Religion and the Rise of Western Culture: Gifford Lectures; Delivered in the University of Edinburgh 1948-1949*, New York: Sheed & Ward.

1957a, 'The Problem of Metahistory: the Nature and Meaning of History and the Cause and Significance of Historical Change', In: John J. Mulloy (ed.), 1957, *Dynamics of World History*, New York: Sheed & Ward, 287-93.

1957b, 'Arnold Toynbee and the Study of History', In: John J. Mulloy (ed.), 1957, *Dynamics of World History*, New York: Sheed & Ward, 394-404.

1960, *The Historic Reality of Christian Culture: A Way to the Renewal of Human Life*, London: Routledge and Kegan Paul.

1961, *The Crisis of Modern Education*, London: Sheed & Ward.

1972, *The Gods of Revolution*, London: Sidgwick & Jackson.

DAY, David, 1979, *A Tolkien Bestiary*, London: Mitchell Beazley.

DILLON, Myles and Nora CHADWICK, 1967, *The Celtic Realms*, London: Weidenfeld & Nicolson.

Du CHAILLU, Paul, 1889, *The Viking Age : The Early History, Manners, and Customs of the Ancestors of the English-speaking Nations*, New York: Charles Scribner's Sons, London: Murray.

DUMÉZIL, Georges, 1973, *Gods of the Ancient Northmen* (ed. by Einar Haugen, introduction by C. Scott Littleton and Udo Strutynski), Berkeley, California: University of Berkeley Press.

EKWALL, E., 1951, *The Concise Oxford Dictionary of English Place-Names*, 3rd ed., Oxford: Clarendon Press.

ERLINGSSON, Thorsteinn, 1899, *Ruins of the Saga Time: Being an Account of Travels and Explorations in Iceland in the Summer of 1895*, London: David Nutt.

EVANS, Jonathan, 2000, 'The Dragon-Lore of Middle-earth: Tolkien and the Old English and Old Norse Tradition', In: George Clark and Daniel Timmons (eds.), 2000, *J.R.R. Tolkien and his Literary Resonances: Views of Middle-earth*, Contributions to the Study of Science Fiction and Fantasy 89, Westport, Connecticut, etc.: Greenwood Press, 21-38.

FARMER, David Hugh, 1978, *The Oxford Dictionary of Saints*, Oxford: Clarendon Press.

FEIST, Raymond E., 1988, *Fairy Tale*, London, etc.: Hill House.

FOSTER, Robert, 1978, *The Complete Guide to Middle-earth*, London: Allen & Unwin.

FYNES, R.C.C., 2004, 'Max Mueller', In : *The Oxford Dictionary of National Biography*, vol. 34, Oxford, etc.: Oxford University Press, 107-10.

GEOFFREY OF MONMOUTH, 1848, 'Historia Regum Brittaniae', In: J.A. Giles (ed. and trans.), 1848, *Six Old Chronicles*, London: H.G. Bohn.

1903, *Historia Regum Brittaniae (*trans. by Sebastian Evans), London: Everyman.

GIDDINGS, Robert and Elizabeth HOLLAND, 1981, *J.R.R. Tolkien: The Shores of Middle-earth*, London: Junction Books.

GILES, J.A. (ed. and trans.), 1848, *Six Old Chronicles*, London: H.G. Bohn.

GODFREY, C.J., 1962, *The Church in Anglo-Saxon England*, London: Cambridge University Press

GORDON, George, 1912, 'Theophrastus and His Imitators', In: George Gordon (col.), 1912, *English Literature and the Classics*, Oxford: Clarendon Press, 49-86.

1924, 'The Trojans in Britain', In: *Essays and Studies by Members of the English Association* IX (1924), 9-30.

GORDON, Robert Kay, 1926, *The Anglo-Saxon Poetry*, London: Dent, 1954.

GREEN, Roger Lancelyn, 1946, *Andrew Lang: A Critical Biography*, Leicester: Ward.

GRIMALDI, Patrizia, 1981, 'Sir Orfeo as Celtic Folk-Hero, Christian Pilgrim and Medieval King', In: Morton W. Bloomfeld (ed.), 1981, *Allegory, Myth and Symbol*, Cambridge, Massachusetts: Harvard University Press.

GRIMM, Jacob, 1966, *Teutonic Mythology, translated from the fourth edition with notes and appendix by James Steven Stallybrass*, vol. 1, New York: Dover Publications.

GRINSELL, Leslie V., 1936a, *The Ancient Burial-Mounds of England*, 2nd ed. revised and reset (1953), London: Methuen & Co.

1936b, 'Analysis and List of Berkshire Barrows', In: *The Berkshire Archaeological Journal* 40.1 (1936), 20-58.

1958, *The Archeology of Wessex: An Account of Wessex Antiquities From the Earliest Times to the End of the Pagan-Saxon Period, With Special Reference to Existing Field Monuments*, London: Methuen.

1976, *Folklore of Prehistoric Sites in Britain*, London: David & Charles.

GUNN, Battiscombe, 1949, 'Archibald Henry Sayce', In: L.G.W. Legg (ed.), 1949, *The Dictionary of National Biography: 1931-1940*, London, etc.: Oxford University Press, 786-88.

HALL, John R.Clark (trans.), 1950, *Beowulf and the Finnesburg Fragment: A Translation into Modern English Prose*, London: George Allen & Unwin.

HAMMOND, Wayne (with the assistance of Douglas A. ANDERSON), 1993, *J.R.R. Tolkien: A Descriptive Bibliography*, Winchester: St Paul's Bibliographies.

HART, Gillian R., 1983, 'Problems of Writing and Phonology in Cuneiform Hittite', In: *Transactions of the Philological Society* 81.1 (1983), 100-54.

HAWKES, Christopher, 1932, 'Reviews', In: *Antiquity: A Quarterly Review of Archaeology*, vol. VI, no. 24 (December 1932), 488-90.

HITTINGER, Russel, 1984, 'The Metahistorical Vision of Christopher Dawson', In: Peter J. Cataldo (ed.), 1984, *The Dynamic Character of Christian Culture: Essays on Dawsonian Themes*, Lanham, Maryland: University Press of America.

HOLDER, Alfred T. (ed.), 1878, 'Die bouloneser angelsächsischen Glossen zu Prudentius', In: *Germania* 23 (1878), 385-403.

HORSTMANN, C. (ed.), 1883, *S. Editha Sive Chronicon Vilodunense*, Heilbronn: Henninger.

HUIZINGA, Johan, 1970, *Homo Ludens: A Study of the Play Element in Culture*, Introduction by George Steiner, London: Maurice Temple Smith Ltd.

ISAACS, Neil D. and Rose A. ZIMBARDO (eds.), 1968, *Tolkien and the Critics: Essays on J.R.R. Tolkien's 'The Lord of the Rings'*, Notre Dame, Indiana: University of Notre Dame Press.

(eds.), 1981, *Tolkien: New Critical Perspectives*, Lexington, Kentucky: The University Press of Kentucky.

JACKSON, K.H., 1955, 'The Pictish Language', In: F.T. Wainwright (ed.), 1955, *The Problem of the Picts*, Edinburgh: Nelson.

KEIGHTLEY, Thomas, 1880, *The World Guide to Gnomes, Fairies, Elves and Other Little People*, New York: Macmillian.

KELLETT, Arnold, 2004, 'Joseph Wright', In: *Oxford Dictionary of National Biography*, 2004, vol. 60, 464-67.

KELLETT, E.E., 1914, *The Religion of our Northern Ancestors*, London: Charles H. Kelly.

KEMBLE, John Mitchell (ed.), 1847, *The Dialogue of Salomon and Saturn*, vol. 2, London: Ælfric Society.

KER, Neil Ripley, 1974, 'Kenneth Sisam, 1887-1971', In: *Proceedings of the British Academy* 58 (1974), 409-28.

KERSHAW, Nora (ed. and trans.), 1922, *Anglo-Saxon and Norse Poems*, Cambridge: Cambridge University Press.

KIRK, Robert, 1893, *The Secret Commonwealth of Elves, Fauns, and Fairies* (ed. by Andrew Lang, London: David Nutt.

KNOWLES, Dom David, 1973, 'Christopher Dawson, 1889-1970', In: *Proceedings of the British Academy* 57 (1973), 439-52.

KOCHER, Paul Harold, 1973, *Master of Middle-earth: The Achievement of J.R.R. Tolkien*, London: Thames & Hudson.

LANG, Andrew, 1873, 'Mythology and Fairy Tales', In: *The Fortnightly Review* 9 (May 1873), 618-31.

1884, *Custom and Myth*, London: Longmans Green.

1887, *Myth, Ritual, and Religion*, London: Longmans.

(ed.), 1894, *The Yellow Fairy Book*, London: Longmans, Green.

1897, *Modern Mythology*, London and New York: Longmans, Green.

LEWIS, Clive Staples, 1938, *Out of the Silent Planet*, London: John Lane.

1945, *That Hideous Strength*, London: Bodley Head.

(ed.), 1946, *George Macdonald: An Anthology*, London: Geoffrey Bles: The Centenary Press.

1947, 'On Stories', In: *Essays Presented to Charles Williams*, London: Oxford University Press, 103.

1952, *The Voyage of the Dawn Treader*, London: Geoffrey Bles.

1954a, 'The Gods Return to Earth', In: *Time and Tide*, 14 August 1954, 1082-83.

1954b, *The Horse and His Boy*, New York: Macmillan.

1955, 'The Dethronement of Power', In: *Time and Tide*, 22 October 1955, 1373-74.

(ed. by Walter Hooper; ed. originally by C.S. Lewis 1947), 1966, *Of Other Worlds: Essays and Stories*, London: Geoffrey Bles.

LOCAS, Claude, 1973, 'Christopher Dawson: A Bibliography', In: *Harvard Theological Review*, April (1973), 177-206.

MACDONALD, George, 1858, *Phantastes: A Fairy Romance for Men and Women*, London: Smith Elder & Co.

1872, *The Princess and the Goblin*, Philadelphia: J.B. Lippincott & Co.

1882, *Orts*, London: Sampson Low.

MACKENZIE, W. Mackay, 1936-37, 'The Dragonesque Figure in Maeshowe, Orkney', In: *Proceedings of the Society Antiquaries of Scotland* LXXI (1936-37), 157-73.

MAP, Walter, 1983, *De nugis curialium* (ed. and trans. by M.R. James, C.N.L. Brooke and R.A.B. Mynors), Oxford: Clarendon Press.

MAWER, Allen, 1924, *The Chief Elements Used in English Place-names, Introduction to the Survey of English Place-names*, Part 2, English Place-Name Society, Cambridge: Cambridge University Press.

MAWER, Allen and Frank Merry STENTON, 1925, *The Place-names of Buckinghamshire*, English Place-Name Society, vol. 2, Cambridge: Cambridge University Press.

MERIT, H.D., 1954, *Fact and Lore About Old English Words*, Stanford, California: Stanford University Press.

MERTON COLLEGE REGISTER 1900-1964, With Notices of Some Older Surviving Members, 1964, Oxford: Basil Blackwell.

MORRIS, Richard (ed.), 1872, *An Old English Miscellany Containing a Bestiary, Kentish Sermons, Proverbs of Alfred, Religious Poems of the Thirteenth Century: From manuscripts in the British Museum, Bodleian Library, Jesus College Library, etc.*, London: Trübner.

MORRIS, Richard and Walter W. SKEAT, 1885, *Specimens of Early English, Part I: From "Old English Homilies" to "King Horn" [A.D. 1150-A.D. 1300]*, Oxford: Clarendon Press.

1898, *Specimens of Early English, Part 2: From Robert of Gloucester to Gower [A.D. 1298-A.D.1393]*, 4th ed., Oxford: Clarendon Press.

MORRIS, William, 1915, *The Collected Works of William Morris*, vol. 7, London: Longmans, Green and Co.

MÜLLER, Friedrich Max, 1861, *Lectures on the Science of Language delivered at the Royal Institution of Great Britain in April, May, and June*, London: Longman, Green, Longman & Roberts.

MÜLLER, Georgina (ed.), 1902, *The Life and Letters of Friedrich Max Müller*, 2 vols., London, etc.: Longmans, Green and Co.

NEWMAN, John Henry, 1845, *An Essay on The Development of Christian Doctrine*, London: Toovey.

NEWSTEAD, Helaine, 1939, *Bran the Blessed in Arthurian Romance*, New York: Columbia University Press.

NOEL, Ruth S., 1980, *The Languages of Tolkien's Middle-earth*, Boston: Houghton Mifflin.

OBITUARY: PROFESSOR J.R.R. TOLKIEN, 1973, In: *The Times*, September 3, 1973.

OBITUARY: PROFESSOR MAX MUELLER, 1900, In: *The Times*, October 29, 1900.

OLIVER, James and Christina SCOTT (ed.), 1975, *Religion and World History: A Selection from the Works of Christopher Dawson*, Garden City, New York: Image Books, Doubleday.

OLRIK, Axel, 1919, *The Heroic Legends of Denmark*, (trans. and rev. in collaboration with the author Lee M. Hollander), New York: American-Scandinavian Foundation.

ONIONS, C.T., 1958, *A Shakespeare Glossary*, 2nd ed. revised, Oxford: Clarendon Press.

O'RAHILLY, Thomas Francis, 1935, 'The Goidels and their Predecessors', In: *Proceedings of the British Academy* (Sir John Rhys Memorial Lecture) 21 (1935), 323-72.

1946, *Early Irish History and Mythology*, Dublin: Dublin Institute for Advanced Studies.

OXFORD ENGLISH DICTIONARY (NEW ENGLISH DICTIONARY), 1908, 1st ed., vol. VI, Oxford: Clarendon Press.

OXFORD ENGLISH DICTIONARY (NEW ENGLISH DICTIONARY), 1933, vol. XI, Oxford: Clarendon Press.

OXFORD ENGLISH DICTIONARY, 1933, 12 vols. with supplement, Oxford: Clarendon Press.

SUPPLEMENT, 1972, vol. 1, Oxford: Clarendon Press.

SUPPLEMENT, 1976, vol. 2, Oxford: Clarendon Press.

PARTRIDGE, Eric, 1968, *Name Your Child: A Handy Guide for Puzzled Parents*, London: Evans.

PEAKE, H.J.E., 1931, *The Archaeology of Berkshire*, London: Methuen.

PETERS, Robert Anthony, 1961, *A Study of Old English Words for Demon and Monster and Their Relation to English Place-names*, Philadelphia, Pennsylvania, University of Pennsylvania, Diss.

POWELL, Frederick York, 1899, 'Review of Eleanor Hull's *The Cuchullin Saga in Irish Literature*', In: *Folklore* 10.4 (1988), 459-61.

POWER, Norman S., 1975a, 'Tolkien's Walk' In: *Library Review* 25.1 (1975), 22-23.

1975b, 'Tolkien's Walk (an unexpected personal link with Tolkien)', In: *Mallorn* 9, 16-17.

PRICE, Stephen, 1981, *Sarehole, Pamphlet Number 14*, Birmingham: Department of Local History of the Birmingham Museum.

RANKIN, J.W., 1909, 'A Study of the Kennings in Anglo-Saxon Poetry', In: *Journal of English and Germanic Philology* 8 (1909), 357-422.

1910, 'A Study of the Kennings in Anglo-Saxon Poetry', In: *Journal of English and Germanic Philology* 9 (1910), 49-84.

RAU, Heimo (ed.), 1974, *F. Max Mueller: What He Can Teach Us*, Bombay: Shakuntala Publishing House.

RYAN, John S., 1969, *Tolkien: Cult or Culture?*, Armidale, N.S.W., Australia: University of New England.

1978, 'Tolkien's Language and Style', In: *Ipotesi*, 4, no. 9-12 (1978), 361-68.

1983, 'The Origin of the name Wetwang', In: *Amon Hen* 63 (1983), 10-13.

2002, 'J.R.R. Tolkien's Formal Lecturing and Teaching at the University of Oxford, 1925-1959', In: *Seven: An Anglo-American Literary Review* 19 (2002), 45-62.

SAYCE, Archibald Henry, 1880, *Introduction to the Science of Language*, 2 vols., London: Kegan, Paul, Trench, Trübner.

1892a, *The Principles of Comparative Philology*, 4th ed. revised and enlarged, London: Kegan Paul, Trench, Trübner, reprinted Oxford: Kessinger, 2004.

1892b, [A review notice], In: *The Athenaeum*, (25 June 1892), 816.

1923, *Reminiscences*, London: Macmillan.

SCOTT, Christina, 1984, *A Historian and His World: A Life of Christopher Dawson, 1889-1970*, London: Sheed & Ward.

SEYMOUR, St. John D., 1972, *Irish Witchcraft and Demonology*, Dublin: EP.

SHIPPEY, Tom, 1982, *The Road to Middle-earth*, London: George Allen & Unwin.

2004, 'John Ronald Reuel Tolkien', In: *The Oxford Dictionary of National Biography*, vol. 58, Oxford, etc.: Oxford University Press, 903-04.

SHOOLE, Laurence K., 1960, 'The Burial Mound in *Guthlac A*', In: *Modern Philology* 58 (1960), 1-10.

1961, 'The Prologue of the Old English *Guthlac A*', In: *Mediaeval Studies* 23 (1961), 294-304.

SHORTHOUSE, J. Henry, 1880, *John Inglesant: A Romance*, Birmingham: Cornish Brothers.

SHORTHOUSE, Sarah (ed.), 1905a, *The Life, Letters, and Literary Remains of J.H. Shorthouse*, vol. 1: 'Life and Letters', London and New York: Macmillan.

1905b, *The Life, Letters, and Literary Remains of J. H. Shorthouse*, vol. 2: 'Literary Remains', London and New York: Macmillan.

SISAM, Kenneth (ed.), 1921, *Fourteenth Century Verse and Prose, With a Middle English Glossary by J.R.R. Tolkien*, Oxford: Clarendon Press.

SKEAT, Walter W. (ed.), 1881-85, *Ælfric's Lives of Saints: Being a Set of Sermons on Saints' Days Formerly Observed by the English Church*, vol. I, 2, London: N. Trübner & Co.

1882, *A Concise Etymological Dictionary of the English Language*, Oxford: Clarendon Press.

(ed.), 1886, *The Vision of William Concerning Piers the Plowman in Three Parallel Texts*, 2 vols., Oxford: Oxford University Press.

1889, *The Lay of Havelok the Dane. Composed in the Reign of Edward, about A.D. 1280*, London: Trübner.

SLEIGH, Linwood and Charles JOHNSON, 1966, *The Pan Book of Girls' Names*, London: Pan Books.

SMITH, Albert Hugh, 1956, *English Place-name Elements*, Part 2, English Place-Name Society, Cambridge: Cambridge University Press.

SMITH, L.P. (ed.), 1919, *Donne's Sermons. Selected Passages*, Oxford: Oxford University Press.

SPENGLER, Oswald Arnold Gottfried, 1927, *The Decline of the West*, New York: Alfred A. Knopf.

STENTON, F.M., 1943, *Anglo-Saxon England*, Oxford: Oxford University Press.

STOKER, Bram, 1897, *Dracula*, Westminster: Archibald Constable and Company.

STOKES, H.G., 1949, *English Place-names*, 2nd ed. revised, London: Batsford.

SUPPLEMENT TO THE HISTORICAL REGISTER OF THE UNIVERSITY OF OXFORD, 1900-1921, 1921, Oxford: Clarendon Press.

THE SCOTTISH NATIONAL DICTIONARY: CONTAINING ALL THE WORDS KNOWN TO BE IN USE SINCE C. 1700, vol. V, 1960, Edinburgh: The Scottish National Dictionary Association.

THE SHORTER OXFORD ENGLISH DICTIONARY, 1933, Oxford: Clarendon Press.

THOMPSON, Stith, 1955-1958, *Motif-Index of Folk-Literature: A Classification of Narrative Elements in Folk-Tales, Ballads, Myths, Fables, Mediæval Romances, Exempla, Fabliaux, Jest-Books and Local Legends*, 6 vols., Copenhagen: Rosenkilde and Bagger.

TINKLER, John, 1968, 'Old English in Rohan', In: Neil Isaacs and Rose Zimbardo (eds.), 1968, *Tolkien and the Critics: Essays on J.R.R. Tolkien's The Lord of the Rings*, Notre Dame and London: University of Notre Dame Press, 164-69.

TOLKIEN, Christopher, 1955-56, 'The Battle of the Goths and the Huns', In: *Saga-Book of the Viking Society* XIV (1955-56), London: University College for the Viking Society for Northern Research, 141-63.

1956, 'Introduction', In: E.O.G. Turville-Petre (ed.), 1956, *Hervarar Saga ok Heidreks*, London: University College London, for the Viking Society for Northern Research.

(trans. and ed.), 1960, *The Saga of King Heidrek the Wise*, London: Thomas Nelson and Sons, Ltd.

TOLKIEN, John Ronald Reuel, 1915, 'Goblin Feet', In: G.D.H. Cole and T.W. Earp (eds.), *Oxford Poetry* (1915), Oxford: B.H. Blackwell, 64-65.

1921, *A Middle English Vocabulary, Designed for use with Sisam's Fourteenth Century Verse & Prose*, Oxford: Clarendon Press.

1924, 'Philology: General Works', In: *Year's Work in English Studies*, vol. IV, no. 1 (1923), 20-37.

(trans.), 1925, *Sir Gawain and the Green Knight*, (ed. by J.R.R. Tolkien and E.V. Gordon), Oxford: Clarendon Press.

1926, 'Philology: General Works', In: *Year's Work in English Studies*, vol. V, no. 1 (1924), 26-65.

1927, 'Philology: General Works', In: *Year's Work in English Studies*, vol. VI, no. 1 (1925), 32-66.

1929, '*Ancrene Wisse* and *Hali Meiðhad*', In: *Essays and Studies by Members of the English Association* XIV (1929), Oxford: Clarendon Press, 104-26.

1930, 'The Oxford English School', In: *Oxford Magazine* 48.21, (29 May, 1930), 778-82.

1932, 'The Name 'Nodens'', In: R.E.M Wheeler and T.V. Wheeler, 1932, *Report on the Excavation of the Prehistoric, Roman and Post-Roman Site in Lindney Park, Gloucestershire*, London: Printed at the University Press by John Johnson for The Society of Antiquaries, 132-37.

1934, 'Chaucer as a Philologist: The Reeve's Tale', In: *Transactions of the Philological Society* (1934), London: David Nutt, 1-70.

1949, *Farmer Giles of Ham*, London: George Allen & Unwin.

1951, *The Hobbit or There and Back Again*, 2nd ed., London: Allen & Unwin.

1962, *The Adventures of Tom Bombadil and other verses from the Red Book*, London: George Allen & Unwin.

1965a, *The Fellowship of the Ring: being the first part of The Lord of the Rings*, 2nd ed., Boston: Houghton Mifflin.

1965b, *The Two Towers: being the second part of The Lord of the Rings*, 2nd ed., Boston: Houghton Mifflin.

1965c, *The Return of the King: being the third part of The Lord of the Rings*, 2nd ed., Boston: Houghton Mifflin.

1977, *The Silmarillion* (ed. by Christopher Tolkien), London: George Allen and Unwin.

1980, *Unfinished Tales of Númenor and Middle-earth* (ed. by Christopher Tolkien), London, etc.: George Allen & Unwin.

1984, *The Book of Lost Tales I* (ed. by Christopher Tolkien), *History of Middle-earth*, vol. 1, Boston: Houghton Mifflin.

1995, *Sir Gawain and the Green Knight, Pearl and Sir Orfeo*, London: HarperCollinsPublishers.

2001, *Tree and Leaf: Including the Poem 'Mythopoeia' and 'The Homecoming of Beorhtnoth'*, London: HarperCollinsPublishers.

2006, *The Monsters and the Critics and other Essays* (ed. by Christopher Tolkien), London: HarperCollinsPublishers.

TOLKIEN, John Ronald Reuel and E.V. GORDON, 1936, *Songs for the Philologists*, London: G. Tillotson, A.H. Smith, B. Pattison and other members of the English Department, University College, London.

Turville-Petre, Edward Oswald Gabriel (ed.), 1940, *Víga-Glúms Saga*, London: Oxford University Press.

1953, *Origins of Icelandic Literature*, Oxford: Clarendon Press.

1964, *Myth and Religion of the North: The Religion of Ancient Scandinavia*, London: Weidenfeld and Nicolson.

1972, *Nine Norse Studies*, London: The Viking Society for Northern Research.

Tyler, J.E.A., 1976, *The Tolkien Companion*, London: Macmillan.

University of Oxford, 1889-1968, *Examination Statutes / University of Oxford: together with the Regulations of the Boards of the Faculties*, Various annual volumes, Oxford: Clarendon Press.

The University of Oxford Gazette, various issues, Oxford: University of Oxford Press.

Wagner, Heinrich, 1969, 'The Origins of the Celts in the Light of Linguistic Geography', In: *Transactions of the Philological Society* (1969), 203-50.

Wells, John Edwin, 1916, *A Manual of the Writings in Middle English 1050-1400*, New Haven: Yale University Press.

Whitelock, Dorothy, 1952, *The Beginnings of English Society*, Harmondsworth: Penguin.

Willoughby, L.W., 1935, 'Coleridge as a Philologist', In: *Transactions of the Philological Society* (1935), 75.

Wilson, Colin, 1974, *Tree by Tolkien*, Santa Barbara, California: Capra Press.

Wilmart, André, 1938, 'La Legende de Ste. Edith en Prose et Vers par le Moine Goscelin', In: *Analecta Bollandiana* 56 (1938), 5-101, 265-307.

Wood, Steve, 1977, 'Tolkien and the *O.E.D*', In: *Amon Hen* 28 (1977), 10.

Wright, Elizabeth Mary, 1913, *Rustic Speech and Folk-Lore*, London: Oxford University Press

Wright, Joseph (ed.), 1898, *English Dialect Dictionary*, vol. I, London: Oxford University Press.

(ed.), 1905, *English Dialect Dictionary*, vol. VI, London: Oxford University Press.

Yeats, William Butler, 1893, *The Celtic Twilight*, London: Lawrence and Bullen.

ZIMBARDO, Rose A. and Neil D. ISAACS (eds.), 2004, *Understanding The Lord
    of the Rings: The Best of Tolkien Criticism,* Boston and New York: Houghton
    Mifflin Company.

The index contains mentions of authors, works and places with the exception of fictional characters and places as well as works by J.RR. Tolkien himself. Works are, in general, given without introductionary definite and indefinite articles and placed with the author where possible (with crossreferences leading to the authors put under the letter with which the first word – again ignoring definite or indefinite articles – begins).

C

Caedmon 251
Caesar 192
Cambridge 136, 143, 166, 194, 258
    Peterhouse College 166, 175
Canterbury Tales. See Chaucer, Geoffrey
Carmina Scaldica 23, 91
Carroll, Lewis 123
Castle. See Kafka, Franz
Caxton, William 19
Celtic Twilight. See Yeats, William Butler
Chadwick, Nora 133, 136, 137, 138, 194, 244
    Anglo-Saxon and Norse Poems 133, 138
Chaillu, Paul Belloni du. *See* Du Chaillu, Paul Belloni
Charms 243
Chaucer, Geoffrey 18, 19, 22, 30, 68, 80, 108, 160, 175, 256
    Canterbury Tales 18, 22, 160
    Troilus and Criseyde 22
Chesterton, Gilbert Keith 156, 161, 162, 165, 171, 200
Christ Church. *See* Oxford
City in the Sea. See Poe, Edgar Allan
Clark Hall, John R. 121
Cleasby, R. 44, 74
Coleridge, Samuel Taylor 68, 108, 156, 159, 160, 164
    Biographia Literaria 156, 160
Collingwood, Robin G. 120, 194, 195, 198
Collingwood, W.G. 194
Cooper, Susan 179, 185, 186
    Dark is Rising 185
Corpus Christi College. *See* Oxford
Countess Eve. See Shorthouse, J.H.
Craigie, William Alexander 17, 33–46, 72, 84, 90, 95, 136
    Dictionary of American English on Historical Principles 36, 37, 84
    Icelandic Sagas 39, 95
    Scandinavian Folk-Lore 34, 36, 38, 45
    Scottish National Dictionary 36, 136
Crawford, O.G.S. 82, 134
Cromwell, Thomas 85
Cursor Mundi 22
Cynewulf 128

D

D'Ardenne, S.T.R.O. 21

Walking Tree Publishers

Walking Tree Publishers was founded in 1997 as a forum for publication of material (books, videos, CDs, etc.) related to Tolkien and Middle-earth studies. Manuscripts and project proposals can be submitted to the board of editors (please include an SAE):

Walking Tree Publishers
CH-3052 Zollikofen
Switzerland
e-mail: info@walking-tree.org
http://www.walking-tree.org

Cormarë Series

The *Cormarë Series* has been the first series of studies dedicated exclusively to the exploration of Tolkien's work. Its focus is on papers and studies from a wide range of scholarly approaches. The series comprises monographs, thematic collections of essays, conference volumes, and reprints of important yet no longer (easily) accessible papers by leading scholars in the field. Manuscripts and project proposals are evaluated by members of an independent board of advisors who support the series editors in their endeavour to provide the readers with qualitatively superior yet accessible studies on Tolkien and his work.

News from the Shire and Beyond. Studies on Tolkien
Peter Buchs and Thomas Honegger (eds.), Zurich and Berne 2004, Reprint, First edition 1997 (Cormarë Series 1), ISBN 978-3-9521424-5-5

Root and Branch. Approaches Towards Understanding Tolkien
Thomas Honegger (ed.), Zurich and Berne 2005, Reprint, First edition 1999 (Cormarë Series 2), ISBN 978-3-905703-01-6

Richard Sturch, *Four Christian Fantasists. A Study of the Fantastic Writings of George MacDonald, Charles Williams, C.S. Lewis and J.R.R. Tolkien*
Zurich and Berne 2007, Reprint, First edition 2001 (Cormarë Series 3), ISBN 978-3-905703-04-7

Tolkien in Translation
Thomas Honegger (ed.), Zurich and Berne 2003 (Cormarë Series 4), ISBN 978-3-9521424-6-2

Mark T. Hooker, *Tolkien Through Russian Eyes*
Zurich and Berne 2003 (Cormarë Series 5), ISBN 978-3-9521424-7-9

Translating Tolkien: Text and Film
Thomas Honegger (ed.), Zurich and Jena, Reprint forthcoming, First edition 2004 (Cormarë Series 6), ISBN 978-3-905703-16-0

Christopher Garbowski, *Recovery and Transcendence for the Contemporary Mythmaker. The Spiritual Dimension in the Works of J.R.R. Tolkien*
Zurich and Berne 2004, Reprint, First Edition by Marie Curie Sklodowska, University Press, Lublin 2000, (Cormarë Series 7), ISBN 978-3-9521424-8-6

Reconsidering Tolkien
Thomas Honegger (ed.), Zurich and Berne 2005 (Cormarë Series 8),
ISBN 978-3-905703-00-9

Tolkien and Modernity 1
Frank Weinreich and Thomas Honegger (eds.), Zurich and Berne 2006
(Cormarë Series 9), ISBN 978-3-905703-02-3

Tolkien and Modernity 2
Thomas Honegger and Frank Weinreich (eds.), Zurich and Berne 2006
(Cormarë Series 10), ISBN 978-3-905703-03-0

Tom Shippey, *Roots and Branches. Selected Papers on Tolkien by Tom Shippey*
Zurich and Berne 2007 (Cormarë Series 11), ISBN 978-3-905703-05-4

Ross Smith, *Inside Language. Linguistic and Aesthetic Theory in Tolkien*
Zurich and Berne 2007 (Cormarë Series 12), ISBN 978-3-905703-06-1

How We Became Middle-earth. A Collection of Essays on The Lord of the Rings
Adam Lam and Nataliya Oryshchuk (eds.), Zurich and Berne 2007
(Cormarë Series 13), ISBN 978-3-905703-07-8

Myth and Magic. Art According to the Inklings
Eduardo Segura and Thomas Honegger (eds.), Zurich and Berne 2007
(Cormarë Series 14), ISBN 978-3-905703-08-5

The Silmarillion - Thirty Years On
Allan Turner (ed.), Zurich and Berne 2007 (Cormarë Series 15)
ISBN 978-3-905703-10-8

Martin Simonson, *The Lord of the Rings and the Western Narrative Tradition*
Zurich and Jena 2008 (Cormarë Series 16), ISBN 978-3-905703-09-2

*Tolkien's Shorter Works. Proceedings of the 4th Seminar of the Deutsche Tolkien
Gesellschaft & Walking Tree Publishers Decennial Conference*
Margaret Hiley and Frank Weinreich (eds.), Zurich and Jena 2008
(Cormarë Series 17), ISBN 978-3-905703-11-5

Tolkien's The Lord of the Rings: Sources of Inspiration
Stratford Caldecott and Thomas Honegger (eds.), Zurich and Jena 2008
(Cormarë Series 18), ISBN 978-3-905703-12-2

J.S. Ryan, *Tolkien's View: Windows into his World*
Zurich and Jena 2009 (Cormarë Series 19), ISBN 978-3-905703-13-9

Music in Middle-earth
Friedhelm Schneidewind and Heidi Steimel (eds.), Zurich and Jena, forthcoming

Liam Campbell, *The Ecological Augury in the Works of J.R.R. Tolkien*
Zurich and Jena, forthcoming

Constructions of Authorship in and around the Works of J.R.R. Tolkien
Judith Klinger (ed.), Zurich and Jena, forthcoming

Rainer Nagel, *Hobbit Place-names. A Linguistic Excursion through the Shire*
Zurich and Jena, forthcoming

Tales of Yore Series

The *Tales of Yore Series* grew out of the desire to share Kay Woollard's whimsical stories and drawings with a wider audience. The series aims at providing a platform for qualitatively superior fiction with a clear link to Tolkien's world.

Kay Woollard, *The Terror of Tatty Walk. A Frightener*
CD and Booklet, Zurich and Berne 2000 (Tales of Yore Series 1)
ISBN 978-3-9521424-2-4

Kay Woollard, *Wilmot's Very Strange Stone or What came of building "snobbits"*
CD and booklet, Zurich and Berne 2001 (Tales of Yore Series 2)
ISBN 978-3-9521424-4-8

Ossie felt the back of his neck go prickly....

LaVergne, TN USA
03 March 2010
174892LV00001B/10/P